Bikes, Toys, & Hot Boyz

WITHDRAWN

WITHDRAWN

Bikes, Toys,
& Hot Boyz

Genesis Woods and Shantaé

www.urbanbooks.net

Urban Books, LLC
300 Farmingdale Road, NY-Route 109
Farmingdale, NY 11735

Bikes, Toys, & Hot Boyz

Copyright © 2018 Genesis Woods and Shantaé

All rights reserved. No part of this book may be
reproduced in any form or by any means without
prior consent of the Publisher, except brief quotes
used in reviews.

ISBN 13: 978-1-62286-220-7
ISBN 10: 1-62286-220-1

First Mass Market Printing December 2019
First Trade Paperback Printing August 2018
Printed in the United States of America

10 9 8 7 6 5 4 3 2 1

*This is a work of fiction. Any references or similar-
ities to actual events, real people, living or dead,
or to real locales are intended to give the novel a
sense of reality. Any similarity in other names,
characters, places, and incidents is entirely coin-
cidental.*

Distributed by Kensington Publishing Corp.
Submit Orders to:
Customer Service
400 Hahn Road
Westminster, MD 21157-4627
Phone: 1-800-733-3000
Fax: 1-800-659-2436

Acknowledgments

To my family, friends, and supporters, I thank you from the bottom of my heart. To my writing partner, Genesis Woods aka Genny Wit' Da' Henny, you the one, boo! This was quite an experience, and I couldn't have chosen a better author to collaborate with. You kept me on my toes and challenged me to bring my A game, and I appreciate you.

-Taé

#SharingTheBeautyOfBlackLove
#OneStoryAtATime

To everyone who has been rocking with me since the beginning, thank you for continuously lending me your mind and allowing me to tell you a story. I appreciate each and every one of you, whether family, friend, or foe, and I can't wait until you read what I have coming up next.

Acknowledgments

To my playa partner Suga Taé—the frick to my frack, the cola to my yak—this has truly been an experience, and I loved every second of it, from our Messenger chats to our IG DMs, our five-hour phone calls, those TDT pics, and our Literary Rejects Clique. There's nowhere else to go but to the top from here. You da best (DJ Khaled voice)!

-Gen

#ExpandYourMind
#ReadABook

Prologue

Ophelia aka Philly

The Hothead Mechanic

"Yo, Phil, there's some dudes out here asking for you."

I looked up from the computer on my desk and eyed my half-ass receptionist and best friend, Natalie. I was convinced she only asked to work here so that we could spend time together, because she didn't do much work. She was my girl, though, so I let her slide.

"Who is it?"

"Hell if I know." She shrugged. "But there's a fat one, a tall, skinny one, and this sexy-ass mutha-fucka who hasn't said a word since they stepped in the garage. The chick hanging on his arm hasn't stopped yapping her gums since they walked in, though."

"Which one asked for me?" I closed down some of the open windows on my computer screen and moved some things around on my desk.

"The fat one, of course. Got the most mouth and the weakest game." She laughed. "A hundred dollars says he tries to pull you with that wack-ass shit he's spitting, too."

I looked at Natalie and smirked. "That ain't no bet. You already know he gon' try me if he tried you."

Natalie and I didn't look that much alike to me, but others often mistook us for sisters. Could have been because our bodies mirrored one another, thick as hell and super curvy. I, however, had a few more pounds on my frame than she did. I was a little chubby, but I thought it looked good on me. Maybe it was because we damn near spent every waking moment of our time together that we'd started looking alike to some people. Her skin was a rich caramel color, which was a few shades darker than my sandy-brown complexion. Her eyes were a golden-amber color, and mine were a light brown. We both wore our jet-black hair in slicked-back ponytails and got our eyebrows threaded by the same Indian girl at the shop up the street. Not only did we work at my shop, Hart of the City, a majority of the day, but we also cohabitated in a three-bedroom, two-and-a-half-bathroom fixer-upper I'd purchased in Boulder City a few years back. The area wasn't ideal for prime real estate or anything like that, but we grew up there, so it was home.

I ran my hand over my left arm and winced when I touched my elbow. After rubbing some of the antibiotic cream over it and popping a few anti-inflammatories, I stood up from my chair and tightened the arms of my coveralls around my waist. The white wife beater I had on was covered in oil and sweat, but I didn't care. My job wasn't the cleanest, so I expected to be a little dirty from time to time.

"Your arm hurting again?" Natalie asked as she walked farther into my office, concern etched across her face. When I went to lace the boots on my feet and winced again, she squatted and tied them for me.

"Thanks. I'm good though. It just still hurts sometimes when I've been working a crazy amount of hours straight. It's been healed for a year, and I'm still rubbing this cream on it to stop the little tingly sensations I feel every now and then."

Natalie licked her lips. Reaching out, she grabbed my arm and traced her fingers over the charred skin that started at my shoulder and went down to my wrist. "I thought the doctor said it would be numb after it completely healed."

"He did. And on some parts of my arm, it is numb. It's just certain areas that still give me a little pain every now and then."

A couple years ago, I was flying down the high-way on my bike, trying to get home, and I ended up getting clipped by a dumbass broad talking on her phone while trying to merge over into the carpool lane. Bitch didn't even have another passenger in the car with her. Needless to say, I hit the median and flipped over a few feet. If that weren't bad enough, my bike caught on fire while I was still on it and burned the left side of my body pretty bad. Well, my arm suffered the most damage with third-degree burns, but I still had some scarring on my hip, thigh, and rib cage. Learning that stop, drop, and roll bit in elementary really helped me out or else my whole body could have been engulfed in flames.

Natalie let my arm go and walked back over to the door. "Well, if you're okay, then I'm okay. Just don't overwork yourself like you usually do." I nodded my head, agreeing with her. "Now, let's go out here and see what these fools want."

"Already on my way," I said, walking out of the door and grabbing one of my lollipops from the candy jar. "But we need to change that bet. I don't like those odds you came up with."

She giggled. "Okay. Well, how about a hundred dollars says you gon' have to smack the shit out of him before they leave?"

I stopped in my tracks and looked back at Natalie and laughed. Could I get through a disrespectful conversation without putting my hands on somebody? I mean, the anger management classes the judge ordered me to sign up for after I beat the shit out of one of our club members had been helping out with my attitude a lot. I hadn't had a physical altercation in about six months now. There was no way in the world I could let this customer bring me out of my new Zen state. I had to keep it together. Especially if I didn't want to go to jail and serve this time. Having complete faith in myself, I took her hand and shook it.

"Okay, bet. And you better have my money, too. I don't wanna hear none of that 'I gotta pay the cable bill' shit, either," I laughed, mocking her as we made our way to the garage.

A euphoric feeling covered my whole body, causing me to forget about the sharp pains in my arm as soon as I stepped into my first love and sanctuary. Hart of the City was my baby and, at times, my life. The vast love I had for bikes, old and new, was on full display everywhere. Motorcycles of all shapes, colors, and sizes were in here being worked on, restored, or maintained in some way. A sea of colors from the custom paint jobs was like a wonderland to my eyes. The smell of burnt rubber was tantalizing to my nose. I sighed in contentment as the sounds of drills spinning, metal banging, and engines revving invaded my ears. Kehlani's song "Gangsta" played in the background but was drowned out by the harmonizing sounds of multiple motorcycles being worked on.

With Natalie on my heels, I bypassed the restoration of the 1968 Ariel Cyclone 650 I was working on and made my way to the front of the shop, speaking along the way to a couple of the fellas whom I employed. When I opened the door to the cool lobby area, which looked like a decked-out living room with its modern furniture and red color scheme, whatever conversation the four guests were having came to a sudden end, and all eyes turned to me.

"I thought you were going to get Phil." The fat one addressed Natalie while still looking at me. His gaze seared my body from head to toe. "Instead you bring this dyke-looking bitch. What? Phil busy or something?" He walked closer to me. "Baby girl, you sexy as fuck and all that, but I need to see that nigga Phil about fixing my bike. Heard he's the best in town."

I opened my mouth to say something but got cut off by the girl who was standing next to one of the sexiest men I'd ever seen in my life.

"I told you we should've gone to my brother's shop. We would've been gone already. We've been here for what?" She looked down at her phone screen and popped the gum in her mouth. "Almost an hour. Babe, you know I got a hair appointment in like thirty minutes that I can't be late for. Can we go already?" she whined.

Cocking my head to the side, I squinted my eyes and looked up at the tall and handsome muthafucka she was hanging on to.

I need a gangsta
To love me better
Than all the others do
To always forgive me
Ride or die with me
That's just what gangstas do

Because we were in the front of the shop and away from all of the noise, Kehlani's song could be heard loud and clear. The lyrics never really mattered to me even though I liked the song, but there was something in that moment that had my body reacting to it, while I stared at a pair of dark brown eyes that were looking right back at me.

"Uhhhh, hello!" The girl snapped her fingers in sexy dude's face to get his attention. "I know you ain't staring at this bitch like that while I'm standing here."

I could feel my fist balling up and my heart rate picking up. I tried to do some of the exercises we learned in anger management to try to stop the rage I could feel building up right now, but nothing was working. Counting, trying to focus on the positive, hell, even ignoring the negativity around me was all going down the drain, especially with this bitch being disrespectful. I looked back at Natalie, who only smirked at me. She already knew I was going to have to pay her that money. Probably why her ass came up with the bet in the first place.

"Shut up, Luscious. Aye, Gideon man, I told you, you should've left her dumb ass at the house," fat boy yelled. He looked back at me and his eyes softened. "Now, if you could, sweetheart, please be a dear and go get Phil for me. As you can see, we have other business to tend to and waiting in this office is throwing off our schedule."

"What can I help you with?" I looked out the window for any new bikes on the lot but didn't see anything. "I don't see any bikes other than the ones that were already out there, so what brings you here?"

"Obviously we need some type of service," the ghetto bird snapped.

"I understand that, but we fix on bikes here," I said, explaining it to her like she was stupid. "And you guys didn't bring any bikes with you."

Fat boy snorted. "We? So what, you fix on bikes too? Shit, here I was thinking that you were just another pretty face to bring us bad boys in, but you out here fixing on shit. How you get this job? Never seen a bitch who could fix on bikes before. Especially not one as fine as you. You fucking Phil or something?"

I laughed, but there was no humor in it. "Nah, I'm not fucking Phil."

"You his old lady?"

"Not an old lady neither."

He walked closer to me and placed his hand on the small of my back and then moved it down to my ass and squeezed. Again, I looked back at Natalie, who was trying her best not to fall out laughing at this point. She already knew what was coming.

"Then who are you, baby girl? Because I would love to get to know you and that tight little pussy I bet you have in between those thighs a little bit better."

Before he could turn his big-ass lips into a smile, I reared my arm back and socked him in his nose, busting it wide open. Blood shot out everywhere. I was all kinds of bitches as he tried to stop the bleeding. I looked at the sexy dude, who now had a smirk on his face, and I rolled my eyes. His ass could get it too if he got out of line just like his buddy here. The tall dude was laughing his ass off and making fun of big boy while Luscious tried to step to me. Sexy dude pulled her back and told her to stand the fuck down with one look.

"You stupid-ass bitch! You lucky I don't hit females. Where the hell is Phil at so I can fuck him up, though? You're his employee, so he gon' take this ass whipping in your place."

Walking behind the counter, I punched a few things into the computer before focusing my attention back on fat boy, ignoring every question he just asked. His eyes darkened, and I could tell he was super mad now.

"So you don't hear me talking to you, bitch? Where the fuck is Phil?" By now, he had the bleeding under control and was throwing the tissues Natalie handed to him on the ground, being disrespectful again. "That's why I can't stand hoes, man. They always wanna put their hands on a nigga and think won't shit happen back to them. Best believe I'ma have some of my homegirls come back up here and whip your ass. Have that other arm fucked up just like that one," he threatened and pointed to my burned arm.

"And when they come up here, tell them to ask for me," I said, walking out the door. I stopped when sexy dude finally spoke.

"And who they supposed to ask for, shawty?"

I sucked my teeth and blew out a short breath. "Me. I'm the owner of this establishment."

"The owner, huh?" He licked his lips with a nod. "I thought a cat named Phil owned this joint."

"You're looking at that cat. Now get the fuck out of my shop before I throw your ass out," I tossed over my shoulder as I walked back into the garage, leaving Natalie to handle them and to get some more ointment for my arm that was now hurting like hell.

Diem aka DiDi
The Foul-mouthed Tycoon

"Damn," I heard one of the ladies call out followed by a series of oohs and ahhs from the others when I revealed my latest masterpiece. I got off on the reactions I received each time I presented a new creation at one of these events.

"This one here is called Pac, ladies. It's an exclusive from my Hart Throb Collection." I beamed proudly as they nodded their heads in approval.

I always gave my sex toys unique names, and I called this dildo I was holding Pac because it was the name of my favorite rapper and also how I envisioned his package to have been when he was alive. It was long, thick, veiny, and made of a material that felt like the real deal. Trust, I'd tested this baby out repeatedly so I knew that every woman who took home their own personal Pac tonight would not be disappointed. I knew I never was when I would put him to use, and honestly, with my schedule, it was quite often. Good thing Pac was as sturdy as they came.

"Sissy, would you pass a few around the room so that the ladies can get a feel of Pac please?" I directed my assistant.

"I'm on it, boss lady," she said before doing as she was told.

There were about fifteen women in attendance, and I knew from the looks on their faces as they rubbed Pac up and down that I would sell every single one I brought here tonight. Once a month I hosted these pleasure parties, and at each one, I made it my business to have something innovative and exciting for my customers to try. My mind was constantly racing and flooding with new ideas and products, and a lot of times it was hard for me to think straight. I had so much going on, and things would get even crazier for me when my second showroom opened up next month. It was twice as big as my current location, and that was where my parties would be held from here on out.

Tonight one of my most loyal customers, Bella, was gracious enough to let us use her brother's home for the event. Could have easily held it at my spacious estate, but I didn't really want these bitches up in my crib like that. My home was my sanctuary, and if your name wasn't Philly or Drea Hart, then you weren't welcome. Half the time I didn't even want my parents coming by. Pops was my ace, but my mother and I had a weird relationship, and I could do without her most times. Because he never went anywhere without her crazy ass, I preferred to just stop by to see him instead of having him come see me. Crazy and weird, I know, but it was just the way I felt.

A few of the women here tonight were cool, but most of them got on my last damn nerve. Especially this siddity ho, Lark, who sat next to Bella, rolling her eyes and checking her watch. Bitch was acting like she was too good to fondle and get familiar with Pac. Best believe her fake ass was going to be first in line to buy one once this was all over. She loved to pretend that she only attended my events as Bella's BFF, but I knew better. Her dick-deprived ass was forever buying two of everything, and I thought it was hilarious. Honestly, Bella was cool and the only one I could tolerate, but I had a feeling that I was going to have to snatch her homegirl up one of these days. Anyway, back to this money and the dick I was holding in my hand.

"Okay, girls, it's demo time for those of you challenged in the oral aspect of lovemaking. I can assure you that Pac makes for great practice while perfecting your technique."

I moved my jaw from side to side to loosen it up as if I were really about to give head to a live man. My mouth immediately juiced up at the thought, and I was ready. I attached Pac to the table by the suction at his base, and he now stood at attention, every glorious inch of him. From my seat at the table, I spat on it nastily before my mouth descended on the dildo like a true headhunter. Slurping and suctioning sounds were all that could be heard throughout the room, and the shit was music to my ears. I was so into what I was doing that I actually moaned a few times. I continued to deep throat Pac with my eyes focused on my audience, who all sat at the edge of their seats, eyeing me in amazement. At that point, I knew I had them, and they would tell a friend who would tell another friend. This Hart Throb line was going to take off just as the others had.

"Gotdamn," I heard a male voice say low.

Looking to the back of the room, my eyes met one of the most gorgeous men I'd ever seen in my life. He had tightly slanted eyes, juicy pink lips, and a full beard just like I fucking liked. He was dressed casually in distressed jeans, a graphic tee, and Vans, and I couldn't tear my eyes away from his fine ass. He stood with his arms folded across his chest, head tilted to the side, biting that pink-ass bottom lip I all of a sudden wanted to kiss and suck so badly. We maintained eye contact while my lips remained wrapped around Pac. Realizing that I was probably sitting here looking a plumb fool in front of the ladies, I became embarrassed. So, of course, I lashed out and began talking shit. With the dildo still in my mouth, it was clear he was having a problem understanding me.

"What?" he asked in amusement as he kicked off the doorjamb he'd been leaning on to move closer to the table.

Sliding Pac slowly out of my mouth, I used my hand to push my long honey-blond hair out of my face before I spoke. "I asked, what the fuck are you staring at, dude? Let me find out you've never seen a bitch deepthroat nine inches before," I scoffed, rolling my eyes in annoyance. The sexy smirk he was wearing was suddenly replaced with an angry scowl. No lie, even that shit was cute to me. It was obvious that he didn't like the way I talked to him, but ask me if I gave a fuck.

"You're right, I haven't, but best believe I've had plenty of bitches deep throat these ten inches," he retorted while grabbing that fat print I was just now noticing.

"Kyrie, stop! Don't come in here causing problems when you agreed to let me use your place for tonight," Bella fussed.

"No, Bella, he's cool." I smiled up at him.

"Yeah, Bells, you heard her. I'm cool." He smiled back with his eyes still locked on mine.

Drea aka Onyx
The Quiet Storm

"Sixteen, eighteen, twenty." I looked down at the order sheet in front of me and furrowed my brow. "Josh!" I called out, eraser end of the pencil between my teeth. I looked behind me when I didn't receive a response. "Joshua!" I called a little louder.

He poked his head from behind the arrangement of sixteen dozen blue roses, a cute little scowl on his face. "Yes," he sang playfully.

"I thought when I spoke to you on the phone earlier, you said there were twenty-two deliveries scheduled for today. I only see twenty."

His head disappeared back behind the beautiful design he was working on for a few seconds before his small but fit body appeared beside it. "There were twenty-two, but we had two cancellations."

Lifting my chin, I could feel the frown forming on my face. "Why were they canceled?"

"Uh-uh. Don't do that, sweetheart. Your face is too pretty to be frowned up like that."

I rolled my eyes, ignoring his advice. "For real. Did they say why?"

"Hell if I know, Drea. Maybe they broke up with whoever the flowers were for, or maybe they didn't want to pay four hundred forty-five dollars for some damn flowers in a box."

I laughed. "You're still shocked at what some people will pay for these arrangements, huh?"

"I just don't get it." He shook his head and walked closer to where I was standing, the cheap Axe body spray he always wore lingering in the air.

"The shit is stupid to me. Men will spend four bills on some flowers for what? Some tired-ass pussy?" he scoffed. "Why not go to the supermarket and get a dozen flowers for twelve bucks? Shit, that's what I would do."

"But will those store-bought flowers last a whole year?" I asked but didn't wait for him to respond. "No, they would wither and die maybe two or three days later, and that would be twelve bucks gone down the drain. The flowers we sell here are preserved and treated to last up to a year if they follow the instructions included with their delivery," I pointed out.

"A year, huh? Who wants to keep some damn roses for a year?"

"Boy, you would be surprised. Do you think I would be in this business for five years if they weren't buying this shit?"

I walked around the counter inside of my flower shop, From the Hart, and picked up one of the bouquets that were ready for delivery: three dozen black roses in our white French hat round box, the cursive From the Hart logo embossed on the front in gold. Not only did we do arrangements for personal reasons, but we also did any kind of floral business needed for weddings, events in the city, ritzy celebrity functions, music videos, and sometimes movies. When I opened this shop five years ago, I never would have imagined that it would take off the way it did. We'd been booming ever since, and I wasn't mad at anything. From wives to mistresses and "I do's" to the director shouting cut, From the Hart was in this floral industry killing shit, and I didn't have any thoughts of stopping anytime soon.

"Where is Marlon? I spoke to him five minutes after I got off of the phone with you," I asked about my right-hand man and best friend who made the deliveries to our elite clientele. He actually owned part of the shop since he loaned me some of the money to start it up. But if you asked him, men didn't own businesses like this, only women. He was a silent partner, so to speak.

Josh rolled his eyes and walked back over to the arrangement he was working on. His khaki pants were a little too fitted for my taste. His From the Hart T-shirt was a little dingy, but that was okay. Josh didn't really too much interact with any customers who would walk in and place orders. He was usually behind some huge arrangement doing what he did best, designing shit. That was the only reason I hired him after Marlon shoved his application in my face. The brother had skills I couldn't deny, and in the six months he had been working here, his intricate designs on our bigger arrangements had my profits and orders going up. The two-toned baby dreads on his head just barely reached the back of his neck and bounced as he started skipping to the beat of whatever song was playing in the background. His smooth brown skin was the same color as oak. Dark spots were on his face from years of picking at it. Josh was indeed a cute young man with his baby face features. He just needed a little help with the way he dressed.

"I don't even know how you've put up with him working here as long as you have. The nigga is always late and always screwing orders up. He'd probably lose his dick if it weren't attached to his body and balls. And what the fuck takes him so long sometimes to get back? It's like he takes the scenic route or something when most of the deliveries aren't but a few blocks away. I better not find out he in these streets being a ho. Nigga got me fucked up!"

Josh continued to rant about Marlon's lack of time management and possible infidelities when the bell from the front door opening went off. Since I was still in search of a new receptionist, I had to play the part for the time being. I had to fire the last girl my sister, Philly, sent over for fucking some of my clientele after business hours.

Walking back up to the front of the store, I made sure that the white long-sleeved button-up I had on was covering my ass in these see-through tights. A poor choice to put on this morning, but I had a long night and didn't wake up in time to iron the pants that I really wanted to wear. After pulling my boots up on my calves, I went to greet whoever walked into the shop.

"Welcome to From the Hart, where our goal is to fill the desires of your heart. I'm Drea. How can I help cater to your vision today?"

I entered the bright room, surrounded by countless displays of the arrangements we offered, from the roses in round or square boxes to the limited-edition collection of luxury acrylic home decor and storage products featuring the Eternity Roses. It was like you stepped into a million-dollar wedding reception designed by David Tutera himself when you walked into my baby, and I was proud of every last dime I spent to make it look that way. The sweet scent of the earth's most romantic flower wavered in the air, enveloping my whole body in its essence. I would never get tired of that smell. I loved it when I was younger, helping my grandma pull weeds in her rose garden, and I loved it even more now. So caught up in my rose high, I didn't notice the tall figure at the shop's entrance a few seconds ago now standing next to me. I looked up into his eyes and got lost for a second in those honey-colored irises, but then I quickly shook it off after he opened his mouth to speak.

"I'm looking for Onyx. Does she work here?" His deep voice whispering my nickname caused a shiver to shoot down my spine.

I swallowed hard and cleared my throat. "Uh, there's no Onyx here. How can I help you?" Him asking for me by that name was kind of weird, seeing as only the motorcycle club family, my sisters, and a few friends called me that. Glancing at his fine ass again, it was safe to say that he didn't belong to any one of those categories.

He licked his lips, and his bright eyes stared into mine without any hesitation. "That's funny you would say that. My boy told that me this was where I could find her."

"Who's your boy?" I asked, professionalism turned all the way off. I was curious as to who would send someone here looking for me. Even though the flower shop was a front for what I really did, everybody knew I did not conduct business this way. A smirk formed on his wet lips, and I couldn't help the way my knees started to buckle.

"Now why would it matter who my boy is if Onyx doesn't work here?" he quipped, cocky attitude turning me the hell on.

This man's whole aura had my body coming alive. My nipples were now pushing through the thin satin of my bra and brushing against the fabric of the white shirt. My panties became moist from my pussy betraying me with my juices and a slow burn building at my core, ready to ignite my entire being. This man was sexy as hell with his smooth pecan skin, menacing but bright eyes, neatly trimmed facial hair, and football-player build. The all-black outfit he had on didn't reveal much of his body, but I could tell he was working with something under the baggy jeans and hoodie. Even the double nose ring was turning me on. Never understood the whole gold hoop and diamond stud on one side thing, but I fell in love with it right then and there.

"Look, man—"

"Simmy," he corrected me.

I rolled my eyes. "Look, Simmy. If you aren't here to buy any flowers for your mama, wife, girl, baby mama, or side bitch, then you need to leave. There's no Onyx here, only myself"—I pointed to my name tag—"Drea, and a few of my employees whose names aren't even close to the one you keep saying." Taking one last lustful glance at him, which I hoped he didn't notice, I turned on my heels to head back to where Josh and my bag were, but I stopped dead in my tracks when I felt the cool metal of a gun pressed at the back of my head.

"You really gonna try to play me like that?" Simmy's warm breath rasped in my ear. His dick pressed into my back because he was standing so close to me. I held my hands up to show that I was unarmed, but I cursed myself for leaving my gun in my bag. "I've been watching you for weeks, Onyx. For someone who should stay under the radar, you sure are out and about a lot. You frequent the same s more than you should, and quite frankly u're terrible at trying to hide who you really are and what you really do." When his lip brushed against my ear, I was positive that he felt the way my body shook. I could feel the smile on his face. "Even with my gun to the back of your head, I still got that pussy thumping, huh? Funny thing is, you done had my dick bricked up since I first saw your fine ass, so the feeling is mutual," he admitted, making me smile.

Yes, with a gun to my head I was cheesing my ass off at his words. Even more so when he pressed his hard dick farther into my back.

"The infamous Drea 'Onyx' Hart. Flower shop owner by day, clean headshot hit woman by night. You know I saw you kill that janky-ass politician the other night, right?" he said, making my body tense up. I was always careful and discreet, so I was lost as to how he knew what had gone down on my last job. "I followed you to the second home he keeps for his mistress and bastard-ass kids. I almost took you out right then and there, but the look in your eyes as you pumped those bullets into that fraud nigga was sexy as fuck. Dick was hard as hell watching that shit. Sorta like it is now," he said low with another quick bump against my ass. I tried to move up a little, but that prompted him to press the gun deeper into my skull.

"Don't even try it. You're not the only one who can do head shots while the target is in motion."

Tired of the taunting, I finally gave him what he wanted: the person he obviously came to see, Onyx. "Nigga, what the fuck do you want with me?"

"Turn around," he told me, completely ignoring my question.

Something in my mind kept telling me that this was the end, so I closed my eyes and said a small prayer. After asking God to forgive me for all of the lives I'd taken over the years, I slowly turned around to face the man who was obviously sent here to kill me. When I looked into Simmy's eyes, I couldn't quite read what they were saying. The look of murder was now evident in them, but it wasn't a look of murder geared toward me. He lowered his lips to my ear again, and that same shiver traveled down my spine.

"In about twenty seconds, some men are going to come in here with guns blazing because I haven't returned to the van yet. Grab the gun tucked in the side of my jeans, and do what you do best. The silencer is already on it, so don't worry about your neighbors or anybody else in this ritzy-ass neighborhood hearing shit."

Before I could fully process what he had just said, the front doors to my shop came crashing open, and the sound of glass shattering echoed in my ear. Three men dressed in all black like him, with semiautomatic weapons in their hands, came barreling in with their guns locked, loaded, and aimed directly at me. Lifting my hand to his waist, I grabbed the butt of the heavy gun he had tucked in his pants and let off three shots, hitting all three of my targets right in the middle of their foreheads before they could even think about getting a shot off on me. This nigga said he was looking for Onyx, and now she was in the mutha-fuckin' building, live and in living color.

"Drea!" Joshua's high-pitched voice yelled from the back, causing me to put some distance between Simmy and me. "What was tha . . ." His voice trailed off when he saw the three bodies laid out on the ground. "What the fuck? Are you okay? Do I need to call the police?"

With the smoking gun still in my hand, I fully turned around to Josh and grabbed his shoulders, shaking him a bit and making sure he was paying attention to what I was about to say.

"Fuck the police, Joshua. What I need you to do is go in the back and grab my bag. Get the red phone that's in the front pocket and press number one. When Marlon picks up, tell him there was a situation at the shop and he needs to call the cleanup woman right now. If he asks any questions, just tell him I'll explain everything when he gets here. Please, can you go handle that while I close down the shop and have Simmy help me get these bodies out of the way?"

Joshua nodded in understanding after a short moment, but he still had a weird look on his face.

"What's the matter?"

"Who . . . Who did you say was gonna help you move these bodies?"

"Simmy's going to help me," I said, turning around and pointing at nothing but air. Just that fast the nigga had dipped out on me and left.

My mind started going crazy with thoughts of who Simmy really was and why he decided to help me rather than kill me. *A hired hit man with a conscience,* I thought as I hit the button for the metal security gates to close over the doors and windows on the outside of the shop. Had that been me, Simmy's ass would've been dead the second I crossed the threshold, regardless of how attracted I was to him. Pussy leaking and all. But I was thankful for his change of heart, and I intended to show him just how much the next time we ran into each other.

Chapter 1

Philly

You ever feel like you're alone in the world? Like your every move is being watched by an audience of people you will never see in your life? Sorta like you're on your own personal *Truman Show*? Well, I'd felt this way ever since I could remember growing up on New Mexico Street with my mama and granny in the single-level home that didn't look like shit to some but was everything to us. My father wanted to put us in a place much bigger and in a different area, but my mother wouldn't hear of it. I remembered when playing hopscotch on the sidewalk in front of the house with Natalie with broken pieces of chalk, or sitting on the front porch with a big glass of lemonade watching the birds fly by, was what I considered fun. Innocent mind wondering where my life would be ten, twenty years from now. Or sitting in the house, watching my granny grease my mama's scalp, or my mother, in turn, helping her rub that smelly ointment on her sore joints afterward were always good times to me. I would give anything to have those days again. But sadly, I couldn't. It's funny how your life could take a turn for the worse in the blink of an eye.

The day my life changed for me was eighteen years ago when I was only nine years old. I had just gotten off of the school bus and was rushing home to show my granny and mama the blue ribbon I had won for the science project I did. I knew Mama would be so proud of me because we'd stayed up late many nights working on it. Even had my pops come over a couple times to help with my thesis of why motors ran the way they did. Of course, after about an hour, he and mama would disappear to her room for the rest of the night, but that was normal to me. Shit. It was normal for us. Our little family. Funny thing was our little family fell apart on one of the most exciting days of my life.

After getting off of the bus and running a couple of blocks to make it home, I stopped dead in my tracks the second the red and blue lights flashing from the police cars surrounding my house caught my attention. Yellow tape roped the yard off from giving anyone access to cross it. When the ambulance pulled up, something inside of me snapped and had me sprinting my little feet fast as hell toward the house I grew up in. I tried to run up to the steps but was stopped short by one of the neighbors I saw my granny talking to on occasion.

"Where's my mama? Where's my granny?" I yelled as tears began to drop from my eyes. I didn't know what was fully going on or why I was crying, but I could feel that something wasn't right.

"Baby, just stay right here with me until your daddy gets here," my neighbor whispered in my ear. But by this time, the adrenaline in my system was kicking in overtime. I wasn't trying to hear anything she or anyone else was saying, so I kicked, punched, and wiggled my way out of her arms and headed straight into the house. A few officers tried to stop me as I sprinted down the broken cement path, but my small feet were a little too fast for them.

The front door was wide open, so I ran straight through and stopped in the living room. Police officers were everywhere, dusting shit off and taking pictures of the broken furniture and glass on the floor. I looked around for my mother for a second, and when I didn't see her, I ran up the stairs and straight to her room. Thinking back now, me running into that house was the worst decision I ever made in my life. Because laid out on the side of her bed with half of her head blown off was my mother. Her small hands were clutching her Bible and my fluffy teddy bear with the missing eye that Daddy had given me when I was six. Her work clothes were still on, and her hair was up in that curly but messy ponytail she liked. And lying next to her in a pool of blood was my granny. Her eyes were open as if she were still here, and she had a halo-like ring of blood beneath her head. She had a faded black apron wrapped around her small frame and flour on her fingertips from the chicken she must've been preparing to fry. My entire soul left my body at that moment, and I let out the loudest, most gut-wrenching scream. Falling to my knees, I crawled over to my granny and laid my head on her lap and continued to cry. My chest heaved up and down so fast I couldn't catch my breath. I must've lain there for an hour or two before my father finally showed up and had to pull me off of her.

That night, I went from being in one hell to living in another one. Sole, my father's wife, wasn't too fond of her husband's love child moving in, but she had no say in it. Because when Julian "Knight" Hart said something, everybody listened, including her hateful ass. My days growing up there weren't all bad, though. My sisters Diem and Drea were there to brighten up the days I was feeling down. Pops treated us all like his little princesses, never putting one above the other. But Sole? That bitch didn't like me for shit and would show it whenever Pops wasn't around. She was always trying to pit me and my sister against one another, but that shit never worked. One thing Pops taught us was to always have each other's backs regardless of what we had going on in our lives, and that's what we'd always done. Case in point, me sitting here in Diem's new sex dungeon, surrounded by all of these fake dicks, pussies, and asses so that we could discuss the things that still needed to be done for our motorcycle club's annual fundraiser.

"DiDi, why couldn't we just meet at your house to discuss this? These dicks are a fucking distraction," Drea scrunched up her face and said. "I'm all for some freaky shit going down, but this is ridiculous."

Mind you, all of this complaining was done as she cupped and rubbed the balls that hung from the silicone sex doll in front of her. I wasn't knocking my sister's hustle, but I would never understand what these women got out of fucking on a damn dildo. And this particular one that Drea was fondling didn't even have a head attached to it. It was just a torso with rock-hard abs and a long dick. Diem made a killing selling this mess, but it was some straight-up freak shit if you asked me.

"I wanted you guys to see my new place. This is where I'll be hosting future pleasure parties, as well as the big orgy fest," Diem piped up.

"Orgy fest?" I asked. "You can't be serious, Di. I know you're not about to be in here fucking a bunch of different niggas!" I hollered.

"Chill the hell out, girl! When have you ever known me to participate? I simply throw the parties and watch the shenanigans unfold before my eyes," she answered, rubbing her hands together like the true pervert she was.

"That better be all you're doing," I retorted, causing Diem to stick her tongue out at me.

"Anywayyyy, I just found out this morning that someone put a bid in on my old location, so things are moving along as planned. And please, please don't forget that I'll need the both of you during the moving process."

"About that—" I started.

"Here we go." Diem rolled her eyes before I could even finish my statement. "What excuse do you have for not being able to help this time? I gave you plenty of notice, and you said you'd help, so what's up? I gotta hear this one," she added sarcastically.

"Chill, bitch! I'm still going to be there. I'll just be running a little bit behind," I said, hoping she wouldn't press any further. I had a good reason, but I was sure it wouldn't be a good enough excuse for DiDi.

"You know what, Philly, don't even bother coming," she dismissed me with a wave of her hand. "First the shit with Brix and now this." That last part was said in a low tone, but I still caught it.

"Brix? What does he have to do with anything?" I was really confused now.

"Y'all, calm the hell down," Drea warned.

"Nah, ain't no fucking calming down. What did you mean by that shit, Diem?" I asked, getting worked up.

"Philly, chill out," Drea interrupted. "Pops already told y'all to put an end to this shit. I don't understand why you two have been going at it the way you have lately."

Ever since we were younger, she was always the peacemaker between Diem and me. Whenever we would argue or at times physically fight, she would always break it up or do something crazy to draw our attention to herself.

"I'll cut it out when she apologizes for sleeping with Brix when she knew I had him on my hit list."

"Di, you sound crazy as hell right now. I don't know where you're getting your information from, but I've never slept with Brix," I tried to explain, but she just scoffed in response.

"Bitch, stop lying. Sissy told me she saw you walking out of that nigga's house twice at seven in the morning. That's walk of shame hours if you ask me." She shrugged.

I shook my head. "So you can't go to a man's house and just talk? And why you listening to other bitches instead of asking me what was up? We're way better than that, and you know it."

Honestly, all Brix and I ever did was just talk, so my sister was tripping over nothing. Once I told him that I wasn't interested in him after we went out for a bite to eat, we sorta just started hanging out as friends. He worked on bikes just like me, so our love for all things motorcycle was what our conversations consisted a lot of. Well, that and DiDi's freaky ass. I mentioned her name a lot while we kicked it. Even told him straight out that DiDi wanted to have sex with him. But he said that my oldest sister by two hours wasn't really his type. Her mouth was too foul for him, and he didn't want to deal with Drea or our pops in the wake of him putting his hands on her. I thought it was funny that his big Adam Rodriguez–looking ass couldn't handle DiDi or that mouth of hers. He said he preferred girls more like me: quiet, laid-back, and playing the background. Three things that DiDi was not and I was pretty sure she would never be.

"Ask you about it? So you could lie about it like you are right now? I'll pass," DiDi replied with an exaggerated eye roll. "Wouldn't be the first time you crossed me behind a nigga."

"Not this shit again," I groaned. "I can't believe you're still tripping over some shit that happened in fucking middle school. You didn't even tell me you liked the nigga, so how was I supposed to know he was off-limits, DiDi? I swear you're petty as hell for bringing that up." I laughed, and so did they.

"Fuck you, heffa," Diem chuckled. "Next time you come for what's mine I'ma fuck you up," she threatened.

"Fuck me up? You've must've forgotten who taught you how to fight."

"Don't matter, Ophelia." She pronounced every syllable of my name while waving the box cutter my way. "Your little hothead ass don't scare me. Never have and never will."

I stood up from the burgundy leather chair I was sitting in, stained work coveralls falling lower on my waist. I rubbed the back of my hand across my nose. The lingering smell of the fast orange hand cleaner was still on my skin. "You don't have to be scared to get yo' ass whooped boo, believe that," I responded. "But, say, I, umm, I'm about to cut out. Got some shit to handle."

"Really, bitch? Been here for all of twenty minutes. Thank you so much for your help!" Diem fumed sarcastically.

"Don't be like that, sis. I promise to be there when you move. I'll even try to rearrange some things so that I'm not late," I tried to compromise.

"Like I said earlier, don't bother. Anytime it has something to do with you, we're there, but you don't seem to give a fuck about what we have going on."

I already knew another round of bickering was coming after I announced that I was leaving, so I prepared myself for it. What I wasn't prepared for was the look of hurt in my sister's eyes. What she was saying was far from true, but I knew that my actions wouldn't support whatever rebuttal I offered, so I kept quiet. Just like the peacemaker she was, Drea stepped in to change the subject and ease the tension that once again filled the room.

"Philly, are you really just going to leave without telling me about the dude who came into your shop?" she asked.

I heard her question, but I couldn't take my eyes off of my oldest sister. She had blond hair with auburn highlights in big curls that framed her smooth chestnut face. Her makeup was done to perfection, her jewelry was on point, and an all-white business suit that looked like it was painted on her body rounded out her look. She was always in CEO mode but quick to turn hood whenever the need was warranted. I loved DiDi to death, and I hated when we butted heads like this. Lately, it had been happening a lot. The look on her face was bothering me to no end, making me feel like shit for disappointing her yet again.

"Philly?" baby sis called out again, her hand cupping my chin and turning my eyes toward her. "Tell me about ol' boy. You said he was fine as hell, right?" I looked at DiDi, who was now waiting for me to respond. No matter how upset she was, her nosey ass wanted the tea just as bad as Drea.

I licked my lips and slowly nodded, my cheeks heating up just thinking about the dude from earlier. Although his little crew got on my last nerve and I had to check his fat-ass friend, I still couldn't get the vision of his fine-ass face out of my mind. As soon as I'd left the front lobby, I'd gone back to my office and called Drea. I needed to talk to someone to cool my temper down since Nats was still out in the front assisting them.

"Well, did you at least get his name?"

"Nah, I didn't get a chance to. He had some ghetto-ass bird hanging on his arm anyway. She tried to check the nigga for staring at me a little longer than she liked, though." I smirked.

"Please tell me you didn't slap that girl too," Drea laughed. She poked my forehead with her finger. "Keep messing around, your ass is going to be in jail for violating your probation."

"Man. I'm not about to be in nobody's jail cell," I countered, pulling the straps of my backpack over my shoulder. Picking up my helmet, I situated it under my arm and leaned my body against the desk. Looking down at my shirt, I made a mental note to stop by the T-shirt store to buy myself some new packs of wife beaters and a couple more pair of coveralls. "I think I handled the situation in a respectable manner. The way fat boy was coming at me was foul as hell. It was borderline harassment if you ask me. So I was well within my legal rights to react to his bullshit."

Drea laughed again. "A'ight, Philly. You know if you go away this time, it will be for some years and not just a few months."

DiDi picked up a few of the boxes that were stacked in the corner and walked them over to her desk. "Damn, you all up in her business. What about you and the mystery dude who sorta saved your life? Did you ever find out who was behind that shit or who he was?"

"Nah, nothing yet. You know as soon as the cleanup crew left I made a few calls to my contacts, but I got nothing. When I checked the security cameras from outside, I was able to get a partial license for the car that he jumped into, but that was it."

"Did you hit Sandie up?" I asked. Sandie was one of our MC sisters who worked at the DMV. We usually hit her up whenever we needed an address for somebody.

"You know I already did. Told me it would be a minute before she can find out some info with just a partial plate number. I also sent the info to Dolly. They put her on desk duty after the little incident with her husband's mistress, but she still has access to the police database." Drea watched me wrapping my skull-face bandana around my neck. "Where you 'bout to go?"

I tightened the arms of my coveralls around my waist and made sure my boots were tied tight. "I'm about to head back over to the shop. I still got some last-minute things to do on the restoration of that 1968 Ariel Cyclone 650 I've been working on. I'm supposed to make the delivery soon, so I want to make sure that everything is up to par, you know?"

"A 1968 Ariel Cyclone 650? I know your ass came a few times while working on that thing. Isn't that your dream bike?"

In actuality, the Cyclone was my dream bike, but it would have to stay that way until I got the money to afford one with the type of restorations and improvements I wanted. The one I was working on now was going to cost the owner a smooth ten grand once I was actually done with everything I was doing to it. The paint work, the new leather seats, tires, lighting, and chrome that I replaced and installed wasn't cheap. Not to mention the engine I rebuilt with some of the parts that I had to order from China. I shook my head. *Maybe I should tack on another five Gs for the extra labor I put into this restoration.* For the last two weeks, I'd only worked on this project, giving my other tickets out to my workers and hoping they didn't fuck shit up.

"Ahhhh, earth to Philly," Drea said, waving her hands in my face, breaking me from my thoughts. "Um, where the hell did you go that fast? One minute you were talking and the next you just zoned out."

My gaze went from hers to DiDi's then down to my helmet. "Y'all know me. My mind is always on some money and these bikes. But let me get out of here. I got some shit to do later on tonight, and I need to count receipts and lock up the shop before I do anything. Call me if you need me, and text me whenever you guys come up with an idea for the annual dance."

"When we come up with an idea? Last time I checked, Hart's Angels was our motorcycle club. Me, you, and Drea," DiDi sassed, placing the open box she had in her hand down and walking closer to me.

"Hart's Angels is our club, but that doesn't mean I have to be present for every decision you guys make," I argued.

"But you're the fucking president, Philly. What the hell would that look like, the president not being here to suggest or finalize shit?"

"'Cause I don't have to be! You're the VP, which means you act as me when I'm not able to be there." Moments ago I was feeling bad for flaking on her, but now she was beginning to get on my fucking nerves. We were now face-to-face with our toes touching, her red Giuseppes to my black steel-toe work boots. "If you don't wanna be VP, maybe I should call a meeting and put in a vote for a new one. We can all meet in Heaven on Friday to find someone else to occupy the position you obviously have a problem adhering to, and we can go from there."

"You wouldn't dare," DiDi gasped.

"I would dare," I threatened. I knew just as well as Diem did that no one else could occupy the top three positions in the club even if they wanted to. I was just saying the shit to piss her off and it seemed to be working.

"Enough, you guys." Drea stepped in, her hips swaying from side to side as she wedged herself between us. "We can all just meet up this weekend at my house. The fundraiser is over a month away, so we don't have to decide anything tonight. Philly, you go on and finish whatever it is you have to do at the shop. DiDi, I'll help you unpack the rest of this freaky shit so we can meet up at Hartland for dinner, okay?"

"Yeah, okay." DiDi nodded with her eyes still trained on me. Turning around, she walked back to the other side of her desk and picked her ringing phone up. With a small scowl on her face, she ignored the call and then looked back up at me. "You still here? I thought you had somewhere to be." When my nostrils flared a little and I pulled my bottom lip into my mouth, she quirked her eyebrow and chucked her chin up. "What? Daddy ain't here to save your ass right now, and Drea can only hold us apart for so long."

"Please just go, Philly. I don't know why she's trippin' like this. We were all cool just a few minutes ago," Drea pleaded.

I nodded slowly and pulled my bandana over my mouth. After placing my helmet over my head and securing the arms of my coveralls one last time, I left DiDi's shop and hopped on my bike. With one earbud in place, I turned on the Evanescence song "Bring Me to Life" and burned rubber out of the small parking lot, merging into the evening traffic.

Swerving in and out of lanes and reeving my motor up to run any yellow light I came across, I flew through the streets with nothing on my mind but getting as far away from DiDi as I could. Sometimes I wondered if she and I would ever rediscover the close bond we had before. Like the bond Drea and I still shared. Like I said before, our father always taught us to have each other's backs and to always be our sister's keeper. Especially after we started the motorcycle club. A lot of people didn't like that we were an all-female club that was dominating our city in more ways than one. Not only did we all have that rough rider side to us, but we were all professional working women in a sense. Some of the all-male clubs tried to run us out of town and even tried to get our chapter erased. But with our father being one of the three elders, it was kind of hard to get rid of Hart's Angels.

Finally making it to the shop, I pulled my bike to the back and opened the small door that had a security pad, which required my thumbprint for entrance. Once in, I turned on the lights and walked straight to the Cyclone. As I walked around the beautiful bike, I lightly trailed my fingers over the shiny chrome and soft leather. A tingle ran down my spine, causing goosebumps to decorate my whole body. Sitting down on my stool, I grabbed the polishing rag that was sitting on top of my toolbox and began to polish the beautiful emerald green paint with the shiny sparkle finish. It had taken me a few hours to come up with this color, and I hoped the owner appreciated every detail that I put into this restoration.

A cool breeze swept over my body and my eyebrows raised. Only one other person had access to the thumbprint security system, and that was Nats. When I talked to her earlier, she was at her boo thang's house, so I knew it wasn't she who could have opened the door and walked in. With my back facing whoever was walking up behind me, I quickly opened my toolbox and grabbed the cool metal handle of my Glock 17. With the safety already off, I turned swiftly toward my intruder with my gun pointed directly at his face.

"You gotta be fucking kidding me," were the words that left my mouth when my eyes finally recognized the nigga standing in front of me. "How the fuck did you get in here?"

Chapter 2

Diem

"I just don't understand why you've been coming at her like that lately, Diem. She's our sister, for crying out loud. Family over everything! You do remember that, right?" Drea stressed the motto.

She went in on me before I could even close the door to my car. I thought we were done with this conversation after leaving my shop, but her ass wasted no time picking up right where we left off. We were now making our way up the marble steps leading to our parents' front door for dinner. This was some shit they could miss me with, but I came because I didn't want to hear my daddy's mouth. Didn't really care what my mama had to say about the shit but whatever.

"Gimme a break, Drea. I love that girl, and you know that. Shit, even she knows that. You also don't have to remind me that she's my sister. Philly's just been getting on my fucking nerves, man," I tried justifying my actions.

Despite the way she came into our lives, I loved her like she'd been there since day one. The situation was fucked up, but I didn't hold it against my sister. Neither of us had control over the dysfunctional position we'd been placed in. Imagine one day out of the blue your father comes home with a girl the same age as you, looks almost identical to you, just with a lighter skin tone, and begins taking up time with your favorite guy. Time that used to only be meant for you. Like, "This is your sister, now deal with it" type shit. No real explanation from our parents, but I was old enough to know that if she was my sister, then that meant my hero was flawed, meaning he'd stepped out on my mom and made a baby with someone else. I already hated sharing him with Drea, but luckily she clung to our mother and didn't give me much competition where Daddy was concerned. Philly, on the other hand, seemed to have her own special relationship with him, and in the beginning, I didn't like that shit one bit. The thing was Pops never switched up on me. On any of us. He made it his duty to shower us equally with love and affection. That right there was the reason I never harbored any ill feelings toward my sister. My current issues with her had nothing to do with Julian Hart or his infidelity.

"She's been through enough though, DiDi, so I would think you'd be more sympathetic. And you can keep trying her if you want to. She gon' beat that ass for real one day," she joked, attempting to make me laugh after low-key telling me about myself. That was just like her ass. Always the peacemaker among us and wouldn't hesitate to tell you off in the funniest or most loving way possible.

"I keep telling y'all that ain't nobody beating my ass! What don't y'all understand about that?" I said, making her laugh out loud. "I hear you, sis, and I promise to try to do better. You have to admit that her fucking ol' boy was messed up though. She knew for a fact I was trying to take that nigga down, and now I can't even get at him. No way I'm fucking behind my sister. No way in hell! Fuck the fact that I ain't fucked nothing in months!" I complained as the door to my parents' home opened. "This bihh . . ." I mumbled, earning a sharp elbow in the side from my sister.

"Why must you speak so nasty all the time, Diem?" my mother asked, shaking her head at me. Clearly she'd heard me talking about not being able to fuck Brix. Hopefully she didn't hear me referring to her as a bitch, because I'd never hear the end of it. She was looking at me crazy, but she was the one standing there dressed to the nines for a casual dinner with her children. I was coming from work, so yes, my outfit was on point as well, but her ass was just being her usual extra self. I was sure all Sole Hart had done today was shop online and track my father's every move, but here she was answering the door looking like the queen of Sheba or some shit. Without my father, her ass wouldn't have a pot to piss in or a window to throw it out of, and I couldn't respect that. I would never respect a female who had absolutely no hustle about herself. Sole Hart irked my nerves like no other, and that was saying a lot considering she gave birth to me.

"'Cause I'm a nasty mutha—'" I started to quote that line from my and Philly's favorite movie, *Life*, but my father's booming baritone voice stopped me.

"Diem, cut that shit out and bring your ass inside. Don't know why you insist on starting up with your mother within five minutes of being here!" he chastised.

Of course, I kept quiet while Drea just snickered. My mother, on the other hand, just smirked, happy that my father had put me in my place yet again on her behalf. In the same way Drea played referee between me and Philly, my father ran interference between my mother and me. I wanted so bad to flip her snooty ass off but thought better of it. I walked over to hug my favorite guy, bypassing my mom altogether. She didn't seem to mind, seeing how she was already caught up in conversation with her baby girl.

"Drea, honey, I just love what you've done with your hair," she gushed and ran her fingers through it. The loose-wave sew-in my sister was sporting was cute as hell, but I still rolled my eyes at how my mother went out of her way to compliment my sister but looked me up and down like I wasn't killing shit with my hair as well. Her ass was too damn old to be a hater, and it was shameful.

"I like it too. Did you see DiDi's? We went to the same chick. She did her thing with Di's color, right, Ma?" Drea smiled over my way. I knew what she was trying to do, and while I appreciated it, it wasn't necessary. To my credit, praise from others never moved me one way or the other. If no one else in the world thought I was the shit, I did, and that was all that mattered.

"Yes, of course. I love hers as well." Sole offered me that fake smile.

"Mm-hmm," I replied, moving toward the dining room. "Pops, what's on the menu tonight? I know you're the one who cooked whatever it is we're about to eat," I said, taking another jab at my mother. I mean, if she didn't want to work, that was fine, but the least her ass could do was cook and clean. Trust she did neither. My pops brought home the bacon and fried that shit up too. Even hired a cleaning lady to come through a few times per week to help my mother out. Help her do what I had no clue, but that was the shit I didn't like. I felt like she didn't really appreciate my dad and she brought absolutely nothing to the table. I honestly didn't know what my father saw in her lazy, materialistic, shallow ass.

"Diem, I'll have you know that your father and I prepared dinner together tonight," she defended herself.

"Where is my other baby?" my father asked, referring to Philly.

I watched as my mom rolled those big-ass hazel eyes of hers. Now, even though we bumped heads, I didn't allow anyone to come for my sister, so hopefully my mother kept it at eye rolling and didn't say anything out of the way about Philly. That's one person not even my father allowed her to speak ill on, and I agreed with him on that. That shit didn't even fly with Drea, so my mother knew better.

"Oh, she had some work to finish up at the shop," Drea answered as she glanced down at her phone.

"She did, but she probably wouldn't have come anyway," I added low.

If you thought my mom treated me fucked up, she treated Philly even worse, but it was only when my father or one of us sisters weren't around. Pops didn't play about his girls. He checked me most times because if my mother and I got into it, nine times out of ten, I'd started it. Philly tended to stay out of my mom's way, but Sole sought her out at times and made it her business to fuck with her. She was the reason that Philly moved out the first chance she got. She and I had probably been eighteen for just a few days, and she was gone. I at least waited until it was time to go off to college, but Philly? Her ass got ghost and hadn't looked back. I couldn't say that I blamed her though. Despite the love she received from the rest of us, it had to be crazy for her living under the roof with my mother.

"That girl works way too hard. I'll stop by to see her after my meeting with a potential new construction company for this new deal I'm working on."

"What do you know about the company?" I asked after praying over the plate my mother placed in front of me. This business shit was something my father and I had in common. We could sit and talk money moves all day long and not get bored.

"Well," he said, slicing into his steak and dipping the medium-rare piece into some A.1. Sauce, "it's a black-owned company, so you know that was a major plus for me. Hopefully their presentation is on point so that I can bring them in on this project. I'm all for uplifting and pulling up other brothers with me. I feel like there's enough money out there for all of us." I just smiled at the man I'd admired my whole life. Was proud to call him Dad. "The owner is a young entrepreneur, so I'm curious to see what he can bring to the table."

"I guess you'll never learn your lesson regarding dealing with these roughnecks. You'd rather do business with them as opposed to going with a more experienced company. I guess you forgot what happened the last time." My mother shook her head.

She was referring to an incident when my father lost tons of money dealing with a black-owned company that didn't make good on meeting deadlines and providing quality work. Since then she'd been adamant about him no longer dealing with companies starting out or companies owned by blacks. Just like my father, I knew that in business you sometimes take losses, but you live and you learn. You couldn't tell my mother that though. She was one of those uppity negroes who liked to forget where she came from and was all about self. Fuck helping others.

"Sole, shut the hell up speaking on things that you have no clue about. All you see is the money," my father spat before I had a chance to say anything. Best believe I was about to go in on her ass, but Pops beat me to the punch.

"Ain't that it!" I concurred while she glared at me.

"I wasn't aware that I couldn't have an opinion, Julian." She just sat there looking like a sad puppy. Ol' fake ass.

"There's a difference between having an opinion and constantly tearing others down. I know what happened last time, but I don't plan to let that stop me from doing business with a company just because the owners are African American. Like I said before, I'm all for pulling other brothers up with me," he said, leaving it at that.

Following that brief back-and-forth, the conversation once again turned positive and continued to flow with my mother adding her two cents every now and again. We discussed everything we'd been up to in the last week as we dined on steak, huge, loaded baked potatoes, asparagus, and some kind of rice mixture that my mother obviously undercooked. Drea, who was preoccupied with her damn cell phone majority of the time, had hardly touched her plate. The only thing that she did show interest in were the yeast rolls she kept grabbing out of the bread basket. My mother kept cutting her eyes and clearing her throat every time her text message alert would go off, and I knew it was only a matter of time before someone said something about it.

"Drea, put that damn phone up. This is family time," my father ordered, wiping the silly-ass grin off my sister's face.

I tried to look at her screen when she placed her phone down on the table, but before I could get a good look at the name of the person texting her, she picked her phone up and stuffed it into her bra. Whoever she was talking to had her cheesing hard as hell, and I was hoping there was a juicy story behind that big-ass smile. My love and sex life was pretty much nonexistent these days, so I was vicariously living through my sister's for the time being.

"So, where are you all at with the planning of the fundraiser?" my father asked.

"We haven't even nailed down a theme yet," I admitted, knowing he was about to have something to say.

"What the hell have y'all been doing?" he bellowed.

"Pop, it's just that we've all been so busy with work that it's been hard coordinating our schedules, but I promise we'll have it together by next month for the ball."

"I understand that, but this is a big deal for me, DiDi. You know how important those children at the group home are to me. I was one of them at one point in my life. If I knew you three wouldn't take it seriously, I wouldn't have passed the responsibility of the fundraiser down to you," he continued. Pops included us all in that statement, but I knew from experience that it was really directed toward me.

I knew how strongly my father felt about his beloved club, and I didn't want to let him down. Every year we came up with something that blew him away, and I wanted this year to be no different. That was why I was on Philly so hard earlier today. They thought it was just me being a bitch like always, but that wasn't the case this time. It was like no matter what they did or what their responsibilities were, my father always looked to me to get things done. That was a good and bad thing for me. Good because it meant that he trusted me to handle business, and bad because a lot of times that left me doing a majority of the work.

"I'll have everything together by next week," I offered with my head down.

"Good! That's what I like to hear." He smiled and continued eating.

I had plans to go out with Bella this weekend, but now it seemed I'd be home working on ideas by myself while my sisters lived it up per usual.

"So how is club business?" Pops asked, referring to our motorcycle club Hart's Angels, wiping the corners of his mouth with his linen napkin and taking a drink of his water. "When's the next meeting?"

I pushed a few pieces of asparagus around on my plate, my appetite slowly dwindling. "Club business is club business. All of the ladies are paying their monthly dues and handling their job titles. Our next meeting is in a few days."

"Has there been any static?"

My eyes cut over to my father. Him asking about static meant something was going on or about to happen. I shook my head and placed my fork down on the side of my plate. "Not that I know of, but why do you ask?"

"Sole," my father's deep voice commanded, "I'd like a glass of my favorite scotch."

"But, Julian—"

"That wasn't a request, dear," he cut her off, with that smile that said he meant business.

My mother looked around the table as all eyes were trained on her. She knew that we never discussed club business in front of her, so I didn't understand what she was trying to argue about.

"I swear I'll be so glad when y'all grow the hell up and leave this bike madness alone. For someone to be retired from that life, you sure do keep your eyes, nose, and ears in it." Her hard eyes turned toward me. "And what respectable woman wants to be out here riding motorcycles anyway? You have a booming business with those toys, Diem, and your sister is doing pretty well with her flower shop. Hell, even Philly's tomboyish ass is making money restoring those old bikes. Why do y'all still function with Hart's Angels? I think it's about time you all give up your seats and just focus on your future. Even though I'm too young to have them right now, I would like to have grandchildren running around one day, and I'm pretty sure your father—"

"Don't speak for me, Sole," my father warned. "Go get my drink. And make sure you put four ice cubes in it."

Their eyes warred for a few seconds before my mom rolled hers to the back of her head and stood up from her seat. The white knee-length and body-hugging cocktail dress she had on hugged every curve of her body. The iced-out watch and bracelet set shined bright under the dim dining room light. She fingered the diamond tennis necklace around her neck and looked down at the table. Her half-eaten plate was almost identical to mine. When my father took another sip of his water and cleared his throat, she pursed her lips and finally left the table with a huff, but not before mumbling something under her breath.

"I don't see how you've put up with her and her attitude all these years," I said low, but loud enough for my father to hear.

He shrugged his shoulders. "It's cheaper to keep her. Your mother and I don't have that fairy-tale type of love that you young folk are so obsessed with, but what we share works. Not everyone is blessed enough to end up with their soulmate, baby."

The distant look in his eyes told me that he was thinking about Philly's mom. I didn't know the extent of their relationship or why he didn't end up with her in the first place, but I did know that she had a large piece of my father's heart that my mom could never fill. The way his eyes would gloss over whenever Philly brought her up or whenever he used to come into our room and see the picture of Philly's mom on the dresser told me that his love for her was far greater than it ever was for the woman who birthed me.

"Are we done here?" Drea asked, bringing me from my thoughts. Her questioning gaze went from me to our father.

"I just need a few more minutes of your time, and then you can go," Pops replied. "I wanted to give you all a heads-up on some things that will be happening in the weeks to come."

"What's up?" I questioned.

My pops sighed and wiped his hand over his face. "You know that big project I'm working on? The one where I was just telling you that I have a meeting with a new construction company in a few days?" I nodded, trying to figure out where he was going with this. "Well, we want to build a new shopping center in the city, and the only prime location to do that is on the north side."

"The north side as in Dragon territory?" I said. The Dragons were a rival all-male motorcycle club that had been in the bike world before I was even thought of. When my pops used to be heavy in the streets, I would hear him and his brothers talk often about whatever beef the Rolling Harts, the original name of Hart's Angels, had with the Dragons. But like any great protector, Julian "Knight" Hart never brought any kind of drama to his front door, so I never got to see firsthand how bad the blood was between them.

However, I did know that some of their beef trickled down into the votes when we presented Hart's Angels to the elders to be acknowledged as a legit motorcycle club. Of the four voting members, Lukas Coleman, an old running buddy of my father's, was the only one who voted against us. Said he could never respect an all-girl crew or take us seriously. Good thing the three other votes were in favor of us, or we wouldn't have been here today. It was funny to me how he felt that way, seeing as his daughter, Elle, couldn't wait to be a part of our club.

Since that time, Lukas had branched off and was now the head of the Dragons. The fact that Pops was about to tear down a lot of their legit moneymaking businesses could possibly cause problems for us, and I was sure he knew that. We would definitely have to call an emergency meeting in Heaven to discuss what we would need to do since it seemed Pops was definitely going forward with this plan. It wasn't that I was afraid, but it was always good to be prepared. If you stayed ready, there was no need to get ready.

"So this is why we had dinner tonight? Why it was so important for us to be here?" I smacked my lips. "See, this is exactly why Philly's ass should've come. How the fuck can we talk about something like this, something that can possibly affect the motorcycle club as a whole, and the president not be here to offer her opinion?" This was the same shit I was talking about earlier when we were at my new office space.

"Calm down, DiDi," Drea cautioned. "You act like demolition started . . ." She trailed off. Her alarmed eyes went to Pops. "Wait, has it started already?"

Pops shook his head and cleared his throat. When our mother walked into the room with his drink, our little conversation came to an abrupt stop.

"By all means, continue," she offered, that stupid-ass smirk on her face as she handed Pops his drink. A small crystal tumbler with four ice cubes just as he requested and his favorite scotch filled all the way up to the rim. I could smell the woodsy scent of the strong alcohol from where I was sitting.

"Dear, will you go ahead and prepare dessert? Bring the pecan praline ice cream as well."

"Pecan praline? Alma told me she put that in the bottom of the deep freezer in the garage. I had her bring out the vanilla ice cream because that's what you said you wanted with the peach cobbler," she complained, her brown skin turning a deep shade of red.

"I did, but I've changed my mind." He patted his belly. "I've decided that I want some pecans with my cobbler tonight."

"Honey—"

"Just go get the ice cream, Sole, damn. Why I always gotta ask you shit more than once?"

The whole room became quiet. Internally I was cheering my father on for checking her spoiled ass. I wanted to laugh at the dumb look on her face, but I didn't want to pour any more salt over the wound she already had open.

"This is why we need to hire a maid full-time. I'm not about to keep fetching your shit like I'm the damn help. This is a St. John Mikado beaded cocktail dress for Christ's sake. You don't wear sixteen hundred dollars' worth of expensive fabric to dig in a deep freezer, Julian."

"Is that how much I paid for that dress?" my father exclaimed. "We seriously need to put you on a budget. We will be broke before we make it to our seventies with you spending money on shit like that."

I snickered as Drea excused herself from the table. Her phone was in her hand, and that silly smile was on her face. While our parents continued to argue about money and my mother knowing her role, I slipped my phone out of my pocket and shot Philly a text, letting her know that we needed to meet up ASAP. I sent another text to cancel the outing with Bella.

After receiving an okay reply from both of them, I stood up and grabbed my things. See, this always happened whenever we tried to discuss any kind of business while Sole was around. Her nosey ass wanted to be privy to everything we were talking about and offer her unsolicited opinion when no one wanted it. That our father brought up the new development at the table told me he had some concerns about what this new deal could bring to not only our MC but our family as well. The fact that we were a bunch of professional women who loved to ride bikes sometimes had these other clubs thinking that we were soft and would bow down when pushed up on. But what they didn't know was that, although we were all book smart in some way, we still had the heart of the streets in us. You don't get raised by one of the most feared men in Vegas and not pick up some of the traits that got him that title.

"Where you off to?" Drea asked, closing the bathroom door behind her and falling in step with me.

"I'm on my way home. I've been up all day with those new shipments and dealing with the new store location. Plus, I have to host all three parties myself this weekend since I haven't found any new hostesses yet."

She nodded and grabbed her jacket from the coat rack. "So what do you think about the shit Pops was talking about? Did he ever say when they planned to begin demolition on the north side?"

I shook my head. "No, he didn't. But I'm sure that when he does, Slim and his little crew will be showing their ugly faces, trying to cause problems."

Drea's body froze. "Wait a minute. What if they started already?"

"What do you mean?"

"Those three men I killed at my shop the other day. I still have no idea who they were working for. I've been fortunate enough not to have any blowback from the hits I've completed over the years. I'm nice with my shit, always in and out. I can't see anything from my past coming back on me like this, so I wouldn't be surprised if the heat is coming from the Dragons," she said.

The wheels in my head began to spin at her revelation. What she was saying made sense. "Did you ever find out who ol' boy was who came through for you that day?"

She shook her head and looked at the screen of her phone. "Naw. That nigga slipping through the cracks something tough. I got my peoples on it and should have some info on him tonight or tomorrow. I gotta pay his ass a visit. We have some unresolved issues we need to discuss."

"Like?" I smirked, loving the look of confusion on her face.

She rolled her eyes and opened the door. "Like who he's working for, for one."

"And?" I teased while walking behind her.

"And what that mouth do before I send two to the middle of his forehead."

We shared a laugh and hugged. "Only you would think about fucking a mark before ending his life."

"Giiiiirrrrrll. If you would have seen how fine this nigga was, you'd be thinking the same thing. Anyhoo, I'll hit you up later. Oh, and when we meet up in Heaven, don't start no shit with Philly. If we're going to get ahead of the static that's coming, we all need to be in this together. Our sister's keeper right?" she asked with her body halfway in her car. The motor was already turned and running, and her high-beam lights illuminated the inside of my Range Rover.

I nodded and blew her a kiss, ending our conversation without answering her question. Yes, I was my sister's keeper, but at what price? Philly needed to grow up and get her shit together if she wanted any type of respect from me. I was always the one picking up her slack, and I was honestly getting tired of it. I had my own life to live just like she had hers. I loved my sister and all, but I would always look out for me before I focused all my time and attention on someone else. It was a decision that might bite me in the ass in the long run, but for my sanity, I would just have to deal with the consequences later. It was time that I started looking out for me.

Chapter 3

Drea

"So how did dinner go with your parents?"

I ignored Lance's question and continued to rock my hips as I rode his dick. From the beginning of our situationship, I'd explained to him that what we had going was simply fucking. Nothing more. I'm talking not even friends but more of a "neighbors with benefits" sort of thing. We may have ordered food twice and caught a flick on Netflix once, but never had we been on any real dates or talked on the phone until the sun came up. Every sexual encounter we'd had over the last year was more than likely initiated by me whenever I was stressed out or needed to quickly calm down from the high I got after killing someone. I would text Lance, and he'd be knocking on my door ten minutes later. Although my neighbor was a nice-looking guy, could fuck like a champion, and could probably make an honest woman out of me, I just didn't see myself being with a square like him. With all of the great attributes he had, he was still missing something as far as I was concerned.

"What did I tell you about asking me personal questionsss?" I hissed as I hit the base of his dick. "Shit!" I'd made the mistake of mentioning going to my parents' house for dinner the last time he and I hooked up, and I regretted that little slipup now. He'd taken that as an invitation to get all up in my business, and he needed to chill.

"Fuck, Drea!" he moaned, his fingers squeezing my thighs. "It's been over a year. You don't . . . Shit," he hissed. "You don't think it's time for . . . Fuck, baby! You don't think it's time for us to be more?"

His dark eyes connected with mine, and I could see the desire he had for me in them. When he opened his mouth to say something else, I leaned over and stuffed my titty into it. Lance latched on to my chocolate nipple like a newborn baby. His skillful tongue swirled around and massaged my round pebble. Another moan escaped from his lips, this one with a little more help from his throat. My phone vibrating on the nightstand had my attention for a second before Lance thrust his hips up and began to drill into me as if his life depended on it.

"Fuck, Drea. I can't get enough of you. Tell me we can be more, baby, please!" he begged desperately.

"Lance!" I wailed, hands gripping the pillow with his head boxed between my arms. "Just be quiet and make me cummm," I whimpered.

I began to move my hips at a faster pace, trying to match his powerful drives into my core. I was almost to the point of ascension when the sound of glass shattering jerked me from my pinnacle point. I scrambled to the side of the bed. Lance's glazed dick was still in the air as I pulled the gun I had tucked under the mattress from its hiding spot, ready to shoot anybody crazy enough to come through my bedroom door. Ever since that little incident at my shop, I'd been on high alert and peeping my surroundings a little more.

"What the fuck was that?" Lance screamed, hopping out of the bed and running toward the closet door. "Where the fuck did you get a gun from, Drea?"

I rolled my eyes at him as I removed my naked body from the tangled sheets. My ears tuned out Lance's scary ass, and I listened for any type of movement on the other side of the door.

"Drea, what are you doing? Grab your phone and call the police. Let them handle whoever is out there," his weak ass suggested.

"Will you shut the fuck up, Lance?" I hissed. "I'm trying to listen."

"Listen for what?" His wild eyes went to the door and then back to me. "Drea, get your ass in this closet and stop trying to be Foxy Brown. I don't know about you, but I don't wanna die. I just made partner at the firm and I—" He stopped talking when I pointed my gun at him.

"Didn't I tell you to shut the fuck up?" I hissed.

Lance looked down the barrel of the gun and then back at me, fear all over his face and in his eyes. I stared at my bed buddy, wondering what the fuck I really saw in him. Yeah, he was fine as hell with his Omar Epps–looking ass, but other than that, I couldn't put my finger on it.

Quietly opening the room door, I stuck my head out to check the hallway and breathed a sigh of relief when I didn't see anyone.

"Drea," Lance whispered low behind me.

Ignoring him, I stepped out of the room with my back pressed against the wall and my gun leading the way. I walked down the dark hall and into my living room, where the noise originally came from.

The sound of Fred Sanford screaming at his son played in the background while the screen from the television highlighted the couch and everything around it. Nothing seemed out of place, which was unusual if someone had broken in, but I still had my guard up. Grabbing the remote, I muted the television and continued to walk through my living room. I did my best to avoid the broken glass that now decorated my hardwood floor from the side window that had been busted open. The cool air from the evening wind caused my nipples to harden. Whoever was in here would sure get an eyeful of my naked body before I did the honors of taking their life.

Continuing with my slow walk through, my steps came to a halt when I heard what sounded like my refrigerator being opened. Redirecting my stride, I quietly crept into my kitchen, ready to blast on whoever was in there. Sure enough, my refrigerator was open, but still, I saw no one. Suddenly, like a moth drawn to a flame, I felt this strong pull as soon as I pushed the refrigerator door closed. In that very moment, I knew it was him. His energy. His smell. I recognized that shit immediately. I didn't even have to turn around to know it was he in my kitchen.

"What the fuck is your stalker ass doing in my home?" I turned to face him with my gun aimed directly toward the middle of his forehead. I wasn't surprised to find his weapon trained on me as well.

He tapped the barrel of his chrome .45 against my rib cage. "If you don't want to die at the same time as I do, I suggest you point your gun somewhere other than my forehead."

I narrowed my eyes and shifted my weight from one side of my body to the other. A smirk was on my full lips. "Nigga, I doubt we will both end up dead. You saw the way I hit those three niggas who ran into my shop that day. Before you could even blink again, my bullet would be through your skull with all of your brain matter splattered on my walls and cabinets."

Simmy stepped back and let his eyes roam over my naked body. A blank expression was on his face. For some reason, I became a little self-conscious as he took in every inch of my frame. Placing his gun on the table, he took his finger and traced the outline of my breasts and then moved down to my belly. Pulling his bottom lip into his mouth, I saw the change in his pupils as his vibe went from curiosity to straight-up lust.

Simmy stepped back into my personal space, his body much closer to mine with my gun still pushing into his forehead. With one swift move, he grabbed my wrist and spun me around, pulling my back into his chest. The hard muscle beneath the black sweater was easily felt when he enveloped me in his arms. My heart started to beat frantically, and my nipples were hard as rocks. The goosebumps that decorated my body revealed how turned on I actually was by this man and how drawn I was to him. I closed my eyes to try to get control of my breathing, but I popped them back open when Simmy's large hand snaked around my throat and lightly squeezed.

"That nigga you was just fucking back there, I want you to dead that shit. He's not the man for you. Understand?"

My body was screaming for me to say yes and agree to anything he requested, but it wasn't like me to give in so easily. "How do you know he isn't the man for me? I'm not about to stop a good thing for some random nigga. I don't even know you."

Simmy chuckled. The grip he had around my neck became a little tighter. Removing my gun from my hand, Simmy placed it on the table next to his and brought his hand back to my chest. After twisting and massaging my nipples for a second, he trailed his fingers over my belly and then down to my pussy. He took my pearl between his thumb and pointer finger, lightly squeezing and applying a little pressure. The combination had my body tingling and my walls contracting like crazy. I was damn near about to have an orgasm from that quick contact. A moan slipped from my lips, and before I knew it, Simmy pulled my head back, stretching my neck and pressed two fingers inside of me.

"You see how wet your thighs and pussy are just from my touch alone?" I nodded as best I could against his shoulder. "That's how I know that nigga isn't the man for you. Your pussy should be that wet when you fucking somebody. I ain't even stuck my dick in you yet and your shit already crying a river," he chuckled, and the deep rumble that vibrated in his chest and against my back caused my knees to buckle. "Too bad you just hopped off of that scary-ass nigga's dick. I would have been tempted to see how sweet that forbidden fruit tastes had you not." He brushed his nose along the length of my neck. "I heard you been asking questions about me? Did you find what you were looking for?"

I licked my lips and shut my eyes, turning my head away from his knowing glare. I didn't want to give this cocky muthafucka anything else to hold over my head. He already turned my body into putty for a second time. Since that little incident went down at my shop, I'd been trying to find out everything I could about Simmy. Where he lived. Who he rolled with. What kind of car he drove. But I couldn't find shit. It was like the muthafucka was a ghost. I even reached out to the PI nigga Marlon fucked with from time to time, and he couldn't find shit either.

"Drea," I heard a low voice call out from behind me, causing my thoughts of the mystery behind Simmy to come to a stop. "Drea, where are you?"

Simmy placed a few kisses behind my ear, and I could feel the smile on his lips. "Are you going to take care of this fool, or should I do the honors?"

I stepped out of Simmy's embrace and moved toward the entrance of the kitchen, waiting for Lance to show his face. I could hear the light drag of his feet and the low mumble of his voice as he walked through my living room, assessing the broken glass and window as he passed it by.

"Shit," he hissed after he bumped into the end table next to the couch. The loud scraping noise causing me to cringe. I knew there were going to be scratches on my hardwood floor. "Drea, where the fuck are you? This isn't funny. I already called the cops, and they're on the way."

Simmy, who had taken a seat on the counter, hopped off of it and grabbed his gun, tucking it in the waistband of the black jeans he had on. The bow in his legs was a lot more noticeable with the light from the night sky shining on him. He grabbed my loose bun on the top of my head and pulled my head back. My chin pointed up to the sky as his darkened eyes looked into mine.

"The next time I come by, that nigga better not be here. Break that shit off or I'ma get rid of him for you . . . permanently," he threatened before placing his soft lips onto mine.

Before I could push my tongue into his mouth, Simmy had moved from behind me and disappeared through the back door. Still lost in his kiss, I jumped when Lance called my name and turned on the kitchen light.

"What the fuck?" His eyes looked around the kitchen and then back to me. "Was someone in here? What took you so long to come back to the room?"

Picking up my gun, I went to the fridge and grabbed myself a bottle of water. Simmy was right. Lance's square ass wasn't the one for me. I drank half of the cold water before turning my attention back to my soon-to-be ex-lover, hoping he wouldn't have a hard time letting go.

"Look, Lance, I had fun with whatever it was we were doing, but I think this is where we need to end things."

"End things?" he screeched, walking closer to me. Lance tried to grab my waist and pull me into him, but I sidestepped his advance. "What the hell happened in the course of ten minutes that would have you wanting to end things with me? I thought we were good. We were just about to make things official before someone threw a rock through your window."

I shook my head and laughed. "Make things official? You can't be serious. Not once have I ever led you to believe that we were getting serious." Lance opened his mouth to object, but I raised my hand, stopping him. "Let's keep it real, boo. We fuck. And we only do that when it's convenient for me. Where do you see things being serious in that?" I shook my head again. "Lance, you are not the man for me, and I honestly doubt you ever will be."

"And how do you know that? You haven't given me a chance to prove it to you."

"Prove it to me? Dude, you hid like a bitch while I came out of my room locked and loaded ready to shoot whoever had the audacity to break into my home. Where were you that whole time, huh?"

"I was calling the police. That's what any normal human being would do in the case of a home invasion."

"Not for me. My normal person would have asked where an extra gun was at or had his own. Ready to shoot some shit up if need be," I schooled him.

My mind drifted to Simmy and how he had extra guns for me that day at my shop. A tingle shot through my body and down to my clit, causing it to thump like crazy. I had to place my palms against the center island in my kitchen to hold myself up.

I was weak in the knees for that nigga Simmy, and he had been gone for almost ten minutes.

"Earth to Drea." Lance snapped his fingers and waved his hand in my face, grabbing my attention. "Did you just hear what I asked you?" I shook my head, my mind still on Simmy but now listening to him. "I asked where the hell did you get that gun from? Don't you own a flower shop? I don't see why you would need to own a gun making floral arrangements every day."

"Me owning a flower shop means I can't own a gun?" I asked incredulously. I swear this man said the dumbest shit at times. I was a young black female who owned her own business, and in my opinion, that was reason enough to own a gun.

"I don't see the need for one. Your shop is in a nice area, as well as your home. You hear that?" The faint sound of sirens could be heard in the distance. "I called the police less than fifteen minutes ago, and they're already on their way."

Lance walked around the island and stood behind me, his hard dick pressing against my back, lips close to my ear. Crazy how I didn't get the feeling I did when Simmy did the exact same thing. My pussy was desert dry and not soaked the way it was when the handsome hit man was behind me.

"Now, I will admit that seeing you with that gun gripped in your hand is a major turn-on, since we know there wasn't a real threat. It actually makes you look like a badass, now that I think about it.

You standing in the kitchen naked with that metal in your hand? Damn, baby. Maybe you can unload it and bring it to the bed with us. We can do a little role playing or whatnot. What do you say?" he asked excitedly.

I was just about to respond with a "hell to the no" at Lance's request when the loud sound of a gun going off rang in my ear at the same time as the window in my kitchen shattered to the floor.

"Shit!" Lance yelped. His arms that were placed on my sides quickly swung to his back. "I think I just got shot," he howled in pain.

"Shot?" I laughed, thinking he was going crazy, but I stopped when I saw a small pool of blood forming at the bottom of his left foot.

"Yes, fucking shot! Oh my God, I'm about to die! I didn't even get to fuck the new white chick they hired in the mailroom. Oh God! My 401K and pension. I never took my ex-girlfriend's name off as a beneficiary. Now she and her new man will be living it up off of me. Where the fuck are the police? Call the ambulance, Drea. Call some-damn-body to save me!" Lance cried like a bitch while I looked on in disgust.

I walked behind Lance and took a look at the two small holes on his left cheek. A clean shot through and through. I didn't even have to look out the window to know who was responsible for that wound. I guessed I was taking too long to get rid of Lance for Simmy's taste.

Grabbing my gun, I laughed the whole way to my room and continued to laugh as I got dressed and ready to deal with the police and whatever questions they had with regard to the break-in that just happened at my house. Like always it was fuck the police, so I didn't know nothing, and I didn't see nothing, so I was sure they wouldn't be here long.

Before returning to the kitchen, I checked my phone and saw that I had a few missed calls from my mom, Philly, and Diem. Opting to take care of the situation at hand first, I made a mental note to call them back just as soon as I kicked the police and Lance's soft ass out. I had just placed my phone back on the nightstand when it vibrated. For some reason, the insane part of me told me to pick it up and look at the message. When I did, a small smirk played on my face, and I could feel the butterflies fluttering around in my belly.

Unknown: In the future, don't take so long doing what the fuck I asked you to do. Things might not go so well the next time.

I bit my bottom lip as Simmy's sexy ass flashed in my mind. My reaction to him was something totally different from what I'd felt for any other nigga before. I didn't know if he had all of the attributes I wanted in a man, but I did know that the something I was missing with Lance was the something I was slowly finding in Simmy.

Chapter 4

Philly

"Wait, so let me get this right. The nigga shot him in the ass because you were taking too long to break things off with him?" I cracked up laughing. Listening to Drea's crazy story about the fine-ass man who saved her life not too long ago was keeping me awake right about now. It was early as hell, and I was tired from being up all night making sure the bike I was delivering a little later was flawless. We were at our clubhouse, Heaven, which was located in the back of my shop, awaiting the arrival of the rest of the crew so that we could get our biweekly meeting started.

"Girl, I was in my house crying laughing. I think I made Lance mad, too, because I kept telling the police I didn't know who could've done it. I don't know how but his ass knew I was lying."

"You are so wrong for that," I laughed.

"I still can't believe he bitched up on me like that. Then had the nerve to talk about us being an official couple. Nigga, please!" my sister scoffed in disbelief.

"He's an okay guy, so I don't see why you won't give him a chance, sis."

"Hell, no! His reaction to someone possibly breaking into my home tells me all I need to know about him. Lance is too weak for me."

"Well, not everyone is like you, killa," I joked.

"It's not about being like me, but at least step up and protect me. Like damn, he stayed in the back the whole time I was out there. Could have been murked fucking with him," she scoffed. "Simmy was absolutely correct when he said Lance was not the man for me." Now her ass was sitting up here smiling.

"I can't wait to hear what happens when dude pops up on you again. The whole situation seems mysterious as hell. Just busting in and rubbing on titties and shit! That's what the hell I'm talking about!" I said, making her laugh out loud.

"What's so funny?" Diem asked as she walked in with her nose in the air, wearing an outfit that belonged on the runway during New York Fashion Week. She'd been acting funny with me lately, but I had to admit that my sister couldn't be fucked with when it came to her style. She was the most fashion-forward chick I knew, hands down, but I'd never tell her conceited ass that. Her head was big enough as it was.

"I was just bringing Philly up to date on the latest happenings with my sexy assassin bae," Drea gushed. I could tell my sis was really feeling this nigga, and she barely even knew him. Made me think about my situation with ol' boy and how he just appeared out of nowhere the other night.

"Have you heard from him again?" DiDi asked, interrupting my thoughts.

"Nope, not a peep as of yet, but I'm just sitting back waiting. I know his ass will be showing up sooner or later," she replied, looking hopeful.

"Or you should find him first. Don't let that nigga have you waiting for him to pop up. Obviously, he likes to play these little games. Him having the advantage of being able to find you gives him the upper hand. Beat him at his own game, and pop up on his ass," Diem suggested as she unbuttoned the red blazer of the fitted trouser suit she had on. The sweetheart neckline of the black lace bustier showed off her D-cup breasts. Diamond hoop earrings matched the solitaire diamond pendant that hung from the thin gold necklace around her neck. I was barely able to see it due to how perfect the gold blended in with her skin. Crossing her legs, Diem pulled her phone from her purse and started to type away on it, no doubt responding to e-mails about her company or some text messages from her assistant.

"That was the plan, but it's been so hard getting info on him."

"Just go back to the basics, sis. There was a time before you came into all that money when you did your own tracking. I know you can find this nigga, and that tells me that you're either afraid of him in some way or your ass just likes that he's out there following you around and stalking your every move," Diem pointed out, and I couldn't agree more. To be so young, baby sis could track down any-damn-body, and I too wondered what was up with her saying she couldn't get a location on dude.

After a deep sigh, she finally replied, "You're right, DiDi. Guess it's time for me to do my own digging and become the hunter instead of the hunted. I can't lie and say that I don't get turned the hell on knowing he's watching my every move." She smirked with a soft bite of her bottom lip.

"Good, because just like Philly, I can't wait to hear how this next encounter turns out." Diem smiled sneakily while Drea sat in deep thought.

"Bitch, I got it!" she shouted, causing us to turn toward her in shock, the sudden outburst catching us by surprise.

"Fuck you yelling for?" I asked, still looking at her like she was crazy.

"My bad, but an idea just came to me." She giggled but failed to elaborate.

"Well?" Diem and I simultaneously snapped moments later. Drea just sat there with that stupid grin on her face while we anxiously waited to hear the plan.

"Calm down, feisty one and feisty two! So impatient," she stalled.

"Girl, if you don't get on with it . . ." Diem ordered, tired of Drea and her dramatics. She always did things like that, and it irked our nerves. Could never just tell a fucking story without all the theatrics.

With a quick roll of her eyes, she continued. "Fine! So, to lure him out of hiding I figure all I have to do is be seen with another man. The way he tripped out about Lance being at the house lets me know he doesn't mind making his presence known or acting a damn fool. And as soon as he makes his move, I plan to flip the script on him." She danced in her seat.

"What guy though? You said you were done with Lance," I questioned.

"Don't know yet, but I'll come up with someone. I have a few standbys I can call on."

"A'ight, player. You better hope that fool don't shoot you and whatever dude you putting in his face," DiDi warned.

"I know, right? Swear that possessive psycho shit turns me the fuck on," she moaned, and she visibly shivered while DiDi and I just shook our heads in amusement.

"Like I said before, I can't wait to hear all about it," I told her.

"Hopefully I'll finally be able to sit on his face then see what that dick do." Heffa was now bouncing up and down in her chair.

"Nasty ass," DiDi teased.

"Hello, angelsss!" Elle's extra ass sang as she sauntered into Heaven, grabbing our attention and causing me to roll my eyes.

"Hey," Diem and I offered dryly in response while sharing a quick smirk between us.

Drea immediately hopped up and hugged her friend. Elle was an okay chick, and we'd known her for years due to the relationship between our fathers, but there was just something about her that always rubbed me the wrong way. She was very condescending and sneaky as fuck, two things that didn't sit well with me, and Diem felt the same way I did. Drea, on the other hand, was blind to the shit. She adored Elle, so to keep down drama we held our tongues on a lot of things when it came to this bitch and her questionable ways.

"What y'all in here talking about?" Elle asked as she set her helmet on the oak table next to the door and took off her vest. The leather pants covering her legs looked like they were painted on, and the black bikini top with miniature diamond skull heads left little to the imagination. Her burnt-orange hair was frizzy at the top from not wearing a scarf under her helmet. A large puffball of nappy curls hung down her back. "What happened now?" she asked, removing her gloves from her hands.

"What makes you think something happened?" Diem asked with her eyes still trained on her phone.

Elle shrugged her shoulders. "I don't know. It seems that all conversation ceased when I walked in, so I'm just checking. G'on and keep your secrets. I'm sure my bestie will fill me in later," she boasted while Drea remained quiet.

Just from the expression she wore, I could tell that I was going to be pissed the hell off by the end of this meeting. This ho just looked like she was ready to start some shit, but I would try my best not to give her the reaction I was sure she was looking for.

We sisters had already met briefly at my shop the day before. Diem and I advised our younger sister to not divulge any info to her bestie regarding what would be happening in the coming weeks in Dragons territory. We were to act just as surprised as she was whenever she found out. The last thing we needed was for Elle to try pumping Drea for information only to turn around and feed it to her father. Baby sis said she understood, and I was hoping she kept her promise to keep things under wraps for now.

"It's nothing, so let's just get the meeting started," Diem said as other members walked in and took their seats.

"Yeah, let's," I agreed and began talking before my sister had the chance to take over and run the whole meeting like she was known to do anytime our club gathered. I wasn't sitting at the head of the table for nothing.

After Drea quickly reviewed the minutes from our last meeting, we moved on to the two big topics for tonight. The first was the annual fundraiser, and the next was New Orleans Bike Week. I'd never admit it to anyone, but I looked forward to going to New Orleans more than I did to the event we put on for the community every year. Great food, fine-ass men, and most importantly some of the baddest bikes I'd ever laid my eyes on. It was months away, but I couldn't wait.

"So, Pops wants this year's fundraiser to top anything we've done in the past. I have a few ideas, but I welcome any input from you ladies. We need something that's going to attract a lot of people and get those donations up. In Daddy's words, we have to remember the reason we do this in the first place. It's not so much about this club but more about the children," Diem stated.

"I agree," I concurred. "Maybe we should have the kids sell some tickets and auction something off. We have a lot of options on what we can give away that I'm sure will make a lot of money. And as far as Bike Week in New Orleans goes, I think that's pretty straightforward. Rooms have already been booked, according to Diem's notes. Sonny agreed to arrange transport of the bikes down there, so we're straight on that. Does anyone have anything to add before I open up the floor to questions?"

"I don't have anything to add, but I do have some concerns." Elle stood from her seat.

"And what might those be?" I asked, trying my best not to roll my eyes.

"I mean, I get that you were here today, and I can't deny that you're doing a good job running this meeting, but how long is this going to last?" she questioned, catching me off guard.

"Elle, what the hell are you about to start bitching about now?" Diem asked, slapping her palm against her forehead.

"No bitching. Just pointing out that Philly hasn't exactly been available much lately. You've basically been running the show, and I think we need to have a discussion about possibly taking a vote to replace Philly as president," she answered like the shit she was saying would ever fucking happen.

My eyes went to Diem then cut over to Drea, and we all had the same shocked expression. I hoped like hell that she knew nothing about this. She looked to be as caught off guard as the rest of us, and I prayed that that was the case, because it was family over everything. If she agreed with this looney bitch or knew anything about her plans to vote me out, we were going to have a problem.

Where the fuck did that come from? I silently questioned my sisters, but before they could even respond, Elle interrupted our eye war.

"Now, Philly, before that little monster that dwells inside of you rears its ugly head, don't go blaming your sisters. I'm sure they aren't the only ones who noticed that your time and dedication to Hart's Angels hasn't been what it used to be. I mean, how many meetings have you missed in the last couple of months?" She slowly walked around the table, her overpowering vanilla scent reaching me before she did. "Diem has conducted a meeting or two in your absence, Drea has acted on your behalf at several events that you were scheduled to be present at, and even Big Gina picked up some of your slack the first couple of days we were at the convention in Little Rock last month. The last time I checked, the MC president is supposed to be present at everything, regardless if anybody else shows up."

Elle stopped a few seats away from me and pulled out a chair. Sitting down, she placed her black wedge boot on the table edge and pushed herself back, while a sneaky smile crept across my face. She just didn't know what a big mistake she'd made sitting this close to me.

"Now, according to the Commandments—" was the last thing that came out of her mouth before her body and the chair hit the ground in a loud thump.

"Philly!" my sisters screamed at the same time.

Before they could even reach me, I hopped on top of Elle and wrapped my hands around her throat. She tried to get a grip on my arms with her nails, but the stains from the oil change I'd done earlier kept causing her fingers to slip.

"Philly, let her go! Did you forget that you are still on probation?" Leave it to Drea to always try to be the voice of reason.

"Philly, please stop!" Diem pleaded. "Bitch, put that phone down before you get your ass whipped too!" Diem threatened someone who, I assumed, was recording my assault on Elle with their cell phone. "I'm not going to say it again, Ophelia! You're only giving them more ammunition to vote someone else into your position. You know these bitches are already scared of you after you beat Trish's ass half to death," she added.

Visions of me hitting Trish with a crowbar started flashing in my mind. I beat that girl so bad that she had to permanently wear a jaw brace for the rest of her life. I didn't mean to work her over as bad as I did, but once I blacked out, I didn't know how to control whatever it was that took over my body. The therapist I was seeing on the low said that if I was able to find a way to balance my rational brain and combat mode, I would get a handle on this blacking out thing. Sucked to say that after a year of seeing her, I hadn't quite learned how to balance the two.

I shook my head and tried to stop my hands from tightening around Elle's neck, but I couldn't. It wasn't until Diem grabbed my left wrist and Drea grabbed my right that I was able to let go. Their closeness kind of calmed me down a bit and broke me from the dark place I was in. Being the dramatic bitch she was, Elle started to cough uncontrollably and grab at her neck. Fake tears sprang from her wide eyes. She managed to sit herself up against the wall and fall into Drea's arms as she kneeled by her to check if she was okay. That shit there had me looking at my sister sideways. Elle's sobs seemed to only get louder when a few more club members walked in late.

"This is what I was talking about. We can't have someone like her running this club. Philly clearly runs off of emotions, and I for one don't want to be killed or thrown in jail because she can't control her temper. She's—"

"Someone like her? Fuck is that supposed to mean? Elle, you better chill before I choke your ass out next," Diem interjected with a smack of her lips. "You're doing way too much right now. Philly's good and you're good, even with her handprints around your neck," she said, making light of the situation. "Everyone just take a seat and let's continue. We still have a few more things to discuss before the meeting is adjourned."

With Drea's help, Elle stood up and slowly walked to a chair on the other side of the table. After taking a few sips of water, she cleared her throat. "If what Philly just did to me isn't a clear sign that we need to have a vote for a new president, I don't know what is."

"We're not going to vote for a new president—"

"And why not?" Elle shouted, cutting Diem off.

"Because I said so, bitch! The name of this motor-cycle club is Hart's Angels, which means you have to be a Hart to run it. And since Drea and I already have our positions and are the only other Harts here, your push to vote for a new president is fucking denied! Fuck I look like letting you vote my sister out?" Diem snapped.

"Fine, boss lady!" Elle threw her hands up in surrender, but her face held tons of sarcasm. "We can put this issue to rest for now, but best believe we'll be talking about it again at the next meeting. Philly is getting out of control, and just because I'm the only one voicing my opinion on it doesn't mean I'm the only one here who feels this way. Huh, Trish?" Elle's messy ass directed across the room. She'd walked in with the late group and probably had no idea what our argument was about.

All eyes turned to her, and ol' girl didn't do shit but sink down into her chair, embarrassed. This was why I didn't like Elle's bitch ass. Claimed I was crazy, but she was always starting shit and being a

fucking drama queen. I was so glad I got to rough
her ass up a little bit a few minutes ago.

Trish and I had long ago squashed our beef, and
I was sure she was pissed that Elle even tossed her
name into this. Her lopsided face was a constant
reminder that coming for me was the wrong fucking move. I didn't feel like she still had an issue
with me, but if I found out these hoes had some
sneaky shit going on within this club behind my
back, I would deal with all of them individually
and discreetly. I was sick of my family reminding
me of what could happen if I got into any more
trouble. I was going to have to learn to control my
temper and go about things differently. Hoes were
still going to get fucked up, but I definitely had to
keep my dirt on the low.

"I'm out," I mumbled after straightening up my
clothes and picking up my helmet. My heart still
beat wildly, and I was resisting the urge to dive on
Elle's ass and finish what I started, so it was a must
that I move around. If I stayed, I was sure to be
hauled off to jail tonight. Plus, I had a quick stop to
make anyway.

"Come on, Philly, the meeting isn't over yet," Diem
groaned, clearly pissed about my early departure.

"Do your thing, VP. Hell, for all I know you taking up for me was just a front and you're really the
one behind the whole 'replace Philly' movement," I
spat, causing both of my sisters to gasp. I regretted

that shit as soon as it left my mouth, but I was mad as hell right now. When I was angry, I was liable to say anything.

"That was a messed-up thing to say, and you know it." Drea shook her head with disappointment.

Surprisingly, DiDi remained quiet, but she was still grilling the hell out of me. I could see through the anger though. My words hurt my sister. Instead of owning up to my mistake and apologizing, I turned to the younger Hart and let her have it.

"Whatever, Drea! It's funny how you're so quick to step in between me and Diem, but when it comes to this ho here, you go mute." I pointed at Elle, who was now wearing an astonished expression. "Fuck her, and fuck you too, baby girl," I spat. To that, she had nothing more to say, so I walked toward the back to make my exit.

Minutes later I was speeding through the city with a special delivery on the back of the truck. Phone on mute. No music. Windows down. The only sound that could be heard was the wind rushing in. The silence was helping to ease my troubled mind.

I hated that I'd let Elle get me out of character. I'd fallen into her trap and had no one to blame but myself. Sometime soon I'd have to apologize to my siblings for what I accused them of, but tonight wasn't the night. My attitude was too fucked up.

Although her delivery was unwarranted and messy as hell, the things Elle said were true. I was aware that I hadn't been pulling my weight, but even before today's meeting, I had plans to start doing better.

No one knew that when I missed certain events or had to leave early, those were the days I was going to see my therapist. I was actually trying to get better, work on my anger, and get back to my responsibilities with the club. That's the reason I ran the meeting instead of letting Diem do it. At times when I wanted to step up, she'd been quick to butt in and push me into the background per usual, and I had kind of gotten used to it. Just like I did earlier, I had to continue to take the initiative and get things done. I just needed her bossy ass to give me a chance.

As soon I was done dropping off this package I was giving my therapist a call. Thank God she was available twenty-four seven, because I needed her right now.

Chapter 5

Gideon

As soon as I stepped into my old bedroom, I dropped my luggage next to the dresser, shut the door with my foot, and sluggishly walked toward the bed. I didn't bother removing my shoes or clothes as I laid my tired body across the cloud-like mattress. My heavy body instantly relaxed and wound down. For the last forty-eight hours I'd been going nonstop and was just now finally about to get some rest.

I closed my eyes, ready to doze off, when there was a light knock on the door. "G?" I heard my brother's voice call out in a hushed tone. I ignored him, hoping he'd leave me alone. "G man, I know your ass ain't 'sleep yet, so stop playing," he laughed, walking into my room and closing the door behind him.

I groaned in frustration, scolding myself for not locking my room door. Turning over on my back, I draped my arm over my face and watched my brother watch me. After several moments of our silent stare-off, he finally decided to speak.

"So what's up? Did you get to meet her?" The excitement in his voice was high, and the look in his eyes was hopeful.

"Yeah, I met her." The sluggish tone of my voice told me that I needed to find sleep soon.

"So how was she? Was she prettier in person? Did her ass look as big as it does on TV? How did she smell? Did she give you a hug?" He was firing off questions back to back, none of which I felt like answering right now.

"My nigga, just let me get a few hours of sleep first, and then I'll tell you everything you want to know."

"Nah, man. I need to know everything now. Right now. You got to meet my future baby mama, and you think I don't want answers?" he scoffed.

I rolled over on my side, crushing my phone in the process, but not really caring. Toeing my shoes off, I pulled the double pillows deeper under my head and laid it back down. All I wanted to do was get a few hours of sleep, but I knew it wouldn't happen until I gave him something.

"All right, Zy. I'ma answer your questions, and then you need to get the fuck out of my room." He nodded anxiously and rubbed his hands together. A low, irritated hum escaped my throat. "She was cool. Way prettier in person. Ass is enormous. She smelled like roses, and yes, she gave me a hug." I closed my eyes and then popped them back open. "Twice."

"Nigga, you put your arms around my girl?" His words were halted by the pillow I threw at him.

"Close and lock my door when you leave. We'll talk later."

"You damn right we'll talk later," he growled over his shoulder. "You know damn well whenever it comes to Onika Tanya Maraj I need all details. And I hope you fucked that nigga Nas's hairline up. Bitch-ass muthafucka loving all on my girl." His voice trailed off as he walked out of my room and closed the door, still talking shit about his imaginary relationship with Nicki Minaj.

I shook my head, thinking about his weird obsession with Nicki, and if he were given the chance to meet her, what his rap would be. Zyhir was my brother and all, and I loved him to death, but if I were to tell the truth, his ass wasn't about shit. The nigga was twenty-nine years old and still lived in our grandparents' house, living off of the amenities provided by them from our grandmother's wealthy lineage. He didn't have a job, his own spot, or a pot to piss in. His trust fund money was probably almost gone, and he had no desire to do anything with his life but party, fuck bad bitches, as he so eloquently likes to put it, and be the next underground rapper to get discovered on social media. I mean, he had a little following and all, but not enough to get the buzz he needed to get the attention of anyone who would take him seriously. With my profession, I had access to a lot of the people he would probably need to meet to make his career happen, but I wasn't going to help him out if he was only going to eventually change his mind once he saw how much hard work, time, and dedication it took to actually have a successful rap career.

My phone buzzed, but I ignored it, already sure who the caller was. Luscious had been calling my shit nonstop since I landed, and I had no idea why. She knew the few times we fucked meant nothing to me and that a relationship between us would never happen. We'd never gone out, we hardly talked on the phone, and she'd never met my family. Three signs that should be very clear to a woman where she stood in a man's life.

After turning my phone off to avoid any other distractions, I'd finally gotten to another comfortable spot on the bed and was about to doze off when there was another knock on my door.

"Aye yo, G." I buried my face into my pillow and groaned. "G!" he yelled the second time. "Aye, man, I know you trying to get some sleep, but there's a delivery here for you."

"Put it on the table, and I'll check it out later," I huffed.

There was silence for a second. "Uh, it's not that kind of delivery."

Not that kind of delivery? What other kind of delivery could it be?

"You have to come down and get it."

I pulled myself up from my bed and sat up, taking a few seconds to get my equilibrium right. Wiping my hand over my face, I focused my eyes on the floor until my vision was straight. Stretching my fingers out, I could feel the slight pain building from years of cutting hair. It was something I started when I was twelve, just playing around and doing a favor for one of my childhood friends who couldn't afford to get his hair cut every week like me and Zyhir.

What began as a hobby later turned into a full-blown and very profitable career once I perfected my craft and built up a huge clientele. I didn't like to brag, but after opening up six successful shops on the West and East Coasts, starting two hair-care lines catered to men, and being on call to over two dozen celebrity clients, your boy was living his best life at the tender age of thirty-one. The most impressive thing about all of this though was that I didn't have to touch a penny of my trust fund money to help me accomplish any of it. All it took was hard work, a lot of networking, a great marketing team, undeniable hustle, and always striving to be the best to get me where I was today.

Finally standing up, I stretched my limbs and walked to the door, pulling my jacket off and dropping it on top of my luggage. "What kind of delivery is it?" I asked as I opened the door to my brother scrolling down some page on his phone. His height, weight, and facial structure were similar to mine. The only thing that separated us in the looks department were his green eyes to my brown and his dreaded hair to my tapered fade.

He shrugged his shoulders. "I don't know. But it's some fine-ass bitch with her hair shaved on the sides in one of those flatbed trucks. I tried to holla at her, but she ignored me and kept asking for you. Said she wouldn't sign off the delivery to anyone other than Mr. Gideon Wells." He used air quotes. "I think it has that motorcycle you got for Gramps under the tarp thingy on the back."

As soon as the vague description of Philly left his mouth, I turned away from him and headed down the stairs, any additional questions from him falling on deaf ears. With the crazy couple of days I just had, I forgot all about the change of plans I made with Philly the night I popped up at her shop unannounced with the help of my mans Casey. Catching her off guard the way I did wasn't as entertaining as I thought it would be. Nevertheless, I got to see a side of her that really intensified my attraction to her.

"*You gotta be fucking kidding me,*" *flew from her pretty little mouth as soon as her hooded eyes recognized me.* "*How the fuck did you get in here?*"

I smirked and walked closer to where she was sitting. "*The same way you did.*"

"*But only two people have access to that security code,*" *she replied. The chromed-out gun in her hand was still pointed at me as I raised my hands up in surrender.*

"*The security system you have is a good one, but it isn't the best. Any level-two hacker can crack into your shit and add a fingerprint.*" *I wiggled my fingers.*

She squinted her eyes, studying me, taking me in from top to bottom. She hiked her eyebrows when she noticed the bulge of the gun on my hip. She gave a slight lick of the lips when she noticed the even bigger bulge between my thighs. Our gazes locked after her full inspection of me. A flick of something flashed in her eyes but changed as fast as the sound of her gun cocking a bullet into the chamber.

"*What the fuck do you want?*"

I stared back at this gorgeous being, anticipating that she would look away at some point, but she never did. Slowly standing up from the stool she was seated on, Philly rose to her full height. Loose coveralls falling down her wide hips gave me a glimpse of the red boxer briefs she had on. A dingy wife beater filled with grease stains hugged her round and very full breasts. Her out-stretched arm pointed right at me while the other was slightly hidden behind her back. The dim light in the room illuminated only enough for me to see that her arm had been scarred in some way.

"You got ten seconds to tell me why you're here, or I'ma put a bullet between your eyes."

I nodded toward the Cyclone 1968 Ariel Cyclone 650. "That fine piece of metal right there belongs to me, and I wanted to make sure you were doing her right since I wasn't able to ask you about it when we were here before." Her eyes finally left mine and went over to the bike. "And I wanna apologize for my friend's behavior, even though you broke his nose. It's not every day he sees a woman as beautiful as you, in this field no less."

Philly lowered the gun to her side once she realized that I was not a threat and backed up until her ass hit the workbench against the wall. Pulling her bottom lip into her mouth, she nodded and crossed her arms over her chest.

"Your boy deserved that and more. But I do apologize for being unprofessional to a paying customer." I could tell she was struggling with admitting her wrong, but I wasn't going to rub it in her face.

"Apology accepted."

Our eyes continued to war with each other as we stood in an awkward yet comfortable silence. The buzzing of my cell phone blended in with whatever song she had playing off of hers. I knew I only had a couple of minutes to discuss the reason for me being here before it was time for me to go and catch this flight, but I was curious to see if she felt the attraction bouncing between us the same way I did.

"Do you feel that?" I asked, trying to deflect the hint of anxiousness in my tone.

She rolled her eyes and scoffed. "Feel what? You finally opening your mouth to tell me why you're here?"

"Nah, not that." I walked a little closer to her. "I'm talking about this attraction between us. I know you feel it now, and I know you felt it earlier when I was in the shop." My fingers traced the leather seat of the motorcycle as I admired the custom paint job. Philly really did her thang with restoring this Cyclone, and I knew that my grandfather would love it.

"Look—" she started to say, but she was cut off when my chest bumped into hers. I heard when her breath hitched in her throat, and I felt the way her heart started to beat a little faster.

"Don't talk, just listen," I whispered into her ear, tracing the rim of her lobe with the tip of my nose. The soft scent of whatever perfume she had on mixed with that strong motor oil smell. "I'm going out of town for a few days, but when I come *back, I want to take you out. We need to have a discussion about possibly exploring the mutual attraction we share. With that rough and tough exterior of yours, I'm sure you'll never admit it, but I can tell by the look in your eyes and the way your breathing pattern changes when you're near me that you're just as intrigued as I am," I told her as she closed her eyes and gripped the front of my shirt.*

Clearly embarrassed by my observations and her reaction to me, Philly flattened her palms against my chest and attempted to push me away, but she stopped when I grabbed her wrists and locked them behind her back. "I see you're a feisty one, but I got something to tame all of that." I knew the threat in that last statement was completely understood when Philly's eyes almost bugged out of her head and she quickly removed her leg from its position against my growing erection.

"Are you done?" she asked through clenched teeth, still flustered by her growing affinity for me. "I still got some shit to do before I get out of here."

I chuckled at the heated look in her eyes and the way her cheeks started to turn red. "If you keep on looking at me like . . . Oh, shit!" I screamed out when the excruciating pain of Philly's knee connecting to my dick zapped through my body. "What the fuuuuuck!" I struggled to get out, dou-

bled over in pain and cupping my most precious jewel.

Philly's laugh echoed throughout the shop. The heavy gun she had placed on the cluttered tool shelf was visibly back in her hand. "Now that we've got that all situated, get the fuck out of my shop, and don't ever come back," she said, walking toward her office door. "Leave your name, address, and the time you want the bike delivered, and I will see to it that it gets there on time. Other than that, get your ass on, and don't forget to pick up your nuts on the way out."

With one eye closed and the other barely open, I watched as Philly walked out of the garage, wide hips swaying with each step. I kept my eyes on her until she disappeared into the darkness. Any other man would've taken what just happened as a sign of rejection, but for me, this was only the beginning of a dysfunctional but sure to be loving relationship for us.

I passed through the kitchen, living room, and foyer until I reached the front door and opened it up. Countless bodies from different companies were running around, trying to get my grandfather's seventy-fifth birthday BBQ together. My grandmother was dressed in her expensive yet casual attire, directing the caterers where to place the huge five-tier cake. Trucks from the different vendors were spread out around the front of the house.

"Oh, Gideon dear. I thought you were asleep."

Her curious eyes followed me as I ignored her question and continued to walk down the winding driveway toward the iron gates. I was already more than sure that my grandmother would pull me to the side sometime today to address the small show of disrespect. I passed the huge garden fountain with the four marble horses, finally making it to the key-code box hidden behind the perfectly trimmed rosebush. I entered the six-digit access PIN to open the gates.

The sound of the flatbed's big wheels rolling over the gravel caught my attention before I looked up and connected eyes with the most beautiful woman I'd ever come across. It was my breath that hitched this time as I got lost in her big brown eyes. Even with the scowl on her face, Philly couldn't have been more breathtaking to me at that moment.

"Muthafucka, are you gonna just stand there and gawk at me, or are you going to tell me where to take this bike?"

Stunned out of my trance by her aggressive tone, I lifted my hand and pointed her in the direction of the driveway that looped around back and led to the two-story steel garage. This space housed over thirty classic cars, and at least seventy-four motorcycles had made their rotation through there as well. Many had since been donated to benefit some cause or charity, but this new bike would be my grandfather's seventy-fifth one to add to his collection. This was something I took over and started doing every year for his birthday as a gift, ever since I made my first six-figure check. When Zy and I were younger, it was our grandparents who stepped in and took on the responsibility of raising us after our father died and our mother decided that being a single parent was not something she signed up for. If it weren't for them, I probably would've ended up in the system and nowhere near as successful as I was today.

The slamming of the truck's heavy door broke me from my engrossed thoughts and had my attention now on the only woman who had ever occupied my mind as much as she had since I first laid eyes on her. Dressed in her usual oversized work attire, Philly jumped down from the metal running board and began to untie the ends of the tarp covering the bike. The leather vest she had on hadn't caught my attention until now. A bleeding heart with angel wings took up the majority of the back. Hart's Angels MC was patched at the top with the state name across the bottom. When she bent over to untie another knot, I caught a glimpse of the president strip above her left breast and a few other patches I couldn't make out.

My interest in Philly was piqued a little higher after realizing that along with working on motorcycles, she actually rode them. On top of that, she was the president of this club her vest was representing. I rested my whole body against the side of the truck's bed with a smirk on my face and my arms crossed over my chest, waiting for her to acknowledge me in some way, but she wouldn't bite. By the time she removed the Cyclone from the bed and rolled it over to the garage entrance, she still hadn't said a word to me.

"So, you're just going to continue to ignore me?" I asked, playfulness evident in my tone.

She took the rag in her back pocket out and wiped it over her face, eyes connecting to mine for a second and then rolling back to the truck. Opening the door, she hopped up into the torn leather seat and grabbed something out of the glove compartment. Folding a few sheets of paper over in a folder, she clicked the top of her pen in her mouth and then wrote something down, before ripping the top sheet off and handing it to me.

"Your ending balance after delivery and everything else comes to $10,862. I do prefer cash payments, but I am willing to accept debit or credit. No personal checks." She looked beyond me to my grandparents' huge home. "Although I'm sure I would have no problems with a check from you bouncing, seeing as how you can afford to live in a place like this."

I followed her gaze and shrugged my shoulders. "One, this isn't my home. It's my grandparents'."

I turned back to her. "And two, you would never have to worry about a check from me bouncing. I make a pretty decent living and can afford to purchase anything I want."

Philly licked her lips, eyes back on me. Cocking her head to the side, she studied me for a few moments before speaking again. "What's up with you?"

I chuckled. "What do you mean?"

She thought of her response for a second. "I don't show you any signs of being interested in you, yet you still try to shoot your shot like shit will somehow change."

"Because it will change," I assured her. "Whether you realize it or not, you do show signs of interest. But for some reason, you keep trying to fight it. You're just as attracted to me as I am to you." A thought suddenly entered my head that hadn't occurred to me before now. "Wait, do you have a man already or something? Is that the reason you're acting like you don't feel what's happening between us?"

I didn't know why those words leaving my mouth caused me to frown, but I could feel the corners of my lips turning down and my brow furrowing. Philly took down the bun at the top of her head and let her hair fall over her face while laughing. Bending at the waist, she combed her long strands with her fingers and then put her hair back in the tight bun. I admired the neat lineup on her shaved sides and wondered who she went to to get her edge ups.

"Are you going to go get my money now, or do I have to put this bike back on the back of my truck and take it back to my shop?" she asked, already walking back toward the garage.

I followed her. "So, you just gonna ignore my question?"

"Basically." Grabbing the handlebars, she kicked the stand up and easily balanced the heavy bike on her side. "Either you gon' pay me now and stay out of my business, or I'm going to leave and take this shit with me. I've always wanted a motorcycle like this." Her eyes wandered over the bike in admiration and pride.

"Hart's Angels?" I nodded toward her vest. "Never knew there were female bike clubs."

"Well, for $10,862 I'll tell you the name of a few more, since you seem more interested in my personal life than paying me for my work."

"Oh, yeah? Well, hold that thought," I said and retreated toward the house before she could say anything else. I ran straight to my luggage in my old room and found the stacks of cash I collected before leaving New York, grabbed a few of those, and ran back out to Philly.

"So this right here is about twelve Gs, give or take a few hundred. You can count it all right now if you don't trust me, although I have no reason to lie or try to cheat you. I got this bike done for my grandfather's seventy-fifth birthday." I waved at all of the chaos going on behind me.

Vendor trucks were still going in and out of the property, as my grandmother stood in the middle of it all, directing the workers where to put things. The smell of grilled meat filled the air, causing my stomach to growl. That sleep I so desperately needed earlier was already forgotten just from being in the presence of my future baby mama. "And as you can see, the party is about to start pretty soon. My gramps has been looking forward to seeing his gift, and I don't want to disappoint him."

Philly kicked the stand back down and fingered the stacks of cash. Walking back over to her truck, she opened the cab and placed the bills in a deposit bag she pulled from under the driver's seat.

"Now that that's out of the way, would you mind staying for a bit and enjoying some of the festivities? I promise I won't ask you that many questions. I just want to get to know you a little better while you enjoy some of this good food, good drinks, and great company," I offered with my arms stretched out, waiting for her to take my hand. "Maybe after we chat for a bit, I can bring you back out this way and let you see my grandfather's collection of cars and motorcycles. If anyone would appreciate the classic beauties, I know it would be you."

I could tell by the look on Philly's face that she wanted to stay. If the offer of free food and drinks didn't close the deal, the mention of seeing everything in the garage did. She hesitated for a second before placing her hand in mine. The tingly feeling that shot up my spine had me shivering a little and wondering what the fuck could be. We were just about to head to the back of the house when my grandmother approached us and pulled my free arm.

"Gideon? Where are you going with this young man, and why are you holding his hand?" she asked. Her voice sounded as innocent as could be, but knowing my grandmother, I could hear the condescending undertone. Her hard eyes went from me to Philly and then to our connected hands. "You know we are Christians in this household and will not tolerate any of that funny business here. Grandson or not."

"Grands, you got it all wrong," I said, coming to Philly's defense. "Phil—"

"Phil?" she shrieked. "Oh Lord, not in my home, Jesus. Not in my family. I rebuke you Satan and all of your twisted ways in the name of Jesus," she cried out to the heavens. "Gideon, if you don't give me some answers right now about this . . . this . . ." She shook her head, too flustered to finish her comment.

I felt Philly's hand retract from mine, a blank look resting on her face, eyes now black as the night. She drew her bottom lip into her mouth. Teeth marks left a white streak from how hard she was biting down. I could tell by her body language that I needed to get this situation under control before things went all the way left.

"Grands, again, you got it all wrong. Philly isn't a—"

I stopped talking when she waved her hand in the air, cutting me off. "Got it all wrong? Gideon, am I not looking at a young man right now? I know I'm considered a senior citizen in some aspects, dear, and I do tend to forget things from time to time, but the last time I checked, my vision still does work rather well." Philly laughed, and my grandmother's unamused gaze turned to her. That privileged Seven Hills tone was now in her voice. "Did I say something funny to you?"

For a second, I thought Philly was going to ignore her and address me about the situation in some way, but when she stopped laughing and that gorgeous smile of hers turned into a frown, I knew that this conversation wasn't going to end well at all.

"As a matter of fact, you did."

"Did I now? And what did I say that was so funny to have you cackling like a wild animal?"

"All of that shit you just said about your vision still being intact. That was some straight bull-shit and also funny as hell. It's obvious that your optometrist lied to your blind ass if you see any signs of a man over here."

My grandmother gasped at her response and had the nerve to look offended. "Pardon me, young man. We don't use that type of language around here. This is a Christian household. How dare you be so disrespectful?"

"So you assuming me to be something I'm not isn't being disrespectful?" Philly chuckled. "I mean, does my demeanor really scream male to you? Because it doesn't to your grandson. Nigga been dreaming about me sitting my pussy on his face since the first time he laid eyes on me," she said, causing my eyes to buck. My fist went to my mouth, and I had to bite down on it to keep from laughing.

"Oh my God! Are you going to really let this ghetto, foul-mouthed boy say these things to me, Gideon? Where is security? Security! Get his ass off of my property now."

"Because you're an old-ass bitch, I'ma try my hardest to not slap the shit out of you. However, if you keep addressing me as a man when I know you can clearly see the titties sitting on my chest, my facial structure, and no visible sign of an Adam's apple along my neck, I might end up in jail today from beating your wannabe Diahann Carroll–looking ass."

"Wait, wait, wait!" I yelled out at the same time my grandmother gasped and grabbed her forehead as if she were about to faint. "Grands. Phil." My voice trailed off at the sight of Philly retreating. "Don't go. This is just all a big misunderstanding," I tried to reason, but Philly wasn't trying to hear shit I had to say.

I ran to the truck and grabbed the door before she could close it. "Wait, at least let me apologize for what happened back there. My grands, she . . ." I shook my head, unable to come up with an excuse to justify the horrible way my grandmother just acted.

Philly laughed. "It's all good. You not my type anyway. Been trying to tell you that from the beginning, and I'm telling you again. You need you one of those proper, Ivy-League, 'Dionne from the movie *Clueless*' type of bitches. Someone like that would be a better fit for your lifestyle than me. Although I did wonder how you ended up with that ghetto-ass bitch who was hanging on your arm in my shop that day. Don't seem like your uppity-ass grandma would be too fond of her either."

"Phil—"

"It's actually Ophelia," she cut me off, "or Philly, but that's neither here nor there." She yanked the door from my hand, closing it hard, and she started the engine. "It was nice doing business with you. And like I told you that night you broke into my garage, stay the fuck away from me and my business, or I'll show you how me and that female bike club you were interested in really get down."

I didn't get a chance to say anything else to her after that, because as soon as Philly gave me her little warning, she pulled off so fast that I was left with my mouth hanging open. I stood in the middle of the driveway and watched as she almost sideswiped a guest's car pulling into the gates.

With a bowed head, a fast-beating heart, and an extremely painful erection trying to push itself from behind the cotton material of the briefs I had on, I couldn't do anything but laugh. Instead of being mad at the way Philly just disrespected my grandma, I was actually turned on at the balls she had for not allowing my grands to disrespect her. That was something I could guarantee Luscious or any of the other women I'd dated wouldn't have ever thought of doing. I shook my head and smiled. Philly was going to see me again very soon. With a little help from my boy Casey, I would find a way to pop up on her sexy ass again.

Chapter 6

Diem

"Dad!" I whined when I realized he wasn't listening to a word I was saying.

"Don't be a brat, DiDi. I hear you, but I'm also working. Just finish what you were saying, baby girl," my father responded to my mild tantrum.

He didn't even bother looking my way, but I couldn't help but take a brief moment to admire the man who was everything to me. Julian Knight Hart was a strikingly handsome man who didn't look to be anywhere close to his sixty-two years of age. The wool pindot-striped Brioni suit fit him perfectly. His salt-and-pepper fade and his beard were trimmed and lined up just right. Pops never slacked when it came to his attire and grooming. I guessed that was where I got my sense of style from. He'd taught his girls to always look the part, and I took that shit to heart.

We were at his downtown office having our weekly lunch date, and I'd been trying to fill him in on everything that had been going on with the club, namely Elle and her minions devising a plan to vote my sister out as president. But he was hardly paying me any attention. Still, I continued with my story.

"So, they're basically trying to vote her out, but I told Elle straight up that it wasn't going to happen. I have Philly's back to the fullest, but it doesn't help that she's not handling up as she should. In fact, she left right after the little altercation instead of finishing out the meeting. Philly is basically giving them all the ammo they need to give her the boot. I'm sure there is something in the bylaws that they can use to remove her, they just haven't done enough digging to find what they need to make it happen. Drea's never really been overly involved with the club, so her lack of input is expected, but Philly is a totally different story. When we first took over she was the heart of Hart's Angels, but something has changed, and whatever it is has not only affected the club but our relationship as well."

I thought I was even more upset about the latter. I mean, Philly and I had always had our issues, but it was never this bad. Now it was like we were down one another's throats every other day, and as hardcore as I seemed, that shit really had me down. I just missed the way things used to be.

"Diem, to me it sounds like you have it all under control," he stated, finally looking my way. The pen in his hand dropped down onto the large stack of papers he was just looking at.

"Under control? Were you listening to anything I said? It's a complete mess, Dad!" I yelled.

"Baby girl, the first thing you need to do is lower your damn voice and remember who you're talking to," he shot sternly, causing me to lower my head. It was crazy how, at my age, whenever I got beside myself and my father had to low-key reprimand me, I would feel like my younger self again. I wasn't trying to be disrespectful or get loud with Pops. I just didn't understand how he couldn't see where I was coming from.

"I'm sorry," I muttered before taking a sip of my drink.

"Apology accepted. Now go on." He nodded, giving me the okay to continue.

"Like I was saying, Philly is slipping, and you seem to think it's okay that I'm left fixing the mess most of the time. I can no longer hold this thing down on my own. Then, on top of all that, you dropped a big-ass bomb on us a few weeks ago, and again you acted like it was no big deal," I added.

"No, I don't think the situation with Philly is okay, but I have faith that you all can work it out on your own. One thing that you girls asked of me when you took over was to let the three of you handle business without me always butting in, and that's all I'm trying to do. Now as far as that other shit goes, you can leave that to me. When I told you about that it was just for your information so that you'd be on the lookout for anything out of the ordinary," he assured me.

"So you honestly think Lukas and his Dragons will let you make it after coming in and tearing all their shit down while forcing them to relocate? Please don't tell me you believe that they're going to let you off that easy." I shook my head in annoyance. There was no way my dad was that naive.

"It's not like they have much of a choice, Diem. This is business, nothing personal, and if anyone understands that, it's Lukas. But like I said before, you and you sisters, along with the Angels, have absolutely nothing to worry about. Just trust me."

"I trust you, Dad." He'd never lied to me, so I had the utmost confidence in him and his word. "And I'm not saying I want you to fix the other issues for us, but I do need you to understand where I'm coming from. I have enough of my own shit going on, and taking on Philly's responsibilities is slowly taking its toll on me." I sighed. People hardly ever saw this side of me. Letting my guard down and being honest about what I was feeling or going through was something only my father and occasionally my sisters witnessed.

"I do understand, DiDi, and I don't want you to think I'm making light of the situation. I'll have a talk with Ophelia myself when I stop by the shop tomorrow evening."

"No, Dad. Please don't speak with her on my behalf. The last thing I need is for her to come at me sideways talking about how I always run to you when we have issues. That will only lead to another big blowup, and we haven't even made up from the most recent one."

"Fine, but whatever you two do, you need to fix this beef or whatever it is you have going on before it escalates any further. What's the motto?" he asked with a genuine yet loving smile on his face.

"Family over everything," I muttered. I couldn't even smile in return when I said it this time. Normally that saying brought me back down to earth and caused me to remember what was most important, but right now I wasn't feeling it. I loved that I could talk to my father about anything, but today was different. I didn't feel like anything was resolved, and it felt as if I was about to walk out of his office with the same weight on my back that I walked in with.

I was wound up too damn tight these days, but I knew what my problem was. I needed some sex, and damn, I needed it badly. Not even my toys were doing the trick these days, and they had always been able to get me right. I guessed what it all boiled down to was nothing could take the place of a hot, warm body. That closeness? That intimacy? That connection? In my case that was something that could only come from a real live man.

"That's my girl." Dad grinned as he walked around his desk to pull me from my chair and out of my daydream.

"And you're my guy," I recited just like I would anytime he'd call me his girl. "So, it's still a go for dinner later this week, right?" I asked, and he nodded. "I'm so glad we're doing it at my house for a change. Do you have something in mind that you'd like me to cook, or do you just want me to make your favorite?" I questioned while I cleared our food containers and condiments from his desk.

"My favorite please, and can you make those bacon-tomato cups, too? Your mother will never admit it to you, but she loves those things."

"I'm not making anything special for her. She's already complaining about dinner being at my place. Called me twice already requesting that we move it to the big house, and I had to shut her down both times."

"Look, Diem, I know your mother can be difficult at times, but I think her problem is that she doesn't feel as if she fits in anywhere. Maybe if we made more of an effort to include her or make her feel special she'd be a little less annoying and bitchy," he said, making me laugh.

"Fine, I'll make them, but she had better not walk up in my spot with that holier-than-thou attitude or I will be turning her fake ass right around at the door," I threatened.

"She's still your mother, Diem, and I expect you to show her respect at all times," he ordered.

"Mm-hmm," I mumbled.

"I'm not playing, DiDi!" he said, raising his voice.

"I'll try, Dad. That's all I can say." There was no use in me promising to be on my best behavior, because I couldn't guarantee that I wouldn't react if she came at me sideways. I wasn't respecting shit or no one who didn't respect me.

After lunch, we'd moved over to the large open window where the lounge area in his office was to talk more. A few steps down from where his beautiful mahogany desk sat was a space that was in total contrast to the rest of the office. The cozy colors, artwork, bookshelves, and plush furniture pieces were so welcoming and relaxing. This area was by far my most favorite spot in his office. Being here made the time I spent with my father that much better, because I didn't have to share his time with my mom or sisters. It was all about us.

Now that we were no longer discussing the club problems, the situation with my sister, or all of our issues with my mother, the conversation flowed, and I was able to take a moment to just chill. I really wanted to talk to him about my recent visit to the doctor, but I didn't want to worry him. He would only overreact, and that's not what I needed from him. If he could just somehow get a hold on the situation with Philly, that would help me out a great deal and surely lower my stress levels like Dr. Mason suggested.

"Julian, I just wanted to remind you that you have about thirty minutes before the start of your meeting with the young man from Anderson Construction," my father's secretary stated over the intercom.

"Thank you, Rhea."

"No problem, sir." Her cheery voice echoed through the room before the call clicked off.

"I'm enjoying our time so much that I almost forgot I still had business to attend to." He smiled lovingly my way.

"Is this meeting with the guy you were telling me about at dinner?"

"It is, actually. I just wanted to speak with him again one-on-one, minus his team and mine so that I could get a better feel for him and how his mind works, you know?"

"Yes, I get it. From what you told me so far he seems to be the real deal. I kind of did my own research on his company, and he is definitely on the rise. It was crazy that I couldn't find any pictures though. Not a single one. That's weird, right?" I asked. I didn't know why I was so interested, but I was.

"And why would you need to see a picture of him, Diem?" My father smirked.

"No reason, Pops. Dude just seemed interesting is all." I shrugged, keeping my face neutral.

"Sure," he retorted with that same sneaky look on his face.

"Whatever, old man!" I laughed. "I'm going to let you get ready for your meeting. Just need to holler at Ms. Rhea before I go," I told him with a quick kiss to the cheek as he remained seated on our favorite couch.

I had to hurry out of here before he had time to dig deeper or speculate further on my reason for researching Ky Anderson. It honestly wasn't as serious as he was making it out to be. The man's story just intrigued me, and I wanted to know more so I looked into his company. His success story was what dreams were made of. Some real rags-to-riches type shit. Grew up in the foster system. Smart as hell and able to put himself as well as his sister through college without help from anyone. According to the article I read, he never even had to take out any student loans because the amount of scholarships he had was ridiculous. The man was just interesting, and there was nothing more to it than that. It was still crazy that I hadn't come across any pictures of him though.

"You sure you don't want to stick around? I could introduce you—" my father started, but I cut him off.

"No thanks, Dad. Call me later though." I didn't even give him a chance to respond as I rushed out of his office, the sound of his low chuckle behind me.

I noticed Rhea wasn't in her chair when I made it to the front, so after placing my belongings on her desk, I took the opportunity to go freshen up a bit. I had just a few things to run by her regarding the fundraiser, and then we would be set.

Rhea had taken her place back at the desk when I returned about twenty minutes later after doing my usual roaming through the office and speaking to a few people. She'd worked for my father for many years, and our family loved her. Well, most of our family. Sole hated Rhea's guts, but my father refused to get rid of her no matter how many times my mother made the request.

Rhea was a petite, brown-skinned woman whose face had that classic beauty. Her posture was always perfect, and she was a lady in every sense of the word. Her signature silky, straight ponytail hung down her back like always, and her light makeup was done to perfection. In all the years I had known Rhea, her beautiful features and style had always stayed the same. The only thing that changed over time was the color of her hair. The once jet-black strands were now replaced with a striking silver color, which still looked gorgeous on her. I could easily see why my mother would be a little intimidated and jealous of Rhea, but she didn't have anything to worry about when it came to the relationship my father shared with his secretary. It was strictly platonic.

"Ms. Rhea?" I sang after sneaking up on her.

"Diem, baby! I was hoping to see you before you left. I missed you when you first got here," she said, getting up from her seat to give me a hug. "How have you been?"

"I'm good. How about you?"

"I'm well, sweetheart. Doing just fine." Her megawatt smile made me smile. You ever been around someone who was just so loving and positive that it rubbed off on you? Well, that was Rhea. She had that whole motherly thing going that drew people in.

"I actually hung around to speak with you. I had a few things I wanted to go over about the fundraiser if you have time."

"I'll make time." She gave me the go-ahead after taking her seat again. "Now shoot."

"Thank you, you're the absolute best. Wait, where is my phone?" I asked, looking around. I could have sworn I set it next to my bag before I walked down the hall. After looking on the floor and turning my purse inside out, there was still no sign of my phone. The last place I remembered having it before coming out here was in my father's office, so I assumed I must've left it there.

"Do you want me to buzz your father? I'm sure he won't mind bringing it out if you left it in there."

"It's fine. I don't want to interrupt his meeting. I think I can remember the last-minute stuff I want your opinion on. I also have notes in my tote so that should be enough." I sighed, pulling a chair behind the desk to sit beside her.

The plan to be long gone by the time my father's meeting was over wasn't going to happen, and if it weren't for the fact that I had my entire life on that damn device, I would have said fuck it and gotten it from him later. Looked like today was the day I was going to come face-to-face with the young CEO Ky Anderson whether I wanted to or not. I didn't know what it was about this man that made me so freaking nervous. Hell, I'd never even seen his face before, and here I was tripping out.

Chapter 7

Kyrie

"Thank you for agreeing to meet with me again, young man," Julian stated, extending his hand out to me, and I gladly accepted.

"It's no problem, sir. No problem at all," I replied after a firm shake of hands.

I was a young nigga just starting out, and I took every opportunity that came my way to soak up game from the OGs. So as you can imagine, I was geeked to be in the presence of greatness once again, and that he possibly wanted me on his team was a bonus. This man was about his business at all times, and I admired that about him. From his bossed-up persona and professionalism all the way down to his handshake, it was all business, which brought me back to the question I'd been asking myself since I got the call from him a few days ago requesting a second meeting.

It wasn't a call from his secretary to set things up. Julian Hart himself called my office to arrange this meetup. I had no clue what it was all about, but I was anxious to find out. Should Hart Enterprises decide to go with Anderson for the work on his new, state-of-the-art shopping complex, his lawyer and team would contact mine, and we'd go from there. In other words, this impromptu sit-down with just the two of us was a bit out of the ordinary.

"Mr. Hart, I was a little surprised that you wanted to meet again. Was my proposal not up to par?" I questioned, taking a seat across from him.

"Please, call me Julian," he requested.

"Okay, Julian. Was there an issue with the proposal?" I knew my shit, so I knew my design was A1. I'd been groomed by the best, and though I'd only been in business a few short years, my work spoke for itself. That, however, didn't stop companies from overlooking me despite how good I was at what I did, so I knew this meeting could go either way.

"Your proposal was exceptional and also in line with my vision, but I'm almost positive that you knew that already," he chuckled, earning a knowing smirk from me. "I'm very impressed with you, Ky, and my request to see you today is simply my way of getting to know more about the man I'm going to be working closely with for the months to come."

"Wait, what?" my voice stammered when I realized what he was saying. "So, you're actually hiring me for the job?"

"Of course I am. And hopefully this will be the first job of many that we get to team up on," he replied.

"There's so much I want to say, but shit . . . I mean, damn." I inwardly chastised myself for my choice of words. "I'm at a loss for words at the moment, so to avoid making a complete fool of myself I'll just say thank you for this opportunity. You have no idea what this means to me, sir," I said, rising to shake his hand once more.

I wasn't shocked, but then again I was. This man was a legend in his field. He could have chosen anyone to help him build his latest masterpiece, someone more established with a much bigger name, but I happened to be the chosen one. Shit low-key made my chest swell.

"Trust me when I say that I do." He gave my hand another firm squeeze before we both took our seats again. I knew a little about his background, so I was sure he'd looked into mine as well. His next statement only confirmed that suspicion.

"We're more alike than you realize. I experienced some of the same trials as you coming up, and to see the way you made it happen for yourself is inspiring. While my competitors may use your lack of experience as an excuse or reason to not do business with you, I, on the other hand, tend to gravitate toward the underdog. I was once in your shoes, and I believe it's my duty as a successful black man to assist young men such as yourself in moving ahead in the game. And trust when I look at you I don't see you as some charity case, because I truly believe that with or without my business your company will continue to flourish."

"Thank you for taking a chance on me, Mr. Hart. You won't regret this," I assured him.

"You're welcome, and I'm confident that I won't," he agreed.

His belief in me meant a lot, and I was certain that I could get the job done, but that didn't stop my mind from going a mile per minute thinking of the possibilities and doors that would open up for me following the completion of a job this big. This was the biggest job I'd been trusted with thus far. Fortunately, my nerves cooled, and I was able to calm down enough to hold a decent conversation with the man while getting to know a little more about him.

He told me all about his daughters, or his girls, as he called them, and I could tell he was very fond of each of them. The Hart daughters each had their own thing going and were running very successful businesses. I wouldn't expect anything less from the offspring of Julian Hart though. In addition to their thriving businesses, they also ran an all-female motorcycle club that had been passed on to them from him. As if being hired for the job weren't enough, he also gave me two tickets to the Hart's Angels annual fundraiser that was a few weeks away. I didn't have a girl at the moment, so I would probably give the other ticket to a homie I went to college with. Hopefully he would be in town when the event rolled around. His ass was always catching flights for work, but he was into bikes and shit, and he was the only one I could think of to invite along.

About thirty minutes into us getting to know one another, his secretary entered, bringing the scotch and glasses that Mr. Hart had requested. We'd already moved to the lounge area, ready to toast to our new venture together.

"Julian, did you happen to see DiDi's phone? She thought she may have left it here after you two had lunch," Ms. Rhea, who I had the pleasure of meeting earlier, asked as she looked around on his desk.

"No, I haven't seen it," he lied, causing me to look at him sideways for a brief second.

"Goodness, that girl is going to lose her mind without that phone."

I distinctly remembered him picking up a cell phone from the desk out front right before we entered his office, but I kept my mouth closed. I didn't know DiDi, nor did I know his reason for saying he hadn't seen it.

As Ms. Rhea exited the room, a familiar laugh floated into the office from outside, causing my head to snap in that direction. However, before I could glance outside to see who that loud-ass cackle belonged to, the door was being pulled shut. Just the sound of it made the damn hairs on my arms stand up. Hoping to get a glimpse of the unknown female before I left, I was now anxious to end this meeting. When I turned back, my eyes met Mr. Hart's, and I couldn't quite read the look he was giving me.

"You good, son?" He smirked.

"Umm, yes, sir. I'm fine," I answered before quickly glancing at the closed door once more.

"Expect a call from Rhea two weeks from today with the date and time of our initial project meeting. We will do an official walk-through of the land before we break ground following that meeting. It's straight to work from there," Julian informed me.

"I'll be ready," I assured him as we stood outside of his office door. Before he could offer a response, that obnoxious-ass laugh tickled my eardrums again.

"Ah, there she is." Julian smiled, causing me to turn in the direction he was now looking. "There's someone I want you to meet before you go, son."

When my eyes finally landed on her, I couldn't help the grin that spread across my face. *There she is, indeed.* I'd been asking my sister for information on her since the night I crashed their little sex party at my house. Bella was being so tight-lipped about her friend that I decided to let it go. I was thinking maybe she had a man or something, and that was why Bella wanted me to stay away from her. Looking at her now, though, I didn't really give a damn whether she belonged to someone else. I don't know what it was about her, but I wanted her ass for myself.

As she moved up the hall, I couldn't tear my eyes away as I took her in from head to toe. She was indeed a gorgeous girl with some unique-ass features, but her body, man, her body was crazy. And believe me, I wasn't one of those men out here looking for perfection or anything, but the sexy-ass frame moving my way was indeed that. Perfect. She was small, but her curves were ridiculous, and the white tank and tight-ass black leather pants she was wearing had them on full display. The black knee-high boots she wore set the whole look off, and I had to say I liked everything that I saw, but it was that hair of hers that had me stuck. Don't ask me about the color or the name of the style because I knew nothing about all of that, but it fit her perfectly. The wild golden and brown curls bounced up and down as she moved, and I had a sudden desire to run my fingers through it. I should have been ashamed of myself for ogling a woman during a business meeting, but I wasn't. Shit was unprofessional as fuck, but I couldn't help myself. My question now was, how was she connected to the man I'd be working closely with for the next six-plus months, according to the timeline he'd laid out for me?

"Sam, get your hands off my child and get back to work. I done told you about that shit," Julian let his hood side slip while unknowingly answering my question. She was his daughter. What were the odds?

I was so caught up in her that I was just now noticing the guy coming up the hall with her, and I didn't know why, but I didn't like the way his arm was draped over my future baby mama's silky brown shoulder either. I was glad Julian said something before I had a chance to. I was sure they all would have thought I was crazy for speaking up on something that wasn't my business.

"My bad, Mr. H. I was just explaining to DiDi how I'll be helping out on this new project," the young, nerdy kid nervously explained as he quickly removed his arm from her person.

"Back to work, Sam," Julian ordered, and this time the young man obeyed.

"Bye, Sammy! I'll see you next time," she called out to him. He turned around and waved shyly before continuing down the hall. I guessed he called himself having a little crush on her, but that was all it would ever be if I had a say in it.

She was chuckling low, but when her eyes traveled from her father and finally landed on me, they slightly bucked in surprise as well as recognition.

"Come, baby girl, there's someone I'd like you to meet." Julian waved her over. "Kyrie, this is my oldest daughter, Diem. Diem, this is Kyrie Anderson of Anderson Construction."

"We've met," we revealed simultaneously.

"Is that right?" Julian asked in surprise.

"Kyrie is Bella's brother, but I had no idea he was who you haven't been able to stop talking about. I can't believe I failed to make the connection before now." She extended her hand with a shy smile. I wasn't buying it because I knew for a fact that there was nothing shy about this girl. We'd flirted heavily the night we met, but she dipped out before I had a chance to get her number. I didn't plan to let the opportunity slip away again.

Taking her hand, I said, "Diem, it's a pleasure seeing you again," as I gently rubbed that soft area between her index finger and thumb. She enjoyed my touch for a few moments before clearing her throat and pulling away.

She turned her attention back to her father. "You mind if I look around the office real quick? I can't seem to find my phone, and I really need to get going," she told him. I was staring a hole in the side of her face, and I knew she could feel that shit because I could see her eyeing me from her peripheral.

"No worries. I found it between the cushions on the sofa," he said after reaching into his pocket to retrieve it.

"Really? I could have sworn I left it on Rhea's desk when I came out."

I was beginning to think that Mr. Hart set all of this up for us to meet, and I for one was glad that he did because I'd been waiting on an opportunity to see her pretty face again.

"Well, now that I have this"—Diem held her cell phone up and looked toward me but cut her eyes as soon as they connected to mine—"I can carry on with my day. Thanks for lunch, Daddy," her soft voice spoke as she kissed him on his cheek.

"No problem, baby girl. Make sure you call your old man before you turn in tonight."

"I will. And, Kyrie, it was good seeing you again. Take care." She smiled sweetly before picking up her belongings along with a motorcycle helmet from the chair.

Once again I forgot all about Mr. Hart's presence as I openly admired his daughter as she sashayed down the hall.

"Sir—"

"Handle your business, young man. I'll see you next week," he cut me off with a smirk before retreating to his office with a snickering Rhea following close behind.

I was inwardly thanking him for saving me the trouble of coming up with a lame excuse as to why I was now rushing to get out of the building. Julian already knew what was up. I needed just a few moments alone with his beautiful daughter, Ms. Diem Hart.

I thought for sure that my chance had passed me by when I made it down the hall only to see the doors to the elevator she now occupied close once I hit the corner. Her face was already buried in her phone, so she didn't notice me coming. Thinking fast, I spotted the stairway to the left of me, but before I could make a move to take that route, the second elevator opened, and I hopped on as soon as the last person got off.

Damn, I'm really out here chasing this girl, I thought as I emerged through the sliding doors at the entrance of Hart Enterprises. I paused my slow jog as my head swiveled from side to side trying to spot her in the crowded parking lot, but she was nowhere to be found. After a few minutes of standing there looking like a complete fool, I decided to leave. Sighing, I made a move to step off the curb and head to my car when I noticed a bad-ass black and hot pink Yamaha motorcycle make a quick circle around the perimeter of the parking lot before coming to an abrupt halt directly in front of me.

"Looking for me?" Diem asked after removing the helmet from her head and giving that hair of hers a quick shake and toss to the back.

"Hell nah," I lied, causing her to laugh, which in turn made me laugh. I didn't know why that chortle of hers affected me so. It was loud as hell and always seemed to come out of nowhere, but I loved it.

"Nigga, you ain't gotta lie," she stated knowingly. Once again my ass was grinning like a kid in a candy store looking at her.

"Let's go have a drink," I suggested out of the blue.

"I can't," she told me, although I could sense that she really wanted to say yes.

"Why can't you?" I asked, taking a few steps closer while maintaining eye contact. After holding it for a while, she bit her bottom lip and looked away.

"My schedule. I have a lot going on, and I don't have time for fun, drinks, or any of that other shit," she confessed.

"All work and no play, huh?"

"Basically." She shrugged.

"So, you're really going to let me celebrate this W all by myself? That's fucked up." I shook my head, trying to guilt her into joining me. When I saw she was contemplating it, I added, "I don't plan to keep you long. It's just drinks, Diem. Come out and play for a little bit."

I stood there and watched her silently go back and forth with herself. If it was that hard for her to decide, then I was going to have to pass. I'd already done the most, chasing her ass out here, so I damn sure wasn't about to stand here and beg for just a little of her time. Right when I started to renege on my offer, she finally spoke up.

"Okay, I'll celebrate with you, but only if you allow me to pick the place," she bargained.

"Whatever you want as long as you park your bike and ride with me," I countered. As sexy as she looked riding her motorcycle, I felt she would look even sexier riding shotgun in my Porsche Panamera, and I was too much of a G to be riding behind her on that thing. No way was that shit happening.

"That's fine. I'll just have my assistant send someone to come pick it up," she agreed.

Right after parking next to the Bentley that occupied the space designated for her father, she joined me, and we made our way to my car. According to her, the place we were going had really good drinks.

We didn't say much to one another on the ride over to her favorite wing spot, because her time was spent making calls, replying to e-mails, and answering texts. It was fine for now, but when we sat down to talk, I wanted that phone and whatever business she had to be put on hold for the time being. I was hoping I was wrong, but I got that independent, "don't need a man for anything more than occasional sex" vibe from her. She seemed to be the type of female who spent most of her time climbing the ladder of success, so she ran through vibrator after vibrator, seeking her pleasures through them instead of making time for the real deal.

I loved an ambitious woman. Shit, I myself was a very ambitious man, but I set aside time for fun and my friends. I even enjoyed the occasional date and traveled abroad twice a year alone and another time with my sister. Although I was about my money, I didn't let it run my life. My world didn't revolve around the almighty dollar. I wanted more from life than that. I was twenty-eight years old, so my playing days were over. A nigga like me was looking for a wife. Someone to spend my life with.

As I watched her do her thing from the passenger seat of my ride, I wasn't sure if Diem and I were on the same page. Our chemistry was undeniable, but as beautiful as she was and as bad as I wanted her, I wasn't about to waste my time on someone who wasn't moving in the same direction as I was. One thing I'd learned from my mentor's sudden death three years back was that life was too short, and I planned to work hard but also enjoy whatever time I had left on God's green earth. I guessed our unexpected date this afternoon would determine if another would follow or if we'd cut our losses and move on.

"This is a pretty dope spot. I've passed by here numerous times and never thought to stop and check it out," I told her once we were seated in a cozy area near the back.

"I know, right? I love this place," she said right as her phone rang. Before she had a chance to look down at the number or answer it, I spoke up.

"Give me that," I ordered with my hand out.

"Wh . . . what? Why?"

"Because I want your undivided attention right now, that's why. I let you do your thing in the car, but that shit is done."

"Fine, Kyrie, I'll turn it off," she said with an exaggerated eye roll as she powered off her phone and placed it inside her crossbody purse.

"Thank you, Diem."

She rolled her eyes in response, but I didn't give a damn as long as she put that phone away. The waitress walked over to introduce herself and take our drink orders before I could check her about that attitude of hers. More eye rolls soon followed when Diem noticed the way ol' girl kept giving me the eye as we told her what we wanted. The jealousy was cute, but she had nothing to worry about. I didn't do thirsty chicks like the one who had just walked away, and at the moment my focus and attention was on the lovely beauty with the golden hair and killer body sitting in front of me.

"Is there anything else I can get for you?" the waitress we now knew as Nina asked as she placed our drinks on the table about ten minutes later. She gave me the quick up and down while biting her lip. Before I could call her out regarding her thotty and disrespectful behavior, Diem was already on it.

"You must be new here," Diem chuckled sarcastically as she reclined into her chair.

"Excuse me?" Nina asked smartly, finally addressing Diem with her hands on those nonexistent hips of hers.

"Bitch, I said you must be new!" she spoke slowly and sarcastically. "Grinning and shit like you don't see me sitting here. I don't take kindly to disrespect. You better ask about me," Diem addressed the woman, who now wore a shocked expression. Hell, even I was taken aback by the sudden change in her demeanor.

"Diem—" I started, but she cut me off.

"Just do your fucking job, lady, and quit drooling over my nigga," she snapped, surprising me with her words. All I could do was smile, while Nina quickly apologized and excused herself from our table.

"So, I'm your nigga?" I questioned.

"Nah, but she don't know that. Thirsty ho," she fumed as she made eye contact with Nina, who was now across the room, talking with another employee while looking our way. The gentleman she was speaking with seemed to be reprimanding her, and I had a feeling it was because of her brief encounter with Diem. I cracked up laughing when my date stuck both middle fingers up in the air for Nina to see. She just huffed and stomped off to the back in response while we laughed. Diem was feisty as hell, and I must admit, I liked that shit.

A little while later, a more professional, less dehydrated waitress came to our table, and I was glad for that. Felt like I might have to end up pulling Diem off of Nina had she continued to serve us.

"One day."

"One day what?" Diem asked, tilting her head to look at me.

"I'm gon' be yo' nigga one day, that's what," I told her with confidence.

"You think so?"

"I know so, but we'll talk more about that later. We're here to celebrate my new gig, so let's get to it," I told her as I raised my glass of Hennessy.

She followed suit with her cute li'l cocktail with the umbrella and pineapple wedge. After about two hours of drinking and talking, we decided to order a few appetizers. Our conversation just flowed, and I was actually enjoying my time with her. When she wasn't glued to that phone of hers, she was more open and really funny. She told me how she met and became cool with my baby sister Bella, and how she couldn't stand Lark, who was my sister's best friend. I decided to keep the fact that Lark had a crush on me to myself. Didn't want to give Diem another reason not to like the girl.

"Damn, these are good." Diem moaned slightly as she chewed the meat of the wing she'd just bitten into. The Buffalo sauce on her lip was begging me to lick it off, but I kept it cool. That was, until she stuck her tongue out and licked it away herself.

"Shit," I mumbled as I watched her eat. Thankfully she was so into her food that she didn't notice me lusting over her mouth. Never in my life had I found the way a woman ate her food to be sexy, but everything this girl did turned me on. I had stopped eating my food just to observe her. My dick twitched slightly as I reminisced on the way her lips and throat molested that dildo the night we first met. It was going to be hard to continue sitting across from her and not imagine her doing that same thing to me. I quickly gulped down some of the lemon water that she'd ordered for me to help with my now-dry mouth.

"You good?" she asked after taking a sip of the meltdown drink she'd ordered.

I just nodded and resumed eating my wings.

"Thank you for this, Kyrie. I really had a good time with you," Diem said once we were back in my ride.

"No, thank you for making time for me. I can tell that you're a very busy lady," I pointed out.

"I am, but it was nice to get a small break from it all," she admitted.

"You do know that you have control over that, right?" I asked. She said nothing, but I could see the question in her eyes, so I continued. "You're an entrepreneur, Diem. You're the boss and the only one in control of your workload. There's absolutely nothing wrong with taking time out for you, and in turn, you'll have more time for me," I said, making her blush.

"I swear I try to do that. You know, make time for myself. But it seems like there's always more to do. Family pulling me in every direction, more money to be made, and crazy ideas that won't let me go until I do something with them," she expressed to me with a new light in her eyes.

I grabbed her hand, interlocking our fingers. "If you let me, I can show you how it's done."

During our talk at the bar, I learned a lot about her, and it was clear that she had many responsibilities in addition to her business. All she needed was to find a balance and realize that she could have it all: her family, the club, the career, and the man. Diem could chase her dreams while living her best life possible. I just hoped to be included in some way.

"I'd like that." She nodded bashfully.

I liked her little shy routine, but even more than that I loved her fiery persona with a dose of hood.

Yeah, I was definitely going to be her nigga one day, and that day couldn't come soon enough for me.

"Damn, that food was delicious." Diem patted her stomach, which now poked out a little after her meal. Her food baby, as she called it, only appeared right after a heavy meal. Why was that shit cute to me though? I found myself digging everything about this woman.

We were parked in front of Seven Seas on Lake Meade Boulevard, trying to recover from over-indulging in some bomb-ass soul food. Today's restaurant was handpicked by me, and I was glad she liked it. We had gone out every day since seeing one another at her father's office, and I was truly enjoying her company. From the goofy smile she wore the entire time we were together, I could tell that she was having just as much fun as I was.

"Hell, yeah, it was," I agreed while pulling out of the lot. Once on the road, I immediately grabbed her hand, interlocking her fingers with mine. It was like I had to touch her in some way any time she was next to me.

"Is it cool to turn my phone on now? Nothing work related, but I know my sisters have probably been blowing me up, and I want them to know that I'm okay."

We had a rule that phones were prohibited during meals. That way we could focus solely on one another. My goal wasn't to make her completely abandon her responsibilities, but I did want her to see that there was more to life than just work. Any time that we spent together we needed to treasure and make it count, since we'd be extremely busy in the coming months. She had her new showroom, and I had this new project for Hart Enterprises.

"I guess I can let you do that," I joked as she took her phone out to power it on. Just as she predicted, her phone began to ding and buzz with incoming text and voice mail alerts.

"You know what? I'm just going to check these when I get home. I'm relaxed, and I want to stay that way at least for a little while," she said before reclining in her seat and getting comfortable.

I smiled inwardly as I hopped on the expressway and headed toward her side of town. I could tell she was tired, so I put my Pandora on the Anita Baker station. As Anita crooned about wanting to know what good love felt like, Diem quickly drifted off to sleep. Halfway into our drive, her phone rang, waking her.

"Hey, sissy," she answered groggily. "Yes, I'm fine. Wait, what are you talking about? I know, but I had my phone off. Are you serious?" Her voice cracked as she sat up straight. Seeing her about to cry was fucking with me tough. Something serious had to be going on, so I pulled off to the shoulder and waited until she finished her call. "Tell them I'm on my way now," she said before disconnecting the call. I waited for an explanation, but she said nothing. She just placed her head in her hands and cried silently.

"Diem, what's going on? Talk to me," I said as I pulled her hands away from her face and turned her chin to face me. "Tell me what you need."

"Right now I need you to take me to my showroom. Or, should I say, what's left of it," she spat before yanking her face away from me.

Instead of making a big deal out of her snapping on me, I pulled off and took the next exit. After a quick U-turn, I headed toward her spot on Las Vegas Boulevard. I wanted to press for more information, but she was upset and needed someone to be angry with. I decided to let her have that for now.

Chapter 8

Drea

"Drea, where the hell are you? It's been almost an hour since I called, and I'm still sitting on this same damn curb waiting," my oldest sister snapped.

"DiDi, I told you I have to handle this business right quick. You know how I rock so I'll be in and out. Is Pops there? What about Philly?" Before she could answer, I heard a deep male voice that didn't belong to my father say something to my sister before fading out. "Who is that talking in the background?"

She covered the phone and responded to whatever his question was before returning to me. "You ain't here, so don't worry about who that was," my sister spat.

"Diem!"

"Ugh, that was Kyrie, nosey-ass girl!"

"Kyrie? Kyrie, who?"

"While you're worried about who I'm talking to, you need to have your ass here to see for yourself. I need you, Drea." My sister suddenly became serious again.

"I feel terrible, but you know there's was no way I can turn around now. Only reason I called again was to make sure you were good," I explained.

Diem smacked her lips and scoffed. "Make sure I was good, huh? If you were so concerned about my well-being, Drea, you would be here, helping me prepare to pick through the ashes to see if there's anything the fire didn't destroy." She sniffed dramatically.

The fire was just put out, so I knew damn well she wasn't sifting through shit, but I decided to appease her for now and not point that out.

After a moment of silence, she started up again. "It's funny to me how the man I just ruined what was becoming a lovely evening with is here helping me, but my sister isn't. Hell, even Philly's missing-in-action ass managed to pull herself away from the bike she was working on to make it here. But you, Drea, you are the first person I thought would be here. What the fuck, man?"

I zipped up my black leather jacket and slipped my gloves over my hands. Pulling my hair into a ponytail at the back of my head, I braided the loose strands into a fishtail and tied a rubber band around the ends. Picking up my helmet, I pulled it over my slicked-down hair and pushed the button on the side to active the built-in Bluetooth feature. After securing my bag on my back and revving the engine of my bike up a few times, I kicked up my stand, pulled on the gas, and slipped into the darkness of the night, blending into the murky background with my all-black outfit and black-on-black Ninja 300.

With my eyes focused on the road and my mind going over what I was on my way to do, I completely zoned out and forgot all about Diem being on the phone until she began to sob in my ear. I had already begun slipping into kill mode. It wasn't that I wasn't concerned about what Diem was going through. It was just that my mind needed to be clear for this job. I knew better than anyone what that shop and those toys meant to her. I just needed her to let me slide this one time for not being there when she needed me.

"DiDi, please don't cry," I told her once I tuned back in to hear her whimpering low. "I promise I'll be there. Just give me an hour, hour and a half tops. Let me handle this business. Go home and get your mind right, and then you got me for the rest of the night. If I have to be out there by myself with a flashlight looking through shit, I will."

"But I don't understand why anyone would do this, Drea," she bawled. "My shop is completely destroyed. Everything is gone. There's nothing remaining of all the inventory that we were supposed to move tomorrow. Nothing. . . ." Her voice trailed off.

"Diem, I promise you, we're going to find out who did this. I already sent a text to Marlon to see if the streets are talking yet. The minute he has a name or some info, you already know we're going to handle that shit, so quit stressing."

There was a loud crackling noise in my ear and what sounded like Diem's phone being shuffled around before Philly's voice came through the line. "Look, go take care of what you need to take care of, Drea. Me and Pops got Diem. There really ain't too much we can do right now anyway. There's still smoke coming from this muthafucka, so until they figure out what caused the fire, we're not allowed to step anywhere near the building, or what's left of it. We're going to be here for a minute."

I pulled up to a red light and slowly came to a stop on the side of this clean-ass Dodge Challenger. The custom paint job was a little too bright for me, but the car looked good. I dropped my feet on the ground and balanced the heavy weight of the bike between my thighs. The sound of gravel and glass crunching together under my boots could easily be heard over the smooth engine. Flipping up my visor, I let the breeze from the cool air hit my face for a second before hiding my eyes back behind the shielding dark tint.

"All right, sis. Let Diem know I'm going to be there. I'll see y'all in a minute."

"I'll let her know, but be careful, Onyx," she said, calling me by my nickname and already knowing what I was on my way to do.

"Always."

"Love you, li'l sis."

"I love you too."

By the time I disconnected the call, the light had just turned green, and I was already across the intersection before any of the other cars moved. I swerved from lane to lane through the slow-moving traffic until I made it to the freeway and was able to take the lead from any car in my way. What would've taken me twenty minutes, had I driven my car, only took me ten to get there on my motorcycle. Lucky for me, there was no highway patrol in sight, so I made it to my destination in record time and ticket free.

A block away from the house I was going to, I parked my bike in the alley on a back street next to a Dumpster and double-checked the poles for any security cameras I may have missed during my intel over the last few weeks. I removed my guns from my backpack and screwed the silencers on to both before tucking one in the back of my jeans and the other on my hip. Walking down the dimly lit street, I pulled the baseball cap I placed on my head lower over my face and pressed the chemistry books and folders I had in my arms tighter to my chest. The green half apron around my waist and my book props made it seem as if I had just gotten off of work and was on my way home for a long night of studying. In a quiet residential area like this, I had to blend in some way to not cause any alarm to the neighbors who may have seen me walking by.

It took me a few minutes to get to the house, but once I did, I easily slipped in the backyard undetected. The dog they had for security was already knocked out, thanks to the steak filled with sleeping pills that Marlon had thrown over the fence not too long ago. I walked to the back door and turned the knob, hoping the door was unlocked, but it wasn't. Pulling my small kit from the front pocket of the apron, I picked the lock and entered the quiet home, ready to do what I came to do.

The lights were off throughout the house, but the TV in the living room and the nightlights in the entrance and kitchen assisted me in not bumping into anything. I held my breath as I pushed my back up against the wall and peeped my head around the corner of the hallway. No sound of movement or snoring could be heard from where I stood, so I made my way to the first door and opened it. It was an empty room with nothing but what looked like an exercise ball and a yoga mat in the middle of it. The next room had a little bit more furniture, but no warm body to occupy it. When I reached the double doors at the end of the hallway, I knew I'd finally made it to the bedroom of the intended target. I never asked why a customer wanted to have someone killed, because it wasn't my business. As long as the deposit was made the day of contact and the rest of my money was deposited after the job was done, I was good.

I pulled both of my guns from their hiding spaces and gripped the handles tightly in my hands. After saying a small prayer, I pushed the already-cracked door open and stepped into the bedroom, ready to kill everything in sight. The minute that metallic smell of blood hit my nose, I knew that something was definitely off. My hand searched the wall for a light switch, but I couldn't feel anything. Slowly walking farther into the room, I noticed an over-turned lamp on the nightstand next to the bed, and I turned it on.

"What the fuck?" I said to myself when the scene before me started to register in my head.

Laid out on the bed was Theodore Wade, my intended target, buck-naked with his arms and legs tied to the four bedposts on the bed. Three bullet holes went across his forehead. His wife, who I was also instructed to kill, was on her knees between her husband's legs with his limp dick still in her bloody mouth. The back of her head was wide open from the shot fired into it. Someone had beaten me to my job, and I was pissed the fuck off. Pulling my red phone from my pocket, I dialed Marlon's number and waited for him to answer.

"Yo, you good?"

"Hell nah, I'm not good," I replied through clenched teeth. I felt myself starting to pace across the dimly lit room. "Who hired me for this job?"

"Some crazy bitch with a lot of money and time on her hands. Why?"

"Do you know if she went to someone else before coming to me?"

"She didn't mention that. Why you asking all of these questions? Where you at?" I could hear the concern in his tone.

"I'm good, Marlon. I'm at the house still."

"For what?" he yelled. "Onyx, get the fuck out of there now before the police show up and catch your ass."

"If they aren't here now, I doubt they'll come anytime soon."

"What do you mean?"

I looked over at the dead bodies. "These mutha-fuckas been dead for some hours now. Their blood is already coagulating and shit. Someone got here before I did."

There was silence on the phone for a second. "Wait. Someone else killed the marks?"

I ignored Marlon's dumb question and began to look around the room to see if the person who was here before me left a calling card or something behind. From the looks of things, there was nothing out of place, just a few things knocked over, which could've happened when Ted and his wife were indulging in their kinky sex act.

"Onyx, did you hear me?" Marlon yelled into my ear, causing me to stop in my tracks, bringing me from my thoughts. "You need to get the fuck out of there now. I don't trust that shit. Might be a setup or something."

"I don't think it's that," I said, squatting down to the floor and picking up a shell casing from the ground. "Aye, Marlon, did you ever get an address or any information on that dude Simmy?"

"Yeah, but what the fuck does he have to do with what's going on right now?"

I twisted the casing between my fingers until the letters engraved on the side were facing me. "'Time's up,'" I read out loud, and I smirked.

"Time's up for what?" a confused Marlon asked.

"You gotta be fucking kidding me."

"Kidding you for what?"

"This nigga."

"What nigga? Onyx, what the fuck are you talking about? And why the fuck are you still in that house? You need to be making your way up the street."

I placed the casing in my pants pocket and made my way around the other side of the bed to turn the light back off. Walking out of the room and down the hallway, I couldn't do anything but shake my head at the thoughts running through my mind.

"Change of plans, Marlon. I'm on my way back to my bike. It's finally my turn to pop up on a muthafucka. Text me the info you have on that Simmy nigga, and I'll hit you up a little later."

"Why do you . . . Wait, you think it was him?"

"I know it was him," I assured him, walking back down the street, headed to my bike. "The casings from the guns I used that day at my shop had the same engraving on them as the one I just found in that room. 'Time's up.'" I laughed. "That nigga's arrogance just cost him his life. Fucking with me is one thing, but fucking with my money is something totally different."

"Maybe I should come with you, Onyx. This nigga already done one-upped you a couple times. What makes you think this wasn't a ploy to get you to come to him? It's doesn't seem weird to you that we've been trying to find this nigga for some time now and could never come up with anything, but all of sudden, boom, we got some info?"

The shit was weird, but I wasn't worried about that right now. My only focus was the $75,000 Simmy just stole from me. I needed my money back in full. Marlon knew by my silence that what I was about to do wasn't up for discussion, so I wasn't surprised when I felt my phone vibrating with a text message from him while we were still on the line.

"Did you get that message I sent you a few seconds ago?" Marlon's voiced echoed through my helmet the second I connected his call to the Bluetooth.

I lifted the visor of my helmet up and brought the phone closer to my face. "I know this address. Seen it somewhere before."

"You should have. That's one of those lofts above the store across the street from Philly's shop," Marlon chuckled. "Nigga been hiding in plain sight this whole time, and you ain't even know it. You really are starting to slip, O."

I bit my tongue to stop the smart response that was threatening to fall from my mouth. Marlon was my man one hundred grand, but sometimes I could do without his sarcastic comments. This nigga Simmy had one-upped me again. Across the street from Philly's shop? Nigga had probably been watching us this whole time, and we didn't even know it. Probably had plenty of opportunities to catch me slipping, and I would've never seen it coming. I made a mental note to bring this up at our next club meeting. We needed to get a handle on our surroundings and tighten up security at some of the places we frequented a little more.

"Have any other information you have on this nigga on my desk at the shop by morning. I'm about to trash this burner, but I'll hit you up from my personal cell when I make it to his spot. I'm sure I'll beat you there," I spoke into my mouthpiece as I revved my engine and sped off in the direction of Philly's shop.

"I'm here."

"Damn, already?"

"You know how I do when I'm riding my bitch," I replied as I looked down the dark and motionless street. "It's kind of quiet around here." My eyes went toward Hart of the City. Usually the lights in the parking lot would be on from Philly working on something after hours, but tonight the area was pitch-black. Only the amber hue from the blinking street lamps gave off a small spot of light. Empty cars lined the street. Some had the windows busted out, and others were alarmed and ready to sound off at the slightest touch. Outside of the black stray cat that Philly fed every evening whining by the entrance of her shop, I was the only person out on the normally busy street. I turned my attention back to the storefronts on the other side of the road and eyed the lofts that sat on top. I wondered how many times this nigga had his gun aimed at the back of my head and never pulled the trigger.

"Onyx!" Marlon's muffled voice yelled into the phone. "Did you hear what I just said?"

"Nah, I'm trying to scope out the scene. What's up?"

"I'm still stuck on the freeway. A fucking car just spun out of control and crashed into the barrier.

Got all of the lanes backed up. Maybe you should wait to run up on this nigga. Catch him slipping some other time. We know where he lives now."

I got off of my bike and placed my helmet on the back seat, ending my call with Marlon without a response. I didn't have time to wait for him. There wouldn't be a best time, because I was getting at this nigga tonight. I made a mental note to call him as soon as I left. He'd be pissed off that I hung up in his face and went into Simmy's house blind and without backup, but he already knew when I had my mind focused on something there was no changing that shit.

Walking up the street a bit, I made it around the corner and into the back alleyway that led to the stairwell for the homes above the stores. Squinting to try to make out the numbers lined on the wall, I slowly made my way to the address Marlon sent me for Simmy. The smell of urine and day-old food filled my nose, as the sound of the water dripping from the rusty pipe above my head echoed around me. Slowly walking up the stairs one step at a time, I pulled my gun from the back of my pants and held it close to my thigh. Depending on how everything played out in these next few seconds, I'd still have enough time to make it across town to Diem's warehouse and help her try to piece together what happened.

Gravel crunching under my boot with each step had me praying Simmy's ass didn't have that bionic hearing. He'd no doubt know about my arrival if he did. I should have gone with my first mind and just walked up the flight of stairs in my socks, but I didn't want to chance stepping on a piece of glass and leaving my DNA anywhere on the scene. I had about six more steps to go until I made it to his door, ready to get shit poppin', but the mumbling sound of different voices arguing back and forth stopped me in my tracks.

"You had one job to do, Simeron. One job. Learn how this bitch moves and then kill her. What the fuck happened?"

Simmy chuckled. "Man, fuck you. All this talking you're doing is really starting to get on my nerves." He coughed. "Either do what you came to do or get the fuck on already."

I could tell by the tone of his voice that he had been injured in some way. There was pain in his tone, but not enough to show whoever was talking to him that he was in any.

The deep voice tsked. "And you were one of the best. Leo practically raised you. Taught you everything that you know about murdering a muthafucka in cold blood. What was it about this kill, huh? Probably had plenty of opportunities to take that cunt out, but for some reason, you didn't." Whoever was talking must've walked closer to the door, because his voice started to become a lot clearer. "What was it, Simeron? What made you change your mind and sign your own death warrant?"

"I think the nigga done fell in love, boss," another voice said while laughing. My breath caught in my throat. "Fell in love with a bitch who would smoke his ass in a minute. Especially if she finds out that he—"

"Shut the fuck up, Mack. Your ass always talking too damn much."

"Talking too much? I'm just fucking with the nigga." He laughed it off.

"That's the problem. Your ass always fucking around when you should be shutting the fuck up. And you wonder why your ass never get to do shit. You lucky I let you come along for this one. I knew you'd take some joy in fucking up Simmy's hogtied ass before I put a bullet in his head, but you have me regretting even bringing you along. Let yo' ass take the lead, and you almost got us both killed with the way he was beating your ass when I came in," the boss, who was obviously in charge, scoffed.

"You act like I couldn't fuck this nigga up if his hands were free."

"Nigga, that patch over your eye and that bullet lodged in your neck should give you that answer. Why you think your job has only been intel all of these years? Ass can't shoot or fight worth shit."

Simmy laughed and then groaned. "Man, are you bitches done arguing or nah? I mean, because I'd rather y'all kill me now than sit here and listen to this weak-ass back-and-forth shit. Especially when we all know that none of you muthafuckas could see me on any level." He coughed and spit. "The only reason you were able to catch me slipping tonight was because I fucked up expecting you to be someone else. But mark my words, if by some miraculous chance I make it out this bitch alive, I won't make that same mistake again."

The sound of flesh being hit and bones cracking sounded off.

"Talk that shit now," the voice I now knew belonged to Mack shouted. "You're a cocky mutha-fucka, and I've always hated your ass because of that." The sound of a gun cocking caused me to hurriedly move up a few more steps. "Do you know how good I feel right now? Nigga, I'm about to end your life and fuck your bitch in the same night. What's her name again, boss?"

"Onyx." I could hear the smirk in his laugh.

"Yeeeaaah, Onyx. That ho got a nice little body on her and some nice lips. You ever see her riding her bike, nigga?"

"Nah, you?" the boss replied.

"Hell, yeah. You know while this nigga was run-ning around catching feelings and shit, I took the initiative to do some additional intel just in case the bitch killed his ass before he could get to her."

"Oh, yeah?"

"Yeah. All I had to do was follow this nigga to find out where she lived. It was all she wrote after that. I would sit outside her place and watch her come and go. Ass poking out so fat when she hopped on her motorcycle," he grunted. "Damn, I can't wait to end this nigga's life so I can go get a sample of that murderous pussy. That nigga Knight sho' know how to breed some fine-ass bitches and pull them, too. I'm gon' fuck the shit out of her ass right before I kill her, something this nigga here failed to do."

My mind went back to a couple of weeks ago when I noticed the black Impala sitting at the end of my block. I knew there was someone watching me, which was why I rode that way, the opposite way to my shop. I tried to get a good look who was behind the wheel, but the tint was too dark for me to see. I thought it was Simmy for a minute, but when he never showed up or broke back into my home unannounced, I knew it wasn't him. I did take precautions though. After I noticed the car sitting there on certain nights, I never stayed. I always left out the back and rode my bike to one of my other spots.

With my back against the wall, I walked up the last two steps and stopped right at the door seal. The overhead light was already shot out, making it easy for me to blend in with the darkness. Taking my chances, I looked through the small crack in the door to try to get a head count on the number of bodies that were about to drop.

A short, bald guy stood in front of a bound Simmy, as his beat-up and bloody body sat up against a wall. The tall, light-skinned dude, who sorta resembled Columbus Short, was leaned back in one of those foldable chairs, with a gun waving around in his hand. Pushing the door open a little wider, I was able to see more into the damn near empty loft. A decent couch and an entertainment center with a nice-size TV were the only things I could make out on the side of the room facing me. In the spot where the two men had Simmy hemmed up were only a burgundy area rug, a few crates, and some empty pizza boxes scattered around the floor. I almost screamed when a big-ass rat ran across the floor and over my boot, but I held that shit down and walked a little farther inside.

"Oh, shit, Mack, I think that nigga mad. You see the look on his face after you mentioned fucking his bitch?" the boss joked.

"I don't give a fuck. I should go hunt that ho down right now and fuck her in front of you. Nut all in that pussy so she can give birth to my seed."

"What you gonna name that little nigga?" the boss instigated, his body doubling over in laughter.

"Shit. I already have a junior, so that's out of the question. Maybe I might name him after this nigga. Thank his bitch ass for introducing me to my future baby mama."

With his arms restrained behind his back and his ankles bonded together, Simmy struggled, but he managed to sit back up from the hit he just endured. Blood fell down his face from the huge gash above his eyebrow, and his right eye was damn near swollen shut. His shirt was ripped open, and the tattoos decorating his frame were barely visible due to the dark purple and blue bruises now covering his body too. Just when I thought the crazy nigga was about to concede to his death and bow out gracefully, he began to laugh a diabolic laugh that sent chills up my spine. The sexy-ass smile on his face had my belly turning flips. Even when he showed his bloody teeth, I was still turned on by the sight of this man. Nigga was a straight warrior.

"What's so fucking funny?" Mack asked. "You think we a joke or something?"

Simmy slowly nodded his head, his laugh growing louder and louder. "You are a joke. A pussy-ass joke. Had I been in your shoes and you in mine, you'd be dead already. What the fuck your scary ass waiting on? Pull the fucking trigga! What? You need your daddy"—his chin lifted in the boss's direction—"to give you the okay? Make sure you don't fuck this kill up like you did that one time—"

Before the words could fully leave Simmy's lips, Mack took the butt of his gun and smashed it into his mouth. Blood instantly began to fill it up. Simmy's jaw twitched, and his eyes turned dark. He stared at Mack with the most evil look before hawking up the biggest glob of spit in his mouth and spitting it directly in his face.

"Muthafucka!" Mack screamed before aiming his gun at Simmy and firing off a shot. "Fuck you, you bitch-ass nigga!" He raised his arm again, this time aiming at Simmy's head. "I should've killed your ass a long time ago when I had the chance. But it's okay, I'ma do that shit now and finish off the job you should've done already. That bitch will be dead by the time the police find your body, and I can't wait to send her ass to hell with you."

Although I was here to deal with Simmy about fucking with my money, the threat this asshole just put out against me had my trigger finger itching in another direction. Before he could get a clean shot off and end Simmy's life, I raised my gun and sent a hot one to the back of his head. When the boss turned around with wide eyes and opened his mouth to say something, I sent a bullet right through that bitch, silencing him for life.

"'Bout time yo' ass killed them niggas. How long were you going to let them fuck me up before you made your move?" Simmy groaned in pain, head falling to the side and popping right back up when I pressed the hot end of my gun against his forehead.

"So, I already knew you were sent to kill me, but you didn't complete the job. Why?"

"I think you already know the answer to that."

I did, but he didn't need to know that, so I went on with my line of questions. "You fucked with my money tonight. Was that a part of some plan to get me to come here so that you could finally kill me?"

"Get you to come here, yes. Kill you? No."

I lowered into a squat and pushed Simmy's head back with my gun so that we were looking into each other's eyes. "You know my intention coming here tonight was to dead your ass for fucking with my money. I wasn't expecting to stumble in on all of this other shit though." I looked over at Mack's and his boss's lifeless bodies and then back at him. "Who are they?"

He smiled weakly. "Thanks to you, a distant memory now."

I twisted my lips, irritated at his cryptic and short response. "Who wants me dead?"

He shrugged his shoulders. "I never ask who. I only request the target's name and my money in cash," he said weakly before spitting out another glob of blood.

We stared at each other after his response. Curiosity was in my eyes, and something else was in his. I could feel the flips in my stomach going crazy again and the goosebumps slowly starting to decorate my skin. The way my body had reacted to his the night he broke into my house was the same way it was reacting now, bloody face and all. My breath hitched, and his one good eye traveled down to my mouth. Involuntarily my tongue slipped out of its hiding spot and swiped across my bottom lip. The groan that escaped the back of his throat was low, but I still heard it loud and clear. The phone of one of the dead men started to ring, which caused our attention to go toward them.

"I need to get you out of here. Take you somewhere and lie low for a few days until you heal up some. I guarantee that whoever is calling that phone is contacting them to make sure you're dead. Him not answering is going to send up a red flag," I told him.

"And you already know that red flag means to send in more men." He nodded in agreement while coughing up more blood.

Conflicted, I cocked my gun back and pressed it harder into his forehead. As much as I was feeling him, I was done playing games and was ready to end this shit once and for all. "You stole my money, which is an instant death sentence in my book. On top of that, you don't have any information on who has a problem with me. Can you give me one good reason why I shouldn't just end your life right now?"

"The duffle bag behind the door."

My eyes zeroed in on the large gray bag sitting against the wall. "What about it?"

"Your money is in there. Your normal fee plus an extra twenty Gs for killing the wife." He tried to smile but winced from the pain of his swollen lip.

With my gun still on him, I walked over to the bag and opened it. Sure enough, bundled bills were stacked neatly inside of it. I lifted the heavy bag over my shoulder and went to stand back in front of Simmy. "This still isn't a good enough reason for me not to kill you."

He shook his head. "Never said it was."

"Okay. Well, any last words before I take your life?"

"Not a word. A reason that you shouldn't," he whispered before dropping his head and lifting it back up.

"And what reason is that, Simmy? Why shouldn't I kill you?"

He chuckled. "You're not gonna kill me, Onyx. Not today. Not tomorrow. Not even next week," he mumbled, now going in and out of consciousness, so it was hard for me to make out what he was saying.

"Come again?" I demanded, putting my ear closer to his lips.

"You're not going to kill me," he said low.

"And how do you know that?"

"Because at some point you wanna see what this dick do just as much as I wanna know how that pussy taste," he cockily retorted.

Nigga was on the brink of death and had the nerve to still have pussy on the brain. He was telling no lies, so I didn't bother offering a response. I wanted this nigga just as much as he wanted me. I simply rose to my feet and dialed Marlon to make sure he was on his way. If we both wanted to make it out of here alive, I needed a little help, and I'd wasted enough time as it was. It didn't make sense killing him right now anyway because I needed him on my team if I had any chance of finding out who was after me. I also had this feeling that Diem's shop catching fire could somehow be related, but I would soon find out. All I knew was that whenever I discovered who was behind this shit, there would be hell to pay.

Chapter 9

Diem

Carefully, I walked through what used to be my office in my old warehouse for the final time. Kyrie and my family granted my request to have a few moments alone to process it all. The smell of smoke, burnt plastic, and wood permeated the air. Ashes flew around aimlessly as the early morning breeze swept through. I heard the low mumble of the crime scene agents talking among themselves as they bagged up and sorted through all the evidence they'd collected. I was just ready for them to get their asses on so that we could begin our own damn investigation. I didn't need them at all, but there was no way to get in the way of them doing their jobs.

Stopping in the middle of the incinerated room, I rolled my head back with a sigh. My hands wrapped around my waist snuggly as I closed my eyes and tried to calm the anxiety I could feel slowly starting to build. My blood pressure would probably be through the roof if I checked it right now, and the pounding headache that usually accompanied those high readings was ever present. Rubbing my temples did nothing to ease the pain.

In through your nose, hold it, then blow it out of your mouth, I repeated in my mind, attempting some breathing exercises to keep my emotions at bay. I didn't want to cry. I wasn't going to cry. At least, not right now. I had to find a way to maintain the tough facade that I was known for. I had to handle whatever I could with this situation now and add anything else to my already ridiculously long to-do list.

"Ms. Hart," the raspy voice of the fire chief called out to me.

Thoughts of my pending grand opening, the two parties I had scheduled for next week, and everything I still needed to do for the fundraiser were placed on pause for the time being. I slowly turned around and acknowledged his presence, my arms still wrapped around my body and my heart hella heavy from the night's and early morning's events.

He cleared his throat. "Sorry to disturb you, ma'am. I just wanted to go over a few things with you before I left."

I didn't really feel like talking at the moment, but I knew that whatever he wanted to discuss would probably help in figuring out how the fire started. All I needed was a lead from them to point me in the right direction. There was no question that this was intentional, and I was determined to find out who was crazy enough to fuck with me. "I'm all ears."

He walked over to the side of the room where the small window used to be. "Do you see this glass right here all over the floor?" He pointed his clipboard down to the ground, and I nodded. "Well, this is only caused from something hitting the window from the outside, which means the person who started the fire had to have entered here, seeing as there is no forced entry anywhere else." He wasn't telling me anything I didn't already know, but I was going to go along with this shit.

"So someone started this? Can't blame it on faulty wiring or anything like that, huh?" I nodded knowingly as I scanned what remained of my business.

He shook his head and continued talking. "Yes, I believe this was intentionally started by someone. You see this line here that starts in this corner and continues down the hall into some of the other rooms?" I nodded, looking down at the scorched pattern as we walked along the wall. "This is where the fire started. An accelerant of some kind was poured here, and lots of it. Whoever did this had to be here for some time, pouring that into all these rooms." He pointed to the ground again.

"And that was done because . . . ?" I motioned with my hand for him to continue.

"Because they wanted the fire to spread faster and basically destroy anything and everything in its path. Had the fire been reported earlier, we probably would've been able to contain it and save some of the building. But unfortunately, by the time we got here the whole place was engulfed in flames. I couldn't even send a team in to check and see if anyone was still in here. Luckily once we were able to put the fire out and do a walk-through, there were no casualties."

"I guess that's a good thing, right?"

His facial expression softened, and he walked closer to me. "It is, it is. But this can also be a good thing for you."

I looked up at him and was a little taken aback by how handsome the fire chief was. White men weren't necessarily my cup of tea, but he was fine as hell, even with all of the soot that covered his face. "And why is that?"

He drew his thin bottom lip into his mouth and smiled. "Because this can be somewhat of a blessing for you. With the insurance policy I'm sure you have on this place, you can rebuild here and start over, or you can find a better location all together. Although it may seem like a total loss to some, I don't see it that way at all."

I only nodded while maintaining eye contact with him. No, I didn't see it as a total loss, and he was right, my insurance policy would pay handsomely for this tragic event. It was the principle of it that bothered me. Not to mention the priceless things I'd lost in the fire. Things that may not have been important to some but to me were my life. There were people who saw what I did for a living as a joke, but it was anything but funny to me. "Haha, she sells rubber dicks for a living." No, what I did to make my money was offer products that spiced up marriages on the verge of falling apart. I provided single women on the move the occasional release to ease those lonely, celibate nights. And how about assisting women in learning their bodies and what could send them to the highest of heights in the bedroom? Like, don't knock me for being in tune and comfortable with my femininity and sexuality. Give me credit for starting this business during my first year of college at only nineteen years of age. It was my baby, and for someone to deliberately come for what I'd built from the ground up was unacceptable.

"Well, Ms. Hart, we're going to pack up and go, but here's my card should you have any further questions, or you know, whatever else," he offered shyly once we neared the front, where everyone stood waiting for me.

"Or whatever else, huh?" I blushed. His ass thought he was slick. I was sure that this wasn't the way this thing went. I was positive that any reports or conclusions that he came to regarding the fire would be communicated to the police and not me, but I couldn't say that I wasn't flattered. And if he kept looking at me like that, he was going to have me scratching something else off my bucket list.

Although fucking a white boy was way, way down on the list, it was still a fantasy of mine, right along with Brix's fine Latino ass.

Before I could say another word, the clearing of a throat snapped me out of the trance ol' green eyes had me in. Expecting to see my father standing there blocking like he normally did, I was shocked to find Kyrie at my side, grilling me like I was his woman or something. The gorgeous firefighter made me forget his ass was even here just that quick.

"Thanks for everything, Chief. I believe we can take it from here," he asserted, removing the card from the man's hand before I could accept it. His hard eyes were still on me.

"Of course." The man simpered in Kyrie's direction before offering me a parting smile.

I saw my father and Philly approaching from my peripheral, so before Kyrie could even attempt to check me about flirting with another man in his face, I spoke up. "Can you take me home, please?" I quickly asked.

"Diem, wait, baby girl. Let me talk to you before you leave," Dad requested.

"I don't believe there's anything for us to discuss. You lied to me," I responded, my pleading eyes still on Kyrie.

"DiDi, please. Just give me a chance to explain," he implored.

"Nah, Pops, fuck that. Diem's right! You told us on several occasions that we had nothing to worry about. That this deal wouldn't affect us in any way. Look at her store!" Philly yelled.

"Girls, I was sincere when we talked about this. I'm just as caught off guard as you are by all that's happened, but trust me when I say that I'll take care of it," he promised.

"Take care of what? And who?" I shouted. "You're basically admitting that you already know who's responsible. How is that, when you just said you didn't expect any of this to happen? I'm finding that hard as hell to believe!"

"Look, I know you're upset, but check yourself and that smart-ass mouth, Diem. Remember who the fuck I am," Pops clapped back, shutting me up immediately. I was pissed, but I wasn't crazy.

"You got that, Dad, but I still don't feel like talking about it right now. I can't even think straight at the moment, and the fact that we still haven't seen or heard from Drea is about to make me lose it. I just want to get the hell away from here." I felt that at any second I would fall apart, and I didn't want Kyrie around to witness it. I needed to get home and away from him as quickly as possible. "Can we do this later?" I begged, hoping he would let me make it.

He didn't respond, just stood there with a mixture of guilt and hurt etched on his face. For some reason that pissed me off even more. It only added to my suspicions that he knew something like this could happen and failed to tell us the truth.

"Look, emotions are on high right now, so why don't we all take a step back and come back together once things have cooled off a bit?" Kyrie mediated, and finally my father nodded in agreement.

"Fine by me," I sassed and walked away.

Why does he keep saying we? I screamed in my head en route to his car. All night and just moments ago with the fire chief, it was "we this" and "we that!" Kyrie included himself in whatever conversation and plans Philly and I discussed.

After snapping off on him in the car, I hoped for and expected him to drop me off and keep it pushing, but he'd been by my side since we arrived to find the last flames being put out by the firefighters. Although I appreciated him, I had no plans to see him again once he gave me a ride to my place. I thought I could do it but I couldn't. He'd convinced me in a matter of days that we could possibly have something with one another, but just that fast I realized that it would never work. I had too much going on, and I didn't feel that I would be able to dedicate the time necessary for us to build a meaningful relationship. From talking with him and getting to know a little about him, I could tell that a situationship or "friends with benefits" arrangement wasn't what he was interested in. Sadly, it was all I had to offer him at this point.

"Hold up, Di!" Philly called out from behind me, causing me to pause midstride.

When I glanced back, I noticed my father and Kyrie standing about fifty feet away, speaking in hushed tones. I was happy that Kyrie was blessed with this opportunity, but I suddenly hated that he was working with my dad, especially on a job that was clearly adding drama to my already-hectic life. I didn't want him involved or possibly hurt in some way due to my father and some unknown beef of his. That was another reason we couldn't be involved seriously.

"You gon' be okay, sis? I can take you home and stay with you for as long as you need," she offered sincerely.

"I'll be fine, Philly, I promise. I just want to be alone for a minute," I told her.

"What about ol' boy? Don't seem like he's trying to let you out of his sight anytime soon." She nodded over at Kyrie, who just so happened to be looking my way.

He tilted his head to the side, and the look he gave me told me that he already knew what I was thinking. I could only sigh when he slightly shook his head no. I quickly turned my attention back to Philly, because if I looked at him any longer, he'd have me changing my mind once again. I had a feeling that this nigga could get me to do just about anything he asked.

"I know, but he doesn't really have a choice. After he takes me home it's a wrap," I informed her convincingly, going against what was in my heart.

"Nah, Di, don't do that man like that." She shook her head disapprovingly. "He's into you like for real for real, and here you go pulling that same shit. 'I'm too busy. I have no time for a relationship. I'm married to the money, honey,'" she quoted in that stupid baby voice with her hand in the air. As much as I didn't want to, I couldn't help but laugh. "We'll be knocking on thirty soon, Diem, so it's timeout for that 'I don't need a man' crap. I know losing this shop was a big blow, but you were moving on to bigger and better anyway. Let this man be there for you like I can tell he's trying to be, and stop dwelling on this shit," she said, motioning toward the burned building.

"That's easier said than done, Ophelia. Would you be saying the same if someone set fire to your beloved motorcycle shop? As much as you love that place, I think not. Don't get me wrong, I understand what you're saying, and in a few days I'm sure I'll see the blessing in all of this, but right now I want to sulk. I want to be pissed off at the nothing-ass individuals who felt they could come and destroy my dream like it was nothing. Once that wears off, I'll be ready to move, and when I say move, you know exactly what I mean. I'm not letting this shit ride," I spat.

"Calm down, girl! I'm not telling you not to be upset, because I know I would be. And hell nah, we not letting this ride. As pissed as I am at yo' daddy, I know he's going to get to the bottom of it."

"Oh, so he's my daddy now?" I chuckled.

"He is today, shit," she joked. After a long pause, she added, "He'll make it right though."

"I know he will, but I still don't have any words for him right now," I said with an eye roll as my father tried making eye contact with me as he slowly pulled away from the curb. I simply ignored him and gave Philly a hug before sliding into the passenger side door that Kyrie was already holding open for me.

"So, this is it, huh?" Kyrie said as soon as he put his car in park in my driveway. He was looking straight ahead at nothing in particular, but even from the side, I could see the irritation he was trying to mask.

"What are you talking about, Ky?" I attempted playing it off.

The entire way to my place neither of us spoke, and I used that quiet time to think of the best way I could break up with a nigga I wasn't even really with. I'd never had a problem dropping a dude, but with Kyrie it was different. The words that I wanted to say didn't quite resonate in my heart, making this a difficult task.

"Come on, Diem, keep it real with me. I could see it in your eyes earlier, and your energy is all off. Speak your mind."

He took hold of my hand and finally looked my way. I could only give him eye contact for a few seconds before I turned my head to gaze out of the window. Why was this shit so hard? Maybe it was the way I felt when he touched me. Or the pounding of my heart being this close to him. Here he was giving me the out I needed, and I was having the hardest time following through. Still not able to look at him, I finally mustered up enough courage to speak.

"I just think the timing is off right now, you know, for you and me. With everything that's going on, I don't thi—"

"You're making excuses, Diem," he groaned before releasing my hand. "I don't give a fuck about what you have going on. I only met your ass a couple of months ago and had only come face-to-face with you on two measly occasions before I knew what I wanted. And what I want is to get to know you. You can front all you want, but you feel the same shit I'm feeling, and you've felt it from day one. Tell me I'm wrong and I'll walk away." He pulled my chin toward him, forcing me to look into his eyes.

"You're wrong, Kyrie. This just ain't what I want right now," I lied to his face.

"A'ight, I won't keep pressing you," he huffed before getting out and walking to my side to open the door.

Why was I pissed that he hadn't put up more of a fight? I didn't want the nigga, but damn if I didn't want him to want me. It was dumb, but I couldn't help the way I felt. Because this wasn't what I truly wanted, I was hoping he would continue trying to convince me to see things his way. But he'd given up, and that legit broke my heart.

Snatching up my clutch, I bypassed his out-stretched hand and stomped to my front door. My unpredictable moods and crazy ambition were a few reasons I was single now. Not many men could put up with it, and I'd had plenty guys stop pursuing me as a result. Kyrie deciding to move on wasn't something I thought I would be able to get over, which was why I was doing it to him first. Still, I wanted him to protest a little more.

"Thanks for everything. Guess I'll see you around," I said without turning around to look at him. I knew that if I did, I would be begging him to stay and forget the stupid shit that I'd just said.

"Diem, baby, wait." He grabbed my wrist.

"Kyrie, please just go." My voice broke as I snatched away from him. Moving as quickly as I possibly could, I unlocked my door, entered, and closed it before he could get another word in.

I placed my belongings on the table in my foyer and moved to my couch, already feeling the side effects of the choice I'd made. Sinking down into the plush material, I held on tightly to one of my decorative pillows, willing my tears to remain in the ducts. These last few days with him had been amazing, and just that fast it was over. Why was I so stupid? Why couldn't I have just taken Philly's advice? At the rate I was going, I was sure to be an old maid with no man and a house full of cats in twenty years.

Glancing up toward the mantle in my living room, I spotted the picture taken of me when I cut the ribbon at my grand opening for Hart Box by Diem. That was a big day for me. I'd purchased that property outright without help from anyone. I arranged the entire grand opening party myself, and it was a big hit. I'd also sold most of my inventory that very first night. I was proud of that fact if no one else was. In the picture, I was surrounded by my family, and it was one of the happiest days of my life.

That image was all that was needed for the dam to finally break. I lost it, and the wail that escaped my body sounded scary and foreign. It was like it was coming from someone other than me. Body shaking and consumed with grief, I stood and moved toward the mantle to get a closer look at the picture. Clutching it to my chest, I fell to my knees and continued my shameful pity party.

The feel of strong arms wrapping around me from behind moments later caused the tears to fall more rapidly and the cries to grow louder. He didn't say a word, just held me tight as I had my meltdown. I realized now that I must have left the door unlocked, and I was honestly glad that he'd come back. Surprisingly, I wasn't as embarrassed as I thought I would be at him being an onlooker to this spectacle I was putting on. If anything, it made me feel closer to him.

Letting go of the frame, I placed my hand on top of his and allowed him to pull me into him even more. In that moment, I discovered that this connection between us wasn't something I was going to be able to easily walk away from.

"Stop trying to push me away, Diem. And don't ever be afraid to show me this side of you. It's okay to cry, baby," he whispered to me. I could only nod and continue doing just that.

"Let me take you away for the weekend," he said into my neck once I was all cried out and only sniffling periodically.

"The weekend?" I questioned. I wanted to say no, because I knew I had things to do, but something about the sincerity in his tone had me responding a different way and without hesitation. "Okay."

"Really?" he asked in surprise.

"Yes, Kyrie, really." I turned to face him so that he could see how serious I was. "Take me away from here, please."

He slowly leaned in to kiss me, and my heart rate skyrocketed, but before our lips could make contact, my phone began to ring and vibrate on the table. He blinked out of the trance he was in and went to release me, but I shook my head no and held on. I didn't feel like being bothered, and I wanted that fucking kiss even more. Whoever was on that phone was killing the vibe. I just wanted to enjoy this moment with him with no interruptions.

"I know you're not feeling it right now, but that may be your sister. I wouldn't want you to miss her call if something is wrong. With the shit that's happening, it's not really the time to shut your people out. That includes your father as well," he added.

"Damn, you had me until you said that last part," I quipped, making him laugh as I got up to get the phone.

Although I was still angry with my father, I appreciated Kyrie saying that, because we needed each other now more than ever, and of course it was still family over everything. I was worried about my baby sister. I knew Drea could handle herself in these streets because she was damn good at what she did. However, that didn't mean that there wasn't someone out there who was better or more skilled. I feared the day that we get a call saying she'd been hurt, or even worse, murdered. I prayed every night that it never came to that, but in her line of work, we were aware of that possibility.

Sure enough, when I picked up the phone Drea's number and picture were on the screen. By the time I answered she had already hung up. I quickly dialed her back but got the voice mail. She was probably calling back, so I walked over and took my place back between Kyrie's legs on the floor by the fireplace. Just like I thought, my phone rang seconds later.

"Where are you?" I hurriedly asked once I picked up.

"I'm off the grid for a minute, but I'm okay," she said low.

"How long is a minute, Onyx? We're over here about to lose our minds."

"I really don't know how long. Some crazy shit popped off, but I'm good." She kept it short.

"Do we need to come to you?" I knew she didn't really do much talking about her business over the phone, but I needed answers. Talking to her on the phone and having her tell me she was okay was fine and dandy, but I needed to lay eyes on her. I had to see it for myself.

"You can't, but I'll be in contact with you soon. Sorry that I wasn't able to follow through with meeting you last night. Also for not being there to help with the final arrangements for the fundraiser. It's less than two weeks away, and then this happens."

"It's cool, baby sis. I'm good as long as you're safe, and to tell you the truth, everything is basically handled. I plan to split the last-minute details between Sissy and Rhea. I need a fucking break from this shit," I said as Kyrie placed a soft kiss on my neck. That simple contact was so damn soothing.

"Good. That makes me feel a little better. And yes, please take a break. You deserve it. I still feel like shit for not being there for you, Di. I really didn't expect things to go the way they did. This last job went all wrong, but I'll work it out."

"I know we can't say much on the phone, but I really feel like everything that's happened is connected in some way. The shit at your shop and the arson at Hart's Box. Pops knows that something's not right, but he's being mum about it, and I ain't really talking to his ass right now, no way."

"I was thinking that too, about this all being related or whatever," she said then suddenly paused. I could hear someone talking in the background, and moments later she spoke again. "Look, DiDi, I have to go, but I'll keep you posted. There's a lot that we need to talk about as a family," she said quickly then disconnected the line.

"Fuck," I hissed, gripping the phone tight in my hand.

"You good?" Kyrie asked.

"Yeah, but I'd be better if I knew where she was or if I could see her."

"I'm sure she'll be fine," he assured me, and I nodded. "So, you still rolling with me, or have you changed your mind already? You're quick to flip-flop on a nigga, and I don't appreciate that shit," he scolded.

"I don't try to do that, but I make dumb decisions when I'm emotional," I admitted.

"I see, and that's why I couldn't leave," he said, brushing his soft lips against mine. "You coming away with me, Diem?"

Staring into his honey-colored eyes, I took his face into my hands and placed my lips fully on his. It didn't take long for him to take my closed-mouth, sweet kiss and turn it into a deep, soul-stirring, sensual one. When his warm tongue parted my lips and entered my mouth, I was out of there. If he could work his dick as good as he worked his tongue, his ass could take me to the fucking Motel 6 off Dean Martin and I wouldn't give a damn. The shit felt just that good. So good that I had to pull back before we got carried away and never left my house.

"Let me go pack a bag," I told him, pecking his juicy lips twice more before rising to my feet. "By the way, where are we going so I'll know what to take with me?" I paused at the entry that led to the hallway and bedrooms.

"Pack whatever you need to be comfortable, a couple swimsuits, and"—he paused for dramatic effect—"make sure you grab your board. I'm taking you to Venice Beach," he informed me with an accomplished look on his face.

My eyes popped open, and my heart suddenly ballooned as I ran and dove on him. As I straddled him, I planted kisses all over his face while he squirmed and laughed heartily. "For real, Ky? We're really going to Venice?" I looked into his eyes.

"We are," he replied, gripping my ass to bring my body up so that our faces were even closer.

My pussy instantly juiced up when it grazed his growing erection. Also causing it to leak was the fact that he'd actually been listening to me. I told him the other day how much I missed surfing on Venice Beach. It had been a while since I had any free time to make the four-and-a-half-hour drive to my favorite place. I always found peace when I visited Venice. This nigga was gone be zaddy for sure if he kept this shit up.

Leaning down, I used the tip of my tongue to trace his lips before covering them completely with mine. A low growl escaped his throat, and he gripped my ass even tighter, moving me up and down his covered dick. Sitting up, I quickly made a move to remove the half-sleeve hunter green cropped top I'd worn to dinner the night before. I shivered when his hands traveled lightly down my arms, which happened to still be extended in the air. Moving a little lower, I watched his expression change once he released the front clasp of my strapless black bra, and my firm breasts were released. Men always seemed to think I'd had a boob job because of how nicely they sat on my chest, but I was proud to say that these babies were natural. All me. It pleased me that Kyrie had quickly become infatuated with them.

"Mmm," I moaned, head thrashing about, as he fondled and squeezed, becoming more familiar with his new besties.

Coming up to a sitting position, he took a nipple into his mouth and began to alternate sucking and flicking his tongue across it while he pinched and squeezed the other between his thumb and index finger. Those sensations, along with the grinding I was doing on top of him, were about to have me releasing. I let him continue doing his thing while I went for the zipper of his jeans. It was like me doing that snapped him out of the sex zone he was in.

"Diem, shit. I'm sorry I got carried away, baby. We ain't gotta do this right now," he said with his hands still caressing my titties.

I looked down and smirked, and his eyes quickly followed mine. Immediately he removed his hands, but his eyes were glued to them. His body was saying one thing while his mouth was saying another, and that was some shit I wasn't trying to hear. This wasn't at all how I planned for this shit to go down, but Kyrie was about to get this pussy before our little road trip to Venice. This was definitely happening tonight, and I knew the best way to guarantee that it did.

His eyes moved with me as I stood up, feet planted on either side of him. Leaning back with his hands extended behind him, he took me in as I unbuttoned then slipped my flattened palms in the sides of the knee-length, ripped denim shorts I was wearing. Sliding them slowly down my hips, thighs, and legs, I kept my eyes on him as he followed my every move. Once they were at my ankles, I motioned with my eyes for him to do the honors, and he obliged, removing the shorts completely, one leg at a time. I now stood before him in nothing but a black lace thong and my red lace peep-toe heels. I watched him scan my body from head to toe for a full minute without saying a word.

Then I just walked away, hips swaying, adding a little extra oomph to each step. Hopefully he took the bait I laid out so that we could get the inevitable cracking. If not, this hot shower I was stepping into would soon turn into a cold one, and the ride to the beach would be an awkward one for sure.

I was in the shower for what seemed like forever but was more like ten minutes before I felt a cool breeze sweep across my naked body. I was standing directly under the water after rinsing my hair following a good shampoo and conditioning, trying to get that burnt smell out of it. I'd almost lost hope that he was coming, and now that he was here I was suddenly nervous as hell.

When those calloused hands wrapped around my midsection and that long dick pressed into my back? Jesus! My knees buckled, and I felt faint. Even more so when he began placing soft kisses on my back and neck. Had it not been for him pushing my chest into the wall and trapping me there,

I would have hit the shower floor. I was being manipulative in my efforts to entice him earlier, but I now saw how he was about to take control of this situation we found ourselves in. Luckily for him, when it came to sex, I had no problem relinquishing all authority over my body.

"You know what I've been fantasizing about since the night we met?" he asked, using his deep-ass sex voice. Damn, why did that shit turn me on so?

"Whattt?" I whimpered as his hand came down between my thighs to palm my waxed pussy.

"The way you sucked off that dildo, never seen anything like it. . . ." His voice trailed off as he really got into what he was doing to my clit.

"Mmm, shit," I moaned when he inserted two fingers inside of me.

"After you bust this nut, you gon' get on your fucking knees and show me how that shit's done," he boldly informed me minutes later, and I swear that was all she wrote.

"Kyyyy!" I wailed, looking for something to hold on to. Although he had me secured against the shower wall, I felt as if my body was experiencing an orgasmic freefall as I came harder than I had in a long fucking time.

There was something about being dominated by my partner that turned me the hell on, and it seemed Kyrie had peeped that shit. Now, a nigga could miss me with the chains and leashes but choke me out, talk dirty to me, or tell me what he wanted me to do to him and the exact way he wanted it done, and I was all there for that shit. Holding me up with one arm, he continued finger fucking me while strumming my clit like a guitar with his thumb until my walls ceased their convulsions. I was a dizzy, wet mess, and I was sure I'd spooked the fuck out of the old folks who lived on both sides of me with all the screaming I'd done, but I didn't care one bit. Once I could feel my legs again, I turned to face him, only to find him licking my essence from his fingers. Yanking my head back by my wet hair, he kissed me sloppily, his big-ass pink lips devouring mine, allowing me to get a taste of myself.

"Get on your knees!" Kyrie demanded, and like a good girl, I quickly complied.

That demo on Pac that he witnessed months back wasn't shit compared to what I was about to do to him in this shower. After kissing and circling the thick tip with my tongue, eliciting curses and moans from him, he began feeding me his dick. I let him tap my tonsils twice before slipping him out again. My oral cavity was super wet, but I spit on him anyway, just for the fuck of it and also because I was nasty like that.

"Fuck, Diem," he groaned, hooded eyes locking with mine.

While I did my thing, I ran my hands up and down his body, which was a fucking dream. He had strong arms, rock-hard abs, and powerful-ass legs. Kyrie was sexy as hell with muscles every-fucking-where, but he wasn't too built, if that made sense. Even sexier was the look in his eyes as I blew him down. Shit had my pussy wetter than the water pouring down on his back.

Getting back to the task at hand, I sucked on the tip a little before taking him back inside, only this time I relaxed my throat all the fucking way. Took a lot of practice to learn how to do that shit, but I had it down pat. When my lips finally reached the base of him, I sucked in my jaws as tightly as I could, then began moving my head up and down while making swallowing motions with my throat. He had to grab on to the rail to keep from collapsing to his knees.

"Gotdamn, baby. Ho . . . hold uppp," he begged hoarsely.

Nigga went to pull me off of him by my hair, but I wasn't having it. His dick was choking the fuck out of me every time I came down on him, and I was loving every minute of it, even with tears running down my cheeks. I began massaging his balls, and within minutes they grew taut and his dick stiffened.

"Diem, baby, I'm gonna cum. Shit! Open up for me," he ordered, and I did.

Like a fat kid waiting for the biggest slice of chocolate cake, I opened my mouth and awaited my treat. There was just something about watching a man release his seeds that did it for me. Seeing him cum made me cum again, with no fucking penetration! My pussy clenched and squirted, while my eyes grew wide in wonderment as he stroked the never-ending flow of thick, white sweetness onto my extended tongue.

"What the hell are you doing, girl?" he damn near squealed when I removed his hand and took over stroking and sucking the tip until I was sure I'd drained him of every single drop. Using more strength this time, Kyrie pushed me back by my shoulders to get me to release him. "What the fuck am I gonna do with you?" He leaned against the wall, panting like he'd just run up ten flights of stairs.

"I have a long list of things for you to choose from." I winked sexily, watching his eyes light up, before standing to my feet.

I was sure to have some bruising from being on my knees on that hard-ass tile, but it was worth it. Kyrie was still staring a hole through me, probably wondering what he was getting himself into. Grabbing my loofah, I applied some body wash so that I could wash up, but Kyrie reached out and took it from me to take over the task. I, in turn, did the same for him, washing his beautifully sculpted body from head to toe. Once we were both clean, Kyrie picked me up, and I quickly wrapped my legs around his waist. Exiting the foggy shower, we engaged in a heated lip-lock, bypassing the towels, opting to fall into my sheets slippery wet. After kissing and sucking every inch of my damp body, Kyrie proceeded to deliver the most thorough, satisfying, life-altering dick down I'd received to date. I knew it was going to be good, but I wasn't expecting it to be fucking phenomenal.

Two rounds later, I was worn the fuck out and ready to say forget the trip and call it a night, but Kyrie wouldn't hear of it. He secured my board and packed my overnight bag then carried it and me to the truck.

As I nodded off in the passenger seat of my Range, I overheard him making calls to my father and Philly to let them know I would be with him for a few days, and then we hit the road. I had no idea what would become of me and the man who was quickly bogarting his way into my life, but I planned to enjoy the ride for however long it lasted.

Chapter 10

Philly

"Stop all of that fidgeting, Philly," Natalie fussed as I pulled at the collar of my fitted tuxedo jacket. "You look beautiful. I don't know why you're tripping."

"I'm tripping because I'm uncomfortable as fuck," I groaned. "Why would anyone want to have this much of their cleavage showing?"

"Because it's sexy. Especially when you possess the kind of curves that you got. I don't know why you choose to hide all of this"—she popped my breasts and ass—"under all of those baggy clothes and coveralls. Bitches is paying big money to have a body that looks like yours. Flying to Miami and overseas just to get someone to give them what God blessed you with naturally. You better embrace that body."

I turned to the side in the floor-length mirror and scrunched my nose up at the way my ass was poking out in the cropped tuxedo slacks I had on. This outfit was totally not my first choice, but after a little persuasion from Natalie, along with Gideon's grandmother's uncertainty concerning my actual gender continuously playing in my mind, I decided to step outside of my comfort zone tonight and take a step into the world of high fashion.

"What's the name of this getup again?" I asked Natalie, speaking in reference to the body-hugging suit I had on. Her small hands pressed down on the lapels of my jacket to make sure the tape she had just placed on top of my breasts would keep the heavy fabric in place.

"It's called a lady tuxedo. Everyone from Gwyneth Paltrow to Kim Kardashian has at least one in their closet."

"Aren't you supposed to wear a button-up shirt or something underneath the jacket?" I tugged at the lapel, trying to cover up more of my exposed breasts.

Natalie playfully rolled her eyes. "No. That's why it's called a lady tuxedo. All you need is your bare skin and some nice, perky boobs to pull it off. Something a man can't do." She walked up behind me and turned me back toward the mirror. A big smile was on her face. Her fingers picked at imaginary lint on my shoulders. "I know I said this a few minutes ago, but you really do look beautiful, friend."

I gazed at my thick frame from top to bottom. Although I was still a little uncomfortable, I had to admit that I did look good. *Bet that old bitch wouldn't have a problem figuring out if I was a man or woman now,* I thought as I placed my feet back into the black pumps I took off as soon as we stepped into the carpeted powder room.

"Thanks for helping me get ready tonight, Nats. I really appreciate it."

She nodded her head.

"I appreciate the compliment as well," I thanked her with a genuine smile.

"You already know."

Outside of my sisters, Natalie was my closest friend and the only link left to my past. She stayed in the home across the street from my grandmother's place, and my father made sure I was able to stay in contact with her even after moving in with him and his family. Our bond sometimes amazed me because she and I were complete opposites, but nonetheless, Natalie was my best friend, and I loved her just as much as I loved my sisters.

My eyes traveled over to Nats, who was applying lipstick to her lips and fluffing up her hair. My girl looked good as hell in the evening gown she wore, but shit like this wasn't new to her. Despite working in a greasy and smelly shop with me day in and day out, Natalie was bougie as hell. She had a degree in marketing and could have the job of her dreams, but for some reason, she chose to work with me. Her man came from money, so she attended events like this on the regular. I, on the other hand, was already over the girly outfit, heels, and thirsty-ass men gawking at me. Shit wasn't my style at all, but I knew that tonight I'd have to look and play the part because if I didn't, I would never hear the end of it from Diem or my father. Next year I planned to spearhead the entire event. It would definitely be held outside. Something casual and fun that the children could attend as well. In an environment like that, I could be comfortable and be myself.

"Have you or DiDi talked to Drea yet?" Natalie asked as we walked out of the bathroom and into the hallway of the luxurious Red Rock casino and hotel. Guests were lined up and down the dimly lit area in their fancy black-tie wear. They had drinks in their hands, and laughter was in the air as they talked among themselves. The sound of the casino slot machines played their familiar tune in the distance. I greeted a few of my father's associates with a handshake and a smile before turning my attention back to Nats, nodding my head.

"Only in a few rushed phone calls, but that was it. Haven't heard from her at all today."

"Well, at least you've heard from her. She probably just needed some rest. Especially with all the shit she does during and after business hours."

Natalie bumped my shoulder with hers. "Hey, stop worrying. I bet you a hundred she shows up tonight. She wouldn't miss your father's event for anything," she assured me.

I was praying and hoping that she wouldn't either. I didn't know what was really going on with Drea over these last few weeks, but something was definitely off. When she never made it out to help me, Pops, and Kyrie look through the debris from Diem's warehouse burning down, I knew that there was a problem then. We were all worried about her whereabouts on top of stressing behind Diem's situation, until finally, she made contact the next day to let us know that she was safe. Although our minds became somewhat at ease, we were still a little concerned about her absence. I intended to keep a watchful eye on the entrance though, just to make sure I was able to see her face the minute she walked in.

"You better have my money, too. You still owe me from that last bet, bitch," I joked as we made our way farther down the hall.

The fundraiser festivities were well underway by the time we made it back to the main ballroom. Servers dressed in their black-and-white uniforms walked around with topped-off champagne flutes on trays, serving guests as they passed by. Appetizer stations lined along the back of the room had a plethora of hors d'oeuvres to choose from, appeasing the hungry guests who couldn't wait until it was time for the sit-down dinner. I looked around at the black, gold, and champagne color scheme and smiled. Diem did her thing with this whole event and the decor in this room. Even with all of the added stress on her back, she really turned this place out. The whole concept and feel matched my father's style and personality to a T, and I knew he was enjoying every minute of it.

Shit, to be honest, I was low-key enjoying the night as well. Standing next to the bar, my whole body relaxed, and that uncomfortable feeling I had earlier was a thing of the past as I sipped on my drink. Natalie stepped away to hit the dance floor with her date, so I was left alone to fake smile and entertain dull conversations with friends and colleagues of my father's. Anyone important or well-known in Las Vegas was in attendance tonight, so I knew donations for the group home would be through the roof.

"Damn, bitch, you fine as hell," a deep voice called out from behind, prompting me to whip my head in that direction, ready to turn the fuck up on whoever was bold enough to disrespect me.

"Nigga, you must be out of your fucking mi—"

I stopped and grilled the hell out of my sister, who was now cracking up laughing along with Kyrie's handsome ass.

"Diem, you're childish as fuck, man. I was ready to kick some ass," I chuckled.

"Baby girl, you couldn't kick my ass on your best day," she teased, twirling her finger around in my face for a few seconds before I smacked it away.

"Kyrie, you may want to have this one checked out. Didn't want to be the one to break the news to you, but Diem used to be our brother Dion before the transition. That voice isn't deep like that for no reason," I lied, causing his eyes to buck and travel straight to Diem's neck, looking for some type of confirmation.

"That shit ain't funny, Philly!" she fussed while trying to swat at me, but I'd already moved out of her way. She was reckless with those hands, so I already knew what was coming. "And if you don't stop checking out my damn neck, I'm gonna add you to my hit list. You know damn well I'm all woman." She smirked in Kyrie's direction.

I could only imagine what she meant by that, but my interest was piqued as I watched him twirl Diem around one good time and pull her frame into his chest, arm snaking around her waist and possessively lying across her stomach. They'd only known each other for a hot minute, and she hadn't told me about them hooking up yet, so I wondered what made him such an expert on what she had between her thighs. I bet they asses had got it poppin' on that quick trip to Venice, and I was gon' fuck her up for not giving me the rundown as soon as they made it back home.

"No word from Drea?" I questioned, and my sister shook her head with a worried look on her face. Kyrie's grip tightened around her midsection, and I could tell by the look that she gave him that she appreciated the comforting. "Don't trip, Di. I know she's fine. I'ma strangle her little ass when I do finally see her though. Got everybody going crazy wondering what the fuck is going on."

"So, you are always this violent? I thought it was just toward me," a familiar voice interrupted before Diem could respond.

A chill ran up my spine when my eyes connected to the last person I expected to see here tonight. I watched as he walked up into the middle of our small circle and dapped Kyrie up, wearing a big-ass smile that for some reason irritated my damn soul. It was clear that they were familiar with one another by their embrace and small conversation, but what I needed to know was what the hell he was doing here? This was my turf, some shit put together by my people, so I couldn't understand how his name made it onto the guestlist on such short notice. It definitely wasn't there when we reviewed it the other day. That's not something I would have missed.

"Damn, sis, close your mouth," Diem all but yelled, causing everyone around us to break out into laughter at my stunned face.

Embarrassed, I pulled my bottom lip into my mouth and bit down hard as I could. I didn't care about my lipstick being smeared off or the attitude I knew Natalie would have once she saw the way I messed up her hard work. More laughter erupted from their lips when I stumbled on the stool behind me that somehow managed to appear out of thin air. I could feel my cheeks flushing and my temperature steadily rising. I tried to calm myself down by taking a big gulp of my drink, and I welcomed the burning sensation that traveled down my throat and chest, but that didn't help. The more I looked at that sexy smirk on his handsome face, the more I wanted to smack the shit out of him for showing up and throwing me off my square.

Diem's ass was on the verge of getting it too. This was clearly the wrong time for her to be cracking jokes at my expense. She had no idea that I'd been having dreams about this nigga every single night since the day he came into my shop. Even more so after I left his grandmother's house after dropping off the Cyclone. The shit was so crazy because I had never had a wet dream in my life until I met him. I mean, I was having the type of dreams that had me waking up in a cold sweat, craving the real fucking deal. A bitch like me wasn't even overly sexual like that, but this nigga was surely bringing it up out of me.

I could feel my nipples pressing against the silk lining of the tuxedo jacket. The dampness in my panties was cool against my thighs. My body was reacting the same way it did when I was having those dreams, and I'd be damned if I let him witness any of that. I needed to get away, find one of the thirsty-ass niggas I curved earlier to distract me and take my mind off of him.

Against my better judgment, I turned my gaze back to the man who had me, Ophelia Hart, feeling like the lovestruck teenage girl in your classic romance movie. The smug look on his face told me that he had an idea of what was on my mind, which made me roll my eyes to the ceiling. Just that quick my guard was right back up, and that giddy bitch who was just here was no more.

"How are you doing this evening, Philly?" His bottom lip disappeared into his mouth as he took in my body from head to toe. He stuck his hand out for me to shake, but I ignored it. A light chuckle and a swipe at his nose followed next. "Although you ignoring my hand was rude as hell, I'm still going to compliment you and tell you how absolutely breathtaking you look tonight."

"What the fuck are you doing here, Gideon?" I huffed out a little harsher than I intended to. I didn't want him to get the slightest inkling of my attraction to him or the pride exploding in my chest from his compliment.

"Why so hostile, ma?" he asked with his hands up, that same annoying smile plastered on his face. "Is it going to be this way every time we meet?"

"Whoa, you two know each other?" Kyrie looked back and forth between us.

"Nah, we don't know each other. Well, at least not in the way you think. He's just some stalking-ass, rich nigga who can't seem to get the hint that a bitch ain't trying to be bothered," I sassed, flipping my curly hair to the back. Natalie talked me into adding a few tracks to my head, and I was starting to regret it. Where this extra shit was coming from, I had no idea. I had never flipped my hair a day in my damn life, but in front of this man I was suddenly switching it up, and that angered me. I'd learned in therapy that anger was just my defense mechanism, but it didn't stop me from reacting. I didn't like the way he made me feel, and the smug-ass look he was still sporting riled me up even more.

Gideon raised his chin in my direction. "This the girl I was telling you about."

Kyrie's eyes widened with a surprised look on his face. "Wait. This is who you were talking about? . . ." He trailed off, and Gideon nodded his head. "Damn. It's a small fucking world."

"Small fucking world indeed." His attention returned to me. "We need to stop running into each other like this, Philly. Sooner or later, you're going to stop this tough act and let me get to know you."

I shook my head and took another gulp of my drink. Him getting to know me could never happen. As much as I wouldn't mind the experience—because let's keep it real, Gideon was fine as hell, and from the little research I did on him via the Internet, he had his shit together and would probably make any woman happy—as far as he and I went, it could never work. We were from two very different worlds. My lifestyle and his snooty upbringing would constantly clash, and I didn't have time for that.

I'd told him this countless times, too. Since the day I delivered the motorcycle to his grandparents' house, he'd been reaching out to me in any way that he could: DMs, e-mails, Facebook, you name it. I had to block him from calling and texting my phone as well. When I asked him how he got my number, he wouldn't tell me. Just said that he'd keep coming for me until I gave him a chance to make up for our first meeting and that little encounter with his grandmother.

"So what did you do to get up in here?" I continued, irritation still present in my tone.

"Chill, Philly," Diem tried stepping in, but of course I kept going.

"Did you use your little money and connections to get tickets? You went through all that to get next to me? Desperation does not look good on you, sir," I insulted him right as a woman I could only describe as a Nubian goddess glided up and grabbed his hand.

The bitch was bad. I'm not even gon' lie. The way that she looked in the little black dress she had on started to make me feel uncomfortable again in my outfit. She was beautiful, tall with a milk chocolate skin tone and a model's features. She exuded absolute confidence, so much so that she had damn near every female in this room second-guessing their looks and their outfit choices for the night.

"I've been looking everywhere for you." She smiled, bumping her slender hip against him playfully.

"Told you I wasn't going far," he said before leaning down to plant a sweet kiss on her cheek.

I honestly felt like crawling into a hole and hiding. I didn't want this nigga for shit, so I didn't understand why I was starting to get so pissed that he was here with this knock-off Naomi Campbell.

She wrapped her arms around his neck and pulled his ear to her mouth, whispering something to him. I watched in pure disgust as the ends of his lips curled into a mischievous smile. The small twinkle in his eyes became brighter when his gaze bounced from over her shoulder to my exposed cleavage and then my face. She giggled and returned a kiss to his cheek. Her hands slowly trailed down his chest to the top of his belt before she hooked her finger in one of the loops and pulled him into her.

He moved out of her embrace and stepped in front of me. The manly scent of whatever cologne he had on clouded my head and senses. "I got you on that, lovely, but first, to answer your question, I was invited by my good friend and brother, Kyrie. I did, however, use my money and those connections you were just talking about to score an extra ticket for my beautiful date," he taunted, ending our conversation. "Ky, I'll catch up with you in a minute," he addressed his friend with eyes still on me. Extending his hand to the woman hanging on his arm from behind, he asked, "Shall we?"

She gladly obliged him, and I was left there looking like a complete fool in front of my sister. I knew by the huge grin on her lips when she turned to face me that I would never hear the end of this shit.

"Mmmph. So that was interesting, Philly. Care to share with the class where you know him from?" Diem pulled from Kyrie's embrace and rested her elbow on top of the bar, shifting the rest of her weight with it. The diamond clutch purse in her hand sparkled under the light. I wanted to smack the goofy look off of her face, but I wanted to change the direction of this conversation and opted to compliment her dress instead. Her fancy ass loved compliments.

"You look good tonight. I really like your dress. The color suits you."

She smoothed her hand down the eggplant knee-length, body-hugging garb with the sweetheart neckline. "Thank you, but don't try to change the subject. Where do you know him from?" Her head nodded in the direction of Gideon on the dance floor, slowly grinding with his date. "He's very good-looking and a little upper crust. So not your type."

"Like you know my type." I rolled my eyes. Curiosity got the best of me as I looked out toward the dance floor. "And how do you figure he's upper crust?"

Diem waved me off. "How can you not? His whole aura screams, 'I come from money.' Plus, I Googled his name once Kyrie told me who he was. Didn't take me long to pull up some very interesting information on Mr. Gideon Wells."

"Gideon Wells?" Natalie repeated, walking up behind me. A light sheen of sweat covered her face from the many songs she just danced to. "Why y'all talking about Philly's boo?"

"So you do like him? I knew it! The way he had your mouth hanging open and the look on your face when his date walked up, I knew it was something." Diem laughed. "How long has this been going on?"

"Nothing is going on."

Natalie nudged me in my back with her hip. "Stop lying, Philly. You haven't stopped talking about him since he first walked into the shop that day you clocked his homeboy in the nose. And don't make me tell them how you are always online, looking at his pictures when you should be ordering supplies and parts for the shop."

"Oh shit! I remember her telling me about their first altercation," Diem damn near screamed in a fit of laughter. "But the cyber stalking is news to me." She looked at Kyrie. "Since you two have been low-key discussing my sister, what has he been saying about her?"

"Nothing really." He shrugged.

"Stop lying, Ky." Diem cut her eyes at him and smirked. "Your boy ain't said nothing about Philly at all?"

He shook his head. His body language told me he was a little uncomfortable with being put on the spot. "Nah, G ain't really said that much. He never went into detail about them meeting or anything like that. Just said he thinks he met the woman he was going to marry." He shrugged like it was no big deal.

I could feel my cheeks heating up at that information. The woman he was going to marry? My eyes traveled over to the dance floor where Gideon and his date were still dancing with each other, her sexual attraction more noticeable than his. When I turned back to Natalie, Diem, and Kyrie, all of their eyes were on me.

"I think you should go cut in," Natalie suggested, her head gesturing toward the dance floor. "Go get your man before she thinks she really has a chance."

"I agree with Nats," Diem added, a slow, teasing smile forming on her face. "Unless you're too chickenshit."

"Chickenshit? A hundred dollars says my girl will go over there and shut down whatever baby Naomi Campbell thinks she's going to have with Gideon."

"I got two hundred that says she won't." Diem took the rest of the drink I didn't finish off of the bar and chugged it down in one gulp. She wiggled out of Kyrie's hold and walked up to me. Her arm slinked loosely around my neck. "Although I'm proud of my sister for keeping up with her court-ordered anger management class, she still has some issues she needs to work out when it comes to her temper. If ol' girl says one thing out of the way, this party will get shut down, and I know Philly doesn't want to disappoint our pops like that. Ain't that right, li'l sis?" Her long lashes fanned against her perfectly made-up face. Her bottom lip poked out in a fake pout.

I playfully rolled my eyes with a laugh and shrugged out of her embrace. "Fuck you, Diem. You're right, but you know damn well I'm not chickenshit."

"Then go over there," Nats urged.

I shook my head. "Nah, I'm good. She got that. Like I told you, he and I would never work."

Natalie's eyes softened. Her facial expression changed to one of concern. "You still tripping on that stupid shit his grandma was saying, huh?"

"What stupid shit?" Diem asked, all playfulness abandoned.

One thing Diem didn't play around with was people fucking with her sisters, so while Natalie rehashed the story to her, I made my way over to my assigned table and sat down. I was already over all this stupid-ass girly drama. This was one of the reasons why I preferred to keep company with the bikes I worked on rather than with a man. All of these up-and-down emotions were draining, and he and I weren't even an item. I could only imagine how much more my feelings would be out of whack if we ever actually started dating or fucking for that matter.

The woman he was going to marry? I shook my head, still mulling over Kyrie's words. Maybe he misunderstood what Gideon was trying to say. How could he know that I was the woman he would someday marry when we'd never even shared a kiss? See? Draining.

I pulled my phone out of my pocket and started looking on different sites to try to find a motor for this new project I just started working on. Anything to keep my eyes off the dance floor and my mind off of Gideon. Of course, anything to do with my job was a pleasant and welcomed distraction for me.

Twenty minutes into my searching and failing miserably at the not thinking of my future husband, I felt a presence behind me. "Mind if I join you?"

Recognizing the voice, I waved my free hand over the seat next to me, never taking my eyes off of my phone screen.

His masculine scent met me before his face did. "You look beautiful tonight, Philly. Never seen you dressed up like this before."

I finally looked up and into the eyes of Brix. His boyish features looked real good in the three-piece suit he had on. The low-cut fade and connecting goatee were trimmed and lined to perfection. He lowered his head and chuckled at my approving nod. When he lifted it back up, his thick lips were wet from his tongue swiping over them. I returned his smile and raised my hand for a pound. Our fists connected.

"Thank you, B. I'm uncomfortable as fuck though," I admitted, and he laughed as I pulled at the lapels of my jacket, trying to cover my breasts again. "But I'm cool with it for this one time." I placed my phone on the table and turned my full attention to him. "How long have you been here? I wasn't expecting to see you at all."

"Why not? You know me and your pops used to do some business together." I nodded my head. "Anytime Julian Hart personally calls you and asks you to attend an event near and dear to his heart, you do." Brix shrugged. His eyes scanned the full room. "Speaking of your pops, where is he? I wanted to say hello before I left."

I had wondered the same thing as well. Earlier I saw him and Sole standing by the entrance in what looked like a heated conversation, but I didn't think anything of it when he stormed out and she followed closely behind him. Arguing was low-key normal for them. That bitch always tried to find a way to make something about her, and if it wasn't, she would throw some kind a fit that would have my dad cursing her the hell out. I told Diem to sit me at a completely different table from her mother if she wanted this event to go off without a hitch.

I tried to stay clear of Sole as much as I could. Even though she somewhat raised me, I still didn't trust that bitch for shit. She couldn't get over the fact that my father's infidelities produced me, and honestly speaking, I didn't think she ever would. My mother had been gone for some years now, and Sole still made it a point to throw it in my face. I respected her because she was my father's wife and my sisters' mother, but outside of that, she didn't mean shit to me. I was hoping one day my father would see her for the treacherous bitch she was and find someone else who made him smile like my mother did. He deserved so much more than what his so-called wife was doing for him.

Brix and I chatted for a few minutes, catching up on the things going on in our lives since the last time we talked. I hadn't seen him since that night Sissy reported to Diem that I was doing the walk of shame out of his house. Between the shop, the club, anger management, and my therapy sessions, I had little to no time to kick it like we used to do, so this conversation was very welcomed. I'd missed him.

"Aye, why aren't you out there on the floor dancing and enticing some of these men with big pockets?" He bobbed his head to the song playing. His knee lightly tapped my thigh.

"Because you know that's not my style. Couldn't care less about a nigga and his money," I shrugged.

As if on cue, my eyes drifted to the dance floor and instantly connected with Gideon's. I could tell by the look on his face that he was wondering who Brix was and why he was so close to me. I knew he wasn't trying to trip over that. Did I look at his date the same way?

"Who's that nigga?" Brix asked, breaking me from my thoughts. He raised his chin in Gideon's direction. "You know him or something?"

I picked up my phone and started scrolling again, my peripheral still fixed on Gideon. "Something like that."

"It gotta be more than something like that. He staring like he got a problem with me talking to you."

"I don't see why. He has a whole bitch out there practically grinding on his dick," I mumbled that last part, but Brix heard me.

"Oh, shit." He raised his fist to his mouth. "You do know him. Got you all in your feelings and shit. Never thought I'd live to see the day."

"I'm not in my feelings."

"Yes, you are."

"And how do you figure?"

"Well, for one, you haven't stopped looking their way since I sat down here." I opened my mouth to object, but he cut me off. "And before you try to fix your face to lie, I've been watching you this whole time. To someone far away, it may look like you're into your phone, but up close, I can see you looking at him from the corner of your eyes." He stood up from his seat, hand stretched out to me. "C'mon."

"C'mon? Where we going?"

"Out to the dance floor so you can get you a few dances in with this nigga before they start serving dinner. I'll run interference with ol' girl while you handle your business."

"What makes you think he's gonna want to dance with me?" I asked nervously.

"Trust me, I know. Nigga look like he's ready to come snatch you up right now."

"But I—" Before I could finish my sentence, Brix grabbed my hand, pulled me up from my seat, and dragged me out to the dance floor, stopping right next to Gideon and li'l Naomi. "Rake it Up" by Yo Gotti was playing loudly in my ear as we moved our bodies to the beat. When the DJ switched the song over to "Have You Seen Her," Gideon abandoned his spot and stepped to Brix's side, his date completely lost as to what was happening.

"Do you mind?" he asked Brix, who bowed his head and backed away with a smile. Immediately taking the vacant spot in front of li'l Naomi, Brix wasted no time taking hold of his new dance partner and spinning her around. She tried to object to the switch, but Gideon had already turned his back to her, motioning for me to come to him. By their own accord, my feet floated into his personal space, and my frame nestled into his embrace. Once my mind caught up with the way my body was betraying me, I tried to pull back, but Gideon tightened his hold around my waist and pulled me closer into his fold.

"You know this is where you belong, right?"

I sucked my teeth. "What about your date?"

"She's just a friend."

I stood on my tiptoes and looked over his shoulder. Although she was now dancing with Brix, her eyes were stapled to us.

"Does she know that?" My eyes went back to him. "I'm telling you now, if she comes over here tripping, she might not make it out of here looking the same."

Gideon smiled, and my stomach started doing flips. "So you beating females up for me now? That money I spent on her ticket and the connection I had to use would be a waste if she doesn't get to enjoy at least half of the night," he laughed.

As we slowly swayed to the beat only we could hear, I tried to make sense of what was going on right now. I didn't want Gideon, didn't want anything to do with him. Hell, I didn't even want to be this close to him. However, something was happening in this moment. All thoughts of us not working out or being compatible seemed to be slipping from my mind, and the stinging words from his grandmother seemed to hurt a lot less. I also thought about the advice I'd given Diem regarding Kyrie. Maybe I needed to practice what I preached and take this chance. One thing I knew for sure was that my feelings were all out of whack right now. I tried to think of anything to get my head out of this fog, but nothing was helping.

Gideon continued to look down at me, his eyes openly expressing what mine refused to. I turned my face to try to hide from his searing gaze, but Gideon grabbed my chin between his index finger and thumb, turning my attention back to him.

"Give me a chance, Philly. I want to know anything and everything there's to know about you."

"I . . . I can't."

"You can," he asserted.

"But we don't—"

"We don't what?" he interjected.

"Mix."

When he reared his head back and squinted in confusion, I knew I had lost him, so I tried to explain. "What I mean is you and I are from two different worlds. A point made very apparent when I dropped the motorcycle off that day at your grandparents' house. The type of girl you need is basically the one you brought here tonight. The type who fits in at parties like this. The type who likes to wear dainty dresses and body-hugging outfits, not the kind who would prefer coveralls and a wife beater to this bullshit." I stepped back, and his eyes lustfully roamed over my body. "If I weren't here right now, I'd be at my shop working on the '67 Shelby GT500 restoration I just started. I love the smell of motor oil and the sound of my tools clicking and clacking against the rusted metal of the old engine." I shook my head. "We just wouldn't work. We could never work."

A thunderous round of applause broke us from the stare-down we were in. When I looked around, I noticed that everyone's attention was turned to the stage, as the master of ceremonies for the night stood in front of the podium, ready to make his announcement that dinner was going to be served. My eyes looked over to the left, and I spotted Diem and Kyrie still hanging around at the bar. My sister giggled at whatever Kyrie whispered into her ear as he held her in his arms and kissed her bare shoulder. When I looked to the right, Natalie excitedly waved one hand, trying to get my attention while holding the thumbs-up with the other. Her boyfriend, Bryce, stood behind her with his attention toward the front of the room. When she mouthed the words, "You owe me a hundred dollars," I rolled my eyes and laughed. Gideon and I hadn't hooked up yet, so I didn't owe her betting ass shit.

Everyone had just been advised to head to their seats, and I turned to head to mine when Gideon lightly grabbed my arm and stopped me in my tracks. Gideon's date must've been more receptive to Brix than I thought, because when I looked around, I didn't see them anywhere in sight. I pulled from his hold but remained facing him, waiting for him to say whatever he was about to say.

He walked closer to me. The back of his hand brushed against my cheek. "Why do you assume we won't be a good match?"

I licked my lips. My chest heaved a little more than I liked. His closeness was affecting me a little more than I cared to admit. "Because you and I are like night and day. Plus, your grandmother—"

"Philly, you're rejecting me based off of your own silly assumptions, and that's not right. My grandmother's opinion does not determine who I choose to pursue. How she feels about someone or something won't stop me from following my heart or mind. I want to get to know you and spend as much time with you as I can. But you would have to stop letting that beautiful mind of yours think the way it does. Give me just one chance. That's all I'm asking."

My mind kept screaming for me to say no, but those crazy-ass feelings I experienced whenever it came to him kept yelling for me to give him a chance.

I was just about to give him my answer, when a loud boom echoed throughout the ballroom, followed by the sound of gunshots going off in every direction. Before I could try to see who was firing the shots, my body was thrown to the floor and covered by an even larger body. The screams of all the guests rang loudly in the air, while a number of lifeless bodies dropping to the ground vibrated the dance floor beneath me. I tried to move from my protective barrier but couldn't. I needed to make sure Diem and Natalie were okay. *What about*

Pops? My mind was going crazy with fear, not for myself but for them.

By the time the bullets stopped flying, the loud voices of the hotel's security could be heard on their walkie-talkies as they rushed into the room, trying to get a handle on the situation. Whimpers from the wounded guests were drowned out by the cries of other guests who must've lost a loved one. I managed to turn my head to the side and get a glimpse of the blood stains splattered everywhere. The floor, the walls, the tablecloths, and people's bodies and faces were covered with the dark crimson hue.

The weight that covered me slowly became lighter, and I was able to move my body and turn around. I didn't know who I was expecting to see when I came face-to-face with my protector, but I was more than surprised when Gideon's worried gaze connected to mine. He searched my face and my body to make sure I was okay before rising to his full height and helping me off of the ground. My body shook as I searched the chaotic ballroom, trying to see any sign of my family and friend.

"Diem!" I screamed out. "Natalie!" My eyes frantically searched back and forth. My nerves got the best of me. "Pops. Diem," I mumbled as I tripped over a body.

Thankfully, Gideon caught me before I could fall. He placed his hand on my shoulders to try to calm me down. "They might not be able to hear you with all of this noise. Do you remember the last place you saw any of them?"

I slowly nodded my head. My eyes still scanned everywhere. "My . . . my dad, I last saw him arguing with my stepmom and heading outside." I pointed.

"So he may not have been in here when the shooting started. What about your sister?"

"She was by the . . . the bar with Kyrie." Both of our heads turned in that direction, and without a second thought, we ran that way, stepping over more bodies and fumbling over furniture. "Diem!" I called out, my voice strained.

"Ky, bro! Can you hear me? Are you okay?"

"We're right here!" Diem hollered, hand waving from behind the bar. When she finally stood up with help from Kyrie, her hair was all over her head with tiny shards of glass in it. Her beautiful dress was ripped at the side, exposing her hip and some of her thigh. She and Kyrie must've hopped behind the bar as soon as the gunfire started. "We're all right," she assured me as Ky and Gideon slapped hands and talked among themselves. "Have you seen Pops and my mom?"

I shook my head. "I don't think they were in here. They left arguing earlier, and I haven't seen them since then."

"Well, we need to go look. What if they were hit before these muthafuckas came blasting their guns in here? Oh my God!" Diem screamed at the top of her lungs. "What the fuck is going on? Who is gunning for us this hard? First, the shooting at Drea's place, my warehouse burning down, now this," she cried, falling into Kyrie's outstretched arms.

Diem was right. Someone was gunning for us, and they were coming hard as fuck. I made a mental note to call an emergency meeting in Heaven as soon as possible, but first I needed to find Natalie and make sure that Pops was straight.

Leaving them at the bar, I walked over to our assigned table, the last place I remember seeing my best friend before the gunfire erupted. "Natalie," I croaked out.

My emotions started to get the best of me. For some reason, I started to feel a sudden heaviness in my chest, and I didn't like it one bit. The last time I felt this way was the day I found my mom and grandma dead. That scared little nine-year-old girl was here, and I had a feeling that she was about to experience that same heartbreak once again. "Nats." My voice cracked this time as I began to hyperventilate. Something wasn't right, and I felt it in my soul.

A hoarse yet masculine cry pierced my ears and caught my attention. By the sound of it, I assumed that death was the cause. I rounded the large table we were supposed to be sitting at, and my eyes zeroed in on Bryce, who was nestled between two overturned chairs, his body rocking back and forth as his face was turned up to the ceiling, tears streaming down his face.

"No, no, no, no, baby. Wake up. Please. You gotta wake up!" his deep voice cried out. "You can't leave me right now. I need you. Baby, wake up. Please wake up."

On the floor cradled in his arms was my best friend. The lower part of her body was under the table, and the top part of her body was riddled with bullets. Blood covered her face and arms. The evening gown that she looked so beautiful in minutes ago was ruined. I opened my mouth to try to say something, but I couldn't. My heart shattered into a thousand pieces, and I couldn't stop the tears flowing down my face. This couldn't be happening to me. Not again. The last connection I had to my past was now gone, and I couldn't bring her back.

Dropping to my knees, I crawled over to my best friend's lifeless body and pressed my forehead to the side of her face. All of the good and bad times she and I had throughout the years played over and over in my mind.

I was so lost in my grieving I must've blacked out at some point, because when I opened my eyes Natalie's body was no longer there and neither was Bryce. I was being hovered over by a paramedic holding up fingers in my face. She was asking me questions, but I wasn't paying any attention to what she was saying. I was too busy looking around the room for my people. Police officers walked around the nearly empty room, still collecting statements, while EMTs attended to some of the wounded who were still there. When I tried to stand up to see where Natalie was taken, a large arm snaked around my waist and pulled me back down. I didn't even realize I was lying between someone's legs until right then.

"The coroner took her already," Gideon informed me, causing me to burst into a fit of tears. I was hoping this was all a dream, but him saying that confirmed that my friend was indeed gone. "Your sister had some kind of episode and had to be taken to the hospital by ambulance. I think they took her to Sunrise, but Kyrie said he would call to let me know. Your mom is okay, and she told me that your dad is on his way. As soon as you let them check you out, I'll take you to see about Diem," he promised.

I loved that I didn't have to say a word. He told me everything he knew I'd want to know when I came to.

On his way back? I had no idea that my father had even left. I didn't even have the strength to correct Gideon at that moment about Sole not being my mom. I was too drained to go into full detail. My heart overflowed with sorrow about the loss of my dearest friend.

Nestling back into his hold, I welcomed the warmth and sympathy he was giving. "Thank you, Gideon." I sniffed.

His nose traced my earlobe, and that flutter thing started up in my belly again. "What are you thanking me for?"

"Being here when you didn't have to be."

I wondered where his date was and if she and Brix made it out alive. As if he had read my mind, Gideon informed me that neither Brix or li'l Naomi were hurt and that both of them had given brief statements and were allowed to leave. A few moments of silence passed between us before he spoke again. I was lost in my thoughts about Natalie, and he was trying to figure out the right words to say.

"I'm sorry all of this happened tonight. I can't imagine what you must be feeling losing your friend. I was serious when I told you I wanted to get to know you. The good, the bad, and the in-between. All I asked for was a chance, Philly. That opportunity presented itself in the worst way, but I'm here, ready to be what you need me to be in this moment, if you let me."

"But do you now see why I said you and I weren't a good mix? Why I said we could never work? Outside of the shop, all of this is also a part of my life." I gestured around at the shooting aftermath. "Although it hadn't happened in a while, it still can.

A lot of people don't like that my sisters and I are heads of one of the baddest motorcycle clubs in Nevada. And that we are all females makes them come for us even harder. I don't want you, or anyone for that matter, to get caught in the crossfire of some shit you can't even begin to understand. We live, breathe, and will die for Hart's Angels. It's the way that we were raised and the law of the land. And the man who chooses to be with me has to respect and understand that, or else it won't work."

Instead of responding to what I said, Gideon kissed my forehead and pulled me back against his chest. The rhythmic beat of his heart unexpectedly synced with mine. Had I been in the right frame of mind, I may have been willing to look more into that synchronization. However, the rage building up in my body at what happened tonight wasn't going to allow me to dwell on it. Like Diem told me weeks back, it was time to move. We'd sat back in the cut long enough, and that shit was over with now. Whatever trip Drea was on needed to be to cut short. She needed to bring her ass home, because it was time for Hart's Angels to handle some business.

Chapter 11

Julian "Knight" Hart

One Hour Earlier

"Dammit, Sole, I'm going to say this for the last fucking time!" I roared once I had her loud ass sequestered in a conference room down the hall and away from the ballroom. She had fucked up royally, raising her voice to me in front of my employees and friends. The mayor was only a few feet from us when she started cutting up, so as you can imagine, I was boiling mad and ready to strangle her at this point.

We'd been arguing for nearly fifteen minutes, and my patience was running thin. I could have been halfway to my destination by now had it not been for her. "Something has come up, and I need to go."

"And there's no one else who can handle it for you?" she questioned suspiciously.

"What the hell did I just say?" I hissed in annoyance.

"I just don't understand why you have to leave on a night as important as tonight," she pouted, aiming to make me feel guilty, but I wasn't going for it.

"Sole, it's honestly not for you to understand," I told her with finality. My business was not her business. That was the way it had always been and always would be.

"Of course not," she sighed dejectedly. "Everything is such a secret with you. I'm your wife, yet I'm treated like a stranger who can't be trusted. I know nothing about what goes on in your life."

Now, that statement hit me right in the heart. Normally I knew when my wife was playing the sympathy card to get what she wanted, but I could actually detect the sincerity in her voice. Real emotion when it came to me was something I hadn't received from her in years, since way before Ophelia's mom, Cassie, came into the picture. I had my reasons for keeping certain things away from my wife, and more often than not it was for her safety, but she didn't see it that way.

When I asked Sole to be my wife I vowed to love and provide for her. I never wanted her to have to lift a finger or worry about anything. To just focus on our home and children was all I asked of her, but she never quite got the hang of that. Sure, she enjoyed the money, houses, cars, and clothes, but our home and children were never a priority. She was quickly sucked up into my lifestyle, and soon her love for it outweighed her love for me.

I truly believed that was the reason it was so easy for me to fall for Cassie. That woman didn't have a selfish bone in her body, and she showed me unconditional love without ever demanding anything in return. All she wanted was me, and for years I strung her along, giving her hope that someday it would happen. It still angered me that the very day I made the decision to give it all up just to be with her, she was taken away from me. To make matters worse, to this very day the murders of Cassie and her mother were still unsolved. I needed that closure, but I knew Ophelia needed it even more, and I hated not being able to give it to her. I missed Cassie so much some days that my heart literally ached in my chest, and I could only imagine how hard it was for my child to deal with, even after all these years.

"Sometimes I wonder why I even bother sticking around," she let slip before her eyes widened in regret.

"You don't know, huh?" I chuckled and took a step back. She quickly grabbed my sleeve to keep me from walking away. I looked down at her hand on me then back up into her eyes, and the look I gave her caused her to immediately release me. "We've been down this road before, Sole. I gave you the option of leaving years ago, and you made the choice to stay. Trust me when I say that that door is still open, baby," I informed her coolly while adjusting my Tiffany cufflinks.

"Julian, honey, I didn't mean . . . I'm sorry." She shook her head emphatically while gently gripping my forearm.

This time I physically pried her hands off of me. "Of course you are, love. Why don't you go back and enjoy the party? I'll be back before it's time to wrap things up," I said with a kiss to her forehead before turning to exit the room.

I'd said all I needed to say, and she had unintentionally done the same. She was just as sick of pretending as I was. We were both going through the motions, and it was no way to live. I guessed not even the money was enough to keep her happy at this point. I felt like a failure, again.

I was nearly to the elevator when my conscience tugged at me. I hated for her to feel that I didn't care about her feelings, because in reality, I did. Things between us were just complicated. As soon as I spun around to go apologize, I caught sight of her finally exiting the conference room. My brow furrowed in curiosity as I observed her.

My wife seemed to be in the middle of a heated discussion on her phone. When I noticed her looking around, I stepped behind a tall column and watched out of her view. Her call continued for another minute at least before she nodded like the person on the line could see her, and she disconnected. Eyes closed with her head tilted back, she sighed while smoothing a hand down the front of the midnight blue, strapless Michael Costello gown she wore.

I had to admit that she looked lovely tonight, but I was more concerned with her behavior right now. *Who the hell was she on the phone with?* After a few moments, she took another deep breath and began to move. Only instead of returning to the ballroom, she moved in my direction, causing me to have to circle the column to avoid being spotted. I continued watching as she pressed the up button on the elevator, which immediately opened, and she hopped on. I only came out of hiding when the doors were fully closed.

I stood there contemplating while staring at the closed elevator doors for a minute. It could have been nothing, but something about that entire scene didn't sit well with me. That coupled with the call I received from Spencer, my wife's driver, informing me of the secret meeting she had at the Palms last week only boosted my suspicions. Hopefully I was overthinking things, but I couldn't help but feel that my wife of nearly thirty years was on some bullshit.

Right now I had more important things to tend to, so I would have to deal with Mrs. Julian Hart at a later time. One daughter was missing in action, and the other two had me on their shit lists. The fact that I had to leave so abruptly probably intensified their disdain. I had so much making up to do, but that too would have to wait.

Entering the newly built establishment, I put my game face on. Everything inside of me hoped I was jumping to conclusions, but the feeling that this nigga was behind the recent attacks on my family were even stronger. I felt like shit because I'd told my girls that they had nothing to worry about, and at the time I truly believed that. Now, I wasn't so sure.

It was after hours, so no one sat at the reception desk. Using the badge I'd illegally obtained, I was able to gain access to the door beyond the desk labeled EMPLOYEES ONLY. Although I'd never been here, the information I received this morning gave me the exact location of his office. According to the men I had sitting on the building all day, he hadn't left since coming in this afternoon. At the end of the long hallway, I came to a stop right outside the door. An entire minute passed without me hearing a word from the other side, so I turned the knob and entered without knocking.

"Knight, my brother. Long time no see," he stated while his eyes remained cast down on the paperwork on his desk.

"Lukas." I couldn't help but feel like he knew I was coming. Like he was prepared for this visit. I was hoping to catch him off guard, but he was too calm, and that was odd to me. The blood between us had been bad for a long damn time, and he was sitting here unfazed like I couldn't have him touched if I wanted to.

"What brings you by this evening?" he asked, finally lifting his head to properly acknowledge me.

Lukas Coleman and I went back a long way. He was someone I once considered a good friend, but things had changed drastically in recent years. The underlying hatred in his gaze was an indication of how bad things had become. This was the first time in a long while that we were in the same room and didn't have to be held back from jumping on one another. Depending on what came from this conversation, that might not be the case when it was all said and done. I had people in place to handle nuisances like him for me, but when it came to my family, I would get my hands dirty to get my point across, the point being that they were not to be fucked with. Period.

"Recent events led me here tonight."

"Recent events, huh?" He nodded. "Well, Knight, since you brought it up, let's discuss how your daughter recently assaulted my Elle. How about we start out with that!" he fumed, tossing his pen to the side.

I laughed, which only angered him further. Nostrils flaring, he stood from his seat and unfastened the middle button on his blazer. "So, my daughter being attacked is funny to you? I had to talk her down from going to the station to file charges on Philly. You should be thanking me, not taking this as some fucking joke!" He pointed a stern finger in my direction.

"It is a fucking joke! Guess she got that police shit from you," I insulted him. "You and I both know Philly could have done Elle way worse than she did, and from what I hear she deserved it. Gathering a clique together in an attempt to oust my daughter from the club? She had to know that shit wasn't going to go over well, and I suggest you advise her not to continue pursuing it," I warned. "There's nothing I can do once my girls get going, so you'd be wise to let her know that."

"A simple disagreement doesn't always have to lead to blows being thrown, Knight! No need guessing where they get that from," Lukas accused.

Yes, indeed! My daughters got that shit from me. We didn't fool with police or waste time doing a lot of talking. The Harts were all about the action, so it was high time for me to move on to the reason for this pop-up visit.

"Simple, huh? Wasn't shit simple about what she suggested, but that's not what I'm here to discuss. I came to talk about my new project out north. When I called you months ago to give you a heads-up on my expansion plan, you were cool with it. Took the money and said you understood it was just business. Now I'm not so sure you were being completely honest with me."

"How do you figure?" he asked, a flash of what looked to me like guilt in his eyes.

"Oh, I don't know. I got somebody literally gunning for my baby girl, and my oldest recently had to stand by and watch as a business she built from the age of nineteen burned to the fucking ground. Then throw in the shit with Elle at the clubhouse, and one can only assume that all these events are related. All I need you to do is tell me that I'm barking up the wrong tree here. Tell me that you and the Dragons didn't have anything to do with any of that so that I can find and deal with the person or persons truly responsible."

Appalled, he said, "Despite the things that have transpired between us, there is no way that I'd bring harm to your girls! I won't lie and say I didn't take a loss with that move you made, but like you said, it's just business. I have no ill feelings about it. If I were in your position, I would have done the same thing. But for you to accuse me of something as low as coming for your children is preposterous, Julian," he stated convincingly.

"I sure hope you're being honest with me, Lukas, because if I find out that you had anything to do with this, I promise you'll regret it. If I even discover that you knew what was going on and didn't give me a heads-up, that's your ass."

"Ease up on the threats!" he challenged. "Like I said, I have no clue who's behind what's going on with your family."

"For your sake, I pray that's the case," I added.

"Knight, man, this doesn't have my name on it, so I'm not worried nor am I afraid," he insisted.

Lukas talked a good game, but he wasn't about the street life. Until I went to college, these Las Vegas streets were all I knew. Don't let the suits and ties fool you. They were still in me. I felt my experience out there made me the successful businessman I was today. I could do my thing in the boardroom or on the block. That was the difference between him and me. Lukas grew up with a silver spoon in his mouth, but after coming with me a few times to visit the old neighborhood while we were on break from UNLV, he was hooked. He had to learn to talk hip because the fellas gave him such a hard time when he first started coming around. He was forever trying to prove he was down, and I was there to get him out of many binds back in the day. He was able to fake being a hoodlum for only so long though. Once he got the label of being a rat, he lost all the artificial respect he'd gained. Despite his reputation, we remained friends until he fucked me over in more ways than one. All bets were off after that, and things hadn't been the same since. We split, and he formed a new crew and established the Dragons.

"If that's all, I have some work to get done before I head home to my wife," Lukas said as he took his seat once again.

"How is Lisa?" I asked, my interest unfeigned. Our beef had nothing to do with our wives and children, so when I asked him how she was, I really wanted to know. Lukas's wife Lisa was a gem and someone I actually liked. Her only flaw was that she'd married a fraud-ass nigga.

"She's well. Pressuring Elle for grandbabies, but other than that she's fine," he answered with an authentic smile.

"Please give her my regards."

He nodded. "Give the same to Sole for me, will you?" he requested.

"Shit, you can do that yourself the next time you meet up with her for lunch." I smirked with my fingers aimed at him in the shape of a gun.

His eyes bucked as I pulled the imaginary trigger. The look on his dumb-ass face was priceless. His mouth opened but just as quickly snapped closed. With that, I was out. I didn't need him to respond. I just needed him to know that I was on his ass and I was going to stay on it until I found the answers to the questions I had. I couldn't make my move until I knew all the facts and every player involved. I still didn't believe he didn't have a hand in the bullshit that was going on, but we would see soon enough.

When I made it back down to the limo, the hired driver rolled down the partition to address me. "Sir, you may want to check your phone. It was going off like crazy the entire time you were inside," he informed me, causing a sinking feeling to form in the pit of my stomach.

When I pulled my cell from the console, I had at least a hundred missed calls from various numbers. Some I recognized and others I did not. Calls from my wife, Diem, and my head of security snatched my attention. "What the fuck is going on now?" I mumbled to myself, deciding to return Sole's call first.

Chapter 12

Drea

"I'm serious, Onyx! I don't think it's a good idea for you to go. I'm sure your sister will understand why you couldn't be there," Simmy tried to reason while his big, fine ass continued to block the door.

"Simmy, I really don't care what you think. I'm sick of everyone telling me what I should and shouldn't do. Between you and Marlon I'm about to go crazy. I got a mind to shoot both you niggas!" I snapped, causing him to jump in my face with the quickness.

The sudden movement must have been too much too soon because he winced and blew out a harsh breath before addressing me. "You ain't gon' shoot shit! If that was the case, you would have done it already." He glowered at me for all of two seconds before he was backing down. "Onyx, please," he said, softening his tone, "these people do not plan to stop until you are dead. How about I just come with you?"

"No! No way. I can handle myself. Besides, you aren't in any position to be running the streets right now. Certainly not with me. All you'd do is slow me down, and I don't have time for that shit. I saved your ass once as a courtesy to myself. I don't know if I'd be willing to be that nice again."

"A'ight." He angrily nodded, stepping away from the door. "I ain't have no problem getting at yo' clueless ass, and I'm sure they won't either, so good luck," he spat.

"You know what! Fuck you, you broke-down, crippled muthafucka. Your fake ass probably got them fools on speed dial so you can give up my location anyway," I lashed out, pissed that he was questioning my skills.

"That's the dumbest shit I've ever heard! If I give you up, I'm giving myself up as well. I am not here to hurt you!" his voice boomed. "And fuck you too with yo' walking-dead ass," he countered, causing my heart to drop. "Fuck that busted-ass wig you got on, too." He pointed, adding insult to injury.

I wanted to say some slick shit in return but couldn't think of anything mean or clever enough to shut him up like he'd done to me. I just pushed past him, elbowing him square in the abdomen on my way out of the door. I aimed right where his wound was hoping to bring his evil ass to his knees. The pained groan I heard him release as I hopped in the car out back let me know that I hit my target.

I hated that I let him hurt my feelings, but he did. I wasn't like my sisters in that way. I was never quick enough with my clapbacks during arguments to shut the other person down. My only solution was to shoot the shit out of you, but I couldn't bring myself do that to Simmy. Regardless of how suspicious I was of him at times, there was no denying that feelings existed on both sides, and I secretly wanted to explore them. That was something I planned to keep to myself for now.

I was so affected by Simmy's hateful words that I mumbled and talked shit to myself the entire way to the church. I swear, I planned and plotted his demise all the way down to where I'd dispose of his corpse. That was just how livid he had me. And I'd clearly been driving like a bat out of hell, because the expected one-hour drive was done in a little over thirty minutes. I honestly needed to get a hold of my emotions, because they would be the very reason I got caught slipping again if I didn't. If that happened, that would mean that Simmy was right, and I couldn't have that. I'd never hear the end of it.

Taking a deep breath, I adjusted my wig, which had a part down the middle, and I placed on my hat and shades. My guns were already tucked and hidden, and my vest was secured under oversized clothing. When I felt I was ready, I stepped out of the basic-ass Maxima that we'd been using for transportation, and I headed up the street toward the church, my neck on swivel and my instincts on high alert. To keep attention off of myself, I took a seat in the back to blend in with the countless mourners. Natalie was loved and well-known in the city, so her tragic death was felt by many.

As expected, I spotted Philly seated next to Nats's parents and boyfriend on the front pew. She had on shades, and her face was hidden by a black veil, but her sorrow was evident in her posture. Her shoulders were slumped as far as they could slump, and her head was hung low. Everything in me wanted to go to her, to comfort her and tell her that everything would be okay and that I wouldn't stop until I handled every single person involved. I still had no idea who was after me or if this was all tied together, but I was determined to find out. For all I knew, our enemies could be right here at this funeral, so I couldn't afford to blow my cover. I just sat back, peeping my surroundings, ready to move if it popped off in here like I heard it had at the fundraiser.

I continued my scan of the room as the pastor opened up the service with a prayer followed by a hymn being sung by one of Natalie's relatives from Mississippi. I was trying to hold it together, but the words of "This Old Soul of Mine" along with her powerful voice pulled moisture from my eyes.

In the morning, when I rise
Shake the dust from my feet, wipe my eyes
And I'll cry
Oh what a day, oh what a day
Oh what a day this will be
I'm going home, I'm going home
One of these ol' days, I'm going home

I was offered a Kleenex from an usher, but I politely declined. I couldn't reach my hand out for it anyway because I was gripping the Glock hidden under the trench I was wearing. The feel of the cold steel reminded me to tuck those feelings back in, and just that fast I shook it off.

I fixed it up with Jesus, fixed it up with
Jesus
Oh long time ago, long time ago

I blinked hard, and when I opened my watery eyes they landed on my parents first, then Diem. Her head was resting on the shoulder of a gentleman I'd never seen before but I assumed was Kyrie. She'd mentioned him the few times we spoke over the phone, and as I watched him pull her closer to him, I couldn't help but smile. I was glad she had someone to help her through this tough time. I was supposed to be there for them, and it pissed me off that I couldn't be. Especially for Philly. While my sister suffered, I was forced to hide out in the open and observe from a distance. Gripping the gun tighter, I wrapped my other arm around my waist, feeling extremely helpless in that moment. Instead of the hunter, I had become the hunted, and that was a bad position for someone like me to be in.

I was able to tune out the rest of the service until it was time to view the body. Being so far in the back, my row was one of the first asked to stand and make our way up to say our final good-bye. Loud cries of grief and sniffling could be heard throughout the church. It was such a sad scene, but that was expected. This wasn't the homegoing service of some ninety-year-old woman who died of natural causes in her sleep. Natalie was young, not even thirty years old. She had so much more life to live, but someone took it upon themselves to dim her light before her time, and it wasn't right.

"I fixed it up with Jesus a long time ago." I hummed along to calm myself.

I was next up to view the body, but I kept my eyes straight ahead. That wasn't the way I wanted to remember her. I only had memories of the bubbly, funny girl who placed hundred-dollar bets on the simplest shit. She was the only chick outside of Diem and me who loved Philly to pieces. I only came up so that I wouldn't look out of place doing anything different.

I bypassed her open casket and waited for my
turn to give condolences to the family. It was the
closest I would get to being there for Philly. She
was right next to Audrey, Natalie's mom, holding
on to her hand for dear life.

"You're in my prayers," I said to each of them,
but I grabbed my sister's hand when I finally stood
before her and recited that same line.

Her head immediately rose, bloodshot eyes locking with mine. Her grip on me tightened instantly.
Releasing Audrey, she stood, and we embraced like
it had been years since we'd last seen one another.
To the bystanders, I probably looked like another
grieving friend, but I knew that my sister had made
me. This disguise didn't fool her one bit. It put
me on edge just a little that it was so easy for her
recognize me, but there was no way I was passing
up the opportunity to touch her and hug her just
once before I went back into hiding.

The line behind me was at a standstill, so I
reluctantly let her go and moved on. Something
in me, however, wouldn't let me walk out of the
church like I was supposed to. I quietly retreated
to the side of the pulpit near the door that led to
the back of the church, my eyes still on Philly.

The usher finally reached their row, and they
were asked to stand. Bryce, Natalie's beau, just
couldn't do it. He'd held it together this entire time,
but when it was time to see her body he just lost it.

He was so overcome with grief that he had to be escorted from the church. Never in my life had I seen anything so heartbreaking, and if that was his reaction, I could only imagine how my sister was going to handle it.

I watched as she shuffled over slowly, her entire being clothed in sadness and despair. Philly drew a quivering bottom lip into her mouth, trying to get a hold of her emotions as she stroked Natalie's cheek. Seeing her like that took me back in time. It was like we were nine years old all over again and she couldn't stop crying about her mom and grandma. I hoped this tragedy didn't put her back in the mindset she'd been in back then. It was terrible witnessing her go through that.

After she placed a soft kiss to her childhood friend's cold cheek, I saw the exact moment that those knees of hers began to buckle, and I was already in motion. A few feet shy of me reaching her, however, the gentleman who had sat next to me during the service was swooping her up in his arms. I had no idea where he had just come from, but I was glad he was there to catch her before she fell. Now I wanted to know who the hell he was and how he knew my sister well enough to be comfortable doing what he did. And why was she so at ease with her arms snaked around his neck, crying softly into his chest? Distracted by their interaction, I failed to notice someone coming up behind me, but when I felt that hand on my shoulder, I relaxed and loosened my hold on the gun.

"Calm down, killer, it's just me. Emergency meeting at Heaven after we come from the cemetery. I know you probably weren't planning to stick around, but you really don't have a choice," Diem said while pointing her manicured finger over my shoulder and into the crowd.

I followed with my eyes until they landed on our father, who stood at the back of the church. Without taking his eyes off of me, he whispered something to my mother, to which she nodded. She made her way to the exit without him. Just that slight lift in his eyebrow told me all I needed to know. He wasn't letting me out of this building until we had a conversation.

Because he was stopped numerous times, it took him a minute to reach me, but when he did, he said nothing. He just brushed past me and walked through the door that led to the pastor's office. Like a disobedient child, I followed him with my head down. *Looks like I'll be postponing going back to the hideaway for a little longer. Simmy will just have to be pissed at me for not returning when I told him I would, but what can I do? I'd rather he be a little worried than to have to face the wrath of Knight Hart,* I thought as I made my way to the back for this thorough tongue-lashing that awaited me.

As I listened to Marlon rant and rave on the phone, I came to the conclusion that today was the day when all of the men in my life decided they would annoy the hell out of me. I'd already gotten into it with Simmy before leaving the house, I was ripped a new one by my father at the church earlier, and now I had to listen to this fool cut up. Marlon wasn't too thrilled with my new living arrangement, nor was he a fan of the man I'd been looking after, but honestly speaking, I was starting to get used to being around Simmy and spending time with him. Marlon, on the other hand, wasn't at all pleased, which he was making perfectly clear right now.

"You're getting too comfortable around that nigga, Drea. Your ass out there cooking dinner, nursing him back to health, and watching movies and shit when things need to be handled here," Marlon complained. "I don't trust that muthafucka, and neither should you."

"I hear what you're saying, Marlon, but what do you expect me to do? We gotta eat, so I fucking cook. We couldn't take him to the hospital. You already know that the laws would've asked tons of questions. And as far as the movies go, you know I hate binge watching shit by myself." I blew out a frustrated breath. "I know you're only worrying because you're my best friend, but you don't have to. I got a handle on our situation, and I think I can handle Simeron if need be."

He scoffed. "Simeron, huh? So y'all on a first-name basis now?" There was a short pause. "I hope you ain't over there fucking that nigga, Drea!" he screeched.

"First off, what I do with my pussy is none of your business. However, the orders coming into the shop should be. Have you been taking care of that?" I didn't like pulling the boss card with Marlon, but sometimes it was necessary. He and I never really discussed my personal life like that, so I didn't get why he was tripping now. I never said anything about him and all of the niggas he was messing with behind Josh's back, so I expected the same from him.

"Drea, I hope you're not being stupid," he continued, ignoring my questions about the shop. "This nigga wanted to kill you two seconds ago. You don't know enough about his background to be giving it up to him already. Sex is not going to stop him from putting a bullet in your head no matter how good it may be to him."

I laughed. "Again, worry less about my pussy and more about my business. Did Josh get the order for that Grammy after-party done? And what about the personal orders that needed to be delivered this week? Did he finish all of those yet?"

"You know he did, and he's already working on next week's orders. I think you should really consider Josh for that manager position you need to fill, too. Especially since you're going to be real busy with our high-end clientele orders when you get back."

"Wait a minute. Now, I'm all for considering Josh as my new manager because he has been working hard and picking up on my slack in my absence, but ain't this a little like the pot calling the kettle black with you pushing him to the top of the list like this?"

"Why you say that?"

"Because you're basically saying it's okay for you to mix business with pleasure but not me."

"My situation is different," he argued.

"How so?"

"Because I don't have to worry about Josh blowing my brains out while he's handling his business. You, on the other hand, do with that nigga you've been shacking up with," he replied, sarcasm dripping from his tone.

"Maybe, but until I cross that bridge, I'm not going to worry about that. Marlon, you know I've never fallen for the okey-doke. My shit has always been on point. Ain't shit changing because I'm attracted to a nigga. Trust me, I got this," I said before ending the call.

There was no need to continue going back and forth. Marlon was going to have his opinion, and I was going to do whatever the hell I wanted anyway. My focus was on getting to the bottom of whatever unknown beef we had so that my family and I could go back to living our lives. Things had been so fucked up lately, and I was ready for it to get back to normal.

Pulling up to Hart of the City, I parked next to the line of motorcycles decorating the street. Harleys, Yamahas, Kawasakis, Triumphs, Ninjas, and Ducatis of all styles, sizes, and colors belonging to other club members were here and ready to ride out at a moment's notice. Seeing this shit had me missing my own bike. It had been a minute since I'd hit the road on two wheels. I looked down the row and spotted Elle's baby. I was glad to know that she was here. It had been weeks since the last time we talked, and I wanted to chop it up with her about some shit that had been bothering me.

Before I stepped out, my phone vibrated in my pocket, and when I pulled it out, I saw that it was my mother. I quickly declined and continued inside. I didn't feel like letting another person curse me out today, and I knew that was what was going to happen had I answered, so I rejected that shit. I'd have to deal with her later.

Before I could put it away, the phone rang again. When I looked down at the number, my heart skipped a beat. It was Simmy, and I knew he was pissed if he was calling. I agreed to be back over an hour ago, so he was probably worried. I had a feeling that I was going to regret it later, but I declined his call as well and made my way inside.

The atmosphere in the shop was somber but not as bad as it was at the church. The mechanics sat around quietly talking among themselves, behaving nothing like the loud and boisterous crew they were known to be. Natalie had worked with them since the place opened, so I know that her death hit them hard. Slipping my backpack from my shoulder, I stopped in Philly's office to change clothes before stepping into Heaven.

"Look at this bitch. Straight tried to slip in the funeral on some incognito shit," Diem teased from her seat at the table while the others broke into a fit of giggles. Even Philly laughed before standing up to hug me.

"Fuck you, Diem," I said with my middle finger up. "How the hell y'all know that was me though?" I wanted to know. I thought I'd done a good job of concealing my identity, but everyone in my family was able to point me out. Everyone except for my mother, that was.

"Chile, you wasn't fooling nobody with that Proud-Mary-keep-on-burnin' wig on!" Diem joked, sending the room full of females into a second uproar. Even I had to laugh at that one. It was safe to say that my wig was retired after today. And to think I thought that shit was cute. I guessed Simmy's rude ass was right.

"Friend!" Elle rushed over to hug me after stepping out of the restroom.

"Hey, Ellie Poo," I laughed lightly while hugging her back.

"And why haven't I heard from you? Are folks really going weeks at a time without talking to their best friends?" she asked with her hand on her hip.

"We'll talk a little later," was all I said.

She gave me a questioning stare, but eventually, she just nodded her head in agreement. Elle then turned her attention to Philly. The look in her eyes told me she was about to be on some bullshit, and today was just not the day for the extras.

"So, Philly, word on the street is that you're fucking around with Gideon Wells. Is that true?" Elle lifted an eyebrow.

"Not that it's any of your business, but no, we're not seeing each other. I barely even know the man," Philly answered with an annoyed expression.

The look that Diem shot her in response to her answer led me to believe that might not be entirely true, and if this Gideon person was the same man she was hugged up with at the funeral, then her ass was definitely lying. They seemed extra cozy to me.

"Seemed to be more to it than that by the way you were clinging to him, but whatever." She shrugged.

"Like I said," Philly said, gritting her teeth, "I barely know him."

"Hmm, that's good to know. A man like that is way out of your league anyway, honey. I might see what's up with him though since you claim to barely know him," she quipped sarcastically, using air quotes.

"Out of her league?" I questioned. "What kind of shit is that to say? Like she ain't good enough or something?" I interjected before Philly could offer a reply. This girl was purposely fucking with my sister, and I wanted to know the reason. She hadn't always been this way, and I wanted to know what the hell was going on with her, because she was becoming more and more blatant with the insults.

"I didn't mean it like that, friend. Hell, for a moment I thought she was into girls." She laughed while her clique snickered lowly. "If you are into dudes, a thug is more your speed, Philly. Not a man like Gideon. You wouldn't have a thing in common with his fine ass." She attempted laughing it off like she hadn't just said some fucked-up shit. The defeated look in my sister's eyes made me snap, and I wasn't the only one.

"Bitch!" Diem and I said simultaneously but got cut off by Big Gina's outburst before we could check Elle's ass.

"Aye, aye, turn that up!" she directed Trish, who along with a few others had her eyes glued to the flat screen that was mounted on the wall above the pool table.

Turning my attention to the television, I, along with everyone else, was once again reminded of the dear friend and club member we'd all laid to rest just hours before.

"Good afternoon, I'm Monica Jackson reporting live for Channel 5 from Victory Missionary, where the funeral of twenty-eight-year-old Las Vegas native Natalie Sykes is being held today. As you can see behind me, hundreds of mourners have turned out today to pay respects to this bright young lady, who I'm being told was loved by everyone she came into contact with. A little over a week ago, Natalie and four other individuals were gunned down at an event held in honor of Open Harts Children's Home. We're still gathering the details, but it's being said that three masked assailants entered the ballroom and opened fire, killing five and injuring countless others. Right now we don't know the reason or who was the intended target, but Vegas PD is working overtime to bring the criminals responsible to justice. We've tried to reach out to Julian Hart, the CEO of Hart Enterprises, for comment but have been unable to do so. We have learned, however, that this service and the combined service for the remaining victims scheduled at this same church on Tuesday at eleven a.m. have been paid for entirely by Mr. Hart. That's all we have right now, but we'll bring you up to date on any new developments as they become available. Back to you in the studio."

"Mmmph, we all know whose fault this is, don't we, Philly?" Elle said, causing every head in the room to whip in her direction.

"The fuck did you say?" Philly said as we both moved slowly in Elle's direction, while Diem stood, all getting in position for the same reason.

If this girl was coming at my sister like Natalie's death and the others were on her, she was getting her ass beat today. I'd been leery of the moves she was making lately, and I planned to talk to her about it, but it seemed we might be beyond a conversation at this point.

"Let's face it," she said, gesturing around the room. "As the president, Philly should've done a better job of making sure that the appropriate security measures were in place prior to the fundraiser. This is all on her. What happened that night should have never happened. Those of us in this room are lucky that we even made it out of there with our lives. Too bad Natalie wasn't as fortunate." She shook her head in disgust.

Before she knew what was happening, Diem had socked her in the face at least three times, snapping her neck back with each blow. I thought Philly was stunned by Elle's conspicuous accusation because she just stood there for a few seconds. But, man, when she checked back in, it was on and popping, and trust I was on the same shit. Say what you want, but the Hart sisters didn't fight fair, and we really didn't give a damn if people didn't agree with our motto. Fuck a one-on-one. If one swung, we all swung. That was why I rushed over and got in on the action right along with them, my growing distrust of Elle fueling my wrath. With all of the shit that had been going on, no one outside of family could be trusted, not even my so-called bestie.

"Wait a minute, Diem, I don't think she meant it like that. Just hear her out," I heard someone yell.

"I don't have to hear shit. This bitch said what she said and meant it. Now move out of the way before you get your ass beat too," my sister barked, connecting her fist to Elle's jaw.

"Somebody stop them! They gon' beat that girl to death!"

Elle tried her best to defend herself, but against us three she didn't stand a chance. After repeated blows to her face and body, she simply gave up, curled up in a ball, and used her hands to protect her face.

"No, let them go at it. That bitch deserves it, always talking that shit. It's high time somebody tagged that ass," Big Gina instigated.

"Nah, this ain't cool. They are going to kill her," Leesha, who was one of the ones laughing at Elle's jokes earlier, said as she came over to break things up.

Gina allowed the fight to continue for another fifteen seconds or so before she helped Leesha pull us off of a battered and bruised Elle. The other members stood around in silent shock, trying to process what had just taken place. Pushing my sisters behind me, I looked down at Elle, who was beyond fucked up.

"Drea, what the fuck?" she cried. "We're supposed to be friends!"

"Yeah, we are, so that's why I don't understand why you feel it's okay to keep coming for my family. If you were really my friend, you wouldn't do that. Oh, what, you thought I was going to keep letting you make it? Nah, it's over for that shit!" I shouted close to her face as she still lay on the floor.

"You act like what I said was a lie though," she said, stumbling to her feet with assistance from Julia and Leesha. One hand held her jaw, and the other clutched her stomach, which had been kicked multiple times.

"To blame the shooting on me? That was a whole fucking lie," Philly shouted, still panting out of control. "My best friend? Bitch, you done lost your fucking mind."

"Elle, you out, baby girl. This the end of the road for you and the Angels," Diem concluded.

"What? No, that's not right. It should be her who's leaving, not me. She's the cause of all the problems." Elle looked around the room at her handful of supporters for some backup.

"Nah, don't look at them. You gotta go," I concurred. "As a matter of fact, Leesha, Deshawn, and Julia, y'all out too. It's clear that you three have been down with whatever movement this bitch been trying to put together, and it stops here. We've been through enough, and we don't need anyone around us on some 'overthrow the government' type shit." I gestured toward Elle. "Unlike this ho, only the three of us have the power to say who stays or goes," I fumed.

"Drea, are you really going to stand here and do this to me?" Elle looked to me with sad eyes.

I didn't have shit for her though. It was family over everything, and she'd already shown she was no real friend of mine. "You heard what I said. Get the fuck up outta here," I voiced with finality, letting everyone in the room know once and for all where my loyalties lay.

To give her and her flunkies an incentive to move a little quicker, I pulled my .22 out and aimed it at their asses. The time for games was over. The remaining members stood quietly, watching the outcasts as they packed up their belongings and made their exit. Elle looked like she wanted to say something, but my weapon pointing at her had her on mute for the moment.

"If anyone here has a problem with what just happened, address that shit right now so that there is no confusion moving forward. People are literally out there trying to take our lives, so we don't have time for any of our own to be smiling in our faces while secretly plotting behind our backs. If you're not built to withstand the storm that's coming our way, now is the time to make it known. We are not going for no more BS in this club, so if you're not with us, you're against us," Diem stated while scanning the room. When no one responded or walked out, she nodded her head and looked to Philly to continue.

"Now that that's over and the weak links have been eliminated, let's get to the reason we were called here today," Philly opened before breaking down for the group everything that had happened up until now and answering questions as she went along.

"So how do we know for sure that the Dragons are behind this? Shit seems kind of shaky. Almost like someone wants us to think it's them," Sandie pointed out.

I had my doubts as well so I decided to speak up on this portion of the meeting. "I feel you on that. I myself am not one hundred percent sold on the idea that the Dragons are behind this, so I came up with a plan to lure their asses out just to be sure."

"Let's hear it, sis. I'd hate to come for them fools and end up being wrong. That would lead to some problems that I'm unsure this small group can handle on our own. This right here is for Nats, so we gotta come correct, and the right people gotta answer for her death. We can't half step with this," Philly stated as she wiped a single tear from her cheek.

In accord, every member walked over to her and wrapped their arms around her for a group hug. We were down four bodies, but the ones remaining were loyal and solid. This was what Hart's Angels was all about. This sisterhood. It was the very reason we wanted our own chapter, and I'd be damned if I was letting anyone tear that apart.

"A'ight, this is what we're going to do," I announced, and everyone gave me their undivided attention.

"I can't tonight, Lance," I giggled as I inserted my key into the lock. "Don't worry about where I'm at or where I've been. I could have sworn that you said you wasn't fucking with me anymore after that shit at my house. How are you even on my phone begging for some pussy right now?" I teased.

I didn't know why I was even entertaining this fool. I had no desire or plan to ever kick it with him again, so I was wasting his time and my own with this conversation. Clicking on the lamp to brighten the dark room, I was startled to see an angry Simmy posted on the chaise, elbows resting on his knees with his hands clasped together. He was sitting there looking like a father waiting for his teenage daughter to come home after a date, and his expression told me he was ready to wring my neck. Standing, he addressed me.

"Hang up the fucking phone, Onyx," he ordered, chest bare with his pajama pants hanging low on his hips.

I wasn't for letting anyone punk me, so guess what I did. I hung that phone the hell up without another word to Lance! The fuck? Simmy's rage was palpable, and I wouldn't even lie, I was scared shitless. I wasn't about to play with him right now. Thinking fast, I produced a gun from the small of my back and pointed it in his direction. Don't ask why that was my first reaction, but this fool had me shaking in my damn boots.

"So, not only do you ignore my calls all day, not bothering to hit me up to let me know that you're safe, but then you walk yo' bold ass up in here, caking with some nigga like shit is sweet? You got life and bullshit fucked all the way up!" he barked, knocking the .22 from my shaking hands. "You need some gotdamn act right, and I'm about to give it to you.

Simmy snatched me by my collar and dragged me toward the back of the house. I knew earlier that I was going to regret not taking his calls, and now look at me. I was being tossed onto the bed, landing right in the middle of his plush mattress, while my heart beat out of control. I rose up on my elbows, looking for something, anything to defend myself with, but it was dark as hell until he flicked on the light. I watched his wild eyes soften when they landed on my face. On the way here I'd noticed a purple bruise forming on my left cheek from an accidental elbow thrown my way by Philly as she swung on Elle.

"What the fuck happened to your face? Somebody put their fucking hands on you?" he roared. He was now at the edge of the bed, gripping my chin while turning my face from side to side to examine it.

"No. I mean yes," I stuttered. "My sisters and I got into a little scuffle with this chick, but this here is nothing," I bragged, motioning to my injury. I guessed I'd relaxed a bit too soon, because that look was once again in his eyes as soon as I finished my sentence.

"So you got time to beat bitches up, but you couldn't take two minutes to call me and let me know you were good or at least tell me what time you'd be back? I been sitting here going out of my mind worrying about you, and you out here parleying and shit!" he ranted angrily while pulling me by my leg to the edge of the bed. He mean mugged me while he removed my shoes.

"Simeron, what are you doing?" My voice quivered.

"And I thought I made myself clear when I told you to get rid of that lame. Guess you thought a nigga was playing with yo' ass. On everything, I'm killing that nigga first thing in the morning," he threatened, completely ignoring my question. He removed my clothing piece by piece until I lay before him in my birthday suit.

"Sim . . ." I began but stopped short when I was flipped over onto my stomach. I made a weak attempt to stop what was happening, but I really wanted him to keep going. He said I needed some act right, and I couldn't agree more. When I say I had never been more turned on and wet in all my life, I'm not lying.

"Apologize!" he demanded, roughly ramming his huge dick into my wet tunnel. I swear, I thought my heart stopped when he did that. I only knew I was still alive because of the pleasure I felt upon his retreat. He pulled back to the tip and repeated the same motion as before. Again, I thought I died and came back to life. "I said apologize to me," he requested once more. How the hell was I supposed to do that with him dipping that monster of a penis inside of me like that? I was barely breathing, so talking was definitely out of the question. "You hard of hearing or something, Onyx? What the fuck did I just tell you to do? Mmm, shit!" he moaned as I tightened my walls around him.

"Apologize for what?" I whined. My ass was crying real tears at this point.

"For having me sitting here worrying about you all day. For not checking in. And last but not least, for caking with that nigga after I gave you strict instructions to dead that shit," he grunted while pummeling my pussy. Simmy was showing me no mercy, and I loved it.

"Oh, my Gawwwd! I'm sorry!" I squealed. I didn't know how much more of this I could take. My entire body was trembling with each and every stroke, and in no time I felt that familiar tightening in my lower abdomen.

"There it is. Cum on this dick, baby," he coached as my walls began to seize. He smacked my ass so hard that I came on contact and fell into the mattress.

"Nah, toot that ass back up, and you bet' not let that mu'fucka fall again," he ordered, making me cream on him even more. "You getting this dick until you act like you got some sense, and I'on give a fuck if it takes all night," he swore.

And dammit, he delivered on that threat. Over and over again.

Chapter 13

Simmy

"What do I have to do to get you to trust me?" I whispered to myself as I observed Onyx.

Of course she didn't reply, but I kept my eyes on her. I'd been sitting up against the headboard staring at her for the better part of the last hour while she pretended to sleep peacefully. It's been said that you should beware of a person who watches you in your sleep because that meant that they were crazy. In my case, that shit was true as fuck, and I wasn't ashamed to admit it.

I was crazy about Onyx, and it hadn't taken me long to realize it. I'd been infatuated with her from the moment I laid eyes on her months back, and with the way she put the pussy on me last night, I was sure I was only going to get crazier. Her plump ass peeking out from beneath the cover was tempting the hell out of me, but I knew I needed to give her body a break after the hurting I'd put on it last night. My own body was still sore as hell from the beatdown them niggas put on me and the bullet I took to my side, but I somehow found the strength to fuck like a champion. By the way she moaned and screamed my name, she was quite pleased with my performance.

Being with her was everything I dreamed it would be and more. What started off as punishment and straight fucking graduated to some slow-grinding type shit that had my feelings all over the place. Her body's response to mine had me feeling like I could have made love to her fine ass for three days straight with no breaks. I'd never made love to a woman before last night. Hell, I didn't even know I was capable of doing it. But Onyx made me want to take my time and enjoy every moment. I shivered just thinking about it, and she had to know that there was no way she was going to be able to get rid of me now. I was bound to turn into a deranged stalker if she tried.

One thing that was fucking me up was that she didn't fully trust me or my intentions, considering I was sent to kill her. I had to practically hold her down the whole night because I kept feeling her pull away from me. I knew for a fact that if I had let her go, she wouldn't have been here when I opened my eyes this morning. I mean, I understood where she was coming from because I'd be a little skeptical myself if I were in her shoes, but the fact that I hadn't taken her life when I had multiple opportunities to do so should have counted for something.

We had some obstacles to overcome, but I just couldn't see myself letting this thing between us go, so I needed to figure something out quick before she stopped fucking with me altogether. Just as I was about to slip out of bed so that I could start my quest for the answers to her questions, a light bulb went off in my mind. I'd come up with a way to prove to her once and for all that I wasn't on no bullshit.

"Onyx," I called out to her. She didn't budge, but I could tell that her ass was faking. Although her eyes were still closed, I knew the exact moment she'd woken up, and that had been a while ago. "Onyx, get up," I said a little louder this time, playing her little game.

When she didn't answer, I removed myself from the bed and walked away. I opened and closed the bathroom door, posted up against the doorjamb, and just waited. After counting out a full sixty seconds, she did exactly what I knew she would: hopped her happy ass up and started scrambling for her clothing. I shook my head, wanting to laugh at how fast she was moving, but I was more pissed that she was trying to dip out on me without even saying good-bye.

"And just where the hell do you think you're going?" I asked, causing her to stop dead in her tracks. Turning around, she looked like a deer facing headlights. She opened her mouth to speak, but nothing came out. "I knew yo' sneaky ass wasn't 'sleep. And you supposed to be some kind of assassin. Ass couldn't even creep up out this bitch right," I made fun of her.

"Fuck you, Simmy!" she spat, angry that I'd called her out on her failed attempt at playing possum.

"I already did that, Onyx! Multiple times," I smugly retorted, causing her to gasp in shock.

For a moment we eye warred in complete silence. If you can't tell by now, I tended to say fucked-up shit when I was upset, and she did as well. That was proven during the explosive fights we had before she left the house yesterday and when she came back last night. Onyx and I were too much alike, and that was either going to hurt us and push us apart, or it would bring us closer. I for one was banking on the latter.

"You sure in the hell did," she said with a shake of her head as she slipped her panties on. "How dumb could I have been to give you access to my body after you tried to kill me? For all I know you were sent for my sisters, too, one of whom just lost her best friend to this shit, and despite knowing that I still let you fuck me dizzy last night. Dumb as hell, right? Bet you got a good ol' laugh about that, huh?" she chuckled sarcastically but continued dressing, refusing to look my way.

Thinking fast, I crossed the room and wrapped my arms around her body from behind. From the look in her eyes as she spoke, I could tell that I may have gone a little too far and only further fueled her distrust of me. I was fucking up. I needed to fix this shit and fix it fast. The only way I felt I could do that was to have her ride along with me as we tried to piece together what the hell was going on.

"Drea," I spoke calmly into the side of her face.

"Don't fucking call me that. I'm Onyx to you! That's who the fuck you came into my shop looking for so that's who the fuck you're going to get from now on," she croaked as she fought against me.

"Chill, Onyx, please. Look, I'm sorry. You know I didn't mean that shit like it came out. And how many times do I have to tell you that I was only given the contract on you? I know nothing about a price being put on the head of either of your sisters," I tried to convince her.

"You gon' have to keep screaming that shit until I believe it, nigga!" she shouted, finally escaping my hold.

I actually had to let her go because I was becoming exhausted watching her tire herself out trying to get away from me. The shit was laughable. Her ass was barely five foot seven and maybe 160 pounds trying to buck against a six foot one nigga pushing 220. Plus, her little feisty ass was making my dick hard with all that fucking wiggling she was doing, and I couldn't let her feel my shit or she'd never listen to a word I had to say. She already had suspicions that all I wanted to do was fuck her before I killed her, and feeling my erection was only going to drive home her point.

"How about I just show you?"

"Show me? How do you suppose you'd do that?" she asked skeptically. She'd stopped trying to slip on her shoes, so I knew I had her attention. Onyx didn't want to believe I had ulterior motives when it came to her, and me telling her wasn't going to be good enough. She needed to see for herself before she would believe it.

"I'm going to do that by bringing you with me while I try to figure this shit out, but before we go let's get a few things straight. Number one, I don't know who paid the money to have you dealt with, and I do not know the reason. You know this fucking business as well as I do. Do the job, get the money. No questions asked. Number two, I'd been watching you for approximately three weeks before I made my move on you in your shop that day. During those three weeks, I was presented with six different opportunities to blow your head off your shoulders, and I resisted every fucking time! You would have never even seen it coming, but a nigga just couldn't do it. From day one there was just something about you that intrigued me. I had to see you every damn day, Onyx. I did no other jobs, just followed you around like a sucker week after fucking week." I mumbled the last part.

"Simmy," she pouted and stomped her foot, upset with herself for letting my words have an effect on her.

"Lastly and hopefully for the final time, your sisters were not included in my contract. If someone is after them, that shit has nothing to do with me. Everything, and I mean everything I just told you is the truth. Now I need you to come with me so that you can see for yourself," I told her before retreating to the bathroom to take a shower, leaving her alone with her thoughts.

I wanted to drag her ass in here with me, but I wanted to see if she would hang around on her own free will. It wasn't like I couldn't find her ass if need be, and I couldn't exactly hold her hostage or make her go on this suicide mission with me, but I hoped that she would. This shit was going to be dangerous as hell, but I honestly didn't trust anyone outside of her to be at my side while I handled it.

She was cold with her shit. It may not have seemed like it because of the number of times I'd caught her lacking, but I was a master tracker and had been doing this shit a lot longer than she had. Caught my first body at twelve so I was a seasoned vet, and since I was a youngster I was known for being able to slip in and out of just about any-damn-where without being detected.

When the older homies around my hood near Donna Street peeped how I got down, they had me robbing corner boys for their stashes and in turn, would split the money with me. The one and only time I got caught was the first time I had to lay a nigga down. That day I learned two things. One was that I could take a life and feel no remorse, and the second was to never get caught. Needless to say, I'd been on my abracadabra shit and laying niggas down ever since.

"Move, jerk," Onyx murmured from behind me once she stepped into the shower.

Like a typical female, she moved to the front, hogging all the gotdamn hot water while my teeth chattered and I fought chills in the back with barely any water hitting my body. Still, I wanted to smile the way them weak-ass, "sucker for love" niggas be doing when their woman did something to make them happy. This fucking girl had me feeling all warm and bubbly inside, but I wasn't even tripping.

After reaching around her to snatch the towel she was using from her hands, I began to wash her body, and she let me. I washed her from the top of her curly head to the bottom of her pretty-ass feet, but I made sure to save the best for last. I swear I was only cleaning between her thighs for a good twelve seconds before I dropped that towel and began massaging her soapy pussy with my hand. Her shit was so fucking plump and warm, and I was dying to slide inside at least once more before we hit the road. I figured busting a few nuts would surely get my mind right before this kill spree we were about to embark on.

Moaning from deep in her throat, she leaned her head against my chest, arched that back, and started grinding. She could complain all day about me just wanting to fuck her, but she couldn't deny that she wanted to fuck me just as bad. Although we connected strongly on other levels, this sexual chemistry we shared was off the Richter scale.

It didn't take me long to get tired of playing in her pussy, so I hurriedly took down the removable shower head and rinsed the soap from her body so that I could bend her over and feast on what had become my absolute favorite dish.

We were deep in the hood, parked at the end of a dark street, just waiting. I eyed this one particular home at the end of the block, knowing that at any given moment my target would be arriving. This was a trip he made every single Sunday evening so I knew that I'd be able to find him here. It was on this very street that he spotted and recruited me, so he should have known that this was where I would come to see about him. I may not have

known anything about the person who hired me to
kill Onyx, but I knew all there was to know about
the nigga who had been depositing big bank into
my account over the last ten years. I'd never considered Leo a friend, but we'd known each other
long enough to call ourselves cool, I supposed.

In this game, you had associates at best but never
true ride or dies. It had to be that way because if at
any time you fucked up on a job or pissed off the
wrong person with one of your hits, that person
you were just screaming the day before was your
partner was the same muthafucka who would be at
your neck the following day if the price was right,
fuck the friendship. That was one reason I didn't
mind rolling solo and also why I wasn't surprised
that the nigga sent shooters for me after I didn't
complete the job on Onyx. I was prepared for that
but ended up getting caught slipping because I was
expecting her to show up to my place and not them.
At least not that soon.

I'd requested more time, and Leo acted as if it
was cool, but I guessed his ass was stalling just like
I was. The plan to kill him was already in place, so I
wasn't even mad at him for coming at me first. The
only thing that stopped me from doing him in was
that I didn't know who had ordered her hit, so it
would have been stupid of me to murk him without getting that info first. I was getting at his ass
tonight though. Onyx had already handled that
wannabe hard nigga Mack and his boss, and now it

was time for the head nigga in charge to meet his Maker as well. I needed to find a way to get him to give up his contact, and that was going to be a challenge. It crossed my mind to use Onyx to get it done, but I refused to take any chances with her life. The men we were dealing with were real killers just like us, and they wouldn't be as reluctant to take her life as I had been.

"Where in the *Tales from the Hood, Nightmare on Elm Street* haunted house hell do you have me, Simmy?" Onyx asked as she cautiously surveyed her surroundings.

I laughed lightly at her extra-ass description of the neighborhood. I was a hood nigga through and through so being around the dopefiends, hookers, and the homeless folks who moved about was nothing new to me. Onyx, however, grew up a far cry from these here streets of Las Vegas. My li'l baby was a stone-cold killer, and although her mouth was reckless at times, she was not a hood chick at all. She was definitely a change of pace for me, but I couldn't say that I didn't like it.

"I know yo' ass ain't scared," I teased.

"I ain't scared of shit, and you know it," she retorted as she screwed on her silencer then placed her gun back in her lap before returning to filing her nails. She was such a fucking girl.

"I'm just fucking with you, but let me ask you something. Like, I already told you the reason that I do what I do. I ain't really have a choice if I wanted to eat and have somewhere to lay my head every night. Crackhead prostitute for a mama. Pimping-ass nigga for a daddy, and I never really knew him like that anyway. Been on my own most of my life, but you? You had it all, baby girl. Why you doing this shit?" I asked. It was something I'd been wondering since I opened the manila folder and read her file. Then I saw that angelic face of hers, and I was confused as to how someone like her even got mixed up in this shit.

"I honestly couldn't tell you," she replied after contemplating it for a minute. "What I can say is that I remember the exact moment that the desire to kill entered my mind. That moment in time when I knew I could take a life and sleep just the same at night." She nodded as if she was going back in her mind to the very day this realization took place.

"When was that?" I asked, turning my eyes back to the house while waiting for her to continue.

"It was a few weeks after my sister Philly came to live with us. Before she showed up, we had no idea she even existed. It was crazy how Pops introduced us, but the three of us fell in love with each other instantly. Diem and I were just so excited to have another sister, so one night we decided we were going to go to her room and have an impromptu slumber party. We had all the good snacks and movies as well as all the other girly shit you bring to a sleepover, but when we knocked, she didn't answer so, we let ourselves in. We got worried when we didn't see her in the room, but we got the shock of our lives when we checked the bathroom and found her passed out on the floor with an empty bottle of sleeping pills beside her. I remember being so angry that she would try to kill herself, leaving us to grieve a sister we hadn't fully got the chance to bond with."

"Damn," I whispered, taking her hand in mine while she went on with the story.

"They made her stay in the hospital for a few weeks to undergo a psych evaluation. Had to monitor her until they felt she was mentally stable, you know. When she did finally come home, I wouldn't speak to her. Straight silent treatment. I was legit pissed off at her because I couldn't understand what could make a person that young so sad that they didn't want to live anymore. Like you said, I grew up with everything, so I knew nothing about her struggles, and that was made painfully clear to me when she told me the reason she had to come stay with us in the first place. Someone had come into her home and murdered her mother and her grandmother in cold blood while she was at school. She ran upstairs to see their bodies lying in pools of blood. My sister lay next to them for hours until our father showed up and had to practically pry her away. Can you imagine how fucked up that must have been for a small child to see?" she asked, wiping a single tear from her face.

I just shook my head in response. Clearing her throat, she went on to say, "Yeah, so that was the day I made a promise to her that I would kill the person responsible for causing her that pain. For taking two of the most important people in her life away from her. For making her so sad that she wanted to die, I was going to make sure that they died."

"Did you get 'im? The person responsible?"

"Nope. I still don't know who did it, but when I find out, it's lights out for they ass," she swore.

"We gon' find them mu'fuckas, believe that," I assured her.

"We?" she asked, trying to mask that beautiful smile of hers.

"Yeah, we, gotdammit. Fuck you thought? Anybody you got a problem with, I got a problem with they ass too, and I don't give a fuck if the grudge started when you was two years old," I stated, putting the car in drive, careful not to get too close to my target, who was now on the move.

"You're crazy. You know that, right?" she giggled.

"You like it though so I'll be that." I blew a kiss at her then focused back on the car ahead.

"Aye, do you see—" she started after we were driving for a while.

"Yeah, I see that shit," I interrupted her while looking out of the rearview and side mirrors.

I was about to instruct her on what to do next, but Onyx had already reached for the other gun that she had resting between her legs and unbuckled her seat belt. I guessed Leo's ass was anticipating me coming for him after the fools he sent to kill me never reported in. He knew the that they were more than likely dead and that he would be next if he wasn't careful. That explained the car that was now tailing us, but they had no idea that they wouldn't be following us much longer.

"Keep your eyes on that car, bae. I got these muthafuckas," she said as she rolled down the window and lifted up and moved her upper body out while aiming directly at the car behind us.

Behind the illegal tint they couldn't see that I had a passenger, so they were more than likely caught off guard by the gorgeous shooter aiming a clean-ass sawed-off shotgun at them. Before they could even react or slow down, she was firing. I didn't want to miss the action, but I also couldn't take the chance of losing Leo. All I could hear were the explosions from the bullets hitting the car and glass shattering, followed by screeching tires and what sounded like the car hitting something hard.

That did it for me. I had to take a look, and when I did the smile that graced my face couldn't be contained. Whoever was in that car was dead, dead, and more dead, and that much I was sure of. The sedan had crashed into a light pole off the side of the road and was now engulfed in flames. I couldn't see anyone making it out of that alive, and if they did, they were going to be fucked up for life.

Switching lanes while continuing to match Leo's speed, I asked, "What did you do?" eyes still wide in amazement and admiration.

"Something I've always wanted to do," she replied, bouncing in her seat excitedly. "After the first couple shots caused them to swerve and that gas tank came into view, I sent a bullet right through it," she told me proudly.

Seemed she got a kick out of this shit as much as I did. Glancing quickly in the rearview, I could still see flames and clouds of smoke in the distance. That was the moment I knew I had found my fucking soul mate. As always, seeing her in action made my dick hard, and I was ready to get this shit over with so that we could get back to doing what we did.

"I'm tired of chasing this nigga," I stated as I put the pedal to the metal to pull up closer to the speeding SUV.

It was now or never. I had to make my move, because knowing him, it was only a matter of time before more of his men would join us on this very road to try taking us out and assisting him in escaping. We were now traveling on I-15 at close to a hundred miles per hour, and Onyx sat next to me, calmly peeping the scene like we weren't in the middle of some super crazy shit.

"You gone ram the nigga or what?" She impatiently motioned ahead of us with her hand.

"I got this shit, baby girl. Just sit back and hold tight," I instructed her while quickly switching lanes to come up on the side of his whip. As soon as the time was right and I was in the perfect position, I slightly swerved, clipping the back of the car, causing it to spin out of control and crash head-on into the barrier.

"That's what the fuck I'm talking about," Onyx piped, blowing my head up a little. I was glad to have done something to impress her, because she'd done the unforgettable when she took care of the fools back down the road a minute ago. There was no way I was topping that shit. At least not tonight.

Throwing the car in park, I undid my seat belt and went to hop out. Onyx was out of the car before I could even tell her to remain inside while I checked things out. Looking around for possible witnesses, I moved toward the smoking vehicle with my Glock by my side and Onyx trailing close behind. The windows were shattered, and the passenger side door was now bent up and hanging open from the collision, so we had no problem seeing inside. We discovered Leo was in the vehicle alone, passed out with his bleeding head resting against the steering wheel. We didn't have time to do anything out here on the open road, so we were going to have to take him with us.

I handed Onyx my gun while I pulled my knife from my pocket and cut the seat belt straps. I looked over to see her already moving backward toward the dummy car we were using for the day with her gun aimed on him just in case he happened to wake up. Pulling him out, I quickly tossed his heavy body over my shoulder and made my way over to the now-open trunk. I dumped his ass in, and we hopped up front and peeled off. I could already hear sirens in the distance, and I wanted to be as far away as possible when they showed up.

"What's that?" I asked, just now noticing the two bags she had in her possession. One was at her feet while she sifted through the other in her lap.

"No clue, but I'm about to find out," she answered. Seconds later she was pulling out stacks upon stacks of money. "For our pain and suffering," she said, waving the money around with her tongue hanging out.

"Back to the spot?" I asked.

She only nodded her response, when something in the other bag grabbed her attention. I watched her brow furrow as she studied the contents of the folders she now held in her hands. Dropping them back inside, she picked up her phone and typed what I assumed to be a text message. Next, she dialed a number.

"Yeah, it's me. Meet me at the address I just sent, and bring your laptop along with any information you have on that Santiago hit I did last year. Don't ask why, Marlon. Just do the shit," she ordered before disconnecting the call. I sped up a little, now very anxious to find out what she'd seen to cause her to react that way.

"How much?" Onyx asked once I placed the last of the money back in the bag.

"A little over two hundred thousand," I replied, tossing the bag onto the table then walking over to a gagged and bound Leo. He must have had a serious concussion, because he was still knocked the fuck out. "Time to wake up, shiesty-ass nigga," I said, pouring a bucket of cold water on top of his head.

He immediately started to come to, eyes blinking and wide as he gasped for air. When those same eyes went from Onyx then landed on me, they damn near bugged out of his head. He had to know that with two of his worst nightmares standing in the same room as him, things weren't going to end well. This was the end of the road, but I still had questions that I hoped he would answer before I took him off the set.

"Simmy, man, look. You know how the game goes. I didn't have a choice. You didn't do your fucking job, my nigga," Leo started explaining before I could get a word in edgewise.

"I ain't even trippin' on that shit. Like you said, I know how the game goes. We already have an idea who was behind the hit ordered on her, but my girl would like confirmation." I nodded over in the direction Onyx was standing. "Which one of Santiago's people did you give her name up to?"

"Come on, Simmy. Man, you know I can't do that," he groaned.

"I'on see why not! You gave them bitches my name first," Onyx butted in.

"I told yo' ass not to fuck with this fool the moment you got the call. We don't do new niggas. I said that. Didn't I say that?" the dude Marlon rambled from across the room, flailing his hands in the air.

"Nigga, chill with that shit. The last thing she needs to hear right now is some 'I told you so' shit. Be a real friend and shut the fuck up!" I yelled.

"Muthafu—" he started but was cut off by Onyx.

"Marlon, please," she hissed.

Something had to be said because this fool was irking the fuck out of me. He had been talking shit since he came in the door, and I could tell he didn't like that Onyx and I were now cool with each other. If his ass weren't gay, I would have thought that his territorial attitude came from a different place. Nigga was acting like he had claims on that pussy or something, and that shit was all me.

"Fine, I won't say shit else," he said with a nod of his head before storming out of the room.

"Bitch-ass nigga," I mumbled, earning me an evil look from Onyx. I just blew her mean ass a kiss in response. "Name," I said, turning my attention back to Leo, but he remained silent, face stoic like he was hard or some shit.

"Fuck it. I guess I'm about to have to shoot yo' ass, and that's a damn shame, because you're cute as hell," Onyx said as she boldly stared him in the eyes. She then used a napkin to gently wipe away some of the blood that dripped from his lip.

Can y'all believe this nigga had the fucking gall to smile when she said that shit? And the way he eyed her from head to toe said that he thought she was cute too. *Hell fucking nah,* I thought as I tossed the gun I'd been gripping onto the sofa. I ran over and rocked the shit out of his disrespectful ass, causing the chair he was in to fall over. His head hit the ground hard as hell, and once again he was out like a light. Onyx didn't even budge, just stood there laughing her ass off. I saw now that she liked to see me act a fool behind her, and there would be plenty of niggas getting their ass beat in the near future. I liked to flex for her, so I wasn't tripping on it.

"How cute is that nigga now, huh?" I bit my lip, getting up in her face. Of course, more laughter ensued.

"Really, Simmy? I mean he is kinda cute," she said playfully once she was done laughing her ass off.

"Stop fucking with me, Drea."

I was surprised when she smiled and failed to correct me about her name. I guessed that meant we'd made progress and she now believed me.

There was nothing in the paperwork or the hard drive we found in the bag that indicated her sisters were a part of the bounty that was on her head. We knew someone in the Santiago family had it out for her, but since Leo wasn't giving them up, I supposed we would just have to kill them all. Eyes locked with hers, I picked my gun back up and aimed it toward the ground where he now lay. Onyx followed suit. At the exact same time, we sent bullets into his body until both of our clips were empty.

"Come here," I demanded.

As soon as she was in my arms I lifted her up, and she immediately wrapped her legs around my waist and her arms around my neck, our guns still in hand. Leaving Leo's dead ass right where he was, she and I engaged in a heated lip-lock as we bypassed an angry Marlon and went right to the bedroom. After we handled our business behind these closed doors, then we could tend to more pressing issues, namely the entire Santiago family.

Chapter 14

Philly

"Philly, why won't you give that man a chance? He seems like he really likes you."

"How can someone who doesn't know me like me?"

Natalie walked behind my desk and grabbed a lollipop from my bowl. "Because they can. Obviously, there's something about you that he's attracted to."

"That nigga ain't attracted to shit but my perceived bad-girl persona."

Her eyebrows furrowed. "Bad-girl persona?"

"Yeah. I'm the complete opposite of the type of female he's used to being with, and that's what has him intrigued. You should have seen the way he got all excited when I told him I was the prez of Hart's Angels."

She sat on my desk and crossed her legs, scrolling through some site on her iPad. Her short shorts showed off the smidge of cellulite on her thighs. "I think any man would be intrigued by a woman who not only rides motorcycles but is the

*president of a motorcycle club. All the power you
hold in your hand and between them thighs might
turn him on."*

I smacked my lips and threw a paperclip at her.
"Whatever."

"Whatever what? You act like his attraction to
you is a bad thing."

"It is for me. You should've seen the way I almost
had to beat his grandma's ass the day I delivered
the motorcycle to their house. It would never
work between us if I was forced to interact with
her on the regular." I shook my head.

"That, I think, was a total misunderstanding or
the old biddie trying to throw some shade. Either
way, didn't you say he stepped in and low-key
checked her ass for being rude?"

I nodded.

"Well see? There you have it. Not too many men
will check their grandmas for a woman they don't
know."

"Yeah, but that was him just—"

"That was him just showing you that he's not
about to allow anyone, including family, to disrespect you in front of him," she cut me off. "If you
ask me, I think he deserves some points for that."

Gideon did deserve points for that, but not
enough to have me fawning over his ass and
falling all in love and shit like Natalie wanted me
to. I got up from my desk and walked over to my
file cabinet, trying to hide the small smile forming

on my face. I'd have been lying if I said I wasn't impressed by the way he handled that whole situation. I'd never tell her that though.

"Oh, snap. Look at you over there smiling and shit. That nigga must've made some kind of impression to have your face lighting up like that," Natalie laughed, busting me out.

"Man." I waved her off. "Ain't nobody over here smiling."

"I can see your reflection through the window, bitch, so stop lying." She laughed harder. "Awwwww. My bestie is about to get some diiiiic-ccck. Heeeeeeey. Let that nigga knock the cobwebs off of that thang, Phil. Don't go too hard, Gideon, when you put it on her," she yelled out while still laughing. "It's been a minute, my nigga!"

"Fuck you, Natalie."

"Fuck me? Nah, don't fuck me. Fuck Gideon's fine ass."

I rolled my eyes and grabbed the clipboard with the work orders off of my desk, giggling at her crazy ass. "See, this is why I don't like telling you shit when it comes to niggas. You always trying to put me in a relationship when it will never happen."

"Why can't it happen?"

I dropped my head and sighed. "Because you already know how I really feel when it comes to that relationship shit regardless of who it is. If a nigga can't move my heart the same way my *bikes do when I'm moving through these streets, nine times out of ten it won't work."*

There were a few seconds of silence before Natalie busted out laughing. "The nigga already has your mind spinning and that pussy of yours thumping. It won't take him long to get to that heart," she joked. Her face turned a bright red from laughing so hard. When her gaze turned to me, I could see the hint of playfulness in her eyes, so I knew what was coming next. "A hundred dollars says you and that nigga Gideon will be fucking and damn near living together by the time your dad's fundraiser is here," she bet.

"A hundred dollars says his ass will be forgotten about by the end of the week," I countered, reclining in my chair.

Natalie was about to open her mouth and say something else, but the phone rang. She took the call from my desk. "Hart of the City, this is Natalie. How can I help you today?" her cheerful voice sang into the receiver. "Uhhhhh, may I ask who's calling?" When her voice changed, I looked up at her. "Oh. Um, just one moment, okay?" She nodded her head with the dumbest look on her face and placed the caller on hold. When she dropped the phone back on the dock, she hopped off of my desk and started twerking.

"What the hell are you so happy about?" I asked, confused by her sudden burst of energy. "Who the fuck is that on the phone, and why are you

dancing like that?" I tried to be serious, but I couldn't do anything but laugh as she stuck her tongue out of her mouth and started twerking harder. *"Natalie!"* I sternly called out, cutting her little celebration short.

"Bitch, I need my money in a crisp hundred-dollar bill when it's time to pay up." She smacked her open palms together. "I can break my own shit."

"Money? What the fuck are you talking about? Who's on the phone?"

She picked up the receiver and handed it to me. "This is for you."

"For me?" Natalie pressed the hold button connecting the call, not giving me a chance to ask her another question. "Uh, this is Philly. How may I help you today?"

"You are a hard woman to get in touch with." A smooth voice floated into my ear. "I've been hitting you up for a minute but can never get a call back or response."

My belly started doing flips. "Gi . . . Gideon?" His silence told me that I guessed right. "How . . . how did you . . . What did . . ."

Natalie started cracking up. "Oh yeah. I'm definitely getting that hundred dollars. Nigga ain't even fucked you yet and got your ass stuttering and shit already." She gathered up her iPad and her can of soda from my desk. "Please have my money by the end of the week. Thank you," she *said over her shoulder as she walked out of my office, still laughing at me.*

I stood over Natalie's gravesite and shook my head at the memory of one of our last conversations, trying not to let my emotions get the best of me. The ground still moist from the dirt being laid over her casket was making it hard. My eyes scanned over the multiple rows of plots that surrounded us. Some spots were manicured and taken care of while others were overrun with weeds and dead floral arrangements from their loved ones. I made a mental note to never allow Nats's space to look like that. She would surely kick my ass in the afterlife if I ever did.

"'In loving memory of Natalie Nicole Sykes. Loved daughter of Harold and Audrey. Loved sister of Philly and loved fiancée of Bryce.'" Wiping at the lone tear that fell from my eye, I read the beautiful gold engraving on the black marble headstone Natalie's mom and I picked out for her. My fingers lightly traced over the picture of Nats's smiling face. I kneeled down and placed the dozen yellow roses I brought into the flower holder and pressed my forehead against the cool marble. With eyes closed and more tears running down my face, I said a silent prayer for my friend's soul and a pleading prayer for my aching heart.

"Baby, wake up. You need to eat something," Gideon rasped in my ear, waking me from my sleep.

I turned over on the couch and stretched my arms above my head. My eyes were still heavy and wet from crying myself to sleep. "How long have I been out?"

"Since last night, so basically for a whole day," Gideon answered, pulling my cover back. "I tried to wake you up a couple times, but you wouldn't budge. Diem came by yesterday and Drea called to talk to you more than a few times, but you were completely out of it."

I finally opened my eyes and was greeted by the most handsome face I'd ever seen in my life. Gideon cracked a smile, and I couldn't help but return the same.

"How you feeling?" he asked, his thumb caressing my cheek before he planted a kiss on my nose and pressed his forehead to mine.

"Better than yesterday and the day before," I admitted honestly. My mind knew Natalie was gone, but my heart wasn't trying to hear that shit.

"Well, you and I both know that it only gets better with time." Gideon softly kissed the bags I knew I had under both eyes before he took a seat next to me on the couch and began removing white containers from the greasy brown paper bag he placed on the coffee table.

"I don't know how many more times I'm gonna say this, but thank you for everything you've done for me, G, since . . ." I trailed off, knowing he would catch on to what I was trying to say. I waved my hands up and down in front of my face in a fanning motion to keep from crying. "I really appreciate it."

He nodded before turning to me. "I told you I got you. I know you're dealing with a lot, but I'm here, and I'll be whatever it is you need me to be whenever you need me to be it. I know I'll never be able to take Natalie's place, but I'd like to be your new best friend, if you'll have me," he said before kissing my forehead gently.

Being his best friend didn't sound like a bad idea at all. Like he said, he could never replace Nats, but I was sure he could help me through the second biggest loss of my life. Hell, he'd been doing that the whole time anyway. Before I could respond, the smell of jalapenos, rice, and very well-seasoned beef started floating in the air, causing my stomach to rumble a little, breaking up our tender moment. Embarrassed, I pulled the blanket back over my body, hoping it would muffle the loud noise if it happened again, and I watched Gideon as he separated each container and opened them up.

The sleeves of his striped shirt were rolled up to his elbows, exposing the titanium bracelet around his wrist and the script tattoo on his forearm. I'd asked him what the passage meant one night when we were chilling and shooting the shit, and he told me that it was a poem he wrote for his mother, who died when he was younger. That small piece of information started a night-long conversation between us about being young and dealing with death as well as learning about all of the things that we had in common.

Gideon popped a tortilla chip in his mouth after dipping it in some guacamole before speaking again. "And you don't have to keep thanking me, Philly. I told you all I wanted was one chance to prove to you that I'm the man you need in your life, and I meant that shit."

I bit my bottom lip and found myself blushing at his declaration. "What makes you so sure I'm the one for you to prove that to?"

Gideon sat back on the couch, the smell of his cologne now surrounding my head. He rubbed his hands up and down his thighs a couple of times in deep thought before turning his attention toward me. "Would you think I was crazy if I told you I felt this weird connection the first time I laid eyes on you?"

I thought about what he said for a second and nodded my head. "I would."

"I figured that." We both laughed. "No, but seriously. There was something about you that drew me in the second you stepped into your lobby and greeted us at your shop. I was digging your style, your aura, and most definitely that right hook of yours. Fucked my boy's face up and everything."

I laughed. "He deserved it though."

"He did," Gideon agreed. Our eyes connected and he licked his lips. "But to keep it real, I felt something I've never felt before with any other female I dealt with when I met you, and I wanted to explore that feeling. Us actually having so much in common was an added bonus." He pointed at the coffee table. "Like our love for Mexican food. Which is the reason I stopped by that little hole-in-the-wall joint we went to by the mall last week. Oh, and before I forget, I made some room in my closet and dresser and put some of your things there. Your vest, helmet, and coveralls are on the coat rack behind the door, and your three sets of keys are in that big bowl on top of the mantel, if you were wondering where your stuff was."

"Oh, damn. I get closet, mantel, and dresser space? Your little girlfriends won't feel some type of way about that, will they?" I joked.

"Philly, you've been here for a little over a month now and haven't encountered one of my 'little girlfriends' yet." He used air quotes. "You come and go as you please and even have a key. If I had a little girlfriend, don't you think your access would be limited?" I shrugged my shoulders, and he shook his head. "I promise you don't have anything to worry about. Between me making sure you're straight and taking care of my businesses, I don't have time to see anyone else, let alone bless them with my time. I was serious when I told you I wanted to see where things could go between us, so those other females became a thing of the past the moment I made that decision."

Damn, it felt good hearing that. I was already questioning what he saw in me considering the type of women he dealt with. I was nothing like them, and although I didn't want to admit it in the beginning, I was feeling the hell out of Gideon, and I wanted him all to myself.

Since the night of the shooting, I'd been staying with him at his apartment in Turnberry Towers. Spending my nights here wrapped in his arms while I grieved was way better than going home to an empty house where memories of Natalie and me would consume my every thought. When this fine-ass man first suggested that I stay with him, I didn't think it was a good idea, seeing as we were just getting to know one another and I was still fighting my attraction to him. But after having the breakdown at the service, I knew that going home was out of the question. Yeah, I could've stayed with Diem or maybe even Pops if I really wanted to, but there was something about being around Gideon that made it a little easier to deal with the loss of my friend. He understood what I was going through, and he knew when I needed time to grieve by myself and when I needed to be comforted and held.

He handed me a plate loaded with green chile barbacoa enchiladas, and my stomach growled again. It had been a while since the last time I ate a full meal. As of late my diet only consisted of vanilla wafers and water, the only things I would eat or drink to satisfy Gideon's mind.

"When are you going out of town again?"

He chewed the food in his mouth and took a sip of his soda. "This weekend. I gotta go up to New York to check on one of my shops and then to Atlanta to see how things are going with the new shop." He took another sip of his drink and then cut his eyes toward me, a small smirk on his lips. "You know, you should come with me. Get out of Vegas for a few days. A change of scenery." He nodded toward the large floor-to-ceiling window. "I know you're tired of looking at this panoramic view of the strip. Even being on the twenty-second floor the shit gets old after a while," he said, sounding just like a rich nigga.

I could never see myself growing tired of his home or this amazing view. However, taking a little vacation away from all of the stress did sound like a good idea. I just didn't think right now was a good time. I still had orders that needed to be worked on and delivered at my shop. Then there was the shit going on with our club and the Dragons. There was no way I could leave my sisters in the middle of a possible war.

"Hey, what's the matter? Why aren't you eating?" Gideon asked, bringing me from my thoughts. "I thought those green chile enchiladas were your favorite."

"They are."

"Then eat," he said, bringing a forkful of the spicy dish to my mouth with his fork. I opened up and took the small serving in, savoring the delicious flavors that danced around on my tongue. I closed my eyes and moaned. When I opened them back up, Gideon was staring at me with a lustful gleam in his eyes.

"Philly, I know I told you that I wanted to take this thing between us slow, but if you keep moaning and pouting those pretty lips like that, I don't know if I'll be able to keep my promise," he said before looking down at his lap. My eyes followed his and landed on the thick print of his dick showing through his jeans. That shit actually made me jump. His face came within an inch of mine, and I could feel his breath lightly pushing against my lips every time he talked.

"Gideon," breathlessly came from my mouth. "I . . . I'm sor—" I tried to get out, but my words were cut off by his lips pressing against mine.

This by no means was our first kiss, but something in this lip-lock felt different. The tenderness he used on the nights he helped me to relieve some of my stress by eating my pussy until I came all over his face and bed was the same tenderness he was using now. All I could say was that the dreams

I'd been having about this nigga didn't come close to the real thing.

The kiss started off with a small and sweet peck and gradually intensified with each passing second. Before I knew what was happening, I felt my body unraveling itself from underneath the blanket I was wrapped up in and straddling my legs over his lap. The bulge in his pants was still there, but it was harder and rubbing against my thigh. Breaking away from the kiss, I let my head fall back, and I enjoyed the feel of Gideon's tongue exploring my neck, shoulder, and chest. My hips started moving on their own, keeping up with the rhythm of our beating hearts. But right when things were about to escalate to another level, our phones started ringing at the same time. Gideon kissed my shoulder one last time before he pressed his head to my chest and groaned. His arms wrapped around my waist, pulling me closer.

"Saved by the bell, huh?"

"Depends on what the bell was saving you from," I returned as I removed myself from his embrace and out of his lap to get my phone. By the time I picked it up to answer, the caller hung up.

"Who was that?" Gideon asked, texting someone on his.

I shrugged my shoulders. "I don't know. They were calling from an unknown number. Who was calling you?"

He played with his phone for a few more seconds. "My grandmother." I cringed at the mention of her. "Probably calling about me coming over for dinner next weekend."

I nodded as I read an incoming group text from Drea.

Onyx: Yo, I think we should make that move this weekend. Just hit the spots Marlon was able to come up with and go from there. What y'all think?

DiDi: I'm down for whatever. But we should make sure Philly's okay with moving. Everything is still fresh with her, and I don't want her judgment getting clouded.

Drea: Clouded? What does that mean?

Me: Yeah. What the fuck does that mean?

Drea: Hey, sis. Gideon's fine ass must be dicking you the fuck down. Your ass don't never answer your phone lmaooo.

I laughed at Drea's crazy ass.

DiDi: Sis, I didn't mean anything by that. You just lost your best friend, so all I'm worried about is you staying focused. Do what we need to do and get the fuck out. No personal vendettas or anything playing out. Just sticking to the plan we already discussed and then figure out our next move later.

I nodded my head as if they could see me, remembering the reason we were doing all of this in the first place. Someone had actually murdered my bestie, and we had to avenge that shit. There was no way we could let this shit go. No fucking way.

"What's wrong?" Gideon asked, coming back from the kitchen and turning on the TV. I could tell by the strong smell of the food again that he had reheated our plates.

"My sisters wanna do that thing I told you about this weekend, but we need a little more information on who we hitting up."

"A little more information like what?" Gideon asked. He already knew a little about what was going on with us and the Dragons. During one of our pillow therapy sessions, I told him all about Hart's Angels and what we currently had going on. Although he didn't too much agree with us going after these assholes ourselves, he accepted that it was a part of the lifestyle I lived and something we had to do.

"We got a couple of addresses to the places in town where they keep some of the guns they traffic through the city, but we can't seem to find the actual location for their main spot they call the Lair. If we can get the drop on where that's located, we will have access to their guns, drugs, money, and everything else they have up in that bitch."

"Hmmm," was all Gideon offered before watching some highlights on ESPN and eating half of his plate. I was still going back and forth with Diem and Drea in our group text when he spoke again. "If you really need someone to get that location for the Lair, I can hook you up with my boy Casey."

"Casey?"

He nodded his head and wiped his mouth with a napkin. "Yeah. My boy is a wiz with the computers and all of that hacking shit. I'm pretty sure he can locate that spot for you."

I stopped texting on my phone and turned my attention to Gideon. "Yo, call him for me right now so I can holla at him real quick."

Gideon shook his head. "Casey ain't cheap, baby. You gotta have some major bread for him to do some work for you, and I'm not talking about a couple of racks either."

I didn't know if I was more offended by Gideon assuming I didn't have money stacked up in my account, or him thinking I was only capable of coming up with a couple racks to offer his friend for his service. Just when I was about to check the fuck out of his ass, Gideon propositioned me with a deal.

"So check it. I know you and your crew really wanna go after these niggas right, and my boy could probably be the key in helping y'all handle y'all business. Now, I'll call my mans and have him come over right now and get that information for you. I'll foot the bill and everything, but only on one condition."

"And what condition is that?"

Gideon hesitated for a second. "I'll get the ball rolling right now if you come with me to my grandparents' house next weekend for dinner."

I stopped chewing the food in my mouth and had a mind to throw back up the shit I already swallowed. Dinner at his grandparents' house? Ahh, hell nah! I vowed to never step foot on that bitch's property ever again, and Gideon knew that. I didn't think I would be able to be as nice as I was the last time. Even if it was a misunderstanding or the bitch throwing a little shade like Natalie said, the shit was still downright rude, and I wasn't going to accept that shit a second time around.

"Aye, Casey said as soon as I transfer the payment in the account, he can be here in fifteen minutes. Do you wanna find this place or just stick with the addresses you already have?" Gideon asked sneakily.

His bribing ass turned his phone screen to me so I could see the conversation between him and Casey. When my eyes scanned over the thread and saw the $10,000 bill he charged for his services, I gave Gideon's invitation to dinner a second thought. I mean, I could afford to pay him that amount and not break a sweat, but did I really wanna pay that for some information I could potentially get later on down the line for free? Deciding to use that ten racks on one of my personal restorations instead, I agreed to go to dinner with Gideon and his grandparents next week and prayed the bitch didn't say anything out the side of her neck again.

"Fine, Gideon."

With a big smile on his face, Gideon sent Casey a few more text messages before telling me that his boy was on his way.

"Does he need any info from me to start his search?" I asked, finishing off the rest of my food as we waited for our guest to arrive.

"Nah." Gideon shook his head. "All he needs is a name to get you tax returns, personal addresses, bank accounts, commercial properties, social security numbers, anything down to their blood type, you name it. That boy Casey is good. You'll see when he gets here. How you think I got all your phone numbers and your security access code to your shop that one time?" He laughed heartily as my eyes widened.

I walked in the back door of Diem's new showroom. The smell of passion fruit lingered in the air. The lights were on, guiding my path down the short hallway and into the main room where my sister was talking to her assistant, who had a stack of boxes in her arms.

"Just put those over there in the corner, Cissy, and we will stock everything up tomorrow."

"What about the other delivery by the door?" she asked, neck straining around the boxes to see Diem's face. When her eyes focused on me, she smiled. "Oh, hey, Philly. I didn't hear you come in."

Diem turned around and nodded her head at me, her eyes taking in the black pants, black tank, and black Tims I had on. My studded helmet was underneath my arm as my skull-face mask hung loosely around my neck.

"How long you been here?" she asked, turning around and scribbling something down on the paper next to the register.

"Not long." I ran my hand through the loose curls at the top of my head, checking out the light-up display cases filled with sex toys, trinkets, and lubes. Curvy mannequins in sexual positions modeled risqué lingerie. "Shit looks good in here, Di. When's the grand opening again?"

"I haven't decided yet. With all this drama I didn't think it would be a good time to have an opening right now. Once shit dies down, then I'll put something together. Until then, come on." She motioned with her head.

I followed closely behind my sister as we passed a few closed doors and rounded the corner to another hallway, where she led me through a set of double doors and into another part of the building. As soon as we stepped into the smaller-scale showroom, Casey looked up from his two laptops and stood.

A small smile was on his lips as his gray eyes bounced back and forth between Diem and me. He stretched his hand out for mine, and I clasped it with his before pulling him in for a shoulder bump and then looking down at the cluttered mess he had spread across the table. When he came by Gideon's house a couple nights ago, at first sight, I was a little skeptical of his skills. I mean, this might be a little shady, but I didn't think his pretty, Ken doll–looking ass could hack into shit. However, he was able to prove me wrong when he not only pulled up my sealed and expunged juvenile record, but he was also able to tell me some information about my mom and grandmother's murder that I didn't know. It was some forensic shit about the scene, but it was something I hadn't come across on my own, so I was sold on him.

"What's this?" I asked, looking down at a blown-up map of Vegas with red markings on it.

"This is the gun shipment route info you wanted and the location for the Dragons' main spot."

"You mean the Lair?" He nodded, a cocky, lop-sided grin on his face. "How did you get that?"

"Easy. By accessing this idiot's text thread and GPS app on his phone. You see right here?" He pointed to a back road near the old Route 66 that I was familiar with. "This is the road the driver takes after he makes a gas stop in Baker. He takes this to avoid highway patrol or any truck jackers who might be up and down the I-15. Once he makes his way to downtown Vegas, he takes a few more twists and turns on back streets only to end up here."

I lowered my face and squinted at the map, trying to make out the streets he was pointing to. "Twain and Paradise?" I rolled my eyes to the ceiling, trying to jog my memory of the area. "Wait, there's nothing there but an old abandoned medical building."

"Old medical building, yes. Abandoned, not so much." Casey typed something on his laptop and then turned it to me, pointing to a document with a list of names. "This is from the bank that initially owned the property. After foreclosing on the original owner, someone by the name of Lukas Coleman purchased it and has been making monthly mortgage payments ever since." He typed something else in his computer, and a video surveillance feed popped up. "This is the real-time security footage in the building now." He clicked through the different camera angles. "I was only able to go back a couple months and look at footage. For the most part, not too much shit goes down here until the second and fourth Saturday of each month." He clicked to a screen where a large moving truck backed up in the parking lot until it reached a big metal gate in the back of the building. We watched as members of the Dragons transferred large crates of drugs, guns, and ammo inside the building from the back of the truck.

"Y'all ready to handle this shit?" Drea asked as she walked into the room followed by Gina, Sandie, Lovely, and a large, hooded figure, obviously not a member of Hart's Angels, dressed in all black the same as us. "Who's the white boy?" She nodded in Casey's direction.

He stood and offered Drea his hand. "I'm Casey."

She shook his hand and looked at me for a more detailed introduction.

"Casey is the dude I told you I was meeting at Gideon's house a couple nights ago. The one who does all that computer hacking, black Internet, illegal shit."

"Ohhhhhh, the nerd?" Drea exclaimed. Everyone in the room giggled except for me. Her eyes flew back to Casey. "You're a little too fine to be one of them brainiacs."

Casey licked his lips, eyes roaming up and down Drea's body. "Well—"

"Drea, please don't make me shoot this nigga too," a deep voice rasped from behind us, causing me to turn around.

"Who the hell are you?" I gripped the handle of my gun, my eyes on the dude who stopped at the door and leaned against the wall, his hoodie covering half of his face. His leg was kicked up with his arms crossed over his broad chest. He chucked his head up at me and smirked.

"My bad," Drea announced, walking back over to dude and sliding her hands down his chest, patting his upper abdomen. "Philly, this is Simmy. Babe, this is my sister Philly. I hope you don't mind this informal introduction, sis, but after the little shootout he and I had the other day, he won't let me out of his sight and insisted on tagging along." She rolled her eyes, but I could tell by the small smile on her face that she didn't mind him being here.

"What shootout?" Diem and I questioned at the same time.

Drea waved us off. "Child, there have been several over the last week, but I'll have to tell you two about that later. Especially if we wanna hit this lick and be back home before midnight."

I nodded in agreement and turned back toward Casey, who was seated back behind his laptop. "Can you pinpoint the driver's exact location right now?"

He hit a few keys. "I can, but I wanted to tell you that this week they are awaiting a larger shipment as well, and it's coming in on a train just a little while after the first truck is set to arrive. Big boxcar full of shit. That's the one I think you guys should intercept," he advised. Casey went on to fill us in on how after they unloaded the boxcar they would then load the items onto an eighteen-wheeler.

"We hitting both them bitches," I said, feeling myself getting hyped.

"You can do that too. I already had a friend of mine set up the small detour the driver is going to have to take to get to Twain once he gets off of the freeway." Casey looked at his watch. "He's going to get there in about an hour with the speed he's driving, so you may want to start heading that way pretty quickly."

I picked up my phone to call Candace and Anique, who were together but running late to the meeting. They were close to the location of the truck, so I would have them follow to handle that while we hit the rail yard for the bigger job. Once I explained to them what needed to be done they headed that way to get in position. With that taken care of, I turned around to the crew and had them gather around me.

"Okay, so we already know what's about to go down. Drea, since you and your bae out here living like Bonnie and Clyde, you two need to be in position here." I pointed at a spot on the map where Candie Girl and Nique would be. "I know they can handle it, but I'd be more at ease with y'all there just in case some unexpected shit pops off.

Once they get control of the truck and whatever's inside, I need y'all to take it to the drop off spot, and Blake will take it from there. Sandie, I need you to stay here after Casey leaves and be our eyes and ears with the police."

She nodded, and I turned to my older sister, who was slicking her thick hair back into a bun. Her outfit was almost identical to mine, except she had on some fancier boots. "Diem, you, me, Gina, and Lovely will take care of the Lair after both shipments are dealt with. The car we're taking is already at the drop-off spot with the jugs of the accelerant in it. Once we get there, we douse the shit, start the fire, and then be out. Anyone have any questions?"

"I do." Lovely raised her hand. "Where will the Dragons be in all of this? I know they should have someone watching the building, right?"

I looked at Casey, and he shook his head. He squinted as he looked at the screen. He pushed his falling glasses up on his handsome face. "They are actually hosting some of their brother chapters at a bar called Hogs & Heifers. Right now, there are only three people at the medical building, or Lair, as you call it, waiting for the trucks to arrive, and there are four at the rail yard. Two are outside the metal gates with some large-caliber automatic guns, and another two are inside. In my opinion, they are slipping big time tonight with a shipment this huge. They should have way more men on hand, but it works in your favor that they don't."

"Automatic weapons? Philly, maybe Simmy and I should go to the yard instead. I know y'all can shoot and shit because y'all learned from the best, but I think my Clyde and I are a little more equipped to handle a gun fight if one breaks out," Drea stepped in.

"You ain't the only one who knows how to handle a gun, sis. I remember saving your ass a few times with my aim too." Drea flipped me off and went back to cleaning her gun.

The heels of Diem's boots clacked against the wooden floor as she walked around the table and behind Casey, her eyes going back and forth between both of his laptop screens. "What's behind that door right there?" She pointed at one of the surveillance feeds. The bangles on her arm sounded like wind chimes with every shake.

Casey stuck a piece of gum in his mouth and then sat back in his chair, folding his hands behind his head. "I'm not sure. For some reason, they don't have cameras behind that door. I've seen a few members go in and out, but I can't see what for."

"Can you bring up a floor plan for the building?" I asked. "Maybe we can see what there is that way."

Casey shook his head. "I already tried that. The Dragons had this room built a couple years ago, without notifying city hall or going through any of the proper channels. There were no permits obtained for the construction and no records on file for what this room actually is."

I went and stood next to my sister, observing one of the armed Dragon members walking into the mystery room and coming out two minutes later. I tried to make out if he was talking to someone over his shoulder when he came out or if there was any kind of light showing from the small crack he walked through, but I couldn't tell. The vengeance in my heart was telling me to just stick to the plan and go light the muthafucka up, take my chances with a shootout and everything, but the sensible side of me decided to take a different route and hold off on torching the place until we figured out what was behind that door. Avenging Nats's death was at the top of my list, but not if it meant I would be putting myself or my crew in harm's way before I had a chance to get it.

I picked up the small communication devices that I had Casey bring in and passed them out, thanking God he thought to bring extra. That way I was able to communicate with everyone within a ten-mile radius if need be. The less we used our cell phones, the better.

"All right, slight change of plans." I addressed everyone as I stood in the middle of the room, pulling my gloves on and tying my skull mask over my face. "Instead of taking down the Lair tonight as originally planned, we'll just intercept their shipments and leave it at that for now. Since we can't see what's behind that door, I don't wanna lead us into something we possibly can't get out of." All heads nodded in agreement. "We go get this truck, grab whatever comes in off that train, and then get ghost. Just stealing this shit will send the message I need it to send and hopefully get me one step closer to finding out who took my best friend."

Pulling my helmet over my head, I didn't miss the look of concern that passed between Drea and Diem. They wouldn't say anything to me right now in front of everyone, but I knew they'd bring it up sometime before the night was over.

I looked at my phone for the time. "Okay. We have a little less than forty-five minutes to get to where we need to be. Once everyone is in position, I'll let you know when it's time to move." My phone vibrated, and I looked down at the screen. I smiled underneath my mask as I read the message Gideon sent.

GBaby: Be safe tonight and come back home to me. See you in a couple days.

Gideon always had a way of being there when I wasn't expecting him to be. Maybe all of that doubt

I had about him was for nothing, like Natalie said. I shook my head thinking about my best friend. *That's another hundred I owe you,* I thought as I stuffed my gun into the back of my pants.

"Any last words for us before we hit this mission, Philly?" Big Gina asked. Her amped voice let me know she was ready to go put in some work.

I thought about her question for a second before I spoke. "Yeah. Only shoot if you have to. We don't need the heat of the police added on to what we're already dealing with," I said over my shoulder as I headed toward the door. "Now let's roll out and remember this is for Natalie."

Chapter 15

Diem

"Can everyone hear me all right?" Philly asked through the earpieces we all had in. "They should be done unloading soon, and we have to be ready. We need to make sure we can all communicate with each other just in case shit don't go as planned."

There was a little static before Drea's voice came through. "Simmy and I can hear you loud and clear from our spot."

My sister and her man, along with Anique and Candace, had already handled their part by securing the first truck. After supervising that situation, they all headed over to make sure we were straight on this end. As we sat here waiting on the truck to pull out, the contents of our first hit was being driven to a location about an hour outside the city.

"Gina and I are good too," Lovely chimed in.

"We're in position, boss lady," Nique responded.

We were all stationed along the route that the big truck would take to get to the Lair for the drop-off. The plan was to take their asses down before they even made it there.

"What about you, Di?" Philly's eyes darted to my spot across the street. When I didn't respond right away, she lifted both of her arms up in the air and started waving them around.

"I can see and hear you just fine, Philly," I responded absently while responding to Ky's text. Between him working overtime on his project and me trying to get the new warehouse together, we hadn't been able to spend much time together. I had to admit that I missed being in his company, and I couldn't wait to see him again. Texting and calling just didn't seem to be enough.

"Please don't tell me you're over there working when you need to be focused on the task at hand. And you were the main one concerned about me being distracted," she pointed out.

I rolled my eyes and slipped my phone into my back pocket. "If you must know, I was not working. Kyrie texted me and I—"

"Kyrie, huh?" she cut me off. "That's even worse, Di." Philly sighed. "Yo, I'm happy you got a man and all to get your uptight ass to relax a little and have some fun, because Lord knows we've tried for years, but right now is not the time. This is big-girl business, so I need all of your attention to be on what we got going right now, sis. I know this is supposed to be a clean job, but you never know what can happen when it comes to unstable niggas like the ones we're dealing with. Especially with the amount of shit we about to snatch from them. I need you to get Kyrie out of your mind for a second and just be here with us, please. If something happens to you, man—" she drawled out, but I stopped her.

"I hear you, Philly. I hear you, and I'm focused now. My phone is silenced and put away," I told her.

Normally I would have cursed her out or put up more of a fight when she tried putting me in my place, but these days I wasn't for all the fussing and going back and forth. I was on some Zen, "Can't we all just get along?" type shit. Fuck all the extras. I thought that getting good dick on the regular was mellowing my ass right on out.

"So while we wait, Anique, finish telling us about Candace and the passenger dude in the commercial truck," Philly requested with a chuckle. I laughed too, and I was sure everyone else did as well.

"O-M-G, I swear I can't take her hot ass any-where! She was really spitting game to the nigga, y'all. Telling him how we don't mean no harm and we're only following orders. How if he wanted to he could call her once all this mess was straight-ened out. I'm like, what the fuck? We jacking this man's whole truck and I'm sure he's going to be held responsible for it. Maybe even killed, but you talking about hooking up when things get ironed out? Bitch, are you serious?" Nique burst out laughing.

"Forget y'all! You bitches didn't see how fine this man was. I'm talking big fine, at least six feet seven, with muscles every-fucking-where. I was rubbing all on his ass once we had him tied up, and not once did he protest," she bragged.

"He couldn't do much protesting being tied the fuck up, Candie girl!" Lovely joked while we all chortled in unison at Candace's expense. She was always doing some crazy shit when it came to these men, and it was funny as hell. The funniest part was that she couldn't care less. If she saw a dude she wanted, she was going for it no matter the situation.

"Aye, y'all hear that?" Big Gina interrupted as the sounds of the train started up again.

"Yup, yup. Our shipment has been loaded and is ready for the taking," I answered, already claiming what was theirs as ours.

"I want everybody to stay put for a moment. Don't make a move until you get the word from me," Philly directed as we watched the truck exit the now-open metal gates. No one responded, letting our silence answer for us. I was just about to say the same thing, but I was glad I held back. This was Philly's show, and I was allowing her to run it without interference from me. "We're going to let them think they're in the clear for the first five miles or so. We don't want them to be close enough to the yard to call for backup. Once they reach that second checkpoint, we'll do our thing.

Nique and Candie Girl, that means that you two need to be ready and waiting."

"We got you," Candace answered.

She was the only one equipped to operate the truck because she had her CDL, which was the reason Philly positioned them there. They would play the same damsel-in-distress routine just as they did with the other truck driver to get him to pull over, and they'd go from there.

"From what I can see there's only one person in the truck, and that's the driver, so you two shouldn't have a problem taking him down. Remember, don't shoot unless it's absolutely necessary. Strip him of any weapons or cell phones then toss his ass out. Let his bitch ass walk back to the yard. By the time he makes it back to tell them what went down, we'll be long gone."

"We're going to pull out last, sis," Drea came across. "Just like we planned, we're going to leave them with something to let them know exactly who they need to look for to get their shit back. They are going to fucking lose it when they walk out to see their property covered in these miniature halos with our club logo," she giggled, making us all laugh as we pulled off one by one.

The night went off without a hitch, which was a big relief. No one was hurt, and we sent the message we needed to send. Now, all we had to do was prepare for the aftermath. It wasn't a thing to us because the Angels stayed ready for whatever.

"Babe, stop playing and show 'em to me," Kyrie begged as he pulled me closer to him by my thick thighs. He was reclining in his desk chair, and I was perched on the desk in front of him with my legs spread wide under my polka-dot midi skater skirt. All I had to do was slide down and I'd be straddling his lap. "We don't even gotta fuck, just let me suck on 'em real quick."

His voice was dripping with lust, and I wanted so badly to grant his request, but I resisted. It wasn't like we hadn't fucked in his work trailer on multiple occasions, but there was something akin to a gut feeling telling me that now just wasn't the time.

"No, Kyrie. Someone might walk innn," I squealed in delight as he slipped his hand under my skirt and into my thong underwear. We'd been getting it in every chance we got, and his ass knew how to manipulate my clit in a way that would have me busting within minutes. "Shit, Ky."

"Diem, why you acting brand new? Ain't nobody coming in here. You act like I didn't have you face down on this very desk just two days ago. Not to mention numerous times on that couch over there, so what's the big deal with me getting some nipple action?"

"I know but—"

"But nothing. Shit, you wet as fuck. I changed my mind. I want some pussy now," he groaned, speeding up his finger motions.

When I say that the moment, I mean the exact moment he went for his belt buckle and I went to remove my blazer, the door to his trailer was being opened. Startled, he quickly retracted his hand and pulled my skirt down to cover up my goodies. Both of our faces were screwed up as we turned to give the unwanted guest a piece of our minds, but we stopped short when our eyes landed on none other than Julian Hart.

"Oh, umm. Hey, Dad, hey," I stammered, not knowing what the fuck else to say.

"Diem, get your fast ass off this man's desk!" he fussed with a disapproving scowl.

"Yeah, Diem. Get up off my desk," Kyrie blurted, as he discreetly adjusted his hard-on and wiped his wet hand on his slacks to remove my juices.

I couldn't believe he completely threw me under the bus like he wasn't the one begging to suck my titties not even a minute earlier. All I was trying to do was stop by with lunch for my man, and he ended up trying to molest me then gon' act like he wasn't the aggressor when we got caught. I swear niggas ain't shit.

"I bet yo' ass won't be getting no pussy tonight," I said in his ear as I hopped off the desk and snatched my purse up.

"I bet I do," he countered cockily before he stood from the chair and addressed my father. "Afternoon, sir. What brings you by?"

"Diem, go speak to your mom while I discuss some business with Kyrie. She's waiting in the car," my father ordered, still shaking his head at me.

I didn't know why he was so shocked. It wasn't the first time he'd caught me in a compromising position with the opposite sex. Only difference was that I was grown now, and he couldn't beat the hell out of me and Kyrie like he'd done to Dylan and me when he caught us fucking around in the guest house when I was sixteen.

"And don't leave, because I want to speak with you regarding that stunt you and your sisters pulled at that rail yard a few nights ago," he said, causing my eyes to buck. "No need to look at me crazy. You already know what the hell I'm talking about," he said in response to the clueless guise I attempted.

"Fine," I grumbled. I pushed up the sleeves to my blazer and tousled my curls. "I'll be outside."

I wasn't at all surprised that he'd already gotten wind of the jack move we pulled on the Dragons, but what could he do besides curse us out? What was done was done, and now we were playing the waiting game. Either they would retaliate or contact us for a sit-down. We were very deliberate with the move we made, wanting to leave no question as to who was behind the stolen shipments of dope and guns. There wasn't shit we could do with the drugs because that wasn't our area of expertise, and no one other than Drea and that crazy fool she was dealing with had use for the weapons. Still, we planned to hold on to their shit as a tool to negotiate with the Dragons. If it turned out that they were indeed the ones coming for us, then we'd proceed with the second part of our plan and burn that entire fucking Lair down to the ground no matter who or what was inside. Then we would let Onyx and Marlon loose on their asses and allow them to pick them off one by one until there wasn't a single Dragon member left.

Walking down the stairs of the trailer, I looked through the front window of my father's car parked out front and noticed it was empty. I scanned the area trying to spot my mother, but she was nowhere to be found. I just knew her siddity ass wasn't over there using one of the portable restrooms. I had to laugh for even thinking something so silly. She would hold her pee for hours before ever setting foot in one of those musty things, and that much I was sure of. Deciding to walk around a little to see if I could find her, I happened upon a familiar face.

"Hey, Sammy! You out here working hard or hardly working?" I yelled to the handsome young intern.

He turned to the sound of my voice and smiled broadly when he saw it was me who was giving him a hard time. If his ass had been just a few years older, I probably would have let him eat me out like he'd been requesting to do since the first day we met at my father's office. He was looking like a young snack in his construction work clothes, with the reflective yellow vest and hard hat.

"What's up, Diem. You look great as usual." He smiled, tucking his clipboard in the crease of his arm while looking me up and down seductively.

"Don't I though?" I boldly concurred, my confidence causing his grin to widen.

"When you gon' stop playing and let me come through?" he flirted, decreasing the distance between us before tugging at the hem of my jacket.

"Sammy, you're so cute." I shook my head in amusement, failing to answer his question. I needed to stop teasing this boy because he really thought he had a chance, and if Kyrie walked up on us, he was liable to curse me out and remove Sammy from this job.

"I see how it is. You done got cozy with the boss man so now the kid can't get no play, huh?" I only shrugged in response. "It's all good. You still fine as hell though. Just like your moms. Y'all damn near dressed alike and everything today."

"Where did you see her?" I asked. The plan to entertain him while he continued to spit his game was cut short. My interest piqued at the mention of my mother.

"Over by that small work shed." He pointed about 150 feet beyond the trailer we were standing in front of. Without offering a response or a thank-you, I began to move in that direction.

"Yo, Diem, wait up!" he called, but I kept moving.

"Where the hell is she," I mumbled when I didn't immediately see her. It was when I went for the handle on the door that I faintly heard her speaking. I walked around the shed and found her standing with her back to me with her phone up to her ear.

"He's getting suspicious," she said before pausing. "What do you mean someone saw us together? No, I don't think he knows about that. Look, that's not what I called you about. I called so that you could reach out to your contact and let him know that I won't tolerate any more mistakes. I paid him good money, so I want this done soon, and I want it done right. No fuckups. Make sure he's clear on the location. . . ." Her voice trailed off at hearing my heels crunching against the gravel as I tried moving closer to get a better listen. "I'm going to have to call you back," she spoke into her phone before disconnecting the call then turning to face me. "Diem, sweetie, is everything okay?" she asked, not missing a beat.

"What the hell was that all about?" I asked.

"It was a personal call, Diem. By the way, it's extremely rude to eavesdrop. I know I raised you better than that," she scolded.

"I don't give a fuck about being rude. I want to know who the hell you were talking to and what you were talking about," I demanded.

The part of the conversation that I was able to hear didn't sit too well with me. Why the hell did she have to come way over here just to talk on the phone if she wasn't on no bullshit? Who the hell was she seen with? If I found out she was cheating on my daddy, I was going to help him throw her ungrateful ass out along with all of her shit.

"Diem Hart, you better watch your mouth when you speak to me. I am your mother, and I'm about sick of you and your disrespect. Who the hell do you think you are to demand to know who I'm speaking with and what my call was in reference to?" she scoffed.

"That's fine. Since you're so reluctant to share I'll just go ask Pop if he can shed some light on your little private conversation," I threatened. The look on her face when those words left my mouth let me know that she was definitely up to something. It wasn't the look of someone innocent.

"Diem, don't." She grabbed my arm to prevent me from walking away. "You can't tell your father."

"And why the hell can't I?" I roughly snatched my arm away.

"Because you'll ruin the surprise if you do. You do recall that his sixty-third birthday is fast approach-ing, and I want to do it up big for him this year," she replied, causing me to relax my mean mug a little. "Last year he wasn't feeling it and wanted to keep the celebration low-key, remember? I went along with it to satisfy him, but this year I won't hear of any of that nonsense. I want my man to be celebrated in the grandest of ways, so I hired an event planner to bring my vision to life. It's going to be one of the biggest parties Vegas has seen in a while." She clapped excitedly.

I wasn't sure if she was excited because she genuinely wanted to make Pops feel special on his birthday or because she was going to be spending tons of his money. I swore that was her favorite pastime.

"Mm-hmm, but you didn't think to include me and my sisters in the planning?" I questioned.

"DiDi, be for real. You hardly tolerate me, and these days I'm lucky if I can get Drea on the phone. And you know Philly holding a conversation with me is out of the question, so I didn't bother trying to include you three." She shrugged sadly.

"Oh, you may as well hang that up. With the things you've said and done to Philly over the years, there is no way she'll talk to you."

"I know I haven't always been the most welcoming and nurturing where she was concerned, but I'm trying to change that. I was in a bad place when I found out about your father's affair, and I didn't react the way I should have. By choosing to stay I should have accepted Philly fully, but my heart hadn't healed from the betrayal. I wasn't ready to move on, but I also had a hard time playing mother to his love child. As the adult in the situation, I should have handled it differently, but I didn't, and I'm sure that's something I'll regret for the rest of my life. I'm hoping that one day she and I can sit down and have a heart-to-heart conversation. Hell, I even hope one day you and I will work out our differences and become closer. I know you're a daddy's girl, but I do love you, Diem. You're my oldest baby," she concluded, pulling a small smile from me.

It felt good hearing my mother say she wanted to change her ways and improve her relationship with all of us. One of the main reasons she and I butted heads so much was her poor treatment of Philly. Well, that and her gold-digger traits. That shit irked me to no end. My sister didn't deserve the cold shoulder she received from Sole, and I was glad my mother was finally recognizing that. Feeling a connection to her for the first time in a long time, I walked over to her and took her hands into mine.

"I know I don't show it, but I love you too, Mom. I mean you work my last nerve, but I do love you." I tossed in the joke to lighten the mood.

"Oh, Diem!" she squealed and hugged my neck tight. "Do you know how long it's been since you said those three words to me?"

"Kill the dramatics. It wasn't that dang long ago," I groaned.

"Child, I remember it like it was just yesterday. You were about fifteen ye—"

"Maaaa!" I laughed dramatically. She was always over the top. I did recall a time when we had a pretty good relationship, but somewhere along the journey she'd switched up, and I wasn't feeling it.

"Okay, okay!" she chuckled. "I really am going to do better, Diem. For your father and for you girls. And when I say you girls, I mean Philly as well. I have a feeling that things will soon be looking up for the Harts. Once all this mess is handled with these lizard Dragon people, I'm hoping our family will grow closer and even stronger," she said, gripping my hand.

"Ma, what you know about some Dragons?" I playfully side-eyed her as we began the short walk back to Kyrie's work trailer.

"Not much, but I hear things." She smirked.

"Damn spy. And got the nerve to get on me about eavesdropping," I teased, making her giggle.

"Can you blame me? Y'all don't tell me shit," she pouted as we watched my father descend the stairs of Kyrie's trailer.

The angry look in his eyes from earlier was replaced with something I couldn't quite read. I glanced toward the door at Kyrie and saw there was a mask of guilt covering his. I had no idea what the hell that was all about.

"You ready to let me have it or nah, Pops?" I joked uneasily.

"No, baby girl, that can wait," he said, closing in on me. When he placed his hands on both sides of my face and placed a kiss on my forehead, I knew what was up. "I wanna see you tomorrow afternoon at my office for lunch. I'm not taking no for an answer, so just be there at our usual time," he spoke softly as he held me tightly in his arms.

I couldn't decide if I wanted to blow the hell up or bust out crying right now. The look I was giving Kyrie as my father embraced me had him shook. Nigga looked like he was about to run back into his trailer and lock the door. I was joking earlier when I told him he wasn't getting any pussy, but I was so fucking for real about that shit right now. When Pops released me, my mother moved in for a parting hug, a look of concern gracing her lovely face.

"Is everything okay, Julian?" I heard her whisper as she sank into the plush seats of the Bentley.

"We'll talk later, dear," he replied low before closing her door.

As soon as they pulled off, I was stomping to my car as best I could with these high-ass heels on. With the way every joint in my body was aching I knew better than to wear these shoes in the first place.

"Diem, wait!" Kyrie yelled in a panicked voice.

"Fuck you, Ky. You had no right!" I shouted as I hit the lock to my truck with my key fob.

"Baby, please. It kinda just slipped," he tried to explain as he grabbed me by my waist from behind. "He was grilling me about where our relationship was going and if I was treating you right.

Of course, I let him know how I felt about you, but I also voiced my concerns regarding the amount of pressure he places on you and how it affects your health."

"I told you that I planned to discuss my diagnosis with them when I was ready. It wasn't your place to do that." My voice cracked as I tried to open my truck door only for him to close it just as quickly.

The last thing I needed was people feeling sorry for me. I hated that shit. I was Diem Hart, baby, and I was tough as fucking nails. I was way too solid to let some dumb-ass autoimmune disease slow me down.

"Look, I know I fucked up, but I care about you. I let my ego cloud my judgment. I mean he practically hooked us up but then turns around and suggests that I could possibly distract you from your responsibilities." He ran his hand down his face in frustration.

"He said that?" I turned to face him in surprise.

"Not outright but practically in so many words. I mean we have been spending a lot of time together, and I guess I just let his accusation get to me," he replied while pressing his forehead against mine. "Do you feel like I'm a distraction, Diem?" His brown eyes searched mine for the truth.

Sighing deeply, I replied, "No, Kyrie. You're not a distraction. If anything I'm less stressed when I'm with you." He released a breath of relief before covering my lips with his in a passionate kiss. He never failed to take my breath away when he did that.

Pulling back before we got too caught up, I told him, "Those lips of yours ain't getting you off the hook, Kyrie. I'm still upset with you for telling my business."

"I know, baby, and I promise to make it up to you. I'll be your personal chef and sex slave until you decide to forgive me, and I don't care how long it takes. How does that sound?" he rasped seductively in my ear.

Now that was something I could get with. In the time we'd been seeing each other, I'd learned that Kyrie could cook his ass off, and the dick was beyond incredible. He'd fucked up with the promise he just made. He was about to be fucking and feeding me until further notice. Now I just had to prepare myself for this lunch with my dad as well as telling my sisters what was going on with me.

Chapter 16

Gideon

The sun was shining bright as I hopped out of my truck, grabbed my bag, and headed straight into my shop. I'd caught a late-night flight from New York back to Vegas last night and hadn't been to sleep yet. My body and mind were both tired as hell, but when you owned multiple businesses, it was hard to sit still while there was money out there to be made.

"What's up, G! I wasn't expecting to see you today," my lead barber, Darren, greeted me as I fist bumped his hand and pulled him in for a shoulder hug. I pulled back from his grip and looked around the shop, giving the rest of my barbers and some of the regulars a quick nod. The sandalwood scent of the shaving cream floated in the air while the sounds of the clippers buzzed. The old-school station played some classics as the customers clowned around.

"I just got back not even an hour ago, man. Jumped in my truck that was parked at the airport and came straight here. No change of clothes or nothing," I said, looking down at my slouch military boots, dark-washed rider jeans, and black V-neck T-shirt I still had on from the night before.

"Oh, yeah?" He eyed my outfit. "Could've fooled me, walking in here looking like a little bit of money. I know for a fact them boots and them jeans ran you a few bills, because I have the same ones," Darren joked, and we shared a laugh. "But for real though, G, you could've gone home to get some rest. We ain't doing shit up here."

I ran my hand over my face and shook my head. "Nah. I needed to check on y'all and handle some shit before I went home. And you know my motto: I can sleep when I'm dead."

"Spoken like a true business owner," Darren commented, turning his client around in his chair to face the mirror. "And speaking on handling some shit, your boy just walked out of here about ten minutes ago. Told me to tell you that he'd be back in an hour tops."

I already knew he was talking about Kyrie because he sent me a text about him leaving before I got here. "Oh yeah? Did he let one of the fellas line him up?" I asked, already knowing the answer to that question. I dropped my bag on the floor at my feet and sat down in the open chair next to Darren's station.

"Hell nah. You know that nigga wasn't about to let anybody but you fade him up." Darren nodded toward one of my new barbers. "But the newbie over there did try his luck."

I pulled my buzzing phone out of my pocket and replied to the text message I'd just received from Philly.

MyBaby: Can we postpone tonight? I really don't feel like dealing with Cruella.

The dig she took at my grandmother made me laugh. This girl didn't give a damn what came out of her mouth most times.

Me: Everything is going to be okay. You already know I got your back.

MyBaby: You've shown that a lot lately. Maybe we could stay in, order some food, and I can finally show you how much I appreciate you having my back.

I shifted in my seat to try to hide my dick, which was getting harder by the second. Just the thought of her showing me her gratitude was turning me on.

Me: You got my shit brick hard right now in a shop full of niggas. Stop saying shit like that.

MyBaby: LOL. My bad. Maybe you should come to my shop and let me take care of that. I'm here by myself. Always had a fantasy to get fucked on my bike. Maybe you could make that happen.

Me: It will happen, sooner than you think. Until then, let me handle my business here, and I'll see you later tonight.

MyBaby: Okay. Oh, before I forget, Simmy should be on his way up there. Play nice. I don't wanna have to kill my sister's man for fucking with mine.

MyBaby: I mean for fucking with you.

I smiled at her little recovery attempt but ignored it. I also made a mental note to be on the lookout for this nigga Simmy. Philly did mention her and her sisters wanting Ky and me to meet this dude during one of our nightly conversations, but I forgot all about it. We'd all be traveling to New Orleans together for some bike shit down there in a few months, so she wanted us to be familiar with each other. I had so much other shit on my mind, including Philly and this dinner at my grandparents', that it slipped my mind. Hopefully the nigga got here within the next couple of hours. If not, I guessed we would have to meet some other time.

"My nigga, are you listening to the story?" Darren waved his hand in my face.

After sending one last message to Philly and confirming that the payment I sent to Casey was received, I tucked my phone into my pocket and turned my attention back to the conversation. "My bad. My bad. I had to respond to that text."

"Awww shit. You had to respond to that text. Somebody done got my boy pussy whipped. Who is the lucky lady?"

"Man, none of your damn business. Now can we get back to the newbie asking my boy to sit in his chair? How did that go?"

The shop went quiet before rolling into a fit of laughter. Darren looked at me and smirked. "We gon' come back to you and this new lady in your life. But as for him?" He nodded in the young barber's direction. "Nigga got turned down like a bitch! I think he had tears in his eyes and everything."

I laughed. "Cut him some slack. He had no way of knowing that Ky only trusts these hands to hook him up." I stood from the chair, taking the focus off of the embarrassed newbie, and I addressed the small lobby area overcrowded with customers. "Speaking of which, which one of you needs a cut right now? My chair is empty, and I have a few minutes before my next head rolls through, so I can hook at least one person up."

Hands and bodies shot up in the air as shouts of "me" and "I do" began to echo throughout the shop. I scanned over the crowd of men until my eyes landed on a cat sitting in the corner with his hood over his head, playing on his phone.

"What's up with you? You waiting on a certain barber, or you just chilling and enjoying the show?"

He moved his phone from in front of his face and sat up in his seat, the two diamond studs on each nostril blinging when the small ray of light seeping through the blinds hit them. His low eyes looked at me and then traveled to everyone around the room before focusing back on his phone.

"I'm good," was all he said.

"You good?" Darren asked, removing the cape from his client and brushing the excess hair from off his neck. "My man, you've been posted in here since we opened and haven't sat in a chair to get your haircut yet. Either you get serviced, or you get gone." Darren pointed at the sign above the door. "There's no soliciting or hanging out here. If you need somewhere to chill, then you need to walk your ass down the street to one of them titty bars or casinos and do it there. This is a barbershop, not a chill spot."

I was just about to add on to Darren's comment when the door to the shop opened up and Kyrie walked in. As if on cue, the song "Wipe Me Down" by Lil Boosie started playing, and the biggest smile formed on his face, cutting through the building tension that was forming between the shop and the nigga sitting in the corner with the hood on.

"This our shit right here, Nupe," Ky yelled out before he started strolling and shimmying his way farther into the shop. Darren, me, and a couple of our other brothers joined the line and did our thing right there in the middle of my spot, while everyone else cheered and laughed at us doing our thing. By the time the song ended and our shoulders stopped moving, half of the shop was trying but failing to imitate our steps.

"What's up, man?" Kyrie asked as we embraced in a brotherly hug. "I ain't seen you in a minute. Where the hell you been?"

I wiped my hand down my face and sighed. "A nigga been everywhere, bruh. I've got so much shit going on right now, I ain't had a minute to myself."

"Word? I feel you, because I've been the same way. Everyday something new pops up with this construction deal, but it ain't shit I can't handle."

I walked over to the chair I vacated a second ago and kicked my bag out of the way so that Ky could take a seat. "Aye, man, congrats on getting that contract. I forgot to tell you that the last time we hung out. I know you wanted it bad."

"I did," Ky admitted, taking his seat. Placing some tissue around his neck, I wrapped the cape around next and then reclined his chair some. "It's a stressful job, but I'm glad Knight trusted me with it. I just hope he's happy with everything once it's all done. Doing this could really sky-rocket Anderson Construction. I mean, we weren't lacking with jobs or anything like that prior, but doing this," he said, shaking his head, "this could be the start of me branching out and being on my bicoastal shit like you."

"You say you want that shit now, but having businesses in other states is a hassle. Especially when you start dating or get into a relationship. Speaking of which, how are things with you and Diem?"

He smiled as my blade gilded against his face, giving his beard the perfect lineup. "Man, Diem. That's my baby right there. We doing good so far. We're both busy as hell, but we make it work. At first it was kind of hard with our schedules and her being so obsessed with her businesses, but everything is cool now." He paused for a second. "What about you and Philly? Is she still taking her friend's death hard? How does she like living up in that deluxe apartment in the sky?"

"Philly's good," I honestly replied and smiled.

Thinking about that text earlier had my dick shifting to the left again. It had been a week since the last time I physically saw her, and I couldn't wait until I laid eyes on her tonight. We FaceTimed a few of the days that I was gone, but that didn't compare to actually being in her presence and inhaling her scent or being able to kiss her soft lips or touch her smooth skin.

"Look at you up here grinning and shit just hearing her name. Let me find out my boy done up and fell in love with my girl sister. I bet you ran home to see her as soon as you landed, huh?"

"Nah." I shook my head. "I wanted to but had to come up here and check on some things. I'll see her later on this evening though. We're having dinner at my grandparents' house tonight."

"Aw shit. Will this be her first time meeting Grands?"

I turned the chair around and started lining up the other side of Kyrie's face. "Nah, this won't be her first time meeting Grands. It will be the first time she meets Gramps though."

"That's what's up, G. Aye, did Philly tell you what time this nigga Simmy supposed to be here to meet up with us? I can't be here all day. I still got to do some work on the site."

I shook my head. "I forgot all about meeting him until Philly just text me and reminded me. Said he would be here in a few." I shrugged my shoulders. "Diem didn't say anything?"

"Nah, I asked her last night, and she said that he would be here by the time I got here, but I haven't seen anyone who looks like the nigga she described. Maybe he changed his mind."

"Maybe." I shrugged.

Ky and I shot the shit with each other for about an hour before I was finished giving him the five-star treatment and showing everyone in the shop why he and the celebrities I had as clients allow only me to cut and style their hair. There was still no sign of this nigga Simmy, and I was starting to think that he was going to be a no-show.

"Now do you see that, newbie?" Darren said while pointing at Kyrie, who was looking at himself in the mirror. "This is why that man denied you earlier when you asked him to have a seat in your chair. You see how sharp his lineup is and how beautiful that fade is cut. You gotta have the Midas touch to do some shit like that and you, my brother, being fresh out of barber college, just ain't on that level yet. As a matter of fact, why don't you try to get him in your chair." Darren pointed to the dude with the hood over his head still sitting in the corner. "Maybe he'll let you line him up since he ain't got his ass in anyone else's chair yet. Aye, bro, you should let my mans over here hook you up. I can't tell what you have all under that hood, but I'm sure he can't mess you up any further than what you already are."

"I see you one of them funny niggas." Dude shook his head.

Darren looked around the shop and smiled. "Well, I am known as the one who likes to clown around here. Don't take what I say too serious, bruh. It's all in fun, especially if I can get someone to finally sit in the rookie's chair."

Everyone in the shop laughed, including the newbie, but all that stopped when the hooded dude spoke again.

"I'm not your bruh, you ugly black muthafucka, so I'd appreciate it if you wouldn't address me as such."

Darren looked at me and then turned his attention back to dude. "Who the fuck you talking to like that?" he asked, removing his apron from around his neck and handing it to the client in his chair. "I said I was just fucking around, but if you wanna get disrespectful, we can easily make this a serious situation."

Ol' boy licked his lips and smirked before standing up from his seat and removing his hood, revealing his full face. My eyes scanned this nigga from head to toe, taking in every tattoo on his head, face, and neck. I didn't recognize him from anywhere and wondered who the fuck he really was.

"Aye, yo—" I started to say but got cut off when the door to the shop opened, grabbing my attention as well as everyone else's.

The shop went deathly quiet as two huge biker dudes dressed in all black walked in as if they owned the place, their eyes taking in everyone who was staring back at them. I raised my head as if to say "what's up," but I didn't get a response. The larger of the two men gathered his dark, wavy hair to the nape of his neck, and placed it in a ponytail before tightening the red bandana around his head. Dragon tattoos decorated every inch of their shirtless bodies, just like the different patches that covered their vests. Big guy's hard eyes scanned every face in the shop until they got to me. Chucking his chin up in my direction, both bikers walked farther into the shop until they were standing directly in front of my chair.

"Gideon, right?" the big one asked, crossing his large arms over his chest.

"Who wants to know?" I placed the brush that was in my hand on the counter next to my blades.

He looked at his friend and laughed. "Yeah, you're Gideon. I remember that pretty little face from the picture I was given." When he didn't get the reaction he wanted from me after his comment, he continued, "I got a message for your little bitch and her Angels that I need you to relay."

"Bitch?"

He smirked. "Must've touched a nerve with that one. But tell Philly she better return the shit she and her sisters stole from us or else."

I walked into his personal space. My fist was already balled up and ready to connect to his jaw if he disrespected Philly one more time. "Or else what?"

"Or else we're going to start knocking those bitches off one by one," he said through gritted teeth.

Before I could react to his threat, the sound of glass shattering rang out through the whole shop, causing everyone sitting next to the windows to run for cover. With my attention now focused on the customers who were covered in glass, big dude took that as the opportunity to swing on me, but he missed. His large body slammed against mine, knocking me into the station behind me and smashing the mirror. Pushing him off of me, I hit his big ass with a three-piece combo before dodging his attempt to fight back, and I ended up hitting him with two more.

"G, watch your back!" Ky yelled as more bikers came running into the shop with bats, heavy gate chains, and metal pipes, destroying all of my hard work and attacking some of the barbers and customers still there.

I grabbed my blades and started slicing every muthafucka who stepped in my way or I caught fucking up my shit. Chairs were overturned, mirrors were shattered, and majority of the barbers' equipment, including mine, was being destroyed. All of my storefront windows were busted out, and there was blood as well as a few unconscious bodies on the floor. We were getting the best of the few bikers left in the shop when another wave of these assholes came in, trying to finish off what the first round didn't. I hadn't been fully informed on why they were here, but I knew with the mention of Philly's name that it had something to do with whatever Casey helped her and the rest of her MC crew do the other night.

I had just tackled one of the muthafuckas who was trying to double team Ky down to the ground when the sound of gunshots rang through the air. My fist continued to pound into the face of the man underneath me, while the rest of the shop froze.

"I'm going to give you muthafuckas to the count of five to get the fuck up out of this shop. After that, I'm doming everybody still in here. One!" the hooded dude in the corner shouted as he kept the gun he just fired aimed to the ceiling with his right hand, while he scanned the shop back and forth with the gold-plated Beretta in his left hand.

One by one the niggas who invaded my shop began to leave with threats to me about Philly returning their shit. By the time the last person made his way out, there were only Kyrie, Darren, me, and a couple other barbers left. The sound of the police sirens in the distance was getting closer by the second. I pushed myself off of the ground and noticed shards of broken glass embedded in my palms and knuckles stained with crimson hues. Flexing my jaw, I winced at the pain that radiated in my face from the hard hit I took from one of the bikers. Kyrie and I looked at each other and nodded a silent thank-you for having each other's back like we always did. I turned to face the hooded dude and was shocked to see his gun now aimed at me.

"If you gon' shoot me, my nigga, then do it. But before you do, I just need to know one thing. Who the fuck are you?" I pressed my hand to my shoulder and rolled it back. It wasn't dislocated, but I had some pain.

He hopped down from the chair he was standing on and placed his guns in the waistband of his pants. His hand smoothed over his tattooed head and jawline before he extended it to me.

"Simmy."

My eyes widened as his name registered in my head. "So you're Drea's—"

He nodded with a proud grin. "Yeah, I'm Drea's. And you must be Philly's."

"I am." I pointed over my shoulder at Kyrie. "And that's . . ."

"Diem's," we all said at the same time with a chuckle.

"Nigga, why you ain't speak up when you first came in here?" Kyrie walked over and asked. The broken glass on the ground crunched with every step.

Simmy looked around at the fight's aftermath and shook his head. "Had to feel you niggas out first. To keep it real, I really didn't want to meet you muthafuckas. I'm not the type of cat who needs to make friends, you feel me? Only doing this as a favor for my lady."

"A favor?" Kyrie laughed. "Man, if Drea's anything like Diem, I know her ass probably threatened to cut off that pussy play. Only reason I agreed to this little meet and greet, to be honest, is because Diem's ass did."

The corner of Simmy's mouth turned up, but the nigga never reacted or admitted to that being his reason for showing up either. The moment turned awkward for a second, but I spoke up and steered the conversation we were starting to have into a different direction.

"Nice meeting you, fam. Again, I'm Gideon, and this is Kyrie, my brother. Thanks for having my back and clearing them niggas out of here before shit got worse," I said, finally shaking his hand. Simmy nodded his head and turned around, assessing the other damage at the back of the shop. I wanted to ask him a few more questions about himself, but I got interrupted when all of our phones started ringing at the same time. Simmy answered his, and so did Kyrie. I wanted to answer mine but chose to send Philly to voice mail instead. I was pretty sure all the sisters had already heard about what happened and wanted to see if we were all okay, but with the police pulling up, I just wanted to deal with them before I had to deal with Philly's concerns.

"Gideon, darling, I wish you would let me call Dr. Samuels over here to look at your face. I can't believe someone tried to rob your shop," my grands fussed as she held an ice pack to my jaw. Because of my dark skin, you couldn't really see the bruising, but the swelling on the side of my face was very noticeable.

"I'm good, Grands. It's only a little pain."

"And what about your shoulder? Every time someone touches it or you move it around, you're wincing."

I looked into my grands's concerned eyes and then kissed her cheek. She'd always fawned over me like this ever since I was a little boy.

"Loretta, give the boy some room to breathe. You act like he's never been in a fight before," my gramps said, walking into the kitchen. He walked past us with his glass tumbler in his hand and went straight to the fridge, dropping a few cubes of ice in his cup. The smell of the tobacco from his pipe lingered behind him. "If you were half the mother hen to Zyhir as you were to Gideon, he'd probably be further along in life right now."

"I do not mother Gideon more than—"

"You do," Gramps snapped, cutting her off. "And we've been over this time and time again. I don't want to discuss it anymore." Gramps walked over to his liquor cabinet next and poured himself a double shot of bourbon. "Gideon, what did the police say? Did they find out who was behind the robbery?"

I shook my head and popped one of the truffle and crab stuffed mushrooms in my mouth. "Not yet, and I doubt they ever will."

"Why not?" Grands asked, her hand over her chest as if I just gave her some of the worst news ever.

I wanted to tell her it was because I lied to the police and acted as if I had been knocked out by one of the intruders who stormed into the shop, but that would lead to my grandmother questioning me about my security cameras and other shit I didn't feel like talking about right now. "Because, Grands. They had on masks, and I wasn't able to get a good look at any of their faces."

"But you weren't there alone. You had your other employees there, right?"

I reached behind Grands's back and grabbed another mushroom, which I got popped on the hand for.

"Those are for dinner. Stop eating them all before your little friend doesn't get a chance to taste one. I'm pretty sure this will be a first for her." The look on her face was of pure disgust, but she straightened that shit it up when she felt me about to say something.

"Dammit, Loretta, don't start that shit tonight either," Gramps interrupted instead. "I'm warning you, you better leave that girl alone when she gets here, and try not to ruin dinner. I need to see what it is about this one in particular that has our grandson here already so head over heels in love."

"In love? Gideon, please tell me you're not in love with that . . . that . . . whatever she or he is. I already told you that we don't condone that type of stuff in this house."

"Woman, didn't I just tell you—"

I held my hand up to Gramps, letting him know it was my turn to address my grandmother and her disrespectful mouth.

"Grands, I've told you more than once that Philly is a woman. So will you please stop saying that? At this point, I know you're just being petty." She opened her mouth to say something, but I continued speaking. "Philly is an amazing woman, and I care for her. I'm not going to allow you or anyone else to mess this up for me. Tonight as well as every night after this, you will show her some respect. You will make her feel welcome in your home whenever I bring her around, and you will make sure she doesn't feel an inch out of place being here."

Grands twisted her ruby-colored lips back and forth before suddenly nodding and turning her attention toward the chef. I guessed because she couldn't continue her little rant with me, she took it out on poor Mike. Although he'd been with the family for over ten years now, I could tell that my grandmother's tongue-lashing still got under his skin a little.

Walking out of the kitchen and leaving my grandparents to argue among themselves, I walked to the front of the house and made my way out to Gramps's garage that housed all of his classic cars and bikes. After dinner tonight, I had a special surprise for Philly, and I wanted to make sure everything was in place before the festivities went down. Just as I was returning to the house, my phone vibrated in my pocket, and I smiled when I saw the text that flashed across the screen.

MyBaby: Five minutes.

I didn't know why I started to blush while reading that message, but I did. Something about Philly meeting my grandparents at this point in our relationship was really starting to set in that I really did have feelings for this woman, and I wasn't ashamed to admit or show it to anyone. I didn't know what it was about Ms. Ophelia Hart that had a nigga's nose wide open and ready to wife her up, but I welcomed it. I'd never felt the way I felt about Philly with any other woman I'd ever dated or spent time with. Her whole aura had consumed every part of me from the first time I met her, and I could honestly say that I needed and wanted more.

The low humming sound of a motorcycle engine, mixed with the rhythmic bass of Doggy's Angels "Baby If You're Ready" blasting loudly from the speakers, grabbed my attention and had my eyes focused on the large iron gate at the front of the property. A small smile covered my face as Philly revved her engine a few times after entering the gates and slowly made her way around the large garden fountain, stopping right next to where I stood in the circular driveway. I threw the ice pack I had against my face in the flowerbed and directed my attention back to Philly.

Cutting her engine off, she dropped the kickstand and swung her thick thigh over the bike. With her helmet still on, she removed her gloves from her hand and came and stood in front of me. The flowery scent of whatever perfume she had on invaded my senses. My eyes scanned her body from head to toe, and I could feel my dick shifting in my pants. Her usual attire of a coverall and wife beater was replaced with some fitted ripped jeans that were cuffed at the bottom, showing off the studded suede ankle boots that gave a small peep of her toes. The white top she wore fit loosely around her breasts and stopped a few inches underneath them, showing off her curved waist and cute belly. Tattoos covered almost every inch of her skin from the neck down. Philly raised her arms to remove her helmet, but I moved my hands a little faster and did it for her. The soft curls in her hair bounced to life when she whipped her head to the side and ran her fingers through it. The shaved side of her head was lined and faded to perfection. I admired the light coat of makeup on her face, lips, eyes, and cheeks. Her extended lashes fanned every time she blinked. Philly had always been beautiful to me, but tonight she was breathtaking. Her eyes connected to mine, and that crazy feeling

I got whenever she looked at me enveloped my body. Raising her chin with my finger, I brought her lips to mine and placed a soft kiss against them.

"You are gorgeous," I whispered in her ear after savoring the taste of her mouth one more time. "Why'd it take you so long to get here?"

Philly stepped out of my embrace after kissing my chin but still held my hand. "I would've been here sooner, but after calling that mandatory meeting in Heaven to discuss what happened today at your shop, getting ready for tonight took a little longer than expected." She looked down at herself. "Is it too much?"

My forehead creased. "Nah. It will never be too much. You look beautiful, babe," I repeated, and she blushed.

"Thank you, baby, but listen, I want to apologize to you again. I hate that my drama brought heat to your front door. When I made that move, I never expected them to come at you instead of confronting me directly. I promise to pay for any damage caused—"

I held my hand up to stop her. "Stop apologizing. I told you I would rather they come at me than you anyway, and as far as my shop goes, I'm not tripping over none of that material shit that they tore up. Besides, by this time tomorrow, it will be right back in the condition it was in before those niggas did that shit, so don't worry." I went to kiss her lips again but stopped when the sound of someone clearing their throat sounded behind us.

"You two going to stay out here all night fooling around, or are you going to come in and join us for dinner?" Grands asked.

I closed my eyes and pressed my forehead against Philly's as we shared a light laugh. After silently assuring her with a squeeze of my hand that she was going to be good, I took her by the small of her back and walked her up the three front steps and formally introduced her to Grands.

"Ophelia Hart, I would like you to meet my grandmother, Loretta Wells. Grands, I would like to introduce you to my girlfriend, Ophelia, or Philly for short," I cleared up when Philly cut her eyes at me.

"Nice to meet you again, Mrs. Wells. I hope this time will be different from the last," Philly suggested as she stuck her hand out.

Grands's hard eyes went to Philly's outstretched hand and then back to her face before looking her over from head to toe. The moment her gaze landed on Philly's charred arm, her lip turned up. "Why do you young women of today's generation think it's cute to have all of that writing and colorful markings on your bodies? You don't think that's a bit mannish?"

Philly looked down at the tattoos on her arm and hand. "Not really. It's all art regardless of whose body it's on."

Grands scoffed. "What respectable job would you be able to get looking like that?"

"Since I own my own business, I don't have those problems. I do what I want," Philly smugly replied.

"Grands, didn't you just say dinner was ready?" I intervened before they could get going. "I think we need to go in so we can get this night rolling. Philly and I have another engagement to get to shortly, plus I want to give her a tour of the place I grew up before we sit down to eat."

I could tell by the way Grands looked at me that she didn't like the tone in my voice, but I didn't really give a fuck. Like I told her earlier, she was going to show my girl some respect and make her feel welcome in this house. If not, she wouldn't have to worry about seeing me until she could.

Chapter 17

Philly

From the outside of Gideon's grandparents' house, I knew that they had a little bit of money, but from the inside, you saw that they were seriously rolling in dough. I mean, Pops and Sole had a nice-sized mansion in Summerlin, but the Wells Estate in the Seven Hills area was nothing short of amazing. From the dramatic grand entry with the twenty-five-foot interior lighted waterfall to the eight bedrooms, ten bathrooms, formal living and dining rooms, two-story great room with a wet bar, gourmet kitchen, gym, and garage, I knew Gideon and his brother enjoyed growing up here. By the time G finished showing me around the humongous space, my feet were on fire, and my legs were about to give out at any second. I made a mental note to slap Diem's ass for giving me these shoes to wear. I wished someone would've told me that Louboutins were only good for walking short distances.

"You good?" Gideon bent over and asked me as he took my hand, and we walked into the family dining room. The smell of some kind of seafood dish hit my nose as soon as we reached the table.

I briefly nodded my head as my eyes scanned over the table that was set for five. Gideon's brother Zyhir was gone out of town for a few days, so I wasn't sure who the fifth setting was for.

"So here you are," a handsome yet older gentleman who was already sitting at the table exclaimed as we walked farther into the room. He smiled at Gideon and then turned his amused eyes to me. "I finally get to meet the woman who has my grandson walking around here on cloud nine and smiling all the time."

"Aww, man, Gramps, don't start that bullshit up again." Gideon chuckled with a smile that had my body tingling. His hand squeezed mine, and I squeezed his back.

"Start what, son? I haven't done anything but speak a little bit of truth. Feel free to correct me if I'm wrong about anything I just said."

Gideon dropped his chin to his chest and shook his head. That same panty-wetting smile was still on his face.

When I looked up at the man who now stood in front of us, he winked at me and pulled me into a hug, his strong, masculine scent mixed with whatever form of tobacco he smoked lingering in his clothes.

"It's so good to finally meet you, Philly. Gideon here has told me a lot about you. I'm his grandfather, Robert Wells, but you can call me Gramps if you like or Robert if you aren't comfortable with the other name yet."

I pulled from his embrace and smiled. "I'm good with calling you Gramps, and it's nice to meet you as well."

He nodded his head and took his seat as Gideon held my chair out for me and then sat down himself. I eyed the stuffed mushrooms, crab cakes with aioli sauce, and smoked salmon canapes sitting on dishes in the middle of the table. I hated seafood and prayed that it wouldn't be a part of the main course, because I was hungry.

"Not a fan of seafood?" Gideon's grandmother asked as she sashayed into the room in a strapless, floor-length gown, an overly made-up face, and diamonds sparkling around her neck, ears, and wrist. It was a totally different ensemble from the slacks and ruffled blouse she had on when we were introduced formally on the front porch earlier.

"Retta, why did you change into that?" Gramps asked, his eyes squinted in curiosity at his wife's attire. "I thought this was supposed to be just a small family dinner where we get to know Gideon's girlfriend."

She waved him off and sat down at her seat across from Gideon. Her small hand smoothed the side of her French-rolled hair, while her eyes stayed focused on me. "Do I need to ask the question again, Ophelia, or are you going to continue to be rude and not answer me?"

"Grands," Gideon scolded, but I grabbed his leg under the table and gave him a gentle squeeze, halting whatever he was about to say.

"Although my birth name is Ophelia, I prefer to be called Philly. Outside of my sister when she's trying to get on my nerves, my mother is the only other person who'd refer to me by my given name, and seeing as she's no longer on this earth I would appreciate it if you respect my wishes. Oh, and no need to ask your question again. I heard you the first time, and had you given me the opportunity to give you an answer, I would have, but since you didn't . . ." I shrugged my shoulders, leaving that open-ended statement for her to figure out on her own.

She rolled her eyes and sat up in her chair as the butler poured everyone a round of drinks. After taking a sip from her topped-off glass, she said something to the maid in French, and seconds later the table was being cleared off.

"Well, I hope you like beef Wellington. I had the chef prepare everyone's just the way Gideon likes his: medium, with extra horseradish on the side."

Instead of acknowledging her comment with a response, I jumped into the conversation G and his grandfather were having about the classic car show coming to Caesar's Palace in January and the new Harley Davidson store being built on the strip.

"You sure know a lot about motorcycles. Did you go to school for that?" Gramps asked as silver trays were being placed on the table.

I took a sip of my wine, and then I placed down the beautiful glass, whose stem was filled with Swarovski crystals. "I did go to school. However, I already knew everything there was to know about a bike by the time I entered middle school. My dad and I used to work on his bikes when I was younger. It was sort of a hobby of ours."

Gramps nodded his head and took a sip of his drink. "I don't think I've ever met a female who could replace a lightbulb let alone fix a bike."

"Philly doesn't only fix bikes, Gramps, she actually does restorations, too. Who do you think I paid to do the job on that Cyclone I got you for your birthday?" Gideon beamed. He licked his lips and gave me that crooked smile that I was starting to love.

"Oh, yeah?"

I nodded my head. "Yeah. I do a lot of restoration work at my shop, Hart of the City, over there on the—"

"North side of Vegas?" Gramps finished off the sentence for me, asking a question at the same time.

"You've heard of my shop?"

"As a matter of fact, I have. Your last name is Hart, right?" I nodded. "Any relation to Knight Hart?"

I looked at Gideon to see if I could get some kind of answers to where this line of questioning was going, but by the look on his face, I could tell he was just as curious as me.

"Uhhh, actually, Knight is my father."

Gramps's eyes opened in shock, but then he slowly nodded his head with a small smile on his face. "Hence your love for bikes."

The butler removed the silver cloches from our plates, and the tantalizing aroma of our dinner had my stomach growling.

"Your father and I have done some business in the past. Years ago, when he was out there riding around with his crew of brothers. Knight always told me that he had three beautiful daughters at home, but I never believed that a man who stayed on the road as much as he did ever had time to produce any kids. I can see now that he wasn't lying. I can only assume that your other two siblings are just as beautiful as you are." Gramps sliced into his dish and took a bite. "Tell your father I said hello and that we should have drinks soon."

"I will," was all I offered before digging into my meal and going to town. The flaky crust melted in my mouth like butter, and the beef fillet in the middle was tender and seasoned well.

For some reason, as I continued to eat, I looked over at Grands, who'd been quiet for the last ten minutes. And when I did, I found her eyes stapled on me. The scrutinizing look on her face as she eyed the tattoos covering my fingers, hands, and arm was funny as fuck. I smiled when her gaze connected to mine, and instead of returning the gesture, she turned her nose up and scoffed. I wanted to flip this bitch off, but I decided to ignore her instead.

An hour into the dinner, my phone started to vibrate in my purse like crazy. A few times I had to excuse myself to answer calls from Diem and Pops about the shit that went down at Gideon's shop. Casey had hit me up as well with a message to call him when I got a minute, but I figured I could do that once dinner was over. Casey could get winded when he got caught up in his discoveries of folks' private lives, and I didn't have time to sit on the phone while he rambled. At least not right now, but I was interested in what his latest findings were.

Ever since he told me about there being a possible suspect in my mother's murder the night we took that shipment from the Dragons, I'd been having him look into the case a little deeper. The police files that he was able to gain access to had a lot of pertinent information either blacked out or missing, which was something that I found kind of odd. I remembered when the detectives came to interview me at Pop's house all those years ago, asking me a million questions about that day but never offering up any information that they had come across during their investigation.

I looked down at my phone as another text message from Casey came in.

"Do you mind turning that thing off while we enjoy the rest of our meal?" Grands demanded. The conversation between Gideon and his grandfather came to a complete stop as all eyes turned to me. Grands rolled her eyes. "That is so rude. Here we are, trying to respect our grandson's wishes by welcoming you into our home and getting to know you a little better, and you spend half of the night on your phone. What could possibly be more important than what we have going on here?"

"Loretta, leave the girl alone and mind your business. If she needs to answer her phone, then let her," Gramps remarked. "Gideon doesn't mind, and if it doesn't bother him, why is it bothering you?"

"Because, Robert, that is just downright rude. We can't even enjoy dessert because of her phone constantly vibrating and her fingers tapping so hard on the screen."

Gideon picked up his glass of wine and swallowed the whole thing in one gulp. After wiping his mouth and hands with his napkin, he threw it down on his plate and stood up from his seat. His hand stretched out to mine, and his eyes focused on his grandmother as he addressed his grandfather.

"Gramps, I think it's time Philly and I head on out."

"Already, son? We haven't had our after-dinner bourbon yet."

He nodded. "Yeah, I think it's about that time. I already told your wife that I wasn't going to tolerate this shit tonight. Come on, Philly."

Removing my napkin from my lap, I took Gideon's hand and stood up from my seat. I tucked my phone in the back pocket of my jeans and picked up my purse.

"Gideon, are you seriously leaving?" Grands's voice rang out as we headed toward the foyer. Her heels clicked like crazy against the marble floor as she tried to catch up to us. "Gideon, I know you hear me talking to you. Don't you dare leave this house without answering me or else."

Gideon, who was walking in front of me, turned around so fast that I almost did a triple axel in the middle of the room. "Or else what, Grands?" he asked through clenched teeth. The grip he had on my hand tightened with each step he took back toward his grandmother. "What are you going to do if I leave this house without answering you, huh? Cut me off? That shit don't work on me anymore, especially since I have my own money. So now what? You gon' threaten to change your will? Go ahead and do that shit. I don't give a fuck. I would rather be broke, homeless, and begging for crumbs with Philly than to be rich and lonely without her. I told you before she got here that you were going to respect her and make her feel welcome here, but you haven't done any of that. From the moment she set foot on this property, you and your uppity attitude have been scrutinizing her and turning up your nose at anything and everything she says or does. When are you going to understand that Philly isn't going anywhere? Philly is who I want and who I'm going to be with. And since you can't respect that, you don't have to worry about seeing me until you can. Grands, I love you with all my heart, but don't let this be the last time you see my face."

Gideon's grandmother stepped back with sadness in her eyes as she looked at her grandson who just checked the fuck out of her on my behalf. The front of the house was deathly quiet as the two eye warred between each other. When she broke their stare-down and looked in my direction, the dislike she had for me could clearly be seen from a mile away.

"This is all your fault," she directed toward me, her voice filled with rage. "My grandson has never spoken to me in that way or tone of voice. Hanging around your tattooed, manly, and disfigured ass has caused him to lose his mind. Gideon, apologize right now and get this hood rat out of my home." She screamed that last part before covering her face and crying.

Gideon's grandfather walked in at that time and waved us off before grabbing his wife and pulling her into his arms, letting her dramatically sob on his shoulder. "You two go on and get out of here. Your grandmother needs a little rest right now. In a couple of days, she'll be fine. You two can talk then."

Gideon shook his head. "I'm not up for any conversation if it doesn't involve her apologizing to Philly. Other than that, she can forget it."

I pulled the back of Gideon's cashmere sweater until his back rested against my front and I was able to snake my hand around his waist. Teetering on my sore feet, I used his body weight to keep me still. "Come on, G, let's go."

When he turned around to me, I could see the light mist of water in his eyes. I cupped his chin with my hand to comfort him in some kind of way, and he winced. The swelling on the side of his face wasn't as much as I thought it was going to be, but I could see that the right side was a little bigger than the left, and even with the smooth darkness of his skin, you could still see the deep purple and blue bruising. I lightly kissed his cheek, and without saying another word to his grandparents, Gideon retook my hand and led us out of the front door. Assuming we were headed to his car, I began to walk in that direction but got tugged back to the pathway that led to the side of his grandparents' property.

"Where are we going?" I asked, my eyes looking over the sparkling outdoor Olympic-sized pool and barbeque area.

"I told you I had a surprise for you after dinner, didn't I?"

My phone buzzed in my pocket, but I ignored it. "You did, but I figured you would give it to me at home. Why are we still here?" I didn't think it was right to still be on his grandparents' property after everything that just went down. I wasn't sure what Gideon had in store with this surprise, but I hoped he hurried up and showed me what it was so that we could leave.

"You'll see," was all he offered as we continued to head into the direction of the building I remembered him telling me was Gramps's garage the last time I was here.

I felt that tingle I got whenever I was around G shoot through my body again. I owed Natalie another hundred-dollar bill. So far, she'd been right about Gideon. He had me falling for him, and I was loving every minute of it.

I felt like a kid in the biggest candy store as my eyes bounced from one classic automobile to the next. Bentleys, Lamborghinis, Chryslers, Jaguars, and other rides from just about every decade were sitting pretty and out for show as we walked down the different rows of cars. The faint smell of leather, wax, and tire polish was in the air, and the sound of W, Hemi, and V8 engines silently played in my mind. The feel of heavy steel was in the palm of my hands. My fingers lightly traced over the hood and emblem of the 1966 Chevy Nova I stopped in front of, and I couldn't help the silly smile that covered my face.

"You like it?" Gideon asked as he walked up closer to me, a bottle of wine and two glasses in one hand, the shoes I removed from my feet in the other. "I told you I'd show you the collection one day."

"You did." I bit my bottom lip and looked around the garage again. "This . . . this is amazing. I don't even know where to start." My brow furrowed as a thought crossed my mind. "You did bring me here to actually sit in some of these cars, right? Maybe look under a few hoods and see what type of muscle or horsepower these babies are working with?"

Instead of answering, Gideon hooked my finger with his and led me to the back of the garage, where aluminum cabinets covered the wall and toolboxes of all shapes and sizes were scattered around. Passing through a row of hanging engines being rebuilt, we walked through a door that led to a second room, and I completely lost it. Cruisers, choppers, tourings, and panheads ranging from BMWs to Harley-Davidsons lined both sides of the room. The shiny chrome from each custom job shined blindly beneath the light. Candy apple red, cerulean blue, burnt orange, and royal purple were just a few of the colors decorating each ride.

Before he knew what hit him, I'd jumped into Gideon's personal space and wrapped my arms around his neck, pulling him in for a kiss that damn near knocked us both off of our feet. The groan that emanated from his mouth into mine was of both pleasure and pain as our kiss deepened. I knew I was a little rough with his injured jaw and shoulder, but at that moment, I really didn't care. My tongue ravished every inch of his mouth until I couldn't breathe a second of my own breath anymore and he was finally able to catch his.

"I take it you like your surprise," he chuckled after I finally released him from my hold. I broke our stare long enough to look back out at the scene before me and nodded. "I was hoping you would. It literally took me a whole week of begging to get Gramps to allow me to do this."

"Where are the keys?" I damn near shouted, anxious to straddle one of these bad boys and feel all of that power between my legs. His grandfather had to have at least over $300,000 worth of custom work and bikes in here.

Gideon laughed. "Slow down for a second. I got something else set up for us before we get into all that."

My face dropped but picked right back up when Gideon walked over to the black convertible 1966 Lincoln Continental sitting in the middle of the bikes. He opened the door, urging me to get into the back. Once he hopped in and got comfortable in his seat, he hit a few buttons on a remote and had a huge projection screen descend from the ceiling. The butler who had served us dinner earlier walked over with a plate full of different kinds of fruit and some chocolate fondue on a silver tray.

"What's all this?" I asked as I pulled my vibrating phone from my pocket and tried to read a message that came in from Drea. Before I could open it though, Gideon grabbed my phone from my hand and placed it in the front seat with his.

"I was okay with you answering your phone earlier, but right now I want a few minutes of your time. No club talk, no conversation about what happened at my shop, and definitely no answering texts from them other niggas who are going to be mad that you are officially off the market."

"There aren't any other niggas, Gideon."

"That's good to know." He nodded. "Now what about me getting those few minutes?"

"Oh, you can have all of that and more," I responded, meaning that both literally and figuratively. Gideon must've caught on to my double entendre too, because before I could question him about what we would be watching on the screen, he pulled my foot into his hand and began to massage it. My head instantly fell back on the soft leather of the classic vehicle, and I enjoyed the gentle touch of his finger kneading the bottom on my feet.

"You should take these off," Gideon whispered in my ear, referencing my jeans, which he looped his finger into.

What took me about three minutes to squeeze into only took me about five seconds to peel off. I wasn't uncomfortable being half naked in front of Gideon because I walked around him in my panties and bra all of the time at home. Plus, I'd lost count of the number of times he'd had his head between my legs, licking me like I was the most delectable flavor of ice cream he'd ever tasted.

"Lie back," he instructed, and I did as I was told. Gideon grabbed both of my ankles and placed my feet on his lap. He began to massage my legs in the same way that he massaged my feet, and I felt my body relaxing again. "Now close your eyes, and don't think about anything else but how my hands feel on your body."

I need a gangsta
To love me better
Than all the others do
To always forgive me
Ride or die with me
That's just what gangstas do

When Kehlani's song and video "Gangsta" began to play on the screen and beat louder through the garage speakers, my eyes popped open and went directly to Gideon. The smirk on his face already told me that he knew what I was thinking, and it had the butterflies going crazy in my belly. He remembered the song that was playing when we first saw each other, the same song I'd envisioned him fucking me to over and over again in my dreams and thoughts. Pulling my foot to his lip, Gideon placed light kisses from my toes all the way to my navel, not skipping an inch of skin along the way. When he retreated down to the spot between my legs, Gideon pressed his nose against my hot spot and groaned. The friction his face caused on my clit as he continued to inhale and nibble on the lace of my panties had my body going crazy.

"Gideon," I whispered, my tone low and raspy. "Please, baby," I begged, not recognizing my own voice but giving him the go-ahead to take what it was he was obviously waiting for me to give. With the green light to go, I felt my panties being pushed to the side and the warm feel of Gideon's tongue expertly digging between my folds, leaving no room for my juices to touch anything other than his chin.

"Ahhhh," I moaned, arching my back and pushing my love deeper into his face. I opened my legs wider, granting him full access. Gideon managed to pull three orgasms out of me just from his mouth alone. By the time he finished his meal and peppered kisses from my belly up to my top lips, I was drained and fully in the clouds.

"I know you aren't tapping out on me already," he whispered in my ear. The scent of myself was all over his face. "I need you here with me," he said, pulling his heavy dick from his lowered pants and pressing it against my entrance.

"Gideon?"

"Yeah, baby."

"I . . . Awwwwwwwww," I screamed as his dick breached and stretched me open. "Baby," I moaned before I bit his lip and pulled his mouth into mine, enjoying the taste of myself on his tongue as he pushed himself deeper inside of me. The second our bodies connected and our souls began to intertwine, everything that had been on my mind as of late easily started to slip away. The grieving of

Nats's death. The stress from being president of Hart's Angels. The shit we had going on with the Dragons. Everything that my therapist tried to help me deal with. It was all gone with just one powerful stroke from Gideon.

> *You got me hooked up on the feeling*
> *You got me hanging from the ceiling*
> *Got me up so high I'm barely breathing*
> *So don't let me, don't let me, don't let me,*
> *don't let me go*

I dug my nails into his back, and Gideon moaned. "I knew your pussy would be golden, Philly. The taste alone has me ready to kill any nigga who even looks at you the wrong way," he mumbled before tucking his face in the crook of my neck. He brushed his thumb over my pebbled nipple, and my body shuddered. The fingers of his other hand massaged my clit, pulling another orgasm from me. I could feel his lips curl into a smile against my neck.

"You know you're mine, right? Mind, body, and soul. I won't accept anything less, Philly. Do you understand?" I nodded my head, and he shook his. "I wanna hear you tell me you're mine. Tell me you understand that everything about you from this moment on belongs to me."

Gideon tightly wrapped his arms around my waist and pulled me up from the cool feel of the leather against my back. Without breaking our connection, he straddled me over his lap as he sat up in the back seat of the car and continued to push his powerful drives into me. My head fell back, exposing my neck to him, and he took advantage of it.

"Tell me, Philly," he groaned as his warm breath tickled my skin. "Tell me you're mine."

Placing my hands on his shoulder, I brought my face back to his and looked him directly in the eyes. "I'm yours, Gideon. I belong to only you," I confessed as my body exploded from another orgasm at the same time. "Only you. . . ." I trailed off. The feel of his dick growing harder inside of me sent me on that mind-blinding high again.

Gideon had me in every way imaginable for the next two hours, and I enjoyed every second of it. From me riding him to oblivion in the driver's seat to him having me spread out over the hood of the '66 Chevy and eating my pussy until my juices blended with the custom paint job, we went at it like two starved lovers who hadn't seen each other in years. All of that built-up sexual attraction and emotional connection came out in one night.

By the time Gideon finished marking the inside of my womb with his seed after we fucked doggie style over one of the Harley-Davidson bikes, my body was exhausted. So much so that my knees collapsed and almost had my overworked body hitting the floor, but thanks to G it never happened. He caught me just in time and carried me back over to the car, where we spent the rest of the night wrapped up in each other's arms.

I didn't know how long it had been since we dozed off, but the loud buzzing of my phone stirred me out of my sleep. When I sat up in the seat, Gideon's arms instinctively wrapped around my waist and pulled me back.

"Don't," his gruffy voice rasped. "I need a few more minutes."

I had to look at my phone though, at least to make sure nothing serious had happened with my sisters or anyone else from the club since the last time I checked it. I knew the shit that the Dragons did at Gideon's shop was only the beginning of more shit to come. But until I was able to find out who was responsible for Nats's death, we'd be warring until I personally put a bullet in the middle of that fucker's head.

"Just let me check my texts. At least make sure everything is cool," I said, reaching over the front seat and reaching for my vibrating phone. When I looked at the screen, I wasn't surprised to see the numerous missed calls and texts from Drea, Diem, and Pops, asking if I was okay and how the dinner went. However, there was one text that stuck out to me the most. It was one from Casey that caught my attention as soon as I opened it.

Casey: Found that information with regard to your mom's death. You need to come see me ASAP!

My eyes bulged out of my head as I reread the message Casey sent over thirty minutes ago again and again.

"What's wrong? Why are you putting your clothes on?" Gideon asked as he sat up and watched me pull my jeans over my exposed ass. "Is everything okay?"

I didn't even know I was crying until he cupped my face in his hands, stopping me from putting the rest of my clothes on, and wiped the tears away with his thumbs. "Philly, what's going on? Why are you crying and in such a hurry to leave? Did something happen to one of your sisters? Your dad?"

I shook my head and pulled from his touch. "Earlier when I was texting on my phone during dinner, your boy was asking me for information with regard to my mom and grandma's case."

"My boy? Casey?"

I nodded and pulled my shirt over my head. "The night we did that shit when you were out of town, Casey told me that he found out about a witness whose name somehow was kept off record. I asked him if he could look deeper into things and he did.

Just got a text from him saying that he found out who was responsible for my mom's death."

I ended the conversation there, because there was no use in further explaining what I was about to do or where I was about to go. I looked around the dimly lit garage until I was able to find my shoes and purse, and I was ready to head out the door to hop on my bike when I felt a gentle tug on my elbow.

When I turned around, a shirtless Gideon was standing behind me halfway dressed, his pants hanging loosely around his waist, showing off his V-shape trail and toned stomach. The tattoos that covered his arms, sides, and chest were almost hard to see against his dark skin. He rolled his cashmere sweater over his head and pulled it over his body, covering the perfect view I just had. Without a word, he grabbed my hand and pulled me back through the garage the way we came last night. Eyes of the early morning yard workers glanced at us as we pushed through the closed doors, but they didn't say a word. We walked straight to Gideon's truck, where he opened the door for me to get in. I opened my mouth to object, but he cut me off before I could.

"We're about to head home to take a shower and change clothes. After which I'll take you over to Casey's spot to hear what he has to say. Don't worry about your bike. I'll have someone put it in

Gramp's garage until I can bring you back out this way to get it."

"Gideon, you don't have to—"

He held his hand up, cutting me off. "I know I don't have to do anything, but as your man, I'm going to make sure you're straight in every aspect of your life. Not just here"—he pointed to my pussy—"but here and especially here." He pointed at my head and heart. "Whatever Casey is going to tell you today might change your life, and I'm going to be there when it happens. You belong to me now, so that means I experience everything you experience. Happy, sad, whatever. Now let's go before we run into that weekend traffic."

I hopped in the passenger seat of Gideon's truck and watched as he made his way to the driver's side after shutting my door.

"Why you smiling like that?" he asked as he pulled out of his grandparents' circular driveway. His eyes went back and forth between me and the road.

I bit my lip before responding. "Because I think I just fell in love with you."

Gideon smiled, and that tingle shot through my body again. When we stopped at the gate and waited for it to open, he leaned over the center console and pulled my face to his, pressing his lips against mine. I closed my eyes and savored the feel of his soft lips. Images of the things we did last night flashed through my mind.

"You've always been in love with me, just as I've been in love with you. It just took a nigga dicking you down to finally get you to admit the shit."

I laughed at his silly ass and playfully punched his arm as we exited the Wells Estate and headed to the freeway.

I made a mental note to add another bill to the money I owed Natalie. She won another one of our bets again when it came to my and Gideon's relationship. Hopefully after I handled this business with my mom, I could finally find out who took her away from me. Until then, I just prayed God would forgive me for the life I was now about to take.

Chapter 18

Knight Hart

"What the hell did this woman spend fifty thousand dollars of my hard-earned money on?" I mumbled to myself as my eyes perused Sole's most recent bank statements.

I was in my office at Hart Enterprises doing something that I didn't normally do, because I honestly never really cared what my wife did with the money I gave her. I was only looking now because my accountant contacted me late yesterday evening to let me know about some suspicious deposits and withdrawals that he'd come across while monitoring her personal account. I always kept at least $75,000 in her account at all times, and normally she managed pretty well, so I didn't receive calls like the one I did last night very often. Not too long ago I recalled her mentioning some painting that she just had to have whose price tag was right around $50,000, so that would explain the withdrawal, but not the deposit of double that amount weeks prior. It was a deposit that I knew damn well I didn't make.

Giving up, I tossed the papers aside and reclined in my chair. Trying to figure this shit out was giving me a headache. The deposit was throwing me because I didn't see where the money came from like it did when I dropped money into her account. Russell was doing a trace on that particular transaction, so I decided to let him do his job and wait for him to get back to me.

I thought the problem was that my mind was still reeling from the conversation Diem and I had over lunch yesterday. Initially, it ticked me off that I had to learn from someone else that a child of mine was sick and going through something so tough. DiDi had only been involved with Kyrie for a short time, but he seemed to be privy to everything that was going on in her life. It hurt that she hadn't confided in me but had with a man I considered a stranger. I'd always been the number-one man in all three of my girls' lives, and I didn't appreciate anyone stepping on my toes.

"Diem, explain to me why I had to find out from someone other than you that you were having health issues?"

"I promise I was going to tell you," she sighed while placing her fork into the Styrofoam container that held the aromatic Thai food we'd had delivered.

"When? And why as your family were we not the first to know?" I inquired as I searched her face. I'd never seen Diem look so vulnerable and fragile. As her father, I knew she kept that tough armor of hers up at all times, and it pained me to see it crumbling right before my eyes. She was makeup free today, and for the first time, I noticed the signature butterfly rash on her face. It was something I was familiar with, seeing as how my mother passed from complications of the same disease. My prayer had always been that the same fate would bypass my babies, but that was a prayer that obviously hadn't been answered.

"I held off because I didn't want you looking at me the way you are right now. As if I'm weak and you feel sorry for me or something," she groaned in frustration.

"I don't feel sorry for you, baby, but I look at you that way because I'm your father. No parent wants to see their child sick, I don't care how old they are, so I'm concerned about what you're facing as well as the fact that you felt the need to keep it from me but chose to disclose it to someone outside of the family. I also feel partly responsible." I dropped my head.

"What? Why? This isn't something you could have prevented, Pop." She looked to me with sympathetic eyes.

"What about the amount of pressure I place on you, huh? You're like my go-to when it comes to you girls. I read somewhere that stress and not resting enough can trigger flare-ups," I told her before moving from my seat across from her to join her on our favorite couch. I draped my arm around her shoulders, allowing her to rest her head on my chest like she always did when we had our heart-to-heart moments.

"You riding me the way you do made me into the success I am today, and I love you for that. This thing"—she cleared her throat—"my Lupus was going to happen anyway. It was just in the cards I was dealt. And for the record, the only reason Kyrie knew first is because he was at the hospital with me the night of the shooting when I had that blood pressure scare, and I had to give them my medical history. What I need to focus on now is slowing down and making some real attempts to manage this illness. Kyrie has been helping me tremendously with that." She smiled bashfully.

"Mmmph," I grunted. I could only imagine what her hot-tail self meant by that.

"Why are you acting like that? Don't tell me you're jealous of Kyrie?" she asked, clearly amused by the thought.

"Not jealous, baby girl. Just worried."

"Yeah, you're so worried that you felt the need to come at him sideways when you two spoke the other day." She side-eyed me with her lips turned up.

"I did not," I denied. *"I simply voiced my concerns in a semi-threatening manner,"* I chuckled.

"Don't be like that with Ky. I really like him, and you do too. Before I even knew who he was, you couldn't stop singing his praises, but now that we're dating you have a problem with him. I mean you practically played matchmaker, Pops," she teased.

Recalling our conversation made me realize how ridiculous I sounded. Putting them together had been a purposeful move on my part because I thought they'd make a dynamic power couple, but from the way things were looking they were on some other shit. Was I being a hypocrite seeing as how I'd basically set it up for them to meet? Probably, but I couldn't help it. I supposed I was a tad jealous. None of my girls had been in serious relationships up to this point, but from what I'd been hearing around town about the other two and what I witnessed firsthand with Diem, it seemed that that's where they were all currently heading.

She was the one who surprised me the most though. She had always been different from the other two when it came to love and relationships. The mystical fairytale love thing never intrigued her. I always thought when she settled down and married it would be for more practical reasons, just because it was expected of her, not because she happened upon the love of her life and decided that she couldn't live without him. I wasn't saying that was where she and Kyrie were headed, but they did seem awful chummy with one another.

"Well hello there, stranger."

The greeting pulled me out of my thoughts, and I looked toward my open office door to see Lisa Coleman standing there. It had been a minute since we'd seen one another. She was as beautiful as ever, but her presence here was an unexpected surprise. It was Saturday and Rhea was off, so I'd left the door open just in case one of my daughters decided to stop by, but this visit definitely caught me off guard. If I didn't have Sole and was a sleazy-ass nigga like the one she was married to, I would have snatched her from him a long time ago. She probably had no idea what type of man she was really married to, but I knew the real Lukas Coleman, and he wasn't shit to write home about.

"Lisa, long time no see. What can I do for you today?" I asked, standing.

"Actually, this visit is more about what I can do for you. Can we talk?"

"Of course. Have a seat." I motioned with my hand.

I was devastated. I was numb. I was broken. I was a lot of things right now, but angry was at the top of the list. I had no doubt that my family would soon experience those same emotions as well, and I was also positive that things would only get worse before they got better.

After standing in the same spot for the last thirty minutes, my feet still refused to move. I needed Cassie right now more than I ever had before. The pain of losing her was more pronounced at this moment than it had been the day she was taken away from me. I came to this place often, those times when I needed someone to talk to or when I was just missing her. I wanted nothing more than to see her beautiful face right now. To feel her. To explain to her that I'd tried my best but had somehow come up short. My mistakes had almost cost our daughter her life. For that reason, I couldn't face her, even though it was merely a headstone. She would probably be so disappointed with me.

Gathering up some courage, I pushed off of my car and began the short trek up the hill. From this distance, I could see a figure sitting Indian style in front of her grave with her back to me. Seemed she was needing her mother today just as much as I was. There was a reason we both ended up here on the same day at the exact same time. That was no one but God's doing. Sharing with her what I found out today wasn't going to be easy, but it was necessary. There was no way I could lie to her.

The closer I got to her, the more my resolve weakened. I could hear the soft whimpers escaping her throat. I could see the slight trembling of her shoulders. By the time I came to stand next to her, my own face was soaked with tears that I quickly wiped away.

Placing my flowers next to the ones she'd placed at the right of the headstone, I called out to her in a shaky voice. "Ophelia."

Her head shot up in surprise. She was so lost in her feelings she hadn't even heard me approach, but when she realized it was me, she began bawling out of control. Getting on the ground, I pulled her into me and held her tight while she broke down. This wasn't like the normal sadness she had when she missed her mother. This was different.

"Sh . . . she killed my mom. She killed them both. How could you let her do that, Daddy?" she sobbed. "How could you?"

"Who, baby girl? Who are you talking about?" I pulled back to look into her eyes. I had no idea what she was talking about right now.

"I never stopped looking. Even when you along with everyone else gave up hope, I kept digging." She ignored my question while wiping her nose and face with the back of her hand. "When I was younger she threatened to do to me what she'd done to my mother, and at the time I didn't understand what she meant, but now I do. She had them killed, and you let it happen." She yanked away from me and hopped to her feet with lightning speed.

"Ophelia Hart, slow down and tell me what you're talking about!" I stood up. "Who threatened you, baby? Who do you think is responsible for killing your mother?" I asked, gripping her wrists tightly.

"Ain't no thinking. I know exactly who did it," she spat.

"So, tell me who it was so that I can take care of it." I tightened my hold, causing her to wince. Her facial expression caused me to snap out of it, and I immediately loosened my grip.

I didn't mean to apply so much force, but if what she was saying was true, I was fucking some shit up tonight. I already had two people on my hit list from the shit Lisa had just shared with me, and now it looked as if I was about to be adding more. My heart was pounding so hard and so fast. For years I hunted and paid outrageous amounts of money searching for Cassie and Nona's murderer. When I wasn't following up on leads myself, I went through numerous private investigators, only to be disappointed time and time again. Now my daughter was standing here trying to tell me that she knew who this person was? No way. I refused to believe that.

"Sole," she answered, breaking me from my thoughts.

"Sole what, baby girl?"

"Your wife killed my mother!" she screamed in my face.

Releasing her, I took two steps back. I glared at her hard as my mind absorbed the words that had just left her mouth. "Who told you that, Philly?"

"My boyfriend paid someone to look into it for me, and I now know every detail about the day they were killed. Even the dumb crackhead muthafucka who was paid to take care of it. All it took was the promise of an eight ball and he was spilling his guts. Even said that Sole recently tracked him down and offered him more money to keep quiet just in case someone came snooping around. The bitch somehow found out that I'd been asking questions, and she was trying to cover her tracks. Thankfully that dopefiend nigga had no loyalty and told me all I needed to know despite taking her money as well."

A rage that I had never known until today consumed my entire being. It looked as though I wouldn't be adding a new person to my hit list, seeing as how Sole's conniving ass was already at the top of it. The Dragons themselves weren't coming for my family, but their elder along with the woman I'd given my last name had concocted this well-orchestrated plan to kill my daughter. I was thinking that after all this time Sole still hadn't been able to get over my infidelity, and it had eaten away at her to the point that she felt that taking my child from me would even the playing field, but that wasn't the case.

When Lisa Coleman walked into my office, I had no idea what she was about to say, but when she went on to tell me a little story of plotting and scheming between her husband and my wife, my whole world came tumbling down. It all made sense now. It explained why she was coming after Philly so many years later. She was close to finding out the truth, and the attempt on her life was Sole's way of silencing her.

"Mmmph, I guess you don't believe me," she scoffed while shaking her head.

"You guessed wrong, sweetheart. I do believe you, and I'm so sorry. This shit is all my fault. I'm so sorry." I embraced her.

"Your fault?"

"Yes, my fault. I should have left her ass a long time ago, but I felt so bad about the things that I had done, and I felt I owed it to her to try working it out. Now look at where we are."

"She ruined my whole life and tried her best to make it a living hell for me living up under her roof. If it weren't for you and my sisters, I would have left years ago and never come back. I just don't understand how someone could be so cruel," she cried.

"Philly, Sole knew that you were close to exposing her, and I learned today that she's the one behind all these attacks on our family. The arson at Diem's shop as well as the fundraiser shooting," I informed her. Her eyes bucked before turning black and filling with intense fury. I knew she was thinking about the fact that she lost her best friend that day and Sole was responsible. Yet someone else was added to the list of people her stepmother had taken away from her. It was a lot to take in, but she needed to know it all.

"The problems you were having with Elle? Also all part of the plan, but it comes to a stop right here and right now. I don't want to you to worry about a thing, baby girl. Daddy is going to take care of this shit once and for all," I promised as I wiped her tearstained face.

"You better, because if you don't, I will," she swore vehemently.

"I promise I'm going to make it right, Philly. First thing we have to do is arrange this sit-down with Slim. It was brought to my attention that they had no knowledge of Lukas's plan, and we have to do the right thing and return what belongs to them. Once we get that situation squared away, I'll handle Sole. You have my word that she won't make it out of this alive, baby girl."

We remained at the cemetery for another two hours, paying our respects to Cassie, Nona, and

Natalie. I left with a very troubled mind. To think of my other two girls and how they would feel about what was about to happen to their mother was fucking with me. I was actually more worried about Drea because she was so close to Sole, but there was no way around it. I just prayed that in the end they wouldn't hate me for what I was about to do. As a family, we had a lot on our plates, but as the head, I was determined to come out on top in all of this. Sole couldn't win, and I planned to make sure she didn't. I vowed that she would never get another opportunity to hurt my daughter. For damn near twenty years, I'd been sleeping with the enemy, and the thought of that made my skin crawl. It made me feel less than a man because I hadn't protected Cassie, and I'd also failed my child. The truth had been staring me in the face, and I'd been too blind to see it.

Chapter 19

Kyrie

"It's about time you showed up. Dinner was about to start without you," Bella stated once I crossed the threshold of her home.

"I told you I had some last-minute things to do at the office when we spoke earlier, Bells. Besides, when have you ever known me to be on time?" I joked as I tossed my keys in the bowl on the table in the foyer and kissed her cheek.

"Never and that's a damn shame, Ky. You're worse than a female sometimes." She shook her head.

"Whatever, li'l one. Back to the matter at hand. I can already smell the Old Bay seasoning, and your big brother is hungry as hell, so I hope my plate is already prepared and waiting on me," I tossed over my shoulder as I entered the dining room.

I stopped short when I realized she had company. A huge smile that I couldn't control formed on my face at the sight of her. She offered a coy nod, and I did the same. Bella failed to inform me that she would be here tonight, but I was happy to see her face since it had been a few days. I actually thought it would be just me and my sister like it was every Thursday night, but looking around I could see that there were several other guests in attendance this evening. Bella's on-again off-again boyfriend, Jaylon, and Lark were both seated at the table as well.

"Finally we can eat," Bella announced as she took her seat. "Kyrie, you remember Diem, right?"

"How could I forget? Diem, how are you?"

"I'm well. It's nice to see you again," she replied with what she thought was a straight face, but I could see the smile in her eyes. I was sure she could see the same in mine. She was looking good as hell, and she was definitely coming home with me tonight. I'd gone one too many days without her, and I was feenin' for her hard as hell right about now.

"Jaylon, it's been a minute." I reached out to dap up Bella's man, who was positioned at the head of the table at the opposite end of her.

"It has indeed. Heard you're doing big things around Vegas though, man. Your sister can't stop talking about you and your accomplishments. She's really proud of you. Hell, we all are," he said.

"Thanks, dude. I really appreciate that," I replied as shot my baby sis a loving smile. She was quite accomplished herself, and I never missed an opportunity to tell her so.

I quickly took the empty seat next to Diem. She looked as if she was about to protest, but my hand on her thigh silenced her. All I heard was the sharp intake of breath the moment I gave her thick leg a tight squeeze. There was another open seat across from her, but I wanted to be as close to her as I could. Maybe feel her sexy ass up as she dined on the huge seafood feast Bella had prepared for us. I knew she hadn't talked to my sister about us dating yet, so I didn't plan to bust her out in front of everyone.

"Well, hello to you too, Ky," Lark addressed me while looking back and forth between Diem and me suspiciously.

"Damn, my bad, Lark. How you doing?" I chucked my head up while continuing to caress Diem's thigh under the table. I wasn't trying to be rude to ol' girl, but once I saw my lady, I lost focus a bit.

"I'm good. Glad you could make it tonight. There's something I would like to speak with you about before you leave." She smiled sweetly.

"A'ight," I responded with an insouciant shrug.

I could feel Diem's eyes on me, but I ignored her. I had no idea what Lark wanted to talk to me about. In all the years my sister had been cool with her she'd had this crush on me, but I had never entertained the shit. She was a good-looking chick with a lot going for herself, but I just had never been interested in her, and I never would be.

"Sorry, everyone. That was one of my baby mamas hounding me," Jaylon's homeboy Troy announced as he entered the room. "Oh, what up, Ky. When you get here?" he asked as he tucked his cell phone in his jacket pocket.

"Couple minutes ago," I replied as I reached out to shake his extended hand.

"That's what's up. I see you stole a niggas seat, but it's all good. Now I can get a better look at the beauty sitting across from me." He winked at Diem, who nervously cleared her throat while my brow furrowed in confusion.

Troy took the seat next to Lark and began piling his plate with seafood pasta, crab legs, and shrimp scampi. Looking around the room, it finally hit me what the hell was going on. The look of unease Diem sported was confirmation. This was a damn setup. The male-to-female ratio was matching up, and the arranged seating was another giveaway. I guessed I was supposed to be next to Lark and Troy next to Diem. No wonder Bella had a whole dinner party setup. She was trying to hook me up with her friend and hook my girlfriend up with a nigga who didn't have no damn job and three baby mamas. I couldn't blame Bella because she didn't know that her friend and I were dealing with each other, but I grilled the fuck out of DiDi. I sat there wondering if she knew anything about this bootleg-ass blind date. Just because we hadn't told Bella didn't mean we weren't together. I know I said I didn't plan to bust her out but fuck that.

"Yo, DiDi, let me speak with you in private real quick." I tossed my napkin aside and stood.

"Kyrie." Diem pleaded with her eyes.

"What are you doing, Kyrie? We're about to eat." Bella gestured with her hand toward the food on the table with a confused expression.

"I'm sorry, but I need to talk to my girl right now. I don't give a damn about no food," I said through gritted teeth as I pulled her chair out for her. I was hungry as hell when I walked through the door, but I'd suddenly lost my appetite.

"Your girl?" Bella and Lark screeched in shock.

Speaking of Lark, the look she was giving me right now as I took Diem's hand in mine to help her up was one of pure disgust and jealousy, but I couldn't concern myself with her feelings. Even Troy was looking like he had a problem, but that fool knew better than to say anything to me. I had to check his ass on several occasions in the past for poking his nose in Jaylon and Bella's business and talking shit about my sister. Nigga already knew how I was coming, so he sat there and kept quiet as I whisked Diem off for a behind-the-scenes conversation.

I barely had the door to the downstairs restroom closed before Diem was explaining herself. "I know what you're thinking, Kyrie, but I had no idea what Bella was trying to do until I showed up," she informed me with her palms up. "I was on my way home from work when she called to invite me over for dinner."

"Why didn't you call me then?" I pulled her into me and nuzzled her neck, relieved that she was just as caught off guard by Bella's attempt at playing Cupid tonight as I was. She smelled heavenly, and her scent had me spellbound.

"I was going to because I wanted to see you tonight, but when she mentioned seafood, I rushed over here. I was hungry, babe," she pouted. "How was work?" she questioned as she pulled back and ran her tiny hands down my chest.

"Work was work. I missed your ass though. Are you feeling okay today? You been taking it easy?" I asked, pulling her back into me to kiss her forehead then her nose softly.

"I missed you too, and yes, I'm good," she said as she wrapped her arms around my neck.

"That nigga was in your ear spitting that weak shit, huh?" I joked as she rolled her eyes to the ceiling.

"Like you wouldn't believe. I'm going to kill your sister. She knows me better than that so she knew for a fact that he and I wouldn't connect on any level. Nigga had the nerve to tell me he's in between jobs. The fuck does that even mean, Ky? Plus his ass stepped away to take calls from two of his three baby mamas in the forty-five minutes that I've been here. On top of all that foolishness, Lark's ass went on and on about you from the moment I came through the door. 'When's Kyrie coming? Bella, are you sure he's coming?'" she mocked, making me laugh. "Oh, so you think that shit is funny, huh?"

"A li'l bit, but you already know I ain't got nothing for that girl."

"Bet' not. Fuck both y'all asses up," she threatened. "I was seconds away from telling her to quit pining over my nigga."

"I'm surprised that you didn't. I remember how you handled that waitress on our first official outing together with your territorial ass. I told you I was gone be your nigga that night, remember?" I pecked her lips a few times.

"Of course I do, but how you gon' call me territorial when you got me hemmed up in the bathroom because you thought I was on a date with Jaylon's friend?" She lifted her brow.

"You damn right! Nigga better find his own and leave mine alone," I said, causing her to blush.

She pressed her mouth against mine again. "Let's get back in there before Bella thinks we're goosing in her bathroom."

"Shit, the way you kissing a nigga and as fine as you're looking right now, I low-key want to bend you over." My dick jumped as I watched her lick her lips before catching the bottom one between her teeth. I already knew she was down for whatever. Diem would never refuse me, but as bad as I needed to feel her insides, I didn't want to cause a scene by having her screaming at the top of her lungs in my sister's restroom. We were just going to have to skip dinner here and pick something up on the way home.

"Come on." I grabbed her hand and hurried back to where the others were. "Aye, sis. Sorry, but we're going to have to take a rain check on dinner. Something came up," I lied as I helped Diem into her blazer, which had been hanging from the back of her chair, ignoring the confused looks everyone shot our way.

"I'm sure it did." Bella smiled approvingly, while her homegirl Lark mean mugged the shit out of us. Being a proper hostess, my sister got up to walk us out. "Miss Diem, your sneaky self better call me first thing tomorrow to explain all this." She motioned between us. Diem only nodded while we smiled goofily at one another. "I have no idea what I'm going to tell Lark when I go back in there. She was damn near in tears the whole time you two were in the restroom," she fussed.

Diem and I both just shrugged our shoulders, unmoved. It wasn't supposed to be some big secret that we were an item. We had just been so caught up in getting to know each other that we hadn't gotten around to discussing it with my sister. Her family knew all about us, and I was glad to finally have Bella in the loop. Hopefully Lark would get the picture and set her sights on another prospect, because I was officially taken. Hell, maybe Bella could fix her up with Troy's bum ass.

"Diem! If you don't bring your ass in here and get this bullshit up out of my restroom! You play too damn much," I griped.

I had just taken my morning leak and went to wash my hands when I noticed this long, penis-shaped soap shit she'd placed above the sink. I loved having a super freak for a girlfriend, but sometimes her ass took things too far. Had the damn thing stuck to my mirror with some type of suction holding it up.

"What are you in here fussing about now?" She poked her head in as I was stepping into the shower.

I could tell by the teasing smirk on her face that she knew exactly what the hell I was fussing about. "Quit playing crazy, girl. Get that shit out of here," I ordered from behind the foggy glass.

"All right, all right. It's just soap, Ky. 'Make your-self comfortable here,' he says," I heard her mumble mockingly. "How the hell am I supposed to be comfortable if I can't wash my hands with my favorite soap? I'll have you know that these are a big hit at Hart Box. They sell out no sooner than I restock."

"That's cool and all, and I'm glad you're collecting those coins, but I ain't trying to rub on no dick just to get my hands clean, baby. Fuck that."

I chuckled to myself as I listened to her talk more shit under her breath before she left the bathroom. I did want Diem to be comfortable in my home, so I would let her put her little dick soap back up. She'd been spending nights here with me since we left my sister's place, and before then she'd been at her parents'. The last thing I wanted was for her to think she was in my way and try going back to her house. With all this beef with the Dragons and the melee that had gone down at G's spot, I felt more at ease with her here. And because we were so busy with work, it helped to come home and have her here waiting for me already.

When I was done with my shower, I skipped moisturizing my body because I already knew I would be needing another shower here shortly. After wrapping a towel around my waist, I walked into my bedroom to find Diem sitting Indian style on the bed with her laptop in front of her. She was only wearing a matching bra and panty set, and her golden-brown hair was loose and bouncy just like I liked it. She looked up to see me staring at her, and she rolled her eyes like a little brat.

"You mad at me, Di?"

"Yup, and I'm packing up my soap along with the rest of my things and taking my ass home tonight," she answered but kept her eyes on her computer.

"You'll do no such thing." I shook my head.

"And who's going to stop me, Kyrie?" she asked defiantly as our eyes connected.

In that moment, as I gazed into her beautiful orbs, I realized something. "What if I told you that I loved you and wanted you to stay? Would that change your mind?"

Her eyes suddenly grew wide in surprise. "Possibly." She grinned.

"Well how about if you bounce you won't be getting any more dick?" I threatened.

"Ky, I have like a hundred dicks at home, so you ain't saying shit right now," she countered playfully.

"I bet they don't do you like I do. They can't take your body to the places I can," I told her with the utmost confidence before dropping my towel. When her eyes landed on my pipe, they nearly popped out of her head. I loved to see that look in her eyes. It was like she'd never seen my dick before or something. Anytime I whipped this bad boy out, her reaction was the same: astonishment and lust all mixed together. That shit low-key made me feel like I was that nigga. Diem talked a good game, but she was like putty in my hands when I served her this dick.

"So you're absolutely positive that you want to go?" I asked with my head cocked to the side. Of course she shook her head this time. Not taking her eyes off of me, she closed her laptop and set it in the chair on her side of the bed. "Take that shit off," I ordered. Watching her remove her undergarments was one of the sexiest scenes I'd ever watched. My lady's body was a work of art, and I doubted that I would ever get tired of her unveiling it to me. "Lie down, Diem. I'm about to feast, so I need you to open up wide for me," I instructed, and she did.

I dove in face first, and her nectar was the sweetest I'd ever tasted. She shivered out of control as my tongue explored every fold and crevice of her pussy. Her body responded so well to me that it only took about ten flicks of my tongue against her swollen bud before she was releasing that good cream into my mouth. We didn't have much time before we needed to be at this meeting, so I immediately rose up to pull her body down beneath mine. When I finally entered her valley, it was like stepping into a whole new world. Hers was the prettiest, juiciest, tightest, fattest pussy I'd ever had and I loved it. Shit, I loved her.

"I love you, Diem," I confessed for the second time.

Her movements promptly ceased, and when I opened my eyes to look down at her, I saw a fear in them that I'd never seen before. Maybe she thought I was bullshitting when I said it the first time. It was truly the way I felt, but it may have been too soon to be confessing it, because she damn sure didn't say it back. I covered her lips with mine and hit bottom with a long, slow stroke.

"Kyrie!" she cried out as her body arched off the bed. I began tapping her cervix with fervor in an attempt to distract her from my admission.

"Nah, I want you to talk that shit you were talking about the number of dicks you have at the crib. Can they do yo' pussy like this, Di?" Her mouth was stuck in an O shape, and no response came out. I was delivering the dick so precisely that she couldn't even moan right now. "That's what the fuck I thought. Matter of fact, I want you to get rid of all them muthafuckas," I grunted as I hit her deep once more. "Pac my nigga and all, but he gotta go too. This the only dick you getting from now on. You hear me?"

"Shit, Ky!" she hissed.

"Did you hear what I said, Diem? You're going to retire those fake muthafuckas, right?"

"Yessss! Fuck yes, baby!" Her pussy gushed and contracted as I expanded inside of her.

Thank God for birth control because this was about to be a big nut, and there was no way I would be able to pull out. I was about to shoot the entire fucking club up with no remorse. By the time

I was done with Diem, she'd agreed to do away with every single one of her toys. The Channing, Momoa, and Chadwick were history as far as I was concerned. Fuck a Hart Throb. Kyrie was all she needed.

"I love you, Kyrie," Diem said softly as she lay on my damp chest.

"You better." I smiled then kissed the top of her head.

"I'm scared though," she admitted.

"Of what?"

"The fact that we're moving so fast. This is all new for me, but I've quickly come to depend on our connection, this bond. Never felt love for a man outside of my father, and even though I'm somewhat afraid, I trust that you won't take my love for granted," she expressed hesitantly as she lifted her head to face me.

"I would never," I promised with a shake of my head. "And try not to worry yourself with the pace. We don't have to follow anyone else's rules or love time table. We move as fast or as slow as we want, and we love the way we choose, okay?" She nodded her agreement. "You staying here, right?"

"Yes, baby," she conceded before snuggling closer to me.

Having established that my place was best for her, for the time being, I was able to breathe a sigh of relief. If I had a say in it, she would never return home. If she decided that that's what she wanted to do, then she needed to be prepared to have me over there all the damn time. Knowing that she felt the same way for me that I did for her also eased my mind. She had me scared for a minute there, but after hearing those three words, I was able to fully relax knowing that we were finally in sync.

"You good?" I asked Diem, who was going from pacing the room to checking the camera for the arrival of our guests.

I didn't know if she was nervous or just ready to get this meeting over with. It could have been that I was here after she asked me numerous times to sit this one out and I refused. The fact that she was meeting with the same vicious muthafuckas who ran up in Gideon's shop not too long ago was all the incentive I needed to be in attendance no matter what. There was no way my woman would be in a room with them and I not be present. It didn't matter to me that Drea along with Simmy, the other Angels, and her father were here. I didn't claim to be a gangster, but wasn't nobody gon' fuck with what was mine, and I had no problem defending that.

"I'm good, Kyrie." She offered a small smile and took a seat on the table in front of me.

"Relax for me. No stress today, a'ight?" I chucked my head up, motioning for her to lean down to kiss me, and she did.

"It's showtime." Drea cheesed as she nodded toward the camera.

Simmy winked at her as he checked the two guns he had secured on each hip as well as the smaller ones strapped to his ankles. Picking up the sawed-off from the windowsill, he draped it over his shoulders and got in position near the door. For the most part, he was a quiet dude, but his presence alone spoke volumes. One look at him and you could tell he was not to be fucked with. The same could be said about Drea, who was normally the cute, reserved sister, but she had the same look in her eyes that her man did. Philly was the only one missing today, and I found that strange seeing as how she was the ringleader in all of this.

"Diem, I know how you can get, so I need you to let me do all the talking. This can be a simple conversation to hash this shit out, or it can turn ugly. With your history with Slim and your smart-ass mouth, I'm hoping to avoid the latter," Julian spoke up, causing her to smack her teeth as we observed four men hop out of an all-black Suburban and point toward the back of the building we were in.

History, huh? I thought as I cut my eyes in Diem's direction. That could have been the reason she didn't want me to come with her today. If that was the case, then she was worried for nothing. I wasn't the type to trip over some fool she dealt with in the past as long as I was the one and only man in her life at the present time.

A few of the girls were waiting outside to pat the men down before allowing them to enter the warehouse. Since the door was already open, the men walked right in, and I immediately recognized two of them from the scuffle at Gideon's barber shop. The taller of the two still had a fat knot upside his head from when my boy G rocked his ass, and the one I'd gone head-on with was grilling the shit out of me. I hit him with a cocky nod, to which he angrily clenched his jaw and turned away. Weak ass.

"Knight, thank you for reaching out," a lanky, fair-skinned dude offered respectfully. He wasn't with his crew at the shop that day, but it was clear that he was the man in charge.

"It's no problem, Slim. I just wanted to get this little situation squared away as quickly and quietly as possible," Julian replied as the men shook hands.

"It's funny that you say that. Off top, you know that I have the utmost respect for you, but I gotta be honest. 'Little' doesn't accurately describe what your girls took from us. The monetary value of what they confiscated was well into the millions. I have people on my ass bitching about product that they've already paid for but have yet to receive, so you as a businessman should surely be able to see my dilemma. I'm not really sure this is something that can be 'squared away,' as you put it," the man I now knew as Slim replied as he eyed Diem while rubbing his hands in a Birdman fashion. I knew right then that I was going to have to put him in his place before it was all said and done.

"So y'all can burn my shit up then turn around and shoot up an entire party full of people where my sister loses her best fucking friend, but it's a violation for us to retaliate? You got the game fucked up, Cornelius," Diem popped off, using his government name.

His response was laughter. "I see not much has changed, DiDi. You still don't know your place." Slim shook his head disapprovingly.

"Hell nah, ain't shit changed. You fuck with my family, my man, or my money, and you'll come face-to-face with an entirely different Diem Hart. I can show you better than I can tell you though, so what's it gonna be?"

I went to speak up, but Knight held his hand up, silencing me. "Please excuse my daughter, Slim." He shot Diem a look, making her back down.

My lady was mad as hell and looked as if she wanted to stomp her feet in protest. My hand at the small of her back relaxed her some, but she was still very heated. So was I. This nigga telling my girl what her place was rubbed me the wrong way. She could say whatever the fuck she wanted whenever she wanted to say it. And in my opinion, she hadn't said anything wrong. The respect I had for Knight was the only thing holding me back right now.

"I totally understand where you're coming from," Knight continued. "And trust me when I say that I'm not trying to minimize the situation at all. But let me ask you something. In addition to the Angels returning everything that belongs to you untouched, what else is it that you feel we could do to make this all go away? What exactly are you looking for?" Knight asked with his arms folded across his chest as he eyed the Dragons' leader pensively.

I'd always admired this man and his work, but I respected him even more in this moment. This was a man who could definitely do both. He was a gangster and a gentleman. Julian Hart had this no-nonsense aura about himself, and even in a meeting where there were discussions of stolen guns and drugs, he remained a boss about his business. He was still dressed impeccably in a suit and tie, but clearly he wasn't one for the games.

"Allowing us to keep our territory would be all I needed to forget this ever happened," Slim propositioned after a long period of silence.

"Son, you know damn well that's not going to happen. You're already well into the thirty-day deadline before you have to be moved out of there already, so you can go right back and tell that nigga Lukas that ain't shit changed. Like I told him before, that was a business move, and it has absolutely nothing to do with this here business we're discussing," Knight asserted. "As a matter of fact, don't tell his ass shit. I'll be seeing him soon enough anyway."

"I mean, we're negotiating so I thought I'd try my luck." Ol' boy shrugged. "And for the record, that request didn't come from Lukas. His dealings with you have nothing to do with us. He's simply the face of the Dragons. Nothing more. Trust that we have it like that for a reason. I'm aware of his recent moves, and I can assure you that we were in no way involved. We won't bat an eye when you decide to go ahead and handle that," Slim said as the two men shared a look of understanding.

"Now, then. I've been gracious, and I've apologized, but outside of returning your shit that's as far as it goes. I have a team of men who should be arriving at the Lair within the hour with everything that belongs to you and a little something extra for your troubles, so you may want to alert your people. They've even been paid to unload it for you, but again, that's all I can do for you."

"The Lair? I could have sworn I saw our trucks out back when we pulled up," one of the unnamed men from the shop questioned stupidly.

"And they pulled out seconds after you entered this building." Knight smirked.

"Should have known," Slim chuckled before setting his sights on Diem again. "Why you looking so mean, DiDi? We worked it out. Ain't no need to be enemies, beautiful. We could even be friends like we used to be. What do you say?" He eyed her frame as she stood sexy as hell in all-black leather, her biker vest snugly hugging her upper body.

"I say it ain't no such thing, my nigga. Like you said, things have been worked out, and there's nothing else for you here. Keep addressing my lady and I'ma check yo' fucking chin like I did yo' homeboy the other day." I nodded over to the stocky nigga with the busted lip.

"Ahh, shit. This you, Diem?" he asked, amused as he looked back and forth between us.

"Aye, man, what the hell I say about addressing her?" I interjected before she could respond.

"You got that, big dog." Turning to his crew, he spoke. "Let's roll. Niggas too hostile up in this bitch," he joked, unbothered by my threats.

"You may have convinced my daddy, but I still ain't feeling this shit. I might get the urge to light your spot up anyway so watch your back, nigga," Diem taunted, moving toward him.

On cue, I moved in as well. When I looked around, I smirked at the fact that every Angel present along with Simmy had made the move too. Good to know her crew was solid and not the least bit intimidated that they were going up against a group of men. Their reaction set Slim's men in motion, but his hand extended toward them halted their movements.

"Slim, you have nothing to worry about. You have my word," Knight stepped in while glaring at his oldest daughter. The man simply nodded and continued out the door with his team.

"We're about to follow them awhile to make sure they're not on no bullshit," Simmy said before grabbing Drea's hand and walking out behind them.

They weren't even all the way in the SUV before Knight was blowing up. "Diem, the next time I ask you to fall back, I expect you to do just that!" he barked.

"Ain't no more falling back, Pops. Those fools could very well be responsible for all of this, and you just let them walk away like it was nothing. Fuck all the lives that were lost. What about Nats?" Diem exploded.

"Babe, calm down," I broke in.

"I let them walk away because they had nothing to do with it, DiDi." He shook his head sadly.

"How can you be so sure, Pop?" She sniffed with tears forming in her eyes.

"Baby girl, I know because everything that has taken place, every single threat against this family was orchestrated by your mother. Sole did this."

Chapter 20

Drea

"Josh," I yelled over my shoulder as I placed the last two roses in the floral arrangement I was designing. "Come look at it now and tell me what you think."

Josh walked to the back of the room, eyes focused on the clipboard of orders in his hand. He bobbed his head and mouthed the words to Jeffrey Osborne's "Only Human," playing low in the background. He paused his stride to write something down and then continued toward me. He wore a white collared shirt that was nice, clean, and neat. His dreads were a little longer and pulled to the back. Tan khaki pants fit his slim frame just right.

I smiled at his name tag, which now had the word "Manager" below his name. Ever since I gave him the title, Josh had been exceeding even my expectations. Not only had he pulled in a shitload of new clientele, but he somehow halved the overhead that was projected for this quarter alone. If that wasn't enough to consider him for the management position, I didn't know what else would have done it.

When Josh reached the end of the work table, he stopped what he was doing and looked up at the large funeral order I'd just completed for the mayor's mother. His soft eyes squinted just a bit as he assessed my work. Stretching his arm out, Josh gently pushed one of the roses that was sticking out a little farther than the others back into the Styrofoam ball and gave the arrangement another once-over before he turned around and headed back toward the front of my shop.

"So you just gonna ignore my question?" I asked, a small smirk on my lips because I knew him not saying nothing meant he was impressed.

"Drea, you already know you did your thing with that shit. I don't know why you even called me back here."

I got up from my stool and wiped down my pants and shirt. I hadn't planned on coming into work today, but with Simmy out handling his business, Diem somewhere off on some last-minute trip with Kyrie, and Philly missing in action, I decided to show my face and get my hands a little dirty, so to speak.

"I called you back here because I wanted you to see the finished product. I also wanted to ask you something with regard to her." I nodded toward the new receptionist he and Marlon hired while I was gone. "Did y'all do a thorough background check on her? Where did she come from? Who are her people?" Although things had kind of died down since the shooting, and the shit we had going with the Dragons was squashed and back in order, I still had my eyes open when it came to people I didn't know.

Josh waved his hand and laughed. "First of all, stop being so paranoid. Second, you don't have anything to worry about when it comes to her. She's good peoples."

"And how sure are you on that?" I asked, picking up my vibrating phone. I was hoping it was Philly's ass finally texting me back, but it wasn't.

"I know because she's my cousin. The girl just moved out here from Jersey to stay with me, and I already told her ass she wasn't sleeping on my couch for free." He walked back over to where I was standing. "After a week of looking for jobs and coming up empty-handed, I had Marlon interview her for the receptionist position. Out of all the ones who applied, he said she was the only one . . . Uh, Drea, how you gon' ask me some shit and not listen when I'm talking to you?"

I was listening to everything Josh was saying when he first started explaining giving his cousin a job here, but the text my father had just sent from his secondary line had my attention more focused on my phone.

Daddy: Penthouse in two hours.

Me: What's going on, Pops? You good?

It took a few seconds for him to respond.

Daddy: I'll explain when you get here. Service entrance.

Me: Say no more.

That was all I sent back, letting my father know that I'd be on my way to the Penthouse, a multi-million-dollar hotel his company developed and helped build about a year ago. The fact that he told me to use the service entrance already had my trigger finger itching. Only time he ever told me to enter through the back instead of the front where all the cameras were was when he needed me to bring a few of my toys to handle something that needed immediate attention.

The sound of the shop door opening had a screwed-face Josh walking back to the front to greet whoever came in, while I dialed Diem's phone to see if she got the same text or knew anything about what Pops had going on at the Penthouse.

"You've reached Diem Hart. Please leave me a detailed message after . . ." When her voice mail picked up, I released the call and immediately tried her again. "You've reached Diem Hart. . . ."

"Fuck," I cursed to myself, trying to remember if I had Kyrie's number stored in my phone somewhere.

"What up, Neeva. Josh," Marlon threw over his shoulder as he walked into the back room.

"Uh, nigga, don't greet my cousin before you greet me. What the fuck you think this is?"

Marlon turned around to Josh and gave him a look that only caused Josh to smack his lips and shift all of his weight to the left side of his body. Neeva clamped her hand over her mouth and giggled before she started wiping down the display case. I stood in the doorway and watched my right hand and his "friend," as he would say, war with their eyes.

"Is this the part where y'all hug and make up or fight and both get shot for fucking my shit up?" I joked, trying to cut some of the tension in the room.

"Nah." Marlon shook his head and looked at me. "This nigga just be tripping. I already told him when we at work, it's strictly business."

"Whatever, nigga. Just make sure you greet me first the next time."

"Oh my God, J, you are so petty," I heard Neeva giggle and whisper as Marlon and I walked back to my office.

Once I opened and locked the door, I turned to my best friend and just stared at him.

"What?" he exclaimed, shoulders shrugging as he plopped down in the chair behind my desk. "I told you not to make that nigga manager. Now he's just taking that shit to the head. Don't talk to his cousin first?" Marlon's lips twisted. "What type of dumb shit is that? Man, I tell you." He wiped his hand down his face and blew out a frustrated breath. "I don't think I can do this too much longer. This whole relationship shit is for the fucking birds."

"It's not all that bad. And why you lying talking about you telling me not to make him manager? Your ass was the main one campaigning for your boo." I laughed over my shoulder as I walked to the safe disguised as one of my file cabinets, and I put the code in. I took out my favorite toys: two silver-plated and engraved Colt .45s with the black pearl grip and silencer to match.

Marlon chucked his head up in my direction. "Whatever, nigga, but what you pulling those out for?"

"My dad just hit me up and told me to meet him at the Penthouse."

"Did he say why?"

I shook my head and began to remove my clothes so that I could change into my black jeans and top. "Nah. Just told me to come through the service entrance."

"Well, you already know what that means." My silence told him that I did. "So where your nigga at? I'm so used to seeing you two attached at the hip now, it's kind of weird not seeing him hanging around you."

I pulled my jeans over my hips and rolled my shirt over my head. After braiding my hair down,

I threw on my Hart's Angels vest and tucked my guns behind my back. "Simmy went to handle that Chavez contract. Today was the only day that he'd be in town at some convention, so he went to take care of it."

Marlon scoffed. "In the daytime?"

It didn't matter what time of the day it was. Simmy always hit his target and finished a job regardless. Whether it was a close-up shot while he was walking past you or at the top of some building scoping you out. That nigga didn't give a fuck. If the money was right so was his aim.

I laughed at Marlon's hating ass. "Don't do my boo like that. Since we started teaming up on these special orders, money has been coming in like crazy. And with Josh doing his thang here and getting us all of this new clientele, it's much easier for us to turn all of this dirty money clean. So instead of you hating on my nigga, you need to be thanking him. Especially since his hard work just helped you with that new ride you just copped," I teased.

Marlon stood from his seat and handed me my helmet. "It did so I'll give him that. But I still don't like the nigga. Just make sure you keep him on a leash whenever he comes around here. I already have to deal with Josh and his bullshit. I'm not about to take it from a nigga I ain't fucking."

I fake gagged at his choice of words and grabbed my keys and phone. "Please don't give me that visual again. Oh, and before I forget," I said, grabbing a stack of orders that came in while he was out, "these are some perspective clients. Check them out and make sure everything is on the up and up before we do the contract. Tell Josh to close up, and remind him to shut down all of the computers. Last time he didn't and the system was fucked up for some reason the next morning."

Marlon nodded his head and followed me out the back door. "You want me to come with you? Just in case?"

I placed my helmet over my head and flipped the visor up and laughed. "I think you can sit this one out, babe. You already know wherever Onyx is Simmy is sure to follow." I stuck my tongue out, causing him to roll his eyes. Hating ass.

Turning my key in the ignition of my bike, my baby roared to life. After pulling on the gas a few times and kicking up some dust, I hit the kickstand and took off, making my way down the street to my father and whatever he had planned for me to take care of.

"Where the hell is everyone?" I mumbled as I gripped my phone tightly in my hand.

On the way over I'd tried relentlessly to reach my sisters with no luck. Unlike myself, it wasn't a habit for them to just up and disappear without notice or at least check in periodically. Not even my own mother was taking my calls. My intuition was telling me that something was terribly wrong, and I couldn't seem to shake the feeling. The cryptic texts from my father only added to my trepidation. I tapped Simmy's name on my phone so that I could check in before going upstairs. I knew he would start tripping if too much time passed without him seeing or hearing from me.

Me: Handling some shit with Dad. Might be late getting home.

Psycho: You good or you need me to come thru?

Before I could type a response, another text was coming through.

Psycho: Don't bother answering that question. I'm OMW.

I could only laugh at that foolishness, because his crazy ass didn't even know where I was but he was talking about he was on his way. I was ready to handle whatever situation Pops had going on and hurry home to my man. When I first met Simmy, no one could have told me that we would be where we were right now. We were dangerously in love and practically inseparable. I honestly couldn't see my life without him. The thought of it alone was depressing as hell.

Shaking the negative thoughts, I hopped off and stabilized my bike then placed my cell in the side pocket of my vest. My heels clicked against the concrete as I made my way to the service entrance. I glanced from side to side as I punched in my personal code to gain entry to the building. Surprisingly there was not one single person moving about at the moment. Not one delivery truck or individual unloaded supplies near the dock. The shit was weird, and the entire scene gave me an eerie feeling.

What the hell am I about to walk into? I thought as I moved down the long corridor.

Of course, no one stopped or questioned me as I walked through the kitchen and food preparation area. The staff here were all familiar with Julian Hart's girls, so they continued with their tasks as if I weren't even present. Dishes clanked and the aromas swarmed as the sizzling of food being prepared was heard throughout. The sound of knives chopping against cutting boards filled the air, while chefs added to the chaos as they barked orders to their team. The feeling of unease remained with me as I entered the service elevator and pressed the button to take me to the penthouse suite. Everything in me was telling me to go back down and get as far away from this building as I possibly could, but there was no way I could do that. Whatever my father needed seemed important, and I would never leave him hanging.

Taking a deep breath, I stepped out of the elevator and made a right to the head to the suite where my father was waiting for me. The closer

I got to my destination, the clearer I could hear raised voices coming from inside. Thinking fast, I removed one of my guns from my back and aimed it straight ahead while using my universal card key to gain entry. The last thing I ever expected to see when I walked in was my very own mother and father pointing weapons at one another in the middle of the room and having a very heated argument.

"What the hell is going on here?" I shouted as I took in the scene before me. Some of the beautiful antique furniture was turned over, and the glass coffee table in the center of the living room was shattered and broken into pieces. Soil from the potted plants was spread all over the floor, and the smell of gunpowder lingered heavy in the air. Glancing across the room, my eyes doubled in size at the sight of a very naked and very dead Lukas Coleman stretched out the couch. I wanted to ask what happened to him, but I didn't get the chance to after my sight zeroed in on a familiar frame lying on the floor a few feet behind my father.

"Philly!" I rushed over to my sister, who was on the ground, wincing while holding her shoulder. It was clear that she had been shot. A small amount of blood stained the graphic tee she wore under her Angel vest, and she was sweating profusely.

What the fuck? I thought as my eyes and hands continued to search her body for any more gunshot wounds. I opened my mouth to ask her what happened but got cut off when she spoke.

"Shoot her ass, Pop," Philly groaned, the grip she had on her injured shoulder tightening, trying to ease the pain.

"Wait, what?" I questioned, her words causing me to release her and stand. "Mom, what are you doing? Put that gun away. The both of you!" I demanded of my parents. "We need to get her to a hospital!" I pointed down at my sister, but neither of them complied. I knew my father was about this life, but seeing my mother with a gun drawn was tripping me out right now. "Somebody please tell me what the fuck is going on! Philly, who shot you?"

It had just dawned on me that there were only two people in the room with guns when I walked in and my sister was on the ground wounded. That meant that my mother, my father, or this dead man was responsible, and none of those scenarios made much sense to me.

"Your mother shot me. Shot me like she wished she could have done to my mother, but her weak ass didn't have the balls," my sister laughed tauntingly through the pain.

"Shut up! Shut the fuck up! Why don't you just die already!" Sole screamed at her with tears running down her face.

My father spoke up for the first time. "The only person dying today is you, sweetheart. Drea, baby girl, I asked you to come here because I knew you wouldn't believe it if I just came right out and told you. What you learn in this room today is not going to be easy. In fact, it's going to be extremely difficult, and bouncing back as a family will take some time, but this has to be done. Just know that I love you and I'm only doing what's right." His voice shook, but he never took his eyes or his gun off of my mother.

"Everyone shut up for a minute!" my voice bellowed. This entire setting I found myself in was overwhelming, to say the least, and all the shouting and talking in codes was about to push me over the edge. "Ma, you go first. Tell me what this is all about."

"She came here to kill me, Drea. I had no choice but to defend myself. She's filled your father's head with lies that he's chosen to believe. They want to hurt me, and I've done nothing wrong," she croaked with more tears spilling down her face.

"You fucking liar!" Philly shouted.

"And what about him?" I nodded toward Lukas's corpse, my finger slipping on and off the trigger of my weapon.

"Yeah, Sole. What about him? Tell your daughter how you've been screwing this nigga for over twenty years. How he put you in contact with the man you paid to kill my Cassie," he said through gritted teeth. Hearing the cracking of his voice caused my heart to pound, and air to become trapped in my throat.

"Your Cassie! Do you hear yourself right now? 'My Cassie!' What about your fucking wife, Julian? What about meeee?" she cried out dramatically.

"She killed my mama, Drea. It was her. . . ." Philly's voice trailed.

"That's not true. That can't be true. Right, Ma? Tell me that they're mistaken and that you'd never do something like that," I pleaded with her as I looked back and forth among my father, sister, and mother, trying to decide who I should believe. I didn't think they would lie about something so serious, but I refused to believe that the woman who gave birth to me had done any of the things they claimed either.

"Oh, it's true. She's been the one behind everything. Her and that dead muthafucka over there. Had us going after the Dragons, but it was them all along. Those men were aiming for Philly at the fundraiser that night, but thank God they missed," my father raged. "They were instructed not to harm you or Diem, just spook you two a little. Her shop burning down? People following you around? All of that wasn't from the Santiago hit. Your mother had people on you too. All so she could take Philly out and have us believe it was Slim and his crew coming for the Angels. We almost fell for that shit, too." He shook his head in disbelief.

"What?" I croaked as my eyes shot back to my mother, who shook her head vehemently but didn't respond to the accusations verbally.

"Drea, we're telling you the truth," Philly groaned in frustration. "She tried years ago and failed, but when she found out I was still asking questions about my mother's and grandmother's murders, she sent people for me again," she explained.

"Years ago?" I gasped.

"Mom gave her the pills that day, Drea."

I looked to my left, surprised to see Diem now standing near the door, looking nothing like her normal self. Her clothing was disheveled, and her eyes and face were puffy and red, looking as if she'd been crying for days on end.

"When I found out about all this shit, memories of that day started flashing in my mind. When we walked in and found Philly passed out, I saw the bottle with Mom's name on it on the floor next to her. By the time the paramedics showed up, it was gone. It's still kind of fuzzy in my head, but I want to say I saw Sole pick it up and put it her pocket as soon as she and Dad rushed into the restroom. All I know is that we couldn't find it anywhere. I didn't see it until months later when I was playing in Mother's makeup. That same prescription bottle was on her vanity," Diem said, wiping the tears from her eyes. "I didn't want to believe it either, Drea, but she did this shit. She's evil." Diem lowered and shook her head from side to side.

"Philly, you never told me that. Why didn't you tell me? I would have killed this bitch long ago if I'd known." My father grimaced. His tone was full of regret.

"Don't listen to them, baby. You know me, and you know I could never do the things they speak of. I love my family. I love you." She pleaded her case convincingly.

In that moment, after listening to all parties, I was no longer Drea. I was Onyx, and I knew what I had to do. From the corner my eye, I could see my father closing in on my mother. A look was on his face that I couldn't recognize, but the grip on his gun was tight.

"This is for Cassie," he declared, applying pressure to the trigger, but he hesitated for a second too long.

Phew!

"Drea, no!" my father's voice roared.

My gun hit the floor at the same time my mother's body hit the ground. She'd taken one to the head, and the bullet had come directly from my weapon. Crushed summed up my current emotional state. I couldn't believe I had pulled that trigger, but it was necessary. I promised Philly, and it was a promise I didn't intend to break. I loved my mother to death, but I knew when she was trying to play people. I'd watched her do it all my life. When she wanted something from my father, she'd toy with him mentally until he gave in. It was the reason her own family didn't fool with her. She'd fucked over too many of them. When she made attempts to pit us sisters against one another, she played with our young minds. As we got older, we began to see through that, and she was no longer successful because of the tight bond we'd formed. I always picked up on the bullshit. Still, I loved her. Sole, on the other hand, loved no one but herself, and she didn't deserve to live.

Philly was now on her feet, and our eyes locked. "I gotta get out of here," I muttered before taking off toward the door.

"Drea, wait!" I heard my sisters call in unison.

"No, let her go. She's going to need a minute," I could hear my father say as I moved down the hall like someone was after me.

I needed Simmy right now more than ever, but I didn't want to be around anyone at the same time, if that makes sense. How was I supposed to move on from this? Taking my own mother's life? She'd done horrible things, but killing her was sure to haunt me for the rest of my days. Maybe some time away would help me come to terms with all of this. The way I was feeling at this very moment, I would probably never return to Las Vegas. Either way, I was getting the hell out of dodge, leaving my heart and my family behind.

Chapter 21

Simmy

"What the fuck?" I wondered out loud as I watched my girl burn rubber out of the alley and down the street.

I cringed as she was nearly sideswiped by a royal blue Camaro. Thankfully she was able to swerve and recover before picking up the pace and continuing at a dangerous speed. I had no idea what the fuck happened inside that hotel, but I was going to lay hands on whoever had her running scared like she was. As bad I wanted to run up in that bitch and shoot it the fuck up, my first and main priority was making sure she was straight, which was why I pulled away from the curb and drove like a madman to catch up with her. Shit was kind of hard, considering the way she skillfully swerved from lane to lane, nearly causing several collisions. When she hopped on the freeway, I was right behind her, grateful as fuck that the police hadn't pulled my black ass over and that neither of us had wrecked out. It didn't take me long to figure out that she was headed to the airport. Where the hell did she think she was going without me?

My brow furrowed as I watched her pull up to the drop-off line and hop off her bike, letting it fall to the side. That was her favorite motorcycle, so I knew that something terrible had to have happened for her to treat it like a piece of scrap metal. Snatching the helmet off her head, she tossed it to the side, and for the first time, I could see the anguish in her face. A fear I'd never known coursed through my body. Not fear for myself, but fear of what could have happened or what would happen to her. Caring for someone else that way was foreign to me, but when it came to her, I was getting used to it.

Rolling down my window, I called out to her in a panic, "Drea!" I needed her to see me, to hear me, and to know that I was here and I had her back through whatever it was she was dealing with.

She didn't even look my way or give an indication that she'd heard me. I was too far back, and the hustle and bustle of life outside the airport drowned out my voice. Folks were everywhere, dropping off and picking up loved ones. I was trying my best to move around these muthafuckas and make my way to the front, but somehow I'd been boxed in. Just when I had the thought to ditch the car altogether, I pulled out my phone to call her instead. My eyes were fixed on her as she pulled the phone out of her pocket, looked down at it for a few seconds, then proceeded to toss it in the garbage bin next to her.

Seeing that shit hurt me like nothing ever had. Defeated, I immediately released the call and watched as she turned to walk inside. It got my hopes up when she hesitated and walked back like she was going to retrieve the phone. However, when she got within a few feet, she shook her head, wiped her tears, and took off running inside. My heart sank to the pit of my fucking stomach when she was no longer in my view.

"Fuck!" I banged my head against the steering wheel, causing the horn to sound off loudly.

When I lifted my head, all the cars that surrounded me before had magically disappeared. I chuckled to myself, thinking, *why couldn't they have done that when I was trying to get to my lady?* Finally, I was able to pull right up next to where she abandoned her Ducati. I got on the phone with my people and made arrangements for them to come pick it up and transport it to my house. Once I saw to it that, I would go to her. There was no need to rush at this point. Call me crazy, obsessive, or a straight-up stalker. Hell, you could even call me a psycho like she did, but there wasn't a place in the world that Onyx Hart could go and I not be able to find her. Believe that.

The signature smell of that Bruce Banner hit me as soon I as entered the house. She must have come across the stash I left here the last time I visited. The fuck was she going through to be smoking something as potent as that? Normally her rookie ass would puff on my shit a few times before she was feeling mellow and tapping out, and that was just on some regular kush.

I headed to the back of the house, knowing I'd find her in her favorite spot. The huge, modernly decorated cabin in Colorado was a purchase I made about two years ago and somewhere I'd come when I needed to clear my head. It became her happy place as well, which was how I knew this was where she would come. She fell in love at first sight with the fireplace and plush chair positioned in front of it. All she needed was a blanket and whatever book she was reading, and she was content in that same spot for most of our trip. When I brought her up here the first time, she acted as if it were the only room in the house.

Her back was to me, but I could see her small frame being swallowed by the smoke as she listened to "My Song" by H.E.R. on repeat. It was one of her favorites. Mine too, but y'all keep that on the low for your boy. I observed her for about five minutes before she acknowledged my presence.

"How did you know I was here?" she said, sniffling, without turning around.

"Nah, the real question is why did I have to hunt your ass down? Why would you just leave without telling me?" I walked around the couch to stand in front of her. She wouldn't even lift her head to face me, which further pissed me off. "You don't have anything to say?"

Silence.

"I know something happened, Drea. Just tell me," I pleaded. "What, you still don't trust me or something?" My voice and eyes were willing her to look at me, but she refused.

More silence.

"You gon' keep running, and eventually I'm gon' get tired of chasing you. That shit was expected in the beginning because of how we started out, but I thought we were in a different place now. A whole fucking relationship and you just skip town on me? Nah, we don't do no shit like that to each other. One thing you'll learn about me is that I love hard, but I don't give a fuck harder. As deep as my love is for you, imagine me putting that same energy into not fucking with you at all. Is that what you want, Drea?"

Nothing.

"Fuck this shit."

"I killed my mother, Simeron," she whimpered, stopping me dead in my tracks. My wide eyes turned back to her as she took another toke of the blunt while a fresh flow of tears poured from her eyes. The pain in her big browns broke my fucking heart, a heart I didn't even have until I met her. "I made a promise to Philly, and I honored it," she added with a nod. "I ain't have a choice," she mumbled.

"Baby, what does that mean?" I moved closer.

"Remember I told you that I vowed to murder the person responsible for taking Philly's family from her?" I nodded my head and kneeled before her. "It was my mother. My dad found out, and that's why he wanted me to meet him at his hotel that day. A lot of shit came out, but it was her the whole time. I mean she didn't do it herself, but she hired someone to . . . to . . ." She paused before pulling on the blunt once more. Leaning her head back, she released a thick cloud of smoke into the air. I was getting lifted off contact alone, so I knew my baby was high as fuck right now, which was completely understandable. If I were in her position, I'd want to check out from reality with the one of the strongest strains of weed as well. She was liable not to come down off that shit for a whole week the way she was chiefing. "She hired someone to do it, so I killed her in that hotel room," she confessed.

"That's why you got up out of there so fast," I said more to myself.

"You were there?" she asked in surprise.

I just looked at her like she was crazy. "You already know that wherever you are, I'm not too far behind," I reminded her as I took what remained of the blunt and placed it in the ashtray.

Picking her up, I cradled her in my arms like a baby, whispering sweet apologies in her ear for how I reacted when I first came in. I held her this way the entire walk to the master bathroom upstairs. I sat her on the counter in the middle of the his-and-hers sinks, and I prepared her bath. She sat quietly and watched me do my thing, sniffling here and there. I fixed her shit up just like she would, adding her favorite bath salt and other ingredients along with tons of bubble bath. She liked to damn near be drowning in that shit while she took her baths.

When that was ready, I walked over and removed all of her clothing then lowered her body into the scalding water. I didn't see how her skin still remained attached to her body in hot-ass water like that, but for some reason she loved it. It relaxed her. After lighting every candle I could find in the drawers, I went to the Tidal app on my phone and played the song she had been listening to downstairs, making sure to put it on repeat.

"Simmy," she stopped me as soon as I went to make my exit.

"Yeah, baby?"

"Please stay." She looked up at me pitifully.

The candles provided the only light in the room, but I could still make out the pain and despair in her eyes. I hated that I couldn't make it better. Her healing would only come with time. I nodded my agreement, trying to hide my smile. My thought was that she needed this time to herself to continue processing everything that had gone down, but I couldn't lie and say that I wasn't happy she was willing to admit she needed me. Going over to the toilet, I put the lid down to take a seat, but she stopped me.

"I want you to get in and hold me, babe," she pouted.

"Dammit, Drea. That water gon' burn my fucking skin off," I complained, but I was already removing my shoes while her crazy ass just smiled. It was the first one she'd given me since I got here and I was relieved to see it. I talked my shit, but there wasn't a damn thing I wouldn't do to see that beautiful smile on her face, even if I had to suffer third-degree burns in a garden tub full of hot-ass water with bubbles reaching the damn ceiling. It was crazy the shit niggas did for love.

Once I was positioned behind her, I wrapped my arms around her torso and pulled her to me. The water was so hot I envisioned my tattoos melting off, but I maintained. Barely.

"Can you sing it to me, too?" she requested low as she settled into my embrace.

I wanted to protest, but hearing the tears in her voice made me swallow my refusal. Like I said before, niggas did crazy shit for love. This was for the only chick in the world who knew I could sing. She was the only one I would ever sing for.

> *When the weight of the world is on my shoulders*
> *You would take away the pain*
> *Through the storm, the sun still shines*
> *With you by my side, I'm not afraid*

I took a moment to stretch my arms in the air as I waited for our bags to come around on the conveyor belt. The short flight from Denver had me stiff as hell. Drea was unusually quiet as she glanced around the airport at nothing in particular, biting off what was left of those long-ass artificial nails she wore. She was slowly coming to terms with the decision she made to take her mother's life, but it was still a struggle.

Three weeks was how long it took me to convince her to come back to see her family. She hadn't talked to or seen them physically since she left, and they were blowing my phone up on the regular wanting to speak with her. She made me promise not to tell them where we were, and as her man, I had to respect that. Only thing I could do was tell them that she was with me and that she was safe.

"Let's just get through these first couple of days, and if you don't want to stay, we can bounce. Just let them see for themselves that you're straight," I told her as I wrapped my arms around her from behind.

"I'm fine, Simmy. I'm actually looking forward to seeing everyone. I missed them," she admitted, pulling my arms around her tighter.

I was happy to hear that because although I loved being needed by her, I knew for a fact that she needed her family as well, and the longer she avoided them, the longer it was going to take her to get over this huge hurdle in her life. Once we made it out front, I immediately spotted the driver her father had sent for us holding up a sign with her name on it. Our first stop was his house, and we would go to my place tonight. Tomorrow she planned to check in with Marlon and Josh at her flower shop while I tended to a job I had lined up. It was just some light work, so I wouldn't be away from her that long.

Pulling up to the mansion that she called home as a child was surreal. Doing the crazy things that she'd done, if you didn't know her personally, you'd never guess that she came from a background like this. Shit looked like that house that dude kicked his wife out of in the movie *Diary of a Mad Black Woman.* I only saw homes like this when I did hits for the rich and famous, but I had never been directly acquainted with anyone living this grand-ass lifestyle. I think that's why I dug her ass so much from the very start. It wasn't the fact that she came from money. I couldn't care less about that part. For me, it was the fact that, despite her upbringing, she was still a fine, down-ass, motorcycle-riding, murdering-ass boss. And from getting to know her siblings, I knew they were one and the same, minus the murder.

It seemed that her sisters were anxious to see her because I could see them standing at the bottom of the steps that led up to the house as our car pulled around the circle drive. Even her father waited nervously at the door. All the gangster stories I'd heard coming up about Julian "Knight" Hart and then to see him standing there looking so edgy and unsure was a trip.

"You ready?" I asked her as I took her hand in mine.

"I'm ready," she replied after taking a deep breath.

I got out and went to her side to open the door for her. She was barely out of the car before I was being shoved aside and the two other Hart girls were hugging her and fawning over her like she'd been gone for years instead of weeks. I couldn't help but laugh.

"I'm so glad to see you, boo." Philly checked her over before hugging her again.

"I'm sorry for staying gone for so long but . . ." She struggled to find the right words.

"No, we understand, sis. We don't even gotta talk about that shit. I'm just happy to see your face. Bitch glowing and shit." Diem shot me a mischievous smirk before kissing her sister's cheek.

I just smiled cockily because even sis knew I was responsible for that bright, refreshed look she had going on. I glanced toward the house to see Knight hesitantly making his way down the stairs toward his family. Sensing his presence, the girls released one another and looked back at him then parted the way for him and his youngest daughter. They locked eyes and held it for a while without speaking. Drea's face was stoic as fuck, and I was almost afraid that she was going to give the nigga the cold shoulder.

"Come on and give me a hug, old man." She finally smiled, causing me to release the breath I was holding. A look of relief washed over him as he rushed over and took her into his arms.

"I love you, baby girl, and I'm so sorry," he whispered as he squeezed her tight.

"I love you too, Pops."

"And thank you, son, for taking care of my baby." He shook my hand while she held on to him.

"No problem, sir. That's my job," I replied. He grinned and nodded in approval.

We remained outside for about twenty minutes just shooting the shit before Gideon and Kyrie pulled up on us. Once we finally made our way inside and out back, we discovered that Knight had a full-fledged BBQ cracking for us out there. We ended up hanging out with the family well into the wee hours of the morning. My baby caught up with her sisters while I got to know her father better.

He gave us the lowdown on what had been happening since we left town, and that shit was crazy. The cleanup crew had taken care of whatever mess was made in that hotel room, and Mrs. Coleman played her part and filed a missing person's report on Lukas two days following the murders. Knight had done the same for his wife. It was later discovered that Lukas and Sole were planning to run off together. During their search of Lukas's office after he went missing, the police found a letter on his laptop stating such, which worked out perfectly for everyone. I'd been concerned that this shit was somehow going to come back on my baby, but I was happy to learn that it wouldn't. It was just one less thing she'd have to worry about.

Knight turned out to be a pretty cool dude, and I could see why his girls were as accomplished as they were and also why they took shit from no one. Drea was behaving like her normal bubbly self for the time being, and I was happy to see that. It was the nights that got to her, when the nightmares came and she'd wake up crying hysterically in a cold sweat. That's where I came in though. She had her family, but I was the one who would be there to hold her tight and assure her that everything would get better, with time.

Epilogue

Knight

I stepped out onto the veranda of the beachfront villa I was staying in, enjoying the beautiful panoramic view of the ocean and the other surrounding islands as the rays from the morning sun began to beam bright. The South Pacific breeze blew coolly as I sipped my coffee and continued to bask in the blessing of this new day. I'd been on this secluded island in Fiji for the last week trying to relax and enjoy my mini vacation as much as I could before returning to Vegas, but for some reason, I couldn't stop my mind from replaying over the crazy events that had happened in my life over the last few months.

Finding out that my wife had been sleeping with Lukas Coleman during our whole marriage did bruise my ego a bit, but if I was being truthful, I couldn't put the blame all on her. Had I chosen who I really wanted to be with back when Cassie was alive, everything that transpired would have never happened. Although my head told me that Sole was the more logical choice to build a life with because she understood the life I was living at the time, my heart still belonged and always did belong to Cassie.

Not only did my selfishness cost me the love of my life, but it caused a rift in my family as well. Drea said she was okay with what she did, but I could tell that she was still mentally battling with ending her mother's life. Diem wasn't so much tripping about the fact that Sole was dead, but I could tell there was some resentment there toward me. It was nothing that couldn't be repaired with time though. As for Philly, she got the closure she so desperately needed, so she was cool for the most part, but she too felt a way toward me for bringing her into Sole's life and not seeing my wife for who she really was. It was going to take a while for things to go back to normal, but I planned to do whatever I had to, to make sure we still remained a family.

The glass door that led to the open-plan living area opening grabbed my attention for a second and had me looking over my shoulder at the small figure walking out. The way Rhea's slim but curvy frame looked encased in the pink one-piece bathing suit already had my dick ready to come to life. When she pressed her breasts against my back and wrapped her arms around my waist, I turned my gaze back out to the rippling ocean and took a deep, calming breath. It felt good to be in the arms of someone who really cared about me and not my status or what my money could do for them. Someone who accepted all of my children and cared about them as she would her own. Rhea reminded me of Cassie in so many ways, and although it was in the early stages of whatever we had going on, I liked where we were heading.

"You out here thinking about the girls again, huh?" I nodded my head, and she kissed my shoulder. "It's going to be okay, Julian. Your daughters love you, that much I'm sure of. They just need a little more time to deal with everything that happened." Her hand slid into mine. "Everything is going to work out fine. You just wait and see."

And that's what I was going to do, give them a little more time and wait. I'd eventually get this family back on track. In the meantime, I was going to enjoy my little vacation and make the best of this private villa.

Meanwhile in New Orleans
Philly

"I'm not playing with you, Philly. You better be careful out there with my baby growing in your belly and shit. I don't know why you feel the need to be on a bike anyway. You got a whole army of riders reppin' Hart's Angels. You could easily ride on the truck with me," Gideon fussed as he helped me put my helmet on.

"Damn, nigga. Just broadcast my business to the world why don't you?" I hissed as I made sure no one was paying attention to us. "And as the president, I have to be on a bike. What the fuck I look like rolling up on the bed of a truck? Me being pumped full of baby don't stop shit when it comes to my bikes, and you know that." I swung my leg over the seat of my custom '68 Ariel Cyclone 650 that I personally customized myself for this week. I wanted to make sure Hart's Angels left a lasting impression of not only being a group of women riders, but a group of women riders who rode some of the baddest bikes this part of the South had ever seen.

Gideon flipped my visor up and looked me in my eyes. "That smart-ass mouth of yours is the reason why you got my seed chilling in your womb now. I stay having to keep your ass in line with this dick. Be careful," he reiterated. "I'll see you at the park. And, Philly, don't make me catch a case out here. Keep them niggas out your grill."

"What are you talking about?" I laughed, acting like I didn't know what he meant. "I was drumming up some business for the shop when I was passing out them cards earlier. You know I need to make as much money as I can now before I have to go on maternity leave or whatever you call it."

I didn't know why I loved that little jealous streak of his so much, but I did. The shit turned me on. I'd admit, I was a little extra flirty while talking to some of the other male riders in attendance at the meet and greet, but it was only for show. That look Gideon got on his handsome chocolate face when another nigga was even next to me made my clit thump like crazy. And now that it was mixed in with these pregnancy hormones, it was even crazier. I was only a little over six weeks, but you couldn't tell my body that. The doctor said that it was natural for my sex drive to increase, and my baby daddy had benefited from that spike religiously.

"Don't feed me that bullshit." Gideon smiled as he removed my helmet and grabbed me by the back of my head, pressing his lips to mine. "These belong to me," he said as he lightly wrapped his hand around my throat, deepening the kiss. I opened my mouth and allowed his tongue to slide in, eliciting a small moan from me. "These kisses, your heart, your body. It's all mine. Keep acting like you don't know what I'm talking about if you want to. Simmy ain't the only one that can get crazy when it comes to his girl."

"I got you, baby. And for the record, you kissing me like that is the reason your seed is chilling in my womb." I winked as he laughed.

Gideon headed toward the heavy-duty truck Kyrie had rented for the week and hopped in with his boys. The smile on his face let me know that he was feeling like the happiest man on earth right now. His businesses were booming. The shop the Dragons destroyed was back up and running better than ever. A large distributing company wanted to invest in his male hair-care line, and he and his grandma were finally back on speaking terms. It took a while for her to get out of her little uppity attitude about me, but she eventually did. When Gideon accidentally let it slip that we were expecting, Loretta's ass did a complete 180. We weren't the best of friends, but whenever I was around her, she was more welcoming toward me. So I guessed that was a start.

After he blew me a kiss and mouthed I was his one and only, I turned my attention to my sisters and the rest of my clique behind me.

"So listen, everybody," I addressed the different chapters of Hart's Angels as all eyes turned to me. We were about one hundred deep, and we all looked good in our red, black, and silver. "I don't know about y'all, but I didn't come down here to play with these muthafuckas about shit. When we get out here, let's show all them why Hart's Angels is one of the baddest motorcycle clubs on the scene. If they wanna see a burnout? Give 'em smoke. If they want a stoppie? Handle that. If they wanna see a wheelie? We got 'em. In whatever you do, make sure you represent that heart and angel wing patch to the fullest. Let New Orleans know who we are, where we from, and what we're about." A chorus of yeah's, screams, and whistling filled the air. Raising my hand in the air, I circled it around a few times before yelling, "Now let's ride out."

Pulling my helmet back over my head, I made sure my skull rag was tied securely around my neck before dropping my key into the ignition of my bike and roaring it to life. After everything that had transpired in the last few months, I didn't think that we would even make it out to bike week. I mean, emotions were so high after Sole's death that we all kept to ourselves for a while. I took on multiple projects at the shop to keep busy, Diem was doing her thing with her new warehouse and sex toy line, Pops was trying to reach out, but we weren't trying to hear it at the time, and Drea just disappeared on us without a word or text to let us know that she was safe. Shit was real crazy for a while, but after some sound advice from Gideon, and Diem being admitted into the hospital, I reached out to my sisters and Pops. I knew we still had a little more work to do with getting our family back on the right track, but I had no doubt that we'd get it together, especially with this new addition on the way. My sisters or father didn't know about my pregnancy yet, but with the way

Gideon's happy ass couldn't stop talking about it, they and the whole city of New Orleans would find out much sooner rather than later.

Diem

"Mmmph, looks like you've taken my place as the workaholic in this relationship, Ky," I teased as I watched my man mess around on his phone. The bike festivities were over for the day, so we broke off from everyone else and made our way to Bourbon Street for some bar hopping and bomb-ass food and drinks.

"Lies, baby. That wasn't about work at all. Just confirming a little something something I got lined up for you for when we get back home." He smirked, knowing I was about to ask a million questions.

"You do this to me every time, Kyrie. Drop little hints then get mad when I constantly badger you for answers. I'd rather you just keep quiet about it then surprise me," I pouted with my arms folded across my chest.

"Fix your face," he ordered, stepping into my personal space to peck my lips several times. "I won't say anything else, but I know you're going to love it," he promised.

"I know I will," I spoke against his lips before he released me and we began walking again. "Babe,

let's make this left right here and go to Deanie's.
I have a taste for some barbeque shrimp," I
instructed before taking a sip of the hurricane I'd
gotten from Pat O'Brien's.

"Baby, have you talked to your dad since we've
been here?"

"No, but I'll call him tomorrow," I lied.

"A'ight, don't make me dial the number on
speaker and force you to talk like I did last time,
DiDi," he threatened. "Quit treating my mans like
that."

I could only roll my eyes. Kyrie and my father
had become real tight since they started working
together, and he was always on my case about
mending our strained relationship. I mean Pops
and I were still cool or whatever, but so much had
changed since Sole died. I had yet to figure out why
I felt a way toward him, but for some reason I did.
Maybe it was wrong, but I couldn't help it. We still
had our weekly lunch, and we talked and laughed,
but it wasn't always authentic on my part, and I
believed he could sense that. However, his efforts
to repair the relationships between him and his
daughters continued despite our resistance, and I
knew that in time we'd be back like we never left,
minus Sole's ho ass. I might sound cold-hearted
but I had no feelings whatsoever about her being
gone, and I doubted that I ever would. As long as
Philly, Drea, and I were still thick as thieves, then
I was good.

Personally, I never suspected my mother could be involved with Cassie's and Nona's murders, but for some reason, I felt like my dad should have known. It also bothered me that if Sole's plan had been successful, Philly would have been dead and gone and we'd be none the wiser, probably still beefing with a group of people who had no hand in the madness that was surrounding us at the time. I was grateful for Lisa Coleman for coming through like she did though. I just hated that we couldn't get our hands on Elle's sickening ass.

According to my father, one of the conditions Lisa had when she spilled the tea on her husband and Sole was that her daughter not be met with the same fate that they had. Her mother would rather she be locked up than dead. For her involvement in the burning of my shop, Elle had been charged with arson along with a few other things. She had yet to go to trial because of crazy motions and delays presented by her attorneys. She was out on bail in hiding, afraid that we were looking for her. I wasn't even tripping on it though. Knowing she was somewhere living in fear was enough for me.

Health wise I was doing good at the moment, and I intended to keep it that way. One hospitalization for a Lupus flare was all it took for me to get serious about my condition. I was trying some natural remedies, and I'd even joined a support group for individuals suffering from the same autoimmune disease.

Things had changed drastically for me. Diem Hart was no longer married to the money, my business, or my phone. I now had a larger team working under me, and surprisingly I was pulling in even more money than I was when I was trying to cut costs by doing everything on my own. These days I was enjoying life, and I was enjoying my man.

Kyrie was still doing his thing, and his company was growing every day. As busy as he was and as many new contracts as he acquired, it didn't stop him from arriving at the beautiful new home we shared at the same time every evening to have dinner with me. Didn't stop him from dropping everything at the drop of a dime to whisk me away to an island or on a quick road trip. He spoiled me like crazy, and since he came into my life, he'd introduced me to a whole new way of thinking and living. And I wanted to continue living this life. With him. For a lifetime.

"I'll call first thing in the morning, babe," I promised as I grabbed his hand and pressed on.

Drea

"You sure you good, Philly?" I asked my sister as I stood at the door of her room. We were supposed to be getting ready to go do some bar bouncing with Kyrie and Diem, but all of a sudden Philly started throwing up everywhere.

"Yeah, she good, Drea. Just had a little too much excitement for the day. I got it from here," Gideon answered for her, walking out of the restroom with a cool towel and laying it on Philly's forehead. He kissed her on her cheek before whispering something in her ear.

"Call me if you need anything okay?" I offered, but Philly and Gideon were so into whatever they were whispering and snickering about that neither one of them acknowledged what I said.

Closing the door, I walked down the hall, headed to my room. Thoughts of the day's events ran through my mind. Enjoying all of this rich Southern culture, great food, even better drinks, and the different motorcycle clubs had me on a high I hadn't felt in a while. Emotionally, I was doing so much better, but I still had intermittent bouts of depression. It was during those times that my man loved on me extra hard and was always able to pull me out of that dark place. Sole was gone, and I didn't regret being the one who sent her away, but it was still hard because of how close we were.

Placing the key card in the door, I unlocked my room and walked in. Simmy had a job to take care of while we were out here, and he had been gone for a couple hours now. I figured I would take a nap until he got back and then we'd figure out what our plans would be for the rest of the night. After removing my jewelry, clothes, and vest in the bathroom, I headed straight for the bed and was about to get in.

"Where you coming from?" His voice startled me. My hand instinctively reached over to the nightstand to turn on the lamp. It was dark as hell in the room with the curtains drawn, and I didn't see his ass at all.

"Simmy, you gotta quit doing that shit!" I blurted when I spotted him sprawled out on the king-sized bed.

"Your ol' retired assassin ass be slipping. A few months back you would have walked in with your gun drawn off top. Now I can't walk up behind you without you jumping," he pointed out.

"I know I done fell off, huh?" I laughed.

Since Sole had been gone, it was like I'd lost the desire to kill. Although I didn't know it at the time, it was her actions that birthed that monster in the first place, and now that she was dead there was no need for me to continue doing the shit. My mission had been accomplished so now my focus was all on From the Hart and this fine-ass nigga stretched out before me. He smirked when he noticed the way the expression on my face switched from being alert to full lust. His usual all-black attire was fitted to his body just right, and I couldn't help the way my eyes kept diverting to the slight bulge in his pants.

"I didn't expect you back this soon," I tried to change the subject. "Did everything go okay?"

"Yeah, same ol', same ol'. Another fifty Gs added to the stack," he replied. I could tell by the expression on his face that something else was on his mind. "I've been thinking though. Kicking it with Kyrie and that nigga G has my mindset changing a bit."

I giggled when I thought about the three personalities I would have never imagined meshing well together but did. Simmy, Gideon, and Kyrie hung out just as much as my sisters and I did. "How so?" I inquired as I joined him on the bed, propping myself up on my elbow.

He stared at me lovingly for a few seconds before he spoke. "Thinking it's time to hang up these guns and invest some of this money. Become a regular, square-ass nigga," he said, making me fall out laughing. Simmy would say the craziest shit sometimes.

"You for real?" I asked when I noticed a more serious expression on his face. The whole atmosphere in the room changed when he nodded. "Did you already have something in mind?"

That sexy bottom lip of his poked out, and he shrugged his shoulders as he twisted his hoop nose ring. "I was thinking I could invest in you first. Open another shop and really get From the Hart on the map. And then maybe look into opening a gun range or some shit like that."

My heart started to flutter. "You would do that for me, Simmy? Invest in my business?"

He grabbed my hand and kissed the back of it. The deadly assassin mask was gone and now replaced with the face of the man I fell in love with the first time I laid eyes on him at the shop.

"I would do it for us." Simmy's face zoomed in on mine, and he placed the sweetest kiss on my lips. I was too caught up to even respond. I just stared at him affectionately. "So that's the plan. I complete the few jobs that I already have lined up, then I go into retirement like you."

"So you gone be my ol' outta-work-ass assassin now?" I laughed as I pulled him in for another kiss.

"Yup, but don't get it fucked up. I'll still lay a muthafucka down about mine. Just ask that nigga Lance."

Keep in contact with us!
www.facebook.com/iamgenesiswoods
www.facebook.com/AuthorShantae

Instagram:
@iamgenesiswoods
@onedimpletae

E-mail:
thebeginning616@gmail.com
BlaqueLovePresents@gmail.com

Web sites:
www.genesiswoods.com
www.authorshantae.com

WITHDRAWN